LACUNA

N.R. WALKER

COPYRIGHT

Cover Art: Bukovero
Editor: Boho Edits
Publisher: BlueHeart Press
Lacuna © 2020 N.R. Walker

All Rights Reserved:

Warning

Intended for an 18+ audience only. This book contains material that maybe offensive to some and is intended for a mature, adult audience. It contains graphic language, and adult situations.

Trademarks:

BLURB

A boychild swathed in green, a distinct tree-shaped birthmark on his wrist. A girlchild enveloped in red, marked with the three lines of the desert winds. A boy bundled in white, the koi mark on his wrist as defined as his shock of red hair. And a boychild wrapped in black, a raven his mark to serve his fate.

Twenty-five years ago, the hand of fate marked four newborns and sent them to the four corners of the Great Kingdoms. They were schooled and trained as rulers of their lands in preparation for the Golden Eclipse ceremony: a festival to celebrate a thousand years of peace and prosperity since the Great War.

Crow, ruler of Northlands, a skilled swordsman and expert tactician, is as reclusive and stoic as the mountains that surround him.

Tancho has spent his life in strict discipline, governing the Westlands with a fair mind and gentle hand. Quiet and unassuming, yet lethal in combat, he is the embodiment of the waters he lives by.

Yet the same hand of fate unknowingly linked Tancho to Crow in ways they cannot comprehend. Ruled by the stars, the Brother Sun and the two Sister Moons above them, and marked by an alchemical sorcery as old as time, their destinies were never their own.

As the eclipse draws near and the festival begins, word comes of another threat. Invaders from unknown lands bring a war no one was prepared for, and Crow and Tancho must decide on which side of the battle line they stand.

In life or death, their destinies will see them joined either way.

TRANSLATIONS AND EXPLANATIONS

Names and meanings

Northlands

Crow – (English) raven
Soko – (Serbian) falcon
Erelis – (Lithuanian) eagle

Westlands

Tancho – (Japanese) breed of koi with red dot
Karasu – (Japanese) breed of koi with black
Kohaku – (Japanese) breed of koi with white
Asagi – (Japanese) oldest known breed of koi
Hikari – (Japanese) breed of koi
Hitode – (Japanese) starfish
Unagi – (Japanese) eel
Iruka – (Japanese) dolphin

Eastlands

Samiel – (Arabic) desert winds
Sirocco – (Arabic) saharan hot winds

Addax – (Arabic) desert antelope
Fazluna – (Arabic) desert flower

Southlands
Elmwood
Oaken
Kearmore
Cardwick

Elders
Maghdlm – (Chaldean) magic
Adelais – (Germanic) noble, soft
Aelfflaed – (Irish) elf, beauty
Gabel - (Germanic) fork

Ascii – plural Latin for one with no shadow

Translation of languages

Please note all Latin phrasing is not exact. To these characters, this is an old, old tongue and they do not speak it or translate exactly.

Aperi ianuam (open the door)
altera ex loco (from one place to the next)
illam cincturam (this compass)
hoc portal (this portal)
revelare (reveal)

Aperire ad orientalum - open to the east
Aperire ad meridianam - open to the south
Aperire ad centrum – open to the centre
Claude ostium – close the door

Demidium - half

Yanam – Arabic for sleep
Mahi (mahicain) – Japanese for numb
Qutil – Arabic for death (the death chili)

Compound meanings

To open doorways - Four elements
    Potassium   (K)   Lanthanum   (LA)   Vandium   (V)
Indium (IN)
    K La V In
    Clavis is Latin for Key

To close the doors - Two elements
    Serenium (Se) Radium (Ra)
    Sera is Latin for door lock

LACUNA

N.R. WALKER

CHAPTER ONE

THE WINTER SUN was at high noon, shining a spotlight on the two men sword-fighting in the open courtyard of the Northlands' castle. Mirroring the rocky outcrops in the snowy landscape, black flags marked with a single white raven shimmered in the cool winds. Dark grey stone bricks gleamed as the sunlight turned icy frost into fleeting jewels, and the clang of metal on metal, grunts of effort, and bouts of laughter echoed skyward.

The broadsword grazed Crow's cheek, the burn of sliced skin and a warm trickle of blood down his cheek made him smile. Soko paused for the briefest moment, horrified that he had struck his king. Crow used the moment of distraction and swung for his neck. Soko parried, and with another bark of laughter, the fight went on.

Plumes of steam escaped with every exhale, sweat cooled on heated skin. Crow's dark hair was damp and clung to his pale face; his dark eyes sparkled with delight as they always did when he sparred with Soko. Friends since childhood, Crow trusted no one as he trusted Soko.

Surrounded by consuls and guards and staff who abided by his every whim, he could count on Soko for his honesty and reason. He told him truths when no one else dared, and he never held back when they fenced or sparred, such as they were doing now.

Crow was bound by responsibility and duty, as kings often were. Even as a small boy, Crow had studied the ancient ways, the lore of his ancestors of the Northlands. Studied, trained, studied, trained when he'd have rather done anything else, and yet it was Soko who had willingly stood beside him. Brothers, even if there was not one drop of shared blood between them.

Soko's hair was ashen blond and shaggy, his eyes blue and sharp. He had a smile of mischief and wit, a keen mind for learning and a keener eye for women, whereas Crow was dark and brooding, and his eye was drawn to the forms of men. Soko was free to act upon his impulses and there had never been a shortage of satisfied women in the North-lands' castle, yet Crow had never been free.

Who wears the mark bears the crown . . .

Bound by responsibility and duty. And the birthmark on his wrist. Even the mere thought of it . . .

He hissed at the pain and dropped his sword, pulling at the leather wrist guard, fumbling to get the straps undone.

"What is it?" Soko asked, immediately concerned. "It itches still?"

"No," Crow breathed. He finally pulled the guard from his arm and covered the birthmark with his cold fingers. "It burns."

"Burns? What the—"

Just then, the heavy wooden doors to the courtyard swung inward. Soko spun into a ready stance with his sword raised to protect Crow, without fault, without question. The young messenger raised his hands in alarm, breathing hard, his eyes trained on the blade.

"What is it?" Soko demanded.

"Excuse me, my lord," the messenger said, bowing his head to Crow. "A lone rider comes. At pace."

A lone rider coming to the city was not uncommon. Villagers traded food and wares all the time. "What of it?" Crow asked, still clutching his wrist. "Why the urgency?"

The messenger swallowed hard. "The rider and horse bear the yellow flag of the Elders' Consul."

Soko lowered his sword and turned to Crow, his eyes wide and face ashen, for it could only mean one thing.

The birthmark on Crow's wrist continued to burn.

DRESSED NOW IN WARMER CLOTHES, Crow and Soko stood at one of the grand hall windows watching as the yellow-clad rider made his way through the gates of the castle. Crow had his guards meet the man, one taking his horse, one escorting the rider inside, out of view, knowing it would take several minutes for the rider to be brought to see him.

Crow held his wrist, trying to ignore the burn.

"It's never caused you pain before," Soko noted. "And I don't think a visit from the Elders' Consul is a coincidence."

Crow winced again and Soko took his hand, inspecting the birthmark. It looked as it always had; dark against his pale skin, oddly beautiful and abstract, the clear form of a raven in full flight, its wings outstretched. The mark which showed Crow's predestined fate appeared no different;

though it had begun to itch at the last full moons, now it burned like fire ants crawling beneath his skin.

Crow tugged his hand away and pulled down his coat sleeve. "I'm fine, and make no mention of it in front of company."

After a brief pause, Soko sighed. "It's time, isn't it? That's what this means? The festival draws near."

Crow gave a nod before the sound of approaching footsteps put an end to this conversation. The two heavy doors opened and a guard appeared and bowed his head. "My lord, messenger of the Elders' Consul."

He stepped aside and the visitor strode forward. He wore the Consul's yellow tunic under a heavy coat of the same colour, with the four-pointed compass rose emblazoned upon his chest. He appeared slightly dishevelled and tired, though he bowed his head. He produced a scroll from inside his coat pocket and offered it to Crow. "My lord."

Crow took the paper from him but did not open it. "Your name?"

"Roulant," he replied quickly.

"You've ridden far."

"Six days."

It was perhaps a seven- or eight-day ride to the Elders' Consul temple, and the ride itself was not an easy one. Northlands was mountainous, rocky roads, and deep snow; hard and brutal land, almost as hard and brutal as the men and women who called it home. Given this rider had done it in six days meant there was urgency. "You rode alone?"

"Yes, my lord. Four riders sent to the four quarters."

The Great Kingdoms had long ago been divided into four quarters. North, of mountains and snow. West, of oceans and rivers. South, of jungles and forests, and East of desert sands and dunes. At its centre, was the *Aequi*

Kentron; a huge moated temple of sorts, where the Elders' Consul presided, upholding the law of the four lands and keeping score.

Formed a thousand years ago after the Great War, nine high priests protected the ancient ways and traditions, ensuring laws remained unbroken and territory borders intact. They overlooked the trade between kingdoms and ensured fairness at every turn, and the last thousand years had been peaceful and prosperous.

Steeped in history and tradition, and by definition the equal centre, Aequi Kentron was the heart of all four kingdoms.

Each of the four rulers was chosen at birth by the birthmark on their wrist. They would each rule their lands independently and in their own right, with their own laws and governance, yet there were some laws they could not ignore.

The law that stated when each ruler was beckoned, they would come.

The law was written when the Consul was established, that when the Brother Sun and the two Sister Moons aligned at the equinox, they would partake in the Festival of the Eclipse. They would abide with honour and with the dignity of the rank they held.

Crow was proud of his title, proud of his people, and he would lay his life down for his kingdom. And he should have been proud to be the chosen one in the time of the eclipse. Once every thousand years and it happened in his lifetime, his rule. Yet destiny was a weight like no other, and unease filled his belly for reasons he couldn't put name to. The fact his birthmark now caused him pain was one he couldn't ignore, and now with the news from Aequi Kentron, it could only mean one thing.

His time was now.

Realisation skittered down Crow's spine like a cold spider. So, it *was* time. Every arrow of his life was pointed to this. He gave a reluctant nod and turned to the guard. "See this man to hot food and warm quarters, and see that his horse is tended to."

Roulant's gaze shot up to Crow's. "My lord, I am thankful."

"As am I." Crow gave him a smile. "Eat and rest as you need."

Roulant gave another nod of gratitude, and he was escorted out by the guard. Soko waited patiently as Crow held the scroll. There was a wax seal atop the Consul's writing in old calligraphy ink.

King of Northlands

Crow slid his finger beneath the seal and unrolled the thick paper. At the centre top was the Consul's four-pointed compass rose stamped in blue ink. The writing was impeccably neat, the strokes delivered with such importance not even the ink dared to bleed.

Your Royal Highness, King Crow of Northlands,

The Eclipse befalls on the Equinox in your twenty-fifth year.

Your attendance is formally requested at the Aequi Kentron one week before the Equinox, for the festival of the Golden Age.

We eagerly await your arrival.

Crow read it again, then handed it to Soko who read it, frowning. "What does this mean?"

Crow stared out the window at the snow-covered valley below, at how the blackened rocky crags tore raggedly through the serene whiteness looking like open claw marks in flesh.

"I ride for Aequi Kentron in two days," Crow replied.

Soko's eyes hardened. "You will not ride alone."

Crow almost smiled at that. "I didn't think I would."

"And the eclipse?"

"A golden sun for a golden age," he replied with a sigh, turning back to stare out the window. "My birthright is finally upon me."

Soko's voice was quiet, as though he dreaded to hear what he already knew. "What will you do?"

Crow took a long moment to answer. Was it fear or dread? Acceptance or resignation? "My choice in this was long ago removed," he murmured, finally meeting Soko's eyes. "I will attend their festival, and when all the fanfare and nonsense is done, I will return as if nothing has occurred."

"It's supposed to be a celebration," Soko replied. "Yet it hangs over you like a dark cloud."

Crow sighed. He would have quite happily been left alone for all his days, but this felt different. This felt ominous and he couldn't explain why. "True metal does not fear the furnace," he murmured.

It was a favoured Northlands saying, cited by the miners who dug ore from frozen mountains and by the blacksmiths who turned it into steel.

Yet Crow feared . . . something. He feared this festival and ceremony; he feared the change he felt would rise with the golden sun. He feared the unknown.

And he feared the greasy dread in his belly and the burn on his wrist that told him his life was about to change forever.

CHAPTER TWO

THE WESTLANDS WAS a vast network of waterways, puddles of land for harvests, villages on rocky outcrops in the north or on stilts amidst the reeds to the south, and arching stone bridges that laced the land together.

The people were born of water. Living according to the tides, the ebb and flow was their pulse, the very lifeblood in their veins. A peaceful people, grateful to the Brother Sun and the Sister Moons, where days of work and nights of rest were a blessing.

Tancho sat in his white robes, cross-legged on the reed mat, with his long red hair tied back from his face, concentrating on the sounds of the water under the floor. How it swirled around the pylons beneath his palace, how it calmed him. He could close his eyes and centre his mind, bringing harmony to his thoughts, preparing him for things to come.

There were almost-silent footfalls outside the rice-paper walls. He wasn't alarmed, for it could only be one of two people, and he knew this sound well. Karasu walked ever so slightly on her toes the way a dancer does, or a well-practised assassin, aiming for stealth and grace. Whereas Kohaku trod heavier, the way a hulking foot soldier would expect to walk after losing a game of di.

The door slid open with a whisper. Tancho never opened his eyes, never moved an inch, though he did smile. "Hello, Karasu."

"We are ready to leave," she said, coming to sit on the floor beside him.

Tancho inhaled deeply and finally drew his eyes to her. Her white guards uniform was crisp, her long black hair fell about her face like ribbons of silk, her dark eyes were as sharp as her blades. She had been his friend and confidant since he could remember. Kohaku too. The three of them were inseparable, despite Tancho's title of king.

They were an unlikely trio. Tancho having long red hair, Karasu black, and Kohaku's long hair was white. Tancho and Karasu were of similar build, tall and lean, both agile and lethal with knives and blades, whereas Kohaku was broad and muscular. His strength was brute force, should anyone be stupid enough to pose a threat.

And both Karasu and Kohaku had been by Tancho's side forever. They had trained with him, learned with him, prepared with him. Every lesson, every class.

As the leader of the Westlands, it was his duty, and one he took in stride. He was proud of his ancestors, of his people, and it was with great honour that he would attend Aequi Kentron in their name.

"And your birthmark?" Karasu asked.

Tancho turned his wrist over, his sleeve falling away to reveal his mark. Since the last full moons, it had begun to irritate him. He suspected then that his destiny drew near, that the moons and sun were aligning in a way fate could not ignore. Then two days ago, the day the messenger had arrived, bringing with him the invitation, Tancho's birthmark had begun to burn. And Tancho knew then, the day he'd trained for had come.

Tancho ran his fingertips over the birthmark, feeling the warmth of the burn. He was barely able to ignore it, even with meditation and well-practised mind control. Even thrusting his arm into cold water had not lessened the heat of it. "It burns still," Tancho replied. "I expect it will get worse the closer we get."

The birthmark itself appeared as it always had: dark against his pale skin, and in the distinct shape of a koi fish. It was his symbol, it was his marking, his destiny. Marked by fate, like all four rulers of the four kingdoms. Tancho had studied all he could on the other three, though there wasn't much to be told.

Eastlands was a kingdom covered by sand dunes and desert-dwelling people. Their queen was a woman by the name Samiel. A tall fierce woman with a birthmark of the desert winds on her wrist.

The King of Southlands was Elmwood. Lands covered by forests and jungle and a tree birthmark on his wrist, he was said to be the size of an elm, though Tancho was sure that was an over-exaggeration. After all, Tancho was named after a fish, but he certainly didn't resemble one.

The last was Crow, King of the Northlands.

And out of the three other kingdoms, Tancho was fascinated with the Northlands the most.

He couldn't fathom living in a land three-quarters ice and mountains. The people had to be resilient and hard, cunning and strong. They didn't just survive in abominable conditions; they thrived.

Tancho could only deduce that Crow would be large in stature and as hard as the alps he called home.

Though if the rumours were true, Crow was a fair and good king, well-liked by his people, and Tancho admired him for that. He too was a fair ruler—as were all rulers of the four lands. There had been twenty-five years of peace across all countries. All trade agreements were mediated through the Aequi Kentron, the island-centre joining all four lands. Everything was equal amongst them.

Each country shared a border with two others but had never had a qualm or quarrel. The Elders' Consul governed and had done since time immemorial. And did so very well.

"Tancho?" Karasu asked. "Is something the matter?"

"No." Apart from the fact his benign birthmark now burned under his skin and his path as king, which had once spread out before him like the oceans to the west, now hung over him like storm clouds.

"You do not wish to leave?"

"I must. Even with my choice removed, I still long to fulfil my destiny. Is this not what we have dreamed about since we were young?"

Karasu gave him a confused smile. "Then why do you still sit here? The sun is risen and the horses are ready. Kohaku will be wondering if something's wrong."

Tancho smiled and rose fluidly to his feet. "Then let us go."

They walked through the quiet halls of his palace to where Kohaku waited impatiently with three horses. "You do realise that breakfast was so long ago, I'll be hungry again before we're outside the city," Kohaku said as he hauled his hulking frame up into the saddle.

Karasu rolled her eyes and took the reins of her horse

and swung herself up on it. "You're always hungry," she argued fondly. "I hope your saddlebag is well-stocked."

Ignoring their constant banter, Tancho went to the grounds' edge where a stone wall met water at the side of the palace. He knelt and put his hand into the water, letting his fingers trail through the cool surface, feeling the power and the serenity of it. He would miss this, no matter how long he would be gone for. Be it half a moon or two full moons, he would miss his home.

With a quiet bow of his head, he took one last moment to ask for the strength to do what was on the path before him. Then he rose and found Karasu and Kohaku watching him. He gave a nod, and without any effort at all, he pulled himself up onto his horse.

He turned back to the palace to find his guards, his council, his staff, standing in a long line. "We trust your safe return," Asagi said with a bow of his head. Asagi was a Westlands elder, a trusted mentor who had been like a father to Tancho. Asagi would never say a farewell tribute like 'good luck' or 'fight well' because Tancho didn't need luck. He had skill. And being told to fight well was implying the possibility that he could fight any other way, like telling the sun to rise well. It knew no other way, like Tancho knew no other way.

So no, Asagi would only say to return safely because that was all there was left to say. Tancho had been taught all there was to know.

He was ready.

He was leaving his land and his people in very good hands.

And if he was honest with himself, Tancho was excited. Everything in his life had led to this point. As all rivers run to the sea, this was his destiny. He nudged his horse with his heel and the three of them rode over the palace bridge into the city, lined with people waving white ribbons and cheering for their king.

He would not disappoint them.

And the closer he got to his destiny, the hotter his birthmark burned.

CHAPTER THREE

AEQUI KENTRON WAS a sight to behold, a picture of peace and order. The citadel itself was as old as time, steeped in history and tradition, built long before the Great War. The sandstone bricks were handcrafted, worn now, but still immaculate. There were potted trees, vines and flowers along the entranceway. Sunshine painted the tall walls and Soko's smile. Crow chuckled at his friend's bright-eyed amazement.

A moated island-castle was built of sandstone with four bridges that linked to each land like ventricles to a heart. Sandstone walls with merlon and embrasures, ornamental crenellations if not for anything else. There were flags and pennants for each land: black for Northlands, white for Westlands, green for Eastlands, and red for Southlands.

If the Great Kingdoms were a large mass of four equal parts, the Aequi Kentron, was the bullseye.

Crow hadn't been to the Aequi Kentron for many years, though it hadn't changed at all. As he and Soko rode over the Northlands' Bridge and into Aequi Kentron, they were officially out of their country and on neutral ground.

A tolling bell announced their arrival, and three guards came to meet them. Each wore the compass rose emblazoned on their chest and a yellow cloak; one held a bell, one stood back with his head bowed, the third stepped forward to greet them.

"Welcome, King of the Northlands. An honour bestowed upon us."

Crow swung his leg over and slid down from his horse, and Soko did the same. The third guard took the horses, and the first waved his hand to the large wooden doors. "To your quarters, if you will. After such a journey, there have been baths and supplies prepared in anticipation of your arrival. This way, to the north wing. The men will bring your belongings."

The seven-day journey itself had been refreshing if Crow was being honest. Yes, his arse could do without meeting a saddle for a while, but seeing his country—the mountain ranges of sheer peaks and snow that gave way to rolling hills before flattening out to grassy plains; the villages, the townspeople waving and cheering with delight at seeing their king—had been something Crow would cherish in his memories forever.

Spending seven days and nights with Soko had been like old times. In their teen years, they would spend nights out under the stars, far removed from castle luxuries, hunting for food, lighting campfires. They'd also had to practise marksmanship and survival skills, but that was what made it all the more fun.

They'd spent the first two nights at inns on the way to Aequi Kentron, needing a hot bath and a warm bed. Only a fool wishing for death would cross the highlands in winter and sleep outside. So while the inns had provided warmth and shelter and bellies with hot food, they'd also provided one too many blackberry wines, which, in turn, provided headaches for the morning's ride.

But as they drew closer to their destination, and as they came out of the mountains, they found the weather a little more forgiving and opted for a makeshift campsite hidden from the road.

Crow could say, without doubt, it was one of the best weeks of his life. He could take off his title and be his true self. Not a king, not one born for greatness, not one chosen by fate. Just a man, with his best mate, riding through the countryside.

But now they were here, where fate awaited, and he couldn't help but feel a little melancholy.

"Is the room not to your liking, my lord?" the guard asked. He'd led them along a warren of well-lit halls to the north wing, up the stairs, to their rather large quarters. They stood in a common room with reading chairs at one end and a table with plates of meats and fruits, two separate bed chambers, a washroom, complete with steaming tub, as promised. It reminded him of home.

"This is fine," Crow replied, affording a polite smile. "Tell me, have the others arrived?"

"One other," the guard replied politely, offering no other information.

"Do you know of my appointments?" Crow furthered. "Am I expected to meet the Consul this day?"

The guard bowed his head. "A feast tonight, to honour all esteemed guests. At sundown. A formal invitation will be forthcoming with details, and a messenger shall come to escort you to the grand hall."

Just then, the other two guards appeared carrying their bags. Struggling to carry was a more appropriate term. They stepped inside the door and lowered them to the ground with relief. "I bet the horses were thankful," Soko said, half a grin in place.

The guard, who had earlier led the horses away, gave a nod. "I believe so, sir. Though the mare attempted to bite me."

Soko laughed. "A slice of apple will change her tune."

The man smiled. "I'll remember that, kind sir."

It was not unlike Soko to befriend everyone he met.

Somewhere across the courtyard, another bell rang. "Someone else has arrived," Crow deduced.

The first guard gave a nod. "Indeed. We shall leave you be. Bathe and rest well, eat and drink all you desire."

They backed out of the room, pulling the doors closed behind them, and Soko chuckled. "I think he was trying to tell us we stink."

"Why do you say that?"

"He told us three times about the bath." Soko picked at some berries on the table. "Mustn't be a fan of horse sweat."

The truth was, they probably did look a little worse for wear. Sleeping the last five nights under the stars without a proper wash was probably unbecoming of his title, but Crow couldn't bring himself to care. He had enjoyed the last week, niceties and royal expectations be damned.

Crow picked up a sliver of meat and bread and smiled as he ate. Soko inspected the room, the bed chambers, the views out the windows. He was very obviously impressed.

"This is the room I've stayed in before," Crow said as he picked at the plate of fruits. "It's the northern wing, so I guess that makes it ours." Not much in the room had changed at all. There was a tapestry on the wall, of snow-covered mountains and blue sky. A rug covered half the floor, the chairs were upholstered with linen, the table hand-carved wood, a fireplace was unlit. It was all very pleasant and welcoming, reminiscent of his home. But this was Soko's first time.

"You're impressed," Crow noted.

Soko came back to the table, choosing some meat and cheese this time. "I am. It's everything I imagined from your stories. You've been here three times before?"

Crow gave a nod. "As a newborn. Then as a small boy, and again at sixteen."

"I remember the last. I wanted so badly to go with you."

"Instead you had to stay behind and help Scaevola in the kitchen."

Soko gave a wink. "Wasn't the only place I helped her either, I'll have you know."

Crow laughed and shook his head as he ate some more. "She helped you was more like it. I can guess who was getting the lesson that day."

He laughed. "She schooled me well."

Crow shoved more sliced meat in his mouth, chewing and smiling at the same time proving rather difficult. "You are without shame."

Grinning, Soko mock-bowed. "Thank you." He picked at some meat and fruit, then collected the bags from the door. "I shall put your belongings in your room, if you wanted to bathe while the water is still hot."

"Now *you* would tell me I stink?"

Soko froze. "No, I wouldn't—"

Crow laughed again. "The look on your face . . ."

Soko huffed, disappearing into one of the bedchambers with two bags and came out with one. "Because I'm certain mocking one's king, in the Aequi Kentron, no less, would see my head parted from my neck."

Amused, Crow gave a shrug. "Well, you wouldn't see it." Soko's mouth fell open, making Crow laugh. "Relax,

Soko. No one's been tried for treason in a few hundred years. And at any rate, you can't mock me for the same stink you wear."

Soko shoved the bag he was holding into Crow's chest. "It's a fine line, I'll have you know. Being best friend to a king, and his personal guard, and his personal advisor. On one hand, I must treat you as any subject treats a king. On the other hand, as your best friend, it is also my duty to laugh at your expense. So you see—"

"Personal advisor?"

"Yes. To personally advise you when you smell like a horse's arse."

Crow barked out a laugh just as there was a knock at the door. Soko unsheathed the sword from Crow's bag and spun on his heel in one swift move, putting himself between Crow and any possible threat.

Crow chuckled. "It's a line you straddle well, my friend," he said. Then he spoke to the door. "Enter."

The door opened and a guard appeared, head bowed, with a piece of paper in his hand. "The Consul's invitation, my lord."

Lowering his sword, Soko stepped forward and accepted the note. The guard backed out with no further word and closed the door. Soko put the sword on the table, handed the note to Crow, then proceeded to take Crow's bag from him and carried it to Crow's bedchamber.

Crow read the invitation out loud.

"In honour of the presence of all rulers of the Great Kingdoms, the Elders' Consul invites you and your guest to the grand hall at sundown. An informal introductory meeting and meal before initiation tomorrow. Stately attire, no weapons."

Soko stood in the doorway to Crow's room, frowning. "No weapons?"

"Stately attire," Crow groused.

Soko looked Crow up and down. "Speaking of which," he began, then turned Crow by his shoulder and gave him a shove toward the bathroom. "Bath."

Crow did as he was instructed, stripped and stepped into the deep, hot bath, and as soon as he'd sat down, he regretted not getting in the second he arrived. It was divine. Every minute he'd spent on horseback melted away, and he sank down, enjoying the bliss and silence—

Until Soko barged in, the invitation in one hand, a half-eaten apple in his other. He sat on the counter, not looking up from his note. "What do you think they're like?"

Crow didn't even bat an eyelid. "Who?"

Soko took a bite of apple. "The others. The Queen of Eastlands and the King of Southlands. We know enough on the Westlands, but the others. What do you think they look like? Should we make a wager?"

Crow snorted. "A wager?"

"Sure. I bet you a bottle of elderberry wine that the Southlands' king has twigs for hair."

Crow laughed incredulously. "That's a bet I'll be willing to take. And I don't even like elderberry wine, but have you gone mad? Twigs for hair?"

"Well, his name's Elmwood, isn't it?"

"Yes."

"And he's king of the forest people."

"Doesn't mean he's made of twigs. My name is Crow and do I look like I have feathers?"

Soko glanced up then. "No, but your hair is raven-black." He gave a second look. "Needs washing, by the way."

Crow rolled his eyes. "Thanks."

"And Eastlands. What kind of name is Samiel?"

"It means desert wind," Crow explained. "The East-lands is of the desert people, Southlands is of the forest people, Westlands the water people, and we, the North-landers, are from the air. We learned this when we were three years old, Soko."

"We're not really from the air, though, are we?" he replied.

"We live in the highest mountains and spend a good part of the year surrounded by cloud."

"Mm, yes," he allowed.

"Just like the people of the Westlands don't live *in* the water. They live on it."

"What do you think he looks like?" Soko pressed.

"The Westlands' king? I have no idea."

"Fancy he has gills?" Soko joked, his eyes bright with humour. "Scales, perhaps?"

"I would wager not." Though Crow smiled at the thought.

"How's your birthmark? Still burning?"

Crow lifted his arm out of the water and inspected the mark. Had it lessened? Or had he just got used to it? "Yes."

"It will be interesting to see how your birthmark fares tonight when you meet the others for the first time, don't you think?"

"Hm." Crow frowned at the birthmark, at the circum-stance he found himself in. "Yes."

"Do you think their birthmarks burn as well?"

"I assume it's some kind of guarantee to ensure we all turn up. I'm hoping tonight will be some ceremony to stop the pain. With a bit of luck, we can say hello, get rid of this stupid birthmark, then we can all leave early."

Soko snorted. "I don't think that is allowed."

Crow grumbled and sank down lower in the tub.

Soko pushed off the counter and made his way to the door. "Hurry up, or the water will be cold by the time I get in it. Don't forget to wash your hair." Crow rolled his eyes as Soko disappeared into the common room, but then Soko called out, "And don't piss in the water."

Crow chuckled, then closed his eyes and slid down below the surface.

CHAPTER FOUR

TANCHO, Karasu, and Kohaku dismounted from their horses and walked across the stone bridge to meet the three guards of Aequi Kentron. One guard rang a bell to signal their arrival, just like they did the last time Tancho had been here. He'd been to Aequi Kentron before, thrice, and the familiar castle looked as welcoming as it always had.

Kohaku's eyes were wide with excitement, having never been this far from home.

Karasu, on the other hand, looked around uneasy.

"Welcome, King of the Westlands. An honour bestowed upon us," the first guard said, wearing the Kentron yellow cape, the compass rose on his chest plate.

Another guard took their horses, but not before Karasu took her saddlebag. "We will deliver it to your quarters on your behalf," the guard said.

She looked him right in the eye. "Thank you for the offer, but I am able to carry it."

The guard was a little taken aback and looked to protest, but the first guard waved his hand to let the matter go. "This way to the west-wing quarters, if you please. After such a journey, there have been baths and supplies prepared in anticipation of your arrival. The guards will bring your belongings."

The castle itself was picturesque with the turrets and flags. Time and untold number of feet had worn the sandstone like smooth river pebbles, which made Tancho smile. History and tradition were an honour he prided himself on, and he could only imagine who had walked these halls before him, and how long ago.

The Aequi Kentron castle was well over a thousand years old, built over and fortified as the years allowed. The ancient scrolls and artefacts were somewhere in the vaults, deep in the underbelly of the castle, with the original crypts and catacombs guarded by legions of Elders' Consuls over the centuries.

Tancho felt as though he was walking on sacred ground.

Kohaku still grinned with excitement, though Karasu eyed everything with caution. She always was the serious one, but her behaviour was a little odd. When they were shown their quarters and finally left alone, Karasu inspected the rooms, the view, and Tancho knew she was determining which rooftops were accessible from which windows, angles and distances, and then she sniffed the foods spread out on the table.

"Okay, Karasu," Tancho said. "What bothers you? You refused to let them take your belongings, you already have our escape plans worked out, and now you suspect our food might be poisoned?"

Kohaku spun to stare, bread already halfway to his mouth. "Poisoned?"

Tancho shook his head to put him at ease, but Karasu crossed her arms. "I do not like this place. It feels . . . off."

"Off?"

"Something is not right here."

"This is old land," Tancho explained. "It is sacred. Perhaps our ancestors know you're here."

He'd meant it is a joke, but Karasu didn't smile. "You can ridicule me if you choose . . ."

Tancho went to her and put his hand on her arm. He trusted Karasu and her intuition, but this was the first time she'd been so far from home. "We are seven days from home, seven days from our oceans and from the push and pull of the water. Seven days in the saddle—"

"And I have not complained once," she replied. "Kohaku, on the other hand, complained like an infant from the moment we left the palace."

"I did not," he said, his mouth full of food.

Tancho and Karasu both stared at him because he had, indeed, complained like a wailing infant for most of the journey. Tancho eventually turned back to Karasu. "I would ask you to give it time. We are here for just one week. Maybe tomorrow we can inspect the grounds and perhaps that will put your mind at ease. It really is very beautiful."

She held his gaze for a long moment before resigning with a hint of a sigh. "Fine. Though I don't like it."

Tancho gave a nod. "Noted."

"This is really good," Kohaku said, shoving a slice of fruit into his mouth. "You should try it."

"We would if there was any left," Karasu said, swatting his hand away. "Tancho eats first, you know that."

"I was starving," he cried.

"It is fine," Tancho said, waving them off. "There's more than enough for all of us." He picked at some meat and fruit. "That bath is calling for me anyway," he said. "You two can eat all you need."

He could hear them bickering while he sank into the

hot water, and with a deep breath, he closed his eyes and centred his mind. He was here for the most important task of his life. He needed to treat it as such.

When he was freshly washed and dressed, he went back out into the common room. "The invitation for dinner arrived," Karasu said.

"Poor guy almost died of fright," Kohaku said with a laugh. "Opened the door and almost had his throat cut by Karasu here, just to deliver a message."

"He should have waited," Karasu said with a sniff.

Tancho ignored them and read the invitation.

In honour of the presence of all rulers of the Great Lands, the Elders' Consul invites you and your guest to the Grand Hall at sundown. An informal introductions meeting and meal before initiation tomorrow. Stately attire, no weapons.

Tancho's belly tightened with anticipation and nerves. This was what he was waiting for. This was what he'd waited for his whole life. The Golden Eclipse was finally upon them; his time had come to honour his destiny. And he would finally meet the man called Crow.

The man, who had been no more than a name, would finally have a face. The mystery, the enigma, would finally be over. And perhaps that was what Tancho was nervous about. Would it make it easier? To see him as just a man? Or would it make it harder?

The birthmark on his wrist heated to the point of pain, so he closed his eyes and tried to lock the pain away.

"Tancho," Karasu whispered, now beside him.

"I'm fine," he replied in a whisper. "The bath is free," he added, closing any hope of conversation. He went to the window and sat on the floor, cross-legged, his face in the sunshine. He closed his eyes, and with a deep breath, he quietened his mind. He put any discomfort, the pain and the anxiousness, into a box, closed the lid, and exhaled.

THEY LOOKED elegant and formidable dressed in their official state attire. Black pants, shirt and jacket, covered with a white robe, the insides lined with silver brocade, a black koi emblem on the back, hoods raised to cover their hair.

Tancho filled with pride as they followed the messenger to the grand hall.

Karasu grumbled beside him. "I can't believe we are forbidden to bring our blades."

Kohaku snorted quietly on Tancho's other side as they walked. "If this is a meal, my dear Karasu," he murmured, "the silverware shall include a knife."

Tancho withheld a sigh. "Karasu will not stab anyone with the silverware."

Karasu bit back her smirk as they crossed a grand foyer and strode up a wide set of marble stairs to the largest set of wooden doors Tancho had ever seen. Tall, wide and smooth, and hinged with cast iron. Each must have weighed a sizeable sum, and he dared not guess at the age of the wood. They opened inward upon their arrival, without effort, like magick.

And before them lay the grand hall. Wide enough for forty men to stand abreast, three storeys tall, marble floors and carved stone pillars lined the walls, and a platform at the rear of the room. A huge compass pattern in the floor tiles marked the very centre of the room, a glass dome directly above it. But the most striking feature were the nine yellow-cloaked figures standing on the stage in a line formation.

Tancho had never seen all nine together.

He had, over the three times he'd visited the Aequi Kentron, only met a few of them.

"King of the Westlands," the centre figure called. She was tall, wearing the official yellow cloak, the hood barely covering her wheat-coloured hair. She had high cheekbones and a knowing smile. Tancho wouldn't dare guess her age. Sixty? Six hundred? The elders were a mysterious people. "Welcome."

Tancho felt Kohaku stand a little taller beside him, but Karasu hissed, almost inaudibly, yet a sound of distaste, nonetheless. No, not distaste.

Distrust.

But Tancho strode forward as though he owned the grand hall and they were his guests, not the other way around.

"Queen of Eastlands," the centre figure called this time, turning to a door from the south. "Welcome."

And to Tancho's left, three dark-umber red-cloaked figures entered. They appeared to almost glide across the floor, smooth and synchronised. Their hoods were also up, so Tancho could not see their faces.

"King of the Southlands," the centre figure said to the door in the west of the room. "Welcome."

Three dark green cloaked figures entered next. They were tall and broad, and their faces hidden by their hoods also.

Tancho's belly tightened to the point of nausea. There was only one more to be introduced . . .

"King of the Northlands. Welcome."

Though from the corner of his eye he could see two men stride in, Tancho kept his face straight ahead, chin raised. From the periphery, he could see their cloaks black as the night without stars, hoods up, faces cast in shadow.

The birthmark on his wrist felt as though it might catch fire. Now there was pain. Not a mild burning as there had been, now it burned like a blacksmith's forge. He wanted to scream and curse but choked it back. He dared not even flinch.

He couldn't show any weakness.

"My name is Adelais," the centre figure said. "I stood in this very room when you were but four newborns destined for greatness, and it is an honour to stand before you again. The Consul of Elders have been guardians of the Aequi Kentron, equal centre of the Great Kingdom, and this grand hall, the very centre of the compass, joining all four lands.

"Once every thousand years, and on the equinox of your twenty-fifth year, we will witness the Golden Eclipse. A truly wondrous celestial event, where the two Sister Moons eclipse the sun, and for one week, the skies turn everything golden."

Adelais looked at the four groups, smiling. "Our ancestors mapped the stars and, from this, found the north star," she said to the men in black robes. Then to the others, "The south star, the east, and the west, the Great Kingdom was divided equally. Even Aequi Kentron follows the lines of the compass."

Tancho knew all this. It was part of his teachings, and he assumed everyone knew this and Adelais was reiterating the details for theatrics. He wished she'd get to the point, and that she'd stop talking about the birthmarks. Because the more she talked about it, the more he thought about it, and the more it burned.

"Your birthmark marks you as the true ruler of your land," she went on. "As it is claimed in our traditions and laws, 'Who bears the mark wears the crown.'"

A buzz burst through Tancho's blood. Hearing those words, making it official. It was beginning. His fate was now.

"Speaking of your birthmarks," Adelais continued with a smile. "They burn, do they not?"

None of the four regals nodded, none dared show weakness.

Adelais' smile twisted as though she expected such a reaction. "Tancho, Samiel, Elmwood, Crow. Please step forward. Hold out your wrists," she said. "Maghdlm will attend them."

Tancho could feel Karasu's unease beside him, but he knew she would keep herself in check. He walked toward the centre, his chin held high, and was joined by the others. Samiel and Elmwood stood to his left and the black-cloaked man stood at his right. He didn't dare look. He didn't have to.

He could feel him.

Beneath the pain of the birthmark, there was something else . . .

A pull. A drawstring between them being pulled tight. And that fascination he'd always had with the King of the Northlands became a tangible thing.

Physically they did not touch—there must have been a foot between them—but the birthmark on Tancho's wrist burned as a white-hot branding iron. He shied away from the tall figure, as much as he could without being obvious, and gritted his teeth and held out his wrist. He could feel how his body reacted to Crow being close, how his skin heated, how his blood warmed as if trying to pull him closer.

Crow was a half-head taller than him, much broader. His mere presence was intimidating and intoxicating.

What is this?

In all his teachings, in all his training, no one had prepared Tancho for this reaction.

Samiel and Elmwood both held out their right arms and it reminded Tancho of the instruction he had been given. He lifted his arm, his hand upturned, exposing his wrist, expecting to see the birthmark red and burning, yet it looked just the same.

Crow held out his hand as well, showing no sign of discomfort.

Could he feel it? Did his burn the same?

Maghdlm, one of the other yellow-cloaked figures, came forward then. Much shorter, and when Tancho saw her face, he realised, much older as well. Wrinkled like linen, creased with time and a number of years Tancho could not fathom.

She put her hand to Samiel's wrist first, her knuckles gnarled, her skin like crumpled paper, lightly touching the birthmark. Samiel gasped quietly and Maghdlm smiled up at her. With a nod, she moved to Elmwood and did the same. He let out a quiet sigh, and Tancho was relieved that it was not only he who would find relief.

Maghdlm stood in front of Tancho, looked up at him, and smiled. But when she touched his wrist, it was she who hissed. Her gaze shot to Tancho's; her old, dark eyes flashed with shock before she gripped his wrist.

"*Demidium*," she whispered.

She let go of his wrist, but the birthmark still burned.

He wanted to beg her to make it stop—it was getting worse —but she moved to Crow next, mumbling something . . . No, not mumbling.

Chanting.

She took Crow's wrist and looked up at him. Her chanting grew louder.

Their birthmarks began to glow red, the pain grew hotter, impossibly so, and Tancho couldn't bear it any longer. He let out a pained gasp, though somehow, through sheer will, he kept his arm out as instructed. Crow bit out a groan at the same time, just as Maghdlm's chant became a shout and she let his wrist go.

Sparks danced above their now-red birthmarks, sparking across their palms as if someone had kicked the embers of a campfire. Tancho turned to look at Crow, seeing his face for the very first time. Seeing how ruggedly handsome he was, his pale skin and square jaw, his pink lips, and how the sparks danced in his black eyes . . .

Then, just like magick, the pain was gone.

CHAPTER FIVE

CROW COULDN'T REMEMBER what they'd eaten for dinner. If, in fact, he'd eaten at all. What had happened with the birthmarks, the pain and the sparks, was not supposed to have happened. And not just because he'd never been taught it, or practised it, or learned about it.

He'd never heard of any such thing.

But from the bewildered look on Maghdlm's face and how she'd grown wary and alarmed, how she'd cast Adelais an incredulous sidelong glance as she'd hurried out of the grand hall, it seemed she hadn't expected such a thing either.

Two other yellow-robed elders left with her, and a brief look of outrage crossed Adelais' face before she calmly schooled her features and continued with her parade. They'd been shown to tables and food had been brought out, but Crow's appetite, along with his ability to concentrate, had disappeared.

For across the room sat Tancho, with his white hooded robe pulled up, his head down, and in deep conversation with the two who sat either side of him.

It was very clear he knew nothing of what had happened either.

Every so often Tancho would glance at Crow, as did the woman beside him, and Crow became angrier each and every time. When Adelais declared the evening formalities were over and they would reconvene in the courtyard after breakfast, Crow stood up so fast, his chair scraped the floor. He stalked out of the grand hall with Soko at his side, ignoring the many eyes on his back, and he barely held his temper until they'd reached the north quarters.

He shoved open the doors to their room and he wanted to throw and smash something, and he would have, only nothing in the room belonged to him, so he pulled at his cloak and threw it at the chaise. Though his aim was fine, it was a soft projectile and lacked satisfaction. "What in all the blue skies was that?" he yelled. "What kind of sorcery are they playing at?" He stomped over to where his cloak had half-spilled onto the floor, collected it into a rough ball, and this time threw it at the wall.

"Did the cloak offend you somehow?" Soko asked, still standing near the door.

Crow spun to face him. "What kind of magick did that woman use on me?"

Soko raised one eyebrow. "Did you not hear what Adelais called it?"

"I didn't hear anything after she did that thing—" Crow moved his hand like he was sprinkling dust.

That drew a frown from Soko. "She called it stella-arcane. Maghdlm draws her power from the stars."

"I'd not felt a pain like it!"

"I don't believe she was the cause of—"

"It burned like ore in a forge. White-hot."

"I think Tancho felt the same. He seemed to be hurting. The woman with him was furious."

"And what gives him the right?"

Soko stared at him. "The right . . . ?"

"Yes, the right! How *dare* he."

Now Soko was lost. "He seemed as confused as you, Crow. I don't think—"

"He has no right to come here and to look at me. The nerve."

"Are you feeling okay, my lord?" Soko asked quietly, cautiously.

"With his perfect skin and his perfect eyes and long red hair!" Crow was annoyed, but Soko finally understood.

"Ah."

Crow put his hand to his forehead; his gaze met Soko's. "What colour even is that? The colour of fresh blood? Or last year's redberry wine?" He was genuinely outraged. "What kind of man appears so perfect?"

Another rhetorical question, but Soko couldn't help himself. "Well, you've used the word perfect three times, so I'm going to go with perfe—"

"How dare he!"

"Yes, quite," Soko said, amused now and relieved his king hadn't succumbed to lunacy, and he was, it seemed, quite simply, enamoured. He went to the table and poured two goblets of blackberry wine, thankful—and a little disappointed, but mostly thankful—it wasn't redberry wine. He held one out to Crow. "Here. Drink."

Crow took the wine, still angry. "He looked right at me. I've never seen eyes like his. And his mouth. The audacity of him to have lips like that."

Soko smiled behind his goblet. "The audacity."

Crow took a long drink of wine and seemed a little

calmer on the other side of it. "And it still doesn't explain the arcane fire that woman drew from my wrist. I've seen healers work all kinds of magick, but this was sparks, as if she summoned the fire from my skin."

"Does the mark still burn?"

Crow showed his wrist and scowled at it. The birthmark appeared unchanged, but the pain was gone. Mostly. "The pain is absent, though it still buzzes."

"The spell was supposed to numb it for the duration of dinner, that's all. Whatever happened to you and Tancho was not expected," Soko said. "And I'd guess that all nine elders are, at this very moment, sitting around a table, reading scroll after ancient scroll, trying to figure out what it means."

Crow's brows furrowed and he conceded an angry nod. "I should hope so."

"I hope so too," Soko said. With a tap of his goblet to Crow's, he gave him a cheeky smile. "And I hope they figure it out soon. Because come sun-up, after breakfast, you get to see King Perfect again. And perhaps you'll see his hair in the sunlight so you can get a better likeness."

Crow bristled and was about to remind Soko of his manners, but Soko laughed and collected the wine from the table. "I joke with you, that's all. Apologies, my king." He poured Crow some more wine. "But I will remind you, Crow," Soko said, serious now. "That while what happened tonight was a far cry from normal, there's still a chance that tomorrow you will need to meet Tancho in the arena. To fight."

Crow's eyes hardened; his jaw bulged. And with a low growl in the back of his throat, he drained his wine, then held out the empty goblet for more.

DAWN CAME FAR TOO EARLY. A platter of breakfast foods was delivered to their quarters, which Soko gratefully received while Crow dressed. He also grumbled incessantly, scowled at everything, and cursed his wretched headache.

"Whose lapse in judgement was it to drink last night?" he mumbled, walking out to the common room.

"Well," Soko began. "I could say the first goblet was my idea, but the remainder and the second bottle was yours." He held out some bread with a spattering of marmalade. "This is good. You should eat."

Crow took it and, after a few mouthfuls, reluctantly agreed. It was good, so he ate some more, then some cured meats and fruit, and a pot of *valngi angelica* tea. It tasted like home. They had made the effort to source foods from the Northlands and that should have comforted Crow somewhat.

But it felt like an overreach.

An apology, perhaps.

A knock at the door drew Crow from his thoughts, and Soko was quick to answer. It was the messenger from the day before. He stood, dressed in his yellow cloak, hood up, head bowed, and handed Soko the note. "From Adelais, herself."

Soko closed the door and handed the paper to Crow. He read it aloud. "The Consul requests your attendance in the grand hall prior to formal proceedings in the courtyard, if you will."

"To discuss what they found out about last night," Soko surmised.

Crow absentmindedly rubbed at his wrist. "Yes. One would think so."

Soko nodded to Crow's birthmark. "Does it bother you again this morning?"

Crow made a face. "It doesn't burn, though it's . . . uncomfortable. It feels as though it moves under the skin, like a nest of tiny spiders has hatched and squirm beneath the surface."

Soko grimaced. "Well, let's hope today puts an end to it. One way or another. Perhaps the little old witch-woman has found out how to remedy it for good." He sheathed his sword and slid a smaller blade beneath his arm guard, then another in the leg of his boot.

Crow watched on, amused. "Do you think all that is necessary?"

"The note did not mention weapons, lest not to bring them," Soko replied. "I would suggest you do the same. We don't know what this day holds, but I would advise to be prepared."

Crow picked up his broadsword. His favourite weapon; the hilt was made for his hand, the blade handcrafted from the finest Northlands' steel, weighted and balanced for his swing. "I will only need one."

Soko smiled and picked up Crow's smaller dagger, handing it to him, hilt first. "Don't forget you'll be facing Tancho this morn."

Crow's nostrils flared, and his birthmark grew warmer at the mention of Tancho's name. He took the dagger and sheathed it in his boot. Then he added another to his belt. "Curse this day."

Soko chuckled and threw Crow's cloak to him, then waited for him to slip it on. "Are you ready?"

Crow squared his shoulders and focused his mind. This is what he'd trained for, and he wouldn't allow the beauty of his opponent to distract him. Was he truly ready? Crow was no longer certain, but he had little choice. He *had* to be ready.

"I am."

Soko went to the door and pulled it open, only to find the messenger still waiting. He hadn't moved. "I am to escort you," he offered.

So, they followed him back to the grand hall, two black cloaks following one yellow. The halls looked different in the morning light. Not so ominous, not so cavern-like. Crow caught a glimpse out a passing window to the blue sky beyond. It looked like a pleasant day, and everything around him was welcoming.

But it did little to quell the unease in his belly.

He couldn't shake the feeling that something wasn't right, and it had nothing to do with the wine he'd had to drink the night before.

They reached the huge doors to the grand hall, and as they had done last night, they opened inward, seemingly of their own accord. The room was so much brighter than it had been last night, and when Crow looked upward, he saw why. The ceiling had a stained-glass dome, fracturing sunlight onto the huge compass tiled into the floor.

He and Soko walked to the north point of the dial and stopped. Before them, five yellow-robed Consul Elders stood, Adelais at the front. She smiled. "Good morning, King of Northlands."

Crow was about to make a point of addressing Soko, but the doors to his left opened, and three white-cloaked figures walked in to stand at the tip of the western point on the compass. Tancho in the middle, the woman to his right, and the tall large man to his left. They were all strikingly beautiful, though Tancho was a standout.

Crow shot his gaze back to Adelais and the other elders,

two of which, were watching Crow. Were they gauging his reaction? Were they assessing something in his behaviour?

"Good morning, King of Westlands."

From the corner of his eye, Crow saw Tancho bow his head.

Adelais smiled. "When Maghdlm tended to your birth-marks last night, the reaction was not only unexpected but also unforeseen. Meaning we, here on the Consul, had never seen such a reaction. Maghdlm and others searched the archives all night and what they found was not . . ." She paused, her face uneasy. "Not in the writings about the Golden Eclipse, or in battle conduct, or in any scroll pertaining to the birthmark ceremony."

Crow noticed Soko cross his arms, not in a defensive posture. It was so he had better access to the knife at his wrist. Soko, very clearly, was as fond of this whole circum-stance as Crow.

"Where we *did* find mention of it," Adelais continued. "Was in Maghdlm's compendium, more specifically in the alchemy of alignment."

Crow frowned. *What in the blue skies was the alchemy of alignment?*

"Maghdlm is an alchemist but also a student of the stars, and she is the oldest amongst us. Her powers are strong and true." Adelais paused a moment, then bowed her head. "My kings, what she found is binding."

"Forgive my impatience, kind Adelais," Crow said. "But if you have answers to give, I would like very much to hear them."

One of the other yellow-cloaked figures strode forward then. A man with warm brown skin, grey hair, and ice-blue eyes. "My kings, I am Gabel, Aequi Kentron's historian. I was with Maghdlm this past night when we found the answer. The alchemy of alignment tells us that the chosen two will meet when their stars align. Marked by fate, as you both are. When your stars align with the sun and the moons, as they will in coming days, the power of the compass will draw you together. As magnets behave, so will you. Your choice no longer applies, I'm afraid."

"Clarify," Tancho said, his voice musical and sharp.

"I dare not explain the alchemy, for fear I misspeak or tangle truths I myself do not understand. But what I know is this," Gabel said, "the markings on your wrist will choose for you."

"Choose for me?" Crow asked, not caring for manners now.

"On the day of the Golden Eclipse, you will be drawn to one another, and the mark of your birth upon your wrist will give you the answer you seek."

"To which question?" Crow snapped back. "Answer I seek for what?"

"As magnets are," Adelais replied. "Whether you will be repelled or joined forever by the mark you bear."

"I know my answer," Crow barked.

"As do I," Tancho said. "I will not be joined with a Northlander. I would rather fight."

Crow turned to him then. "You would fight *me?*" That was almost laughable to Crow. He stood taller, broader, stronger. The reach of his arm would easily outmatch his in a sword fight. He'd fought countless men smaller than him, and he'd bested every one. Easily.

In one swift movement, Tancho reached into his cloak and produced two katanas as if they were extensions of his hands. He stood in the strike pose, the two figures in white with him also stood guard, weapons ready.

Soko had his daggers out in an instant, and Crow

unsheathed his broadsword, swinging it for good measure. He smiled at Tancho. He could ignore the man's beauty when he raised a sword at him. "Your three against our two, and I still don't like your odds, little fish."

Tancho bared his teeth and crossed his swords. "Karasu?"

"Yes, Tancho," the woman at his right said, unflinching, unblinking.

Tancho stared right at Crow. "Did you ever hear a pretty blackbird sing?"

Karasu grinned, and the tall brutish man with them laughed.

Crow growled and swung his sword—

"Enough," said a small, papery voice. Maghdlm walked in, her steps uneven as though her hips gave her grief, an old book in her hands. "You'll get your chance to spill blood, but it is not this day." She strode toward them like a weary grandmother putting an end to the bickering of children. "Put the blades away or I'll render them to iron."

She was half of Crow's height. A slight woman, elderly and soft, yet for some reason, Crow didn't doubt her powers. He lowered his sword and stood taller. "Apologies." Soko stood down as well, sheathing his daggers.

Tancho lowered his katanas, as did Karasu, but the oaf alongside them did not. He made one last show of raising his blade as a silent warning aimed at Crow and Soko. Maghdlm simply raised her hand, murmured some ancient chant, and the blade in his hand turned to rusted iron.

He gasped in shock, his eyes wide, sorely about to protest, but Tancho raised his hand. "Kohaku, you were warned."

Maghdlm smiled up at Kohaku. "I don't know exactly

how much iron is in your blood, boy. But ignore me again and we will find out."

Crow chewed the inside of his lip so his smile didn't escape him. Last night, he wasn't overly fond of Maghdlm, but he liked her this day.

"I am the daughter of an alchemist and an astronomer, born in an eclipse many lifetimes ago," Maghdlm said. "Gifted by the hand of fate in the ways of old magicks, and in all my years, I didn't think to see this. The golden sun is not rare enough, yet to have your stars aligning at the same time . . . there are not enough stars in the sky to count the odds."

"Is this an alchemical bond?" Tancho asked, his head tilted slightly. It gave him an innocent boyish look that Crow didn't find disarming at all. Or attractive.

One of the yellow-robed elders cleared her throat. She appeared elvish-like, with brown curly hair and a beautiful face, and she was smiling at Crow as though she could read his mind.

"I am Aelfflaed," she said, bowing her head, her voice musical. "Seer of truth."

"You both have many questions," Aelfflaed said.

"Which we need answered," Crow snapped. "If you are a seer, how did you not foresee this?"

"I see the truth," she replied. "Not the future. I see if your words or actions match your heart."

Crow repressed a growl. So she could see that Crow found Tancho beautiful?

Great.

"Alchemical bond? Yes," Maghdlm said, ignoring Aelf-flaed and answering Tancho's question.

Tancho gave a nod. "Then it can be broken."

"But the stars are at work here as well," Maghdlm

replied. "The basis of alchemy is the process of change by which to fuse or reunite with the divine or original form. As I did with the boy's dagger, you see. The reaction of your birthmarks we witnessed yesternight was of the old, *old* ways. Before my time, before even my magick's time. Your bodies are elemental, we all are. But you two are different. The metals, the elements, are one and the same. From the same source, and this golden sun, when the stars align to complete the alchemy, your stars must meet again, and they will decide your fate."

"Our stars?" Crow asked. This was becoming more absurd . . .

The old woman opened the book and ran her gnarled finger down the page to a heading. It was in ancient script that Crow could not read.

"Yes," Maghdlm said, reading the words. "Demidium, meaning half. You are two halves of the same whole. Fate has left its mark on you both. Not only for the golden sun, but the lacuna as well."

"Lacuna?" Tancho repeated.

"Yes," Maghdlm said, her voice a whisper. She looked up at Crow, then Tancho, then went back to her book and read the ancient words out loud. "The space between. The part that is missing," she said, "from each of you, is found in the other. Your fate will choose either way, but the space between you will be no more, and as it is done in alchemy, returned to its original form."

Crow tried to get her words to make sense. "Returned?"

Maghdlm referred back to the ancient script and hummed. "There is a line that connects the crow to the fish, Corvus to Pisces." She smiled up at them. "The stars will align during the Golden Eclipse."

Crow had lost patience with the riddles. "What does that mean?" he barked at her.

She met his gaze with a cool indifference. "It seems fate has already rolled the dice. Your destiny is chosen. The lacuna is done."

Crow was about to lose his temper completely when Tancho looked at him, meeting his gaze. And the fire in his eyes was gone, replaced with resignation.

He understood.

"What does that mean?" Crow asked.

"Our birthmarks have already chosen," he whispered. And finally it dawned on Crow what it all meant, though it was Tancho who spoke it out loud. "And they have chosen that we cannot be apart."

CHAPTER SIX

MAGHDLM ASKED for more time for further studies, to be absolutely certain of her findings. There were scripts and scrolls in the belly of the Aequi Kentron that she was yet to go through. Even though Tancho wanted all doubt removed, time seemed to be something they had very little of.

The Golden Eclipse would be upon them soon, so either way, Tancho had little choice but to wait. Training all his life for this one moment, only to have it all change moments before he was to take the stage was unsettling.

He prided himself on his control—self-control and control of that around him—and to have that taken away from him left him uncertain and a little lost. He felt . . . off-kilter and ill-composed.

Maghdlm, Gabel, and two other elders hurried out of the grand hall back to the library with promises to relay any new findings immediately.

They were no sooner out the door than a messenger came in. He stood before Adelais in his pristine yellow robe. "Apologies, but the King of the Southlands and the Queen of the Eastlands grew tired of waiting in the courtyard," he said ruefully. "They've taken to fighting."

"Fighting?" Adelais asked, unable to hide her stricken surprise.

"Ah, yes. Each other. It appears to be in good spirits, though the commander suggested I let you know."

She gave a hard nod. "Thank you." Then she looked up at Tancho and Crow. "Please follow me." Without another word, she turned and strode out of the hall. Karasu moved to follow on her heels, but Tancho held her arm, allowing Crow and his friend to go first.

"I'd rather not have him at my back," Tancho whispered. He gave them a few yards start, then fell into step, the remaining elders at the tail. They walked along a sandstone corridor with filtered sunlight, and soon enough, Adelais passed a large opening and Tancho could hear laughter coming from outside.

They came to a wide set of stone steps, which led the way down to what had to be the courtyard. And there, in mock battle, were Elmwood and Samiel. Elmwood wore his dark green pants and a leather vest, showing his huge biceps as he swung his axe at Samiel. Samiel wore a red sleeveless tunic overtop umber pants. She held a scimitar to his axe, deflecting and parrying, as graceful as Elmwood was lumbersome. Both of them grinning and laughing, and even their entourages sat looking on highly amused.

"Apologies for keeping you waiting," Adelais said, her yellow cloak billowing in the breeze. Elmwood and Samiel stopped sparring and lowered their weapons, but they gave both Tancho and Crow curious looks, and Tancho didn't blame them. They must have felt kept on the outer, and Tancho would have felt disadvantaged if the elders had taken any of them aside for a secret meeting.

"There's been a development," Adelais explained. "Something unforeseen, which may change the direction we move forward in. We are, as yet, still awaiting finer details and we cannot start official proceedings until all doubt is removed."

"A development?" Samiel asked, her dark eyes as sharp as her blades. She was tall and thin, her rich brown skin and long, dark, braided hair matched perfectly with her red and umber clothes. She was all the colours of the desert sands from which she came, and she was beautiful.

"You witnessed the unusual reaction to their birthmarks last night," Adelais said, gesturing regally to Tancho and Crow. "Theirs is an ancient connection we are yet to fully decipher. We hope to know more this day, and we shall delay official ceremonies until then."

"We can still fight, yes?" Elmwood asked. He was a strange man, Tancho thought. More in his element here than anyone else, it would seem. He was King of the Southlands, lands of forests and jungles, warmer in climate and more prone to rain. He wore shades of dark green leather, his brown hair was artfully dishevelled, appearing almost like tree roots. His arms were the size of tree trunks, and his eyes and smile had the air of a satyr or the forest elves Tancho had read about in their histories. He liked Elmwood with barely a word uttered between them.

Then Tancho reconsidered his earlier assessment of Elmwood being more in his element than any other leader. Yes, Elmwood was very much an embodiment of his land, his people, but Samiel was that too. And perhaps Tancho was indicative of his lands and his people; he was named after a fish, after all. Sleek and quiet, tranquil, but powerful too.

And what of Crow?

His black hair shone in the sunlight, his black cloak danced in the breeze as a bird's wing. His eyes were as sharp as a bird of prey, Tancho allowed. And when they'd drawn weapons on each other in the grand hall, neither of them had given an inch, and Tancho liked that. In fact, he liked squaring off against Crow more than he ought to.

And much to Tancho's surprise, he found it as arousing as it was thrilling. Perhaps it was the adrenaline and the heightened senses from their near fight . . .

"I think we shall," Adelais said.

Shall what?

Tancho had been so lost in his own thoughts, he'd lost track of conversation.

"I think exhibition sparring sounds fun," Adelais furthered. "Exhibition only, no blood drawn. Any malice or ill-intent will see your position forfeited." She turned to Crow and Tancho. "Perhaps you two should not engage?"

Crow smiled at Tancho, that conceited smirk that Tancho wanted to wipe from his face. That fire in his gaze that Tancho wanted to see more of when they fought, when they fucked.

Wait.

What?

Crow unsheathed his sword and swung it, still smirking . . . Oh, those lips . . . Tancho shook his head.

"What's the matter, little fish?" Crow asked. "Too scared to spar with me?"

Before he even knew what he was doing, Tancho pulled out his katana and swung it in an infinity loop, letting the weight of it guide his hand. "Not at all, pretty blackbird."

The man with Crow, the blond Northlander, stood between them, hands up, staring at Crow. "My king, I don't think it wise to start this."

"Soko," Crow said, not taking his eyes off Tancho. "I don't think it wise you stand in between us."

"The rule was no blood. I don't fancy seeing either of you forfeiting this day," Soko countered.

"The rule was no malice or ill-intent," Tancho replied staring at Crow, raising his sword. "There will be no malice, and my intent is pure."

Karasu slid next to Soko but faced her king. "Tancho," she whispered, her hand out as if in front of an injured animal. "This is not who you are. The mark on your wrist draws false bearing. Remember why you are here."

Adelais raised her hand. "Kind kings," she said serenely. "It is clear we do not know the full effect of your birthmarks or what the pull of the Golden Eclipse does to your self-control. I should suggest you not partake in these games against the other. Tancho, please partner off with Samiel. Crow, face Elmwood. Perhaps Soko and Karasu should also like to showcase their skills."

Tancho lowered his sword and bowed his head at Adelais. He knew Karasu's words to be true. This was not who he was. He had more self-control than that, but something about Crow set him off. Even being near him had him on edge. Tancho's usual cool demeanour fell into chaos. He wanted to fight him, hurt him, make him bleed and cry out in pain, in ecstasy. He wanted to fuck like animals, wild and unbidden.

Tancho froze at the thought. What had made him think that? Imagine it, picture it . . . want it?

Karasu's hand on his snapped him from his thoughts. "Tancho, what is wrong?" she asked. "This plays tricks on your mind."

He gave a curt nod. "I do not know," he whispered. "I want to do things . . . I cannot control . . ."

She took his hand and upturned his wrist to inspect the birthmark. "How does it feel?"

It was so hard to describe. It felt as though it should be on fire, but the pain wasn't allowed to surface. "Agitated."

"Come," Karasu said. "We shall try some distance." She led him toward where Samiel and her two companions stood. Kohaku followed, but Tancho saw how he kept an eye on Crow. It was clear Kohaku wasn't fond of him either.

"Greetings," Samiel said, her smile wide. She waved her hand to the two women beside her. "Fazluna and Addax."

Tancho gave a polite bow of his head. "Greetings to you, also. This is Karasu and Kohaku."

Samiel glanced around the courtyard. "A day of mock battles instead of ceremonial proceedings. Unexpected, is it not?"

"It is," Tancho replied. "Unexpected and concerning."

Then, all of a sudden, his birthmark grew warm, and warmer still. It buzzed and burned, growing warmer again, then hot . . . too hot. Pain ripped up his arm.

He spun around to search for Crow and found that he and Elmwood had begun to move to the far end of the courtyard. Crow was stopped, his hand out, glaring at his wrist, then up at Tancho.

"What is this?" he roared.

"I would ask you the same thing," Tancho yelled back, trying to keep his temper in check.

"The distance between you," Adelais called out. She had both hands out to them. "Close the distance between you."

Tancho's feet moved, almost without his permission. Anything to make the pain stop. Crow took a few small steps toward him, staring at his upturned wrist. And sure enough, as they drew closer, the pain lessened.

Tancho stopped moving and gave Adelais a nod. She turned to the yellow-cloaked guard beside her. "Seek out Maghdlm in the archīvum and ask her to join us. Please hurry."

Crow turned his livid gaze from Tancho to Adelais. "What is this? We can't be parted by more than twenty strides?"

"I'm sure Maghdlm will have some kind of remedy, even if only short term."

"Short term?" Crow barked. Then he mumbled something and spun on his heel, taking long strides back to Soko. Only, he didn't get far.

Tancho cried out, holding his wrist, and Crow gripped his as well, glancing at Tancho. Pain etched his face, but there was something else as well. Soko went to him and pushed him back toward Tancho, and the pain was gone. "Give me your dagger," Crow said to him. "I'll cut it off."

"Cut what off?" Soko cried.

"The birthmark. My whole hand if need be."

Soko laughed, but when he saw Crow was serious, his smile fell away. "Have you fallen into madness?"

"Give me your dagger," Crow hissed at him.

"My king, I will not," Soko said quietly. "I dare not defy you, but I cannot allow—"

Adelais interrupted curtly. "The ties between you are in your blood. The only thing cutting your arm off to be rid of the birthmark will ensure is that you'll require assistance to lace your boots for the rest of your days while your blood still burns." She recomposed herself. "I would ask for patience until Maghdlm arrives."

"And I would ask for this to be gone," Crow replied, holding up his wrist. "It's been weeks."

Adelais cocked her head. "Weeks?"

Crow gave a nod. "Yes."

"It began last full moons," Tancho added. "For me at least. First, it itched. Then it grew warm. I thought it might burst aflame."

Crow gave a nod, and for the first time since they'd met, they actually agreed with each other. Crow turned to Elmwood. "Does your mark give you no grief?"

Elmwood held out his right hand, palm up. His birthmark was the shape of a tree, of course. "Not at all."

Samiel held up hers, showing three zigzag lines. "Mine neither. I forget I have it. And you say yours has troubled you for weeks?"

Both Tancho and Crow nodded, but Adelais became concerned. "I assumed the marks became troublesome upon your arrival."

The guard returned with Maghdlm scurrying behind him. She was out of breath, and her cheeks had some colour. Tancho could see her eyes better in the daylight and they appeared a dark, cloudy blue. "What troubles?" she asked.

"They cannot have a distance between them of more than twenty paces without immense pain," Adelais explained. "And they say this began at the last full moons."

Maghdlm looked up at both of them, concerned, confused. She mumbled something in an ancient tongue and shook her head. She took Tancho's wrist and covered his birthmark with her hand, mumbling, chanting, and then she did the same to Crow.

Her fingers danced above their skin and sparks glittered again, but this time their birthmarks glowed red. There was no pain, they stood too close for that. But there was . . . something. As though Maghdlm was drawing the bond out of them or closer together, Tancho couldn't be sure.

Then it was over. Maghdlm let her hands fall away, the

echo of her chant still lingered, and her eyes were wide. Tancho recognised fear when he saw it. "What is it?"

"Something evil comes," Maghdlm whispered.

"Evil?" Tancho asked, a shiver running down his spine.

Crow's hand went to the hilt of his sword. "From where?"

"From far and near, and we are not ready," Maghdlm replied, frowning as if she didn't like that at all. Then her eyes grew fierce. "Remember the lacuna. You must stay together, so the distance between is no distance at all."

Just then, a guard came running into the courtyard. "Elder Consul!" he yelled as he ran toward them. "Four riders come, at pace."

Adelais gasped, and everyone drew their weapons. "From where do they ride?"

"From the Westlands," he replied, his gaze falling on Tancho. "They come from the Westlands."

Tancho's blood ran cold, his belly turned to ice. And from somewhere deep in the castle, a bell tolled.

CHAPTER SEVEN

ADELAIS AND TANCHO led the way back to the grand hall, Crow and Soko close on their heels, Elmwood with his two guards, Kearmore and Cardwick, as well as Samiel and her two guards following behind them. Not that Crow could go any distance from Tancho, it would seem, but this time he didn't want to.

Evil was coming, Adelais had said, and then riders came at pace from the Westlands.

This couldn't have been a coincidence.

They burst into the grand hall as other elders arrived at the same time, faces ashen, eyes wide. Before Crow could demand to know what was going on, the western doors opened and the four riders, wearing the Westlands white cloaks, were escorted in by a guard.

"Hikari," Tancho said, going to them. "Hitode, Unagi, Iruka. What brings you?"

The first, who Tancho had called Hikari, bowed his head. He was pale and beautiful with long brown hair. Were they all so damn pretty?

"My king," Hikari said. "We bring news. Beings, creatures we cannot describe, came. They appeared overnight on the first day after your leave."

"Beings?" Adelais asked.

Hikari met Tancho's gaze. "Please don't fear me mad, my king. Creatures, ill-formed and grotesque. They had snouts and tusks like boars. They came from the ocean, north of the castle."

"The north?" Tancho repeated and many eyes went to Crow.

"I know of no such thing," he said defiantly, offended, affronted. "I wouldn't force attack from the water, at any rate, when that is your domain, when I could cross the mountains and flatten you from our advantage. Only a fool would—"

"No one is blaming you," Adelais said. Then she turned to the four guests. "Are they?"

Hikari bowed his head again. "No. These creatures are a likeness we have not seen before. Pale blue with mottled skin."

Pale blue?

"They came ashore?" Tancho asked, his voice quiet. "What did they do?"

"Asagi ordered us to ride with this message. We do not know, my lord. But . . ."

"But?"

He looked at Tancho, then to Karasu and Kohaku and back to Tancho. "But we believe that was their intent. They came toward the castle in military lines, with purpose, my lord."

Tancho put his hand on Hikari's arm, but he looked to Karasu and Kohaku. "We must return."

Karasu nodded hard, and Kohaku straightened his wrist guard. "We can leave now."

"Wait, please," Adelais said. "We will find out what information we can." She turned to one of the elders. "What do we know about these . . . creatures? We must check our archives. Where is Gabel? As the keeper of history and culture, perhaps he will know something."

"Apologies, kind Speaker Adelais," Tancho said. "But we are leaving. If my lands are under attack, if my people need me . . . I care not for a lesson in this enemy's history but would rather meet them at the end of my sword, sooner rather than later. Please have my horses ready and four fresh horses for my fellow men."

And with that, white cloak billowing out behind him, he turned to walk to the western doors . . . and got no further. He cried out the same time Crow did, gripping his wrist in pain. The pain was worse, shooting to his elbow, and his birthmark burned. Tancho's guards went to his aid. The four new riders were shocked to see their king in pain.

Soko went to Crow, holding his arm and dragging him a few steps toward Tancho until the searing pain eased. "Crow, you cannot have distance between you," he whispered. "That much is clear."

"What of the Golden Eclipse?" Adelais asked, her voice loud and clear, her gaze aimed at Tancho. "If you leave . . ."

Tancho raised his chin, defiance and anger burning in his eyes. "If I leave, I forfeit. But if I do not defend my people, my kingdom is forfeit anyway. My honour is forfeit, along with any right to be called king." He swallowed hard and his gaze turned to steel. "And I promise, if any enemy has taken aim at my people, I will defend them. And I will kill all who stand in my way."

Crow's heart thumped and a smile tugged at his lips at Tancho's words. He liked this Tancho, this livid and proud king, and he felt oddly protective of him because he understood this Tancho. Because if someone posed a threat to Crow's land, to his people, Crow would unleash a whole world of horrors.

"Tancho, wait," Crow said, his hand outstretched. Tancho stared at him, clearly out of patience, but Crow turned to Adelais and held up his wrist. "Speaker, can this birthmark be removed?"

Adelais paused, her quiet reply loud in the silence. "No."

"Then my choice is removed also. As the lacuna dictates and as we have witnessed, the Westlands' king and I cannot permit a distance between us. I must go with him."

"Do you know what this means?" Adelais asked, her tone disappointed and cold.

"Does this lacuna not supersede the Golden Eclipse?" he asked. "Which takes precedence?"

"Our history is long and our laws are resolute. The Golden Eclipse occurs once in a thousand years."

Crow bristled at that. "Are we being held hostage here?"

"No," Adelais replied softly.

"Right." Crow stared at her, unblinking. "Because should anyone be fool enough to try and take my kingdom from me, my reply will be swift and without mercy." He waited for Adelais to reply, but when none was forthcoming, Crow looked to Samiel and Elmwood. "Though it has been brief, our meeting at long last has been an honour."

Elmwood and Samiel both bowed their heads. "Likewise," Samiel said. Her expression was cautious, as was Elmwood's.

Crow turned to Tancho then, to find him staring at him. Resilience and something akin to understanding flashed in Tancho's eyes, and he gave Crow a nod. Then both kings walked out of the grand hall toward the western wing. Soko followed quickly alongside Karasu and Kohaku, and the four riders scurried to keep up.

"Ah, Crow?" Soko said as they hurried along. "Are we really going to the Westlands?"

"Still your tongue," Karasu hissed, "lest these walls have ears."

Crow shot a glance back at Soko and smiled at his scowl, and he couldn't help but notice the slight lift at the corner of Tancho's lips.

He also couldn't help but notice how quiet the Westlanders were on their feet. As they made their way down stone halls, they barely made a sound. Crow and Soko, on the other hand, with heavy boots made for snow, sounded like their own army.

They arrived at a set of wooden doors, much like those to the north wing, and Tancho pushed through them without stopping. As soon as Crow was inside, he stood to the side while everyone filed in, and he felt intrusive being in another king's quarters.

The common room was much like his own, with some long seats and a large table, topped with plates of food. Tancho called the four riders over to it. "You must be hungry after your ride. Please eat and drink. Rest while you can."

The first rider bowed his head in gratitude. "We will be ready to ride when you are, my king."

"Tell us what you know of the creatures that arrived," Tancho said, pouring them each a cup of water.

Hikari took the cup, bowing again, almost embarrassed. Crow could only assume it wasn't every day their king fetched them a drink. "We did not see them too closely. They came and Asagi sent us at pace to bring the message."

"I told you something was wrong," Karasu murmured. "From the moment I set foot upon the bridge to this land, I felt an unease in my bones."

"I know," Tancho replied, so calm, so serene. "The regret for not taking heed is mine, though I don't know what could have been done. This"—he held out his wrist, birthmark showing—"was a path I was already on. As much as I wish otherwise."

"I didn't ask for it either," Crow said. They were talking about him as if he wasn't in the room, and he didn't care for that at all. "And believe me, had my choice not been removed, I'd not be here in this room, and I certainly wouldn't be looking headlong into lands that aren't mine with those who would quicker see me dead."

Tancho gritted his teeth, and if he wanted to fire back well-aimed words, he chose not to. Instead, he turned to Karasu and Kohaku. "Please start packing up. We need to leave without delay."

She gave him a nod and shot Crow a look of distaste before skulking off to one of the rooms. Soko waved his hand awkwardly at Tancho. "Uh, I'm not sure if I yet have permission to speak? I was told to hold my tongue. Unless these walls also have ears?"

Crow bit back a smile at Soko's snark, and the bedroom door that Karasu had disappeared behind swung open. She stood, tossed a small bag onto the floor, and shot a murderous glare aimed at Soko. "I vote no."

Crow kept a pleasant expression, but he squared his shoulders and straightened his spine. "He is free to speak anytime he so chooses," Crow said coolly. If there were to be some ranking pissing contest, he held equal authority with Tancho, and Crow refused to take orders from anyone.

All eyes drew to Soko, and he cleared his throat. "I was, uh.

I was just going to say that Crow felt something was not right also. Mention was made earlier that Karasu believed something to be wrong. Crow did also. This morning he said something felt not right. Not to deride the statement of Karasu as less than Crow's." He waved his hand. "I just thought it worth a mention that two out of five from our lands combined thought something was ill afoot." All the Westlanders stared at him. So he cringed and added, "Which is less than half but still a considerable percentage, and one worth noting, one would think."

Crow fought a smile. "One would, yes."

Tancho walked to the far door and he and Crow both hissed at the fresh blaze of pain. "This cursed thing," Tancho hissed, holding his wrist.

Crow rubbed his birthmark, and Soko took Crow's hand, inspecting the offending mark. "There has to be some way to break this bond."

"Yes," Kohaku said, eating some kind of meat off a bone. "One of you must die."

Soko shot him a look. "Some other way." He lifted Crow's hand, inspecting the skin closely. "It is alchemical, is it not? Maghdlm can get a reaction out of it, and I feel Adelais knows more than she's letting on."

"I agree with that," Tancho said, angrily shoving belongings into a rucksack. "If one has an interest in considerable percentages."

"One does," Soko murmured, probably too smug a reply to a king. He was still inspecting the birthmark and didn't see Tancho's murderous glare, but Crow caught it.

Tancho roughly folded some clothing, as if the shirt had offended him and not Soko. "If you intend to come with us, should you not be packing your belongings?"

"I would need you to accompany me," Crow said, taking

his hand from Soko to show Tancho his birthmark. "Remember?"

Soko snatched Crow's hand and brought it back to the end of his nose, inspecting the birthmark so closely Crow wondered if he was looking at it or smelling it.

Tancho picked up a leather strap and began coiling it around his hand to pack it away. His jaw was clenched, his nostrils flared, his red hair seemed to catch the rage in his eyes. "Perhaps he could make a start without you."

Crow snarled. "Perhaps he—"

Tancho snatched up the bag. "And perhaps Soko could keep his fucking hands to himself!"

The room fell as quiet and cold as a tomb. Everyone stared at Tancho, and Crow's impulse to meet rage with equal rage was quelled when he saw the look on Karasu and Kohaku's faces. They were as stunned as he was.

Tancho let out a frustrated growl, directed inward, it was plain to see. He threw the bag to the floor and stalked to the window. Crow could see his shoulders rise and fall with what he guessed were deep, calculated breaths.

This was clearly out of character for him. And it was out of character for Crow to like it. Despite the stress and worry about his homelands, this pull between them was the birthmarks' doing. Crow pulled his hand from Soko's. "Tancho is right. Soko, perhaps you could make a start on our belongings."

Soko's gaze searched his. "I will not leave you in here, outnumbered and alone," he hissed.

"Take Kohaku with you," Crow obliged. "If that's amenable with his king."

Tancho turned his head, just slightly, and gave the slightest of nods.

"I don't like this," Soko said. "Whatever is in our quarters can stay behind."

"Soko," Crow said, and that was all he needed to say. Crow wasn't asking.

Soko knew this was an order from his king. "I don't like this."

"I know you don't. Though I am mortally wounded that you think me unable to best six on my own."

Soko rolled his eyes and almost smiled. "I will return at once. Do not leave without me."

"I would never."

Soko gave a nod, then turned to Kohaku. "You're with me."

Kohaku, the huge, hulking Westlander who hadn't stopped eating since they'd walked into the room, wiped his mouth with a napkin and smiled. "Or is it you with me?"

Just then, there was a knock at the door. Everyone drew their weapons, but the four riders stepped backwards into the corner, unarmed and wary.

Karasu stood in front of Tancho, putting herself between him and the door, and Soko did the same to Crow. Kohaku went to the door. "Who comes?"

"It is Samiel" came a female voice.

"And Elmwood" followed in a deeper tenor.

"Let them in," Tancho said.

Kohaku opened the door with one hand, his sword in his other. Samiel and Elmwood and their entourages filed through with some pageantry, though they stopped when they saw the room full of swords. Samiel smiled. "You have the same sentiment as us. Unease, uncertainty," she said. "Things are not what they seem here."

"This is not what we trained for. This is not our

destiny," Elmwood said. "There is no honour in these walls."

"I concur," Crow said, relaxing a little to know they all felt the same. "It feels manufactured. I can't describe it any other way."

Tancho met Crow's eyes and gave a nod. "I agree."

"My king?" Soko asked, his tone uncertain.

"Yes, please go. But don't waste daylight." Crow looked to Samiel and Elmwood to explain. "He and Kohaku are going to gather our room. We need to leave."

Elmwood raised a tree branch-like arm and pointed to the door. "Kearmore, attend with them," he said to his guard.

"And Addax," Samiel added, nodding to one of hers. "Be watchful."

The four of them left the room, one wearing black, one white, one red, and one green; all lands united. It made Crow smile. "Thanks to you both."

A silence fell over the room until Samiel broke it. "So, you two are joined by the string of fate?" she said, looking between Crow and Tancho. "Unexpected, yes?"

"You could say that," Crow replied. "I came here for the tradition, as I was born to do. But this . . ." He held his wrist forward, showing the birthmark. "This was not expected. Adelais also found it so."

"Mm, yes," Elmwood said. "It seems an inconvenience to her."

Tancho walked closer, his brow furrowed. "Samiel, you mentioned the string of fate? Do you know of it?"

She smiled, her eyes alight. "In my qasr, I was raised by my own elders. Generations of women who teach the stories and traditions as we worked. I trust you had your own teachings. But according to lore, the red string of fate is invisible to the eye, but the soul can see. It stretches from one soul, out in the world to find the soul it connects to," she flitted her hand in the air. "It is an old tale told to ease the worried hearts of those who long for love. They will find their one."

Crow was about to protest that, and Tancho sputtered something unintelligible. *Love? Had Samiel succumbed to madness?* She laughed and waved them both off. "It is not always love. The string of fate ties you to someone who will bring change to your life, a friend, merchants, neighbours. It can mean many things. Were you not taught this?"

Crow, Tancho, and Elmwood all shook their heads.

"We don't know what it is," Crow said. "Red string or not, it's something entrenched in alchemy. Maghdlm brought about a reaction, and I don't believe anything here is a coincidence."

"You're suggesting she can eliminate this but chooses not to?" Tancho asked.

Crow gave a nod. "Perhaps she orchestrated the whole thing. Perhaps this was always the ploy."

Tancho asked them what Adelais and the other elders had discussed after he and Crow had left, and the answer was not much. The way they skirted around truths and feigned surprise of a possible attack on the Westlands had not sat well with Samiel and Elmwood, and as the elders left to seek information or insight, Samiel and Elmwood had come directly here.

But Crow only listened with half an ear because his mind was racing . . .

Perhaps she orchestrated the whole thing. Perhaps this was always the ploy.

"Crow?" Tancho asked. "Are we boring you?"

Perhaps this was always the ploy . . .

"That's it!" Crow said. "It's all a ploy."

"What is?" Tancho asked. Even Karasu paused her packing to look at him.

"This Golden Eclipse comes but once in our lifetimes. Our whole lives are dedicated to this."

"So?" Samiel asked.

"We would be here without question," Crow explained. "It is insisted that we all leave our lands to be here, in this place. Together. For the first time in our lives, all four of us are here at the same time."

"What is your point?" Elmwood asked.

Crow stared at Tancho, and from the way his face was now devoid of colour, Crow guessed he understood. "Karasu," Tancho whispered. "Forget what isn't packed. We leave at once."

"What is it?" Elmwood asked, more concerned now.

"If you were to invade four connecting lands, would you do one at a time? Or would you wait for such an instance when all four rulers are absent and move in, taking all in one fell swoop?" Crow shook his head. "We left our lands unattended. This whole thing has been a ruse."

"What of the string that binds you?" Samiel said, nodding to Crow, then Tancho. "How do your birthmarks play into this theory?"

"That was unexpected," Crow replied. "And also why she didn't like it. She wants us to still partake in the Golden Eclipse."

"Why?" Tancho said, cinching his bag closed and tying it off. "What purpose does that serve? We're already here."

"I don't know," Crow admitted.

"To divide us," Elmwood said.

Soko and Kohaku and the others arrived back, flushed from running but smiling. Until they saw the looks on their faces. Soko dropped the two bags, his eyes full of worry. "My king, what is it?"

"We leave without delay," Tancho replied instead.

Crow realised then, with ice in his belly, that he wasn't going home. "I can't abandon my people," Crow whispered. "If each land is being invaded in turn, I must go to them."

"Invaded?" Soko cried.

"We don't know if the Northlands are under attack," Tancho said. He spoke with certainty, but there was a hint of understanding as well. As a king, he could sympathise with how Crow must feel. "But we *know* the Westlands are."

Crow knew in his reasoning that if an attack came by the north seas and approached the northern shores of his land, they met sheer mountains and snow. An almost impossible trek, and they'd be fools to attempt it. And the Eastlands was a sea of desert dunes that would take weeks to travel, the Southlands dense and impassable jungles. It made tactical sense to go to the Westlands. They could basically walk ashore and simply keep on walking.

But still, it didn't make abandoning his people any easier.

"My people . . . ," he mumbled.

Soko shook his head. "Don't ask me to go back without you. I swore to never leave you. My life for yours, remember?"

Tancho stared at Soko with barely contained rage before he met Crow's eyes. He seemed conflicted and irate before he turned to his four riders with a sigh. "Iruka and Hitode, you will ride to the Northlands' castle. Relay any message their king needs sent."

Tancho was giving Crow two of his men?

Crow was about to express his disbelief and thanks

when Tancho snapped, "I don't require your gratitude. I would expect the favour returned should you and I be returning to your homelands."

Blue skies above, the man's mood was like a blade. All ashine one moment, killer sharp the next.

"I shall offer my thanks to the men who do your bidding," Crow snarled back at him. "And perhaps give the little fish a lesson in manners before I'm done."

Tancho spun around to glare at him. His long red hair swirled around his head like ribbons, his hand on his sword hilt, but Karasu slipped between them. She gnashed her teeth at Crow but held her hand up, passive. "I care not for you, blackbird. But my king is not himself. Whatever this thing is between you—this lacuna curse—affects you both."

The tension in the room was so thick and caustic, a simple spark would have set it all on fire. So of course, Soko said, "Blackbird on its own is rather plain." He made a face. "Tancho called him pretty blackbird. I like that much better."

Karasu drew her eyes to Soko, and if her eyes were swords, he'd have been slain where he stood.

He held up his hands in surrender. "Or just blackbird is fine." But then he straightened. "Or you could address him as *king*."

Kohaku laughed. "The ride home with you all is going to be so much fun."

Tancho let his head fall back with a groan. "We are wasting time. We must leave."

Bags were collected and Crow slung his over his shoulder, Soko did the same while Kohaku carried two. Karasu helped Tancho strapping on his scabbard, and Crow was blindsided . . .

Irrational anger and jealousy slammed into him like

someone opened a door to a blizzard, seeping through his skin and into his bones. She was touching him. She shouldn't touch him . . . No one should touch him . . . He tried to ignore it, tried to swallow it down, shake it off, to breathe through it, but it was too strong.

Soko grabbed Crow's shoulder and shook him. "Crow? What—"

But Crow couldn't look at Soko. He couldn't take his eyes off Tancho—*his* Tancho—and how Karasu touched him . . . "Remove your hands from him," he snapped, seething. His fingers wrapped around the hilt of his sword.

Karasu turned, and seeing the glowering look on Crow's face, she bristled and reached for her katana. But Tancho pulled her away and put some distance between him and her. "It's not rational," Tancho murmured. "He can't help it. I felt the claws of it earlier."

Soko looked between Crow and Tancho, back and forth. "What in all the blue skies is going on?"

"Nothing," Crow said, almost breathless. He felt better now that Karasu wasn't so close to Tancho, but still . . . "I suggest no one touches him. That is all. Unless they wish to step into the afterlife."

Soko let out a low breath. "Oh, my word. This is . . . indeed, new."

Crow closed his eyes and inhaled deeply. He shook his head when he exhaled, opened his eyes, and hoped he had a better frame of mind. "I don't know what this is. And I like it less than I understand it." He fixed the bag at his shoulder. "Can we move on?"

"Yes," Tancho agreed. "Our horses should be ready."

Crow gave a nod. "Did you encounter many guards when you went to our quarters?" he asked Soko.

"No, none," he replied.

Kohaku agreed with a nod but then cocked his head. "Not any, actually. And that's not good, is it?"

Crow, Tancho, Samiel, and Elmwood all shared a look. "Probably not," Crow said. "If there's been one consistent thing in Aequi Kentron, it's a yellow cloak at every turn."

Kohaku and Karasu opened the door, and after giving the corridor the all-clear, everyone filed out. The halls were empty, the passing courtyard was empty, every room they went past. There was not a guard or elder to be found.

"Something is not right here," Tancho whispered.

Crow agreed. The silence was . . . eerie.

They went past the grand hall; the doors were open and it was silent and bare. A ray of sunlight beamed through the stained-glass dome, casting a lonely spotlight on the marble floor.

"Why do I get the feeling this is a trap?" Elmwood murmured.

"They lured us here so our lands would be without their leader," Crow said. He didn't bother to keep his voice down. There was no one about to hear it. "To the horses."

"West is this way," Tancho said.

They followed the halls to the outside where they had each crossed the bridges from their homelands. The white flags flew above the railings on the westside as the black had flown at the north. The moat looked like it had before, and Crow searched the lands to the west as far as he could see, and he restrained himself from turning north, tempting as it was.

How far could he and Soko get from Tancho before the pain at his wrist consumed him? Would the pain kill him?

Or would leaving Tancho be his end? Would going with him see the same fate?

Crow had no idea. He was so conflicted.

"They took the horses this way," Karasu said, leading the way along the stone path. She kept close to the wall, walking in a smooth crouch, her katana in her hand.

Crow made himself follow. Not that his birthmark gave him much choice, and even though walking away from the north felt wrong in every bone in his body, the idea of leaving Tancho felt the same. So he stayed close to the wall, one step behind Tancho, and followed.

CHAPTER EIGHT

AS THEY CREPT along the sandstone wall in search of
the stables, Tancho felt off-balance. Everything to do with
the mark on his wrist, the lacuna—whatever that was—and
his irresistible draw to Crow was at odds with Tancho's
ingrained need of self-control.

He'd mastered his discipline and restraint. He prided
himself on it.

And now it was in ribbons at the feet of the Northlands'
king.

Yet his urgency to get home drove him forward. Everything was a distraction, and he needed to stay focused. For
his people, for his kingdom.

What Crow had suggested, that their invitation had
been a ruse, felt truer with every step.

But just who exactly was deceiving them? Had it been a
plan twenty-five years in the making? Or did the opportunity present itself with the coming Golden Eclipse?

Tancho was determined to uncover the truth.

Elmwood sniffed the air. "I can smell horses."

Karasu stopped walking, holding her fist up to warn

everyone to freeze. She craned her neck. "I can hear them. This way."

She jogged ahead and turned at a breezeway, rounded another corner, and stopped at two huge wooden doors, wide open, revealing stable stalls down both sides of a long centre walkway. The smell of horse sweat, hay, and shit hung damp in the air. Horses brayed and kicked at their walls, unsettled and agitated.

Tancho knew the feeling well.

"Spooked horses is never a good sign," Crow said, walking down between the stalls. He barely got ten paces before he turned back to Tancho, irritated he hadn't followed him. Ten paces wasn't enough distance between them to hurt, but it was enough to twinge. Reluctantly, Tancho obliged.

Crow found his horse, giving it a rub on the nose, and murmured soothing words to calm it, but then he told Soko to swap their horses with the two riders who would be going north. Soko took Crow's bag and saddled their horses; Karasu and Kohaku did the same. There were no guards, no horsemen, no keepers, no . . . anyone.

Tancho walked to the last stall. It was empty, the stall door open, and instead of a bridle and reins hanging from the wall, were two yellow guard cloaks. Tancho pulled them off, and when he turned around, Crow was at the stall door. Tancho probably should have felt bad for putting distance between them, but he liked that Crow followed . . .

"What have you there?" Crow asked.

"Two cloaks." He handed them to Crow. "This place has been abandoned."

Crow inspected the yellow fabric, then glanced up at everyone getting horses ready. "The question is, where did they go?"

Tancho frowned. "Maghdlm said evil is coming. From far *and* from near. Do you think she knew?"

Crow nodded. "Is she in on it? Or just one arrow in a quiver?"

"My lord," Iruka interrupted, bowing his head, Hitode behind him. "We are ready."

Crow handed them the yellow robes. "Wear these, and my people will think you messengers and give you free passage. Wear your Westland colours and I doubt you'll get far."

They slipped the cloaks on and gave Tancho an apologetic smile as they discarded their Westland whites. "Apologies, my lord."

Tancho patted his shoulder. "The cloak may be Aequi Kentron, but your hearts are Westlands."

They smiled with relief. "We will go with honour, my lord."

Crow looked upon them fondly. "And I acknowledge and appreciate your sacrifice. I know your hearts long to go home." He went to his horse and took a purse from his bag. "Take this. There are inns along the way with warm beds and hot food. Buy coats and fur-lined boots. I assume you're not accustomed to ice and snow. Our horses are bred for it, and as soon as they hit the cold country, they will take you to my home. They know the way."

Iruka bowed his head. "It is very kind, lord." He looked up. "And your message?"

"When you get to the Northlands' castle, ask for Mentor Erelis. Arriving on our horses might cause some alarm, but ask for Erelis directly, and tell him you have a personal message from me. Tell him Soko and I have gone to the Westlands, for we believe them under attack. Tell him what you saw of those creatures and to send scouts to the northern fort to see if any creatures come from our waters. And tell him to ready our armies and wait for my word."

"And if he doesn't believe me?" Iruka asked. "If he thinks I'm lying, that I've stolen your horse and your purse, what then?"

Crow grinned. "Tell him if he does not believe you, I'll recite the works of the Kalevala upon my return. And he'll know it came from me."

Soko chuckled at that. "Oh yes, he'll know."

"I hated that book, and for years he made me read it and study it. We argued over that cursed thing, and I swore to him as king I would have it written into law that the book be banned." Crow's smile turned a little rueful. "He never forgave me for that, even all these years later."

Soko snorted out a laugh. "It was the royal penises you drew in the book that he never forgave you for." He grinned at Iruka. "Tell Erelis *that*. Then he'll know for sure."

Crow laughed. "That is true." Then his gaze cut to Tancho's. "I was young."

Tancho rolled his eyes and turned to his men. "Ride well. Be safe."

The two Westland guards, dressed in Kentron yellow, rode out of the stable and headed north.

His words were cut off by a banging sound coming from somewhere at the end of the stables. On the other side perhaps? A door slamming? Or something falling?

Tancho and Crow both had their swords out in an instant and both pressed their backs to the side of the stall, half-hidden in shadow, as they moved silently to the end of the walkway. There was a set of huge double doors, matching the one at the entrance they'd come through, and Crow slid it open while Tancho stood ready, sword raised.

On the other side was another breezeway, well-lit by an

opening that Tancho thought looked like might have led to another outside courtyard. It was empty, there were no signs of any guard or elder, and no sign of anything out of place.

"Where does that lead?" Crow asked quietly.

"I don't know," Tancho whispered.

They crept along the wall to the opening, and there in the sunlight was a grassed square with potted cumquat trees. Pretty, by all accounts, and perfectly tended, but very strangely deserted.

They ran across the square and down another corridor, and at the end of that one, another going in the opposite direction. "How big is this place?" Tancho asked.

Before Crow could answer, a door banged. The same sound they'd heard before, and without a word between them, Tancho and Crow ran toward it. Tancho was faster and he reached the door first. He pulled it open and Crow took the lead with his sword at the ready.

Tancho didn't want to admit it, but they worked well together. Moving and reacting as if they'd practised these moves a hundred times.

Nothing came out of the door at them, and it took a moment for Tancho's eyes to adjust to the dark inside the room. It appeared to be some kind of communal meeting room, long and rectangular with stone walls and stained-glass windows. There were chairs and long seats and cushions, and unlit oil lamps sat on tables.

And it was empty.

"There is no one here," Crow said.

By this time, Soko, Karasu, and Kohaku were behind them. Samiel and Elmwood as well, and their guards on their heels, covering the rear.

Elmwood swung his axe as though it weighed a feather. "I come from jungles that are never silent, so this is strange to me. But is it odd that it be *this* silent? Not a whisper, not a chirp, not a bird song, not even the leaves can find a breeze. The horses are not happy here, and I can tell you if animals fear a place, it is with good reason."

"I agree," Crow said.

"Something evil comes," Tancho repeated.

"Something evil is already here," Samiel replied.

The faintest noise, a cry or moan, echoed from inside the common room, and all heads turned to the sound. "You heard that?" Soko asked. Karasu nodded, and they went inside. Tancho and Crow followed them in, running to the end of the room, through to another set of doors. They appeared to be in an older part of the castle: the stone walls were a drab grey; the floors were tiled with marble so old there were wear marks from centuries of use. Almost as if this place and the Great Hall were different buildings. There was a small wooden door with cast iron hinges, older than seemed possible, and so small that Tancho wondered if Kohaku or Elmwood would fit through it. There was an ancient inscription carved in the stone above it.

Archīvum

"This is where Maghdlm said she was going," Tancho pointed out, just as another groan echoed through the hall. They were closer to it, but it sounded weaker.

"Through here," Karasu whispered, opening the small door to the archive room. Only it wasn't a room . . .

They found themselves on a mezzanine overlooking an immense library. A spiral staircase wound its way down to floor level. Arcane lamps lit the walls so they could see the stacks and stacks of books, with ladders and crosswalks and catwalks.

Tancho was mesmerised. "There are more books than

stars in the night sky." He could feel Crow beside him, feel his eyes upon his face, but he dare not look at him.

"Why are the lamps blue?" Samiel asked.

"Arcane power," Crow replied. Tancho didn't know if he should be annoyed or impressed that Crow knew that. So he settled on a little of both. "They are lit by magick, not oil."

"Look, down there," Soko said, pointing down underneath their feet. "Someone lay on the floor."

That someone lying on the floor groaned again. The arcane lights flickered and dimmed.

"Hurry," Karasu said as she took to the stairs. They filed down the dizzying drop to the floor below, to find Maghdlm slumped on her side, a pool of dark red blood seeping from her head.

Karasu knelt before her, as did Tancho and Crow. The others took to the stacks searching for anyone else at all. "Maghdlm, can you hear me?" Karasu asked.

The old woman moaned, but it was now Tancho who could see her more clearly. She looked as though she'd been hit in the head by something heavy, with a sharp edge. The bottom of an iron candle holder, perhaps. There was a nasty gash to the side of her head, her face and her hair were smeared with blood, her eye was swollen shut, her face badly bruised. She opened her one good eye and tried to whisper something.

"Maghdlm," Crow said. "Can you tell us who did this? Did you see who hurt you?"

". . . must leave," she murmured. ". . . evil comes."

"Kohaku," Karasu called. He came running back down an aisle of bookshelves.

"We found no one," he said to Tancho.

"Can you carry Maghdlm?" Karasu asked him. "We must hurry."

Kohaku gave a serious nod and sheathed his sword. With more gentleness than belied his size, he scooped up the injured woman and overhead, the blue lights flickered.

"I think she controls the lamps," Tancho said as they headed for the spiral staircase.

And sure enough, as the last of them filed up the stairs and out the door, the lamps at the far end of the library went out. Then the next, and the next, and as the last guard came through the small door, the library fell into darkness.

"Back to the stable," Crow said, and he and Tancho led them back the way they had come.

They encountered no one and heard not a sound. The horses were antsy, and if that was unease from whatever oddity was here, or if they knew they were heading home, Tancho wasn't sure.

But he felt much the same.

Kohaku mounted his horse, Maghdlm at his front. It wouldn't be an easy ride for him, but he was the biggest, the strongest. The only one who could carry her.

Elmwood and Samiel stood to the side, watching as Soko and Karasu ensured the horses were ready. Crow went to them and offered his hand to them in turn. "Your alliance is met with a well of gratitude," Crow said. "I look forward to when we meet again. A feast, perhaps, and a bottle or two of mead."

"We never did get to spar," Elmwood said with a grin, shaking his hand with earnest. "I should like to see your skills with that sword."

"It would be my—"

Tancho slipped in closer to Crow. He wanted to tell Elmwood it would be met with a well of gratitude if he didn't touch Crow, but the handshake was brief and Tancho's irrational rage subsided as quickly as it had arrived. He managed a smile at Samiel instead. "You are leaving also?"

"Yes," she replied with a smirk, as if she'd seen Tancho's barely schooled reaction. "We shall collect our belongings and leave directly after you."

"A suggestion, if I may," Tancho said. "Don't go back inside. Leave whatever you brought with you and ride for your homelands now. Ready your armies. Drawing the four of us away from our kingdoms had little to do with the eclipse. And if trouble has not found your home yet, I fear it is only a matter of time."

Crow stared at Tancho for a long moment before he gave a nod to Elmwood and Samiel. "Send word if you need help," he said. "I cannot promise we won't be fighting our own battles, but please know you have allies in the north."

"We will meet again," Samiel said. She offered her hand to Crow and smiled when Tancho bit back a snarl. Then she clapped Tancho's shoulder and laughed when Crow bristled at her hand on him. "That red string of fate has a sense of humour."

Both Crow and Tancho growled at her, then at each other, and Samiel chuckled. "Ride well, and we will meet again."

Karasu, Kohaku, and Soko were on their horses, unsettled, turning tight circles and trying to control them. Tancho pulled himself up on his horse and Crow did the same, and with a nod, they rode for the western bridge.

The horses wanted to gallop and they were hard to hold back. Tancho half expected to be met by guards, or something more sinister, blocking their escape. He didn't know by what exactly, but he expected to be stopped. Yet nothing came at them. They crossed the bridge without incident and he felt an almighty weight off his back when they were on Westlands' soil.

He had no idea what he would find at his home when they got there, or even along the way. Would his castle be in ruins? Would his people be slain?

What had happened to Asagi? He would have met an invading enemy with honour. He'd have fought like a lethal summer breeze, killing effortlessly, gently, like the kiss of the wind.

But how many could he face?

Was he even still alive? The creatures were first seen arriving six days ago. That was the distance between his castle and Aequi Kentron, and it would take another six days, maybe seven, considering the position of the sun, to ride all the way back. That would make it one half-moon between the creatures arriving and Tancho's return.

Would anything be left standing at all?

Or would Tancho return and find everything as it should be? Were the unknown ships simply passing? Were they innocent merchants from afar?

So many questions and so few answers. Tancho loathed the uncertainty, but one thing was clear.

He was riding into an unknown future with the King of the Northlands at his side. Everything about it was wrong, yet the birthmark on his wrist told him it was right. He felt better the further they got from Aequi Kentron, with every stride west they made. He was going home. Regardless of what he would find when he got there, the waters called him to return.

CHAPTER NINE

CROW DIDN'T WANT to admit that the Westlands were pretty. For the distance they covered before the sun climbed to the afternoon sky, it looked mostly similar to his own lands: green valleys, grasses, fields, and streams. But as it neared dusk, where the Northlands would have begun to climb upward to undulating foothills before the mountains, the Westlands remained flat. The streams grew wider and more frequent. Stone arch bridges wide enough for two horses to cross, or a horse and cart perhaps, linked all pockets of land, and the road followed the path of the river through picturesque valleys.

The constant sound of water running over rocks was peaceful. The songs of the wildlife were ones Crow had not heard before. There were herons and egrets, birds Crow had only seen in books before. There were rabbits, deer, and serow.

It was a different world to his snowy Northlands.

As the daylight began to fade, Karasu led them off the road, through a shallow stream behind a bluff in the valley.

It was well-hidden and invisible from the road, should anyone come looking.

Crow slid down from his horse, and he and Soko helped relieve Kohaku of Maghdlm. The two guards tethered the horses where they could feed on long grass, Tancho began a campfire and Karasu filled canisters from the stream.

Maghdlm looked worse for wear, and the darkening sky hid the true horrors of her injuries. They lay her down near the fire, and she stirred and groaned but didn't wake. "How does she fare?" Tancho asked, kneeling silently beside them.

"Not well," Crow replied. He pulled Maghdlm's cloak up like a blanket. "Morning will tell if she survives. I'll be surprised if she lives to see it."

Karasu handed Tancho a water canister and he gave her a grateful smile before sitting back on some soft grass. He faced the fire and took a long drink. "Ah, the waters of home have never tasted so sweet."

He leaned over and handed the canister to Crow. He sipped it at first, then took a mouthful. It was cool and crisp, fresh. Maybe it was after the long day behind them without a drink, but that was possibly the best water Crow had ever tasted.

He passed the canister on to Soko who took a long swallow, then he tossed it up to Kohaku who had walked over. He drained it in one go and wiped his mouth with the back of his hand. "I'm starving," he said. He grinned right at Soko. "Want to see who can catch a rabbit first?"

Soko jumped to his feet. "Challenge accepted!"

And Crow and Tancho watched them disappear deeper into the bluff, bickering and laughing as they went. He shot a smile to Tancho. "They're like children."

Tancho smiled but it faded fast. His face in the flickering firelight half-hidden in shadows, and Crow realised they were alone.

"Karasu has gone to pick the berries she saw by the stream," Tancho said as if reading his mind. "Hikari and Unagi will take the first shift to sleep."

Crow looked over to where the two Westland guards had been, and sure enough, there were now two sleeping forms in the grass.

Crow kicked himself for not thinking of suggesting splitting shifts so someone could keep watch. He sighed. "I have grown complacent in peaceful times, it would seem. I should have thought of that."

"You learned tactical and combat strategy, I assume," Tancho said.

"Yes, of course. I simply meant that in all my years in the Northlands, no threat ever raised its head."

"None here, either. Yet . . ."

Oh, the blue skies above. Was he always so impossible? "Yet it is not a mistake I will make twice." Crow glared at him, and that irrational anger bloomed in his chest. "I did not wish to come here with you."

Tancho's gaze was fire and venom. "Nor did I wish you to. I did not ask for this," he said, flashing the birthmark on his wrist. "To be joined with yours. Whatever that means."

"And you think I did?" Crow shot back. "You think I wanted this? To be heading further away from my home, from my people? And the only reason we are here with you now is because of the chance an enemy chose your land to hit first. If it were my home—"

"If it were your home, you'd what? Cut your arm off to be rid of me? Isn't that what you asked for?"

"Yes. There is nothing I would not do for my people."

"You think I am not the same?"

"That is why I am here," Crow said, probably too loudly. "Because I know what a king would do. I would expect no less. You give your blood and your life for your kingdom and for your people. That is why I am here with you. So perhaps you could show a little gratitude at the sacrifice Soko and I have made—"

"I apologise if my kingdom being invaded is an inconvenience for you and your lover—"

"My what?"

"Your lover. I've seen how you are with him. How he touches you," Tancho hissed through his anger.

"He is no such thing. He is like a brother; he has been by my side since we were born. And it is of no matter anyway, he favours women." Then it occurred to Crow what this was. "Is that jealousy, little fish? Because I've seen the way you and Karasu are, how her eyes follow you."

Tancho shot to his feet and he drew his katana. Crow leapt to his, drawing his sword in the same sweeping movement. "Do not call me little fish, blackbird," Tancho breathed.

"I've touched a nerve," Crow said with a sneer. His blood was racing, his adrenaline spiked.

Karasu came trudging up from the river, dropped a pouch of berries, and took a sword in each hand, a look of impatient fury on her delicate face. "I will not spend the next seven days settling squabbles," she said. She gave Tancho a pointed glare. "My king, he might be an uncultured Northlander, but he is with us as an ally when we may have too few." Then she pointed her blades at Crow. "And if you disrespect my king one more time, I will part you from your tongue." She took a deep breath and was calmer on the other side of it. "Tancho, this temper is not your own but the result of whatever curse was put upon you. You are better than this."

Crow shook his head, disbelievingly. "Uncultured Northlander?"

"By the very definition," she replied curtly. "Loud, unrefined—"

"Yet still a king!" he boomed, the grip on the hilt of his sword tightened. "Speak to me in such a manner again, and I'll see your blades hung above the gates to my castle with your blood still on them."

She turned to face him and squared her feet as if ready to strike. "You hold no rank here," she said. She raised her two daggers. "And if you think you're good enough to take my swords . . ."

Tancho slipped between them, his katana now aimed at Karasu. "Do not threaten him. I beg of you, Karasu, I cannot control this. The need to protect him burns in my blood. As much as I wish otherwise. Do not aim your blades at him, for I cannot trust what I will do."

She raised her hands, daggers downcast. "Apologies, my king." Taking a step back, she sheathed her blades and nodded to Crow. "May I suggest you caution him to watch his manners."

Tancho turned to Crow and held his katana to Crow's broadsword. "I might be driven to protect you and to defend you, but so the abyss, help me, that does not mean I will not kill you."

Crow grinned at him, daring, amused. Aroused.

What was this madness?

Maghdlm groaned from beside the fire, a welcome distraction. Karasu and Tancho went to her while Crow sat his arse down and tried to get his head in order.

Fighting with Tancho had aroused him?

And from the fire and conflict he'd seen in Tancho's eyes, Crow was almost certain he felt it too. Because as if this whole thing wasn't weird enough . . .

Yes, Crow's attraction had always been to men. But never to men who held a sword to him, and most certainly not to a man whom he was blood-tied to by some lacuna magick and a Golden Eclipse. The same man who wanted to protect Crow *and* kill him, and who Crow wanted to strangle with his bare hands and kiss senseless.

Yeah. Like he said. Weird.

And what right did Tancho have to be jealous of Soko— an absurd notion anyway—when he was with Karasu. They were always together, she was always close to him, touching him . . . like she was right now.

Crow tried to breathe through the jealousy.

They were tending to a sick old woman, Crow reasoned. He had no right to be jealous. He had no claim over Tancho . . . not really. Apart from their bonded birthmarks, which neither of them wanted. Tancho had told him to his face he didn't want this, how he wished it weren't so, how being tied to him was a fate worse than death.

Crow watched him by the fire as the orange flames sang and danced for the sky, casting a red glow over him. He looked even more beautiful, more ethereal, and Crow wanted to do things to him he'd never done with any man. Crow's birthmark grew warm and warmer still, as a pleasant burn that singed up to his elbow.

Tancho shot Crow a confused look, then rubbed at his birthmark. He felt it too. "What is that?"

Crow wanted to pull out his hair, or perhaps find a tree he could punch until his hand broke. It would have to be less torturous than this . . .

"Can you please tell Karasu not to be so close," Crow

hissed, his skin and bones stretched tight as he tried to stay calm. His blood pounded in his ears, his heart raced.

Tancho whispered something to Karasu and she, thankfully, obliged. She moved an arm's length away to the other side of Maghdlm, giving her a sip of water, but only before she'd stopped to glare at Crow. Well, it began as a glare but morphed into something sadder, Crow guessed, when she saw how painful it was for him. How this wasn't their fault.

They'd never asked for this.

Or maybe she was heartbroken because Tancho was now tethered by some invisible bond to Crow. It was no wonder she resented him. This whole mess wasn't fair to her either.

Crow was even more determined now to find a way to break the bond.

"Look at what we scored," Kohaku said as he and Soko walked back to the fire. He was holding three rabbits. "My tally was two."

"I would have got a second one, but Kohaku bumped me," Soko said, grinning.

Kohaku laughed. "He lies like he kills rabbits. Very badly."

Now Soko pushed Kohaku and they laughed again, but Soko's eyes stayed on Crow's, and it was only then he seemed to notice the mood. "Is everything okay here?" he asked.

Crow gave a nod. "Yes, of course. Maghdlm was stirring, that's all."

Tancho's gaze darted to Crow's, silently questioning why Crow would lie to Soko. Because things were most definitely not okay here. A few moments earlier, the three of them had their swords drawn, threatening death.

"You have to help me skin the rabbits," Kohaku said, giving Soko another shove.

Soko gave Crow one more meaningful look, but Crow got to his feet. "I'll go check on the horses," he said, ignoring all the eyes upon him, and was grateful to be surrounded by darkness away from the fire. It wasn't too far away, but his birthmark told him it was far enough.

The horses were all fine, of course, eating and resting, but Crow did check their hooves and legs for soreness. He could hear Soko telling a story and the laughter that followed, but he just didn't have the heart to join them. His heart was heavy. He was confused and shrouded with uncertainty.

He hadn't realised the pain in his wrist had disappeared.

"Did you forget something?" Tancho asked quietly.

Crow turned quickly, surprised. He hadn't heard him approach.

Tancho held up his wrist. "Could you not feel it?"

"I didn't feel the absence of pain. I was distracted, I guess." He stroked the horse's neck. "Is Maghdlm still with us?"

Tancho stood at the horse next to Crow's, rubbing its forehead. "I think she's going to live. She sipped some water."

"I hope so," Crow murmured. "She has answers."

"Who do you think tried to kill her?"

Crow sighed. "Adelais," he answered.

"The Grand Speaker? Leader of the Elders?" Tancho made a face. "Bold choice."

Crow wasn't sure who else it could be. "If she didn't strike the blow herself, she ordered it to be done."

"You didn't like her?"

"She smiled as though she intended to rob us blind." Crow shrugged. "Everything about her felt wrong. The smile, the gesture, the fake surprise at your four riders returning with the message of invaders."

"You think she's a part of it?"

"I'd bet your kingdom on it."

Tancho raised an eyebrow. "You wouldn't bet your own?"

"No, I like mine."

Tancho laughed, and the sound of it flooded Crow's chest with warmth. He found himself smiling despite his sullen mood. He found himself staring at Tancho's beautiful profile in the moons' light, his delicate nose, his cheekbones, jaw . . . and when Tancho caught him staring, he tilted his head. "What?"

"Nothing," he replied quickly. "I've just . . ."

"You've just what?"

Trying to avoid seeing his beautiful face and uttering some embarrassing truth, Crow found himself looking up. "I've never seen the stars from here."

Tancho smiled as if he knew it was a lie but had the good grace not to call him out. "Do they look different?"

He searched the clear night sky, marvelling in its familiar beauty. "No. I mapped enough of the stars in my studies to know I'm not at home, but it's not too different."

"Is that disappointing?" Tancho asked. "I've never seen the stars from any lands but my own. I think I'd be disappointed if they looked the same."

He scanned the sky and the blanket of stars above them. "No. It's a comfort. Something familiar when everything else has changed."

Tancho's gaze fell to Crow then; he could feel the burn

of his stare. But he daren't look at him. He wasn't sure his heart could take it.

"I think the meat is almost cooked," Tancho said, eventually. "If you'd prefer more alone time, I'll have them leave you some."

Crow met his gaze then. Was he so transparent that Tancho could read him so easily?

Tancho smiled. "Though I can make no promises about what will be left. Kohaku likes to eat."

He watched Tancho walk back to the fire, and after a moment, Crow followed. He couldn't sulk all night, as much as he wanted to, and truth be told, he felt better after their little chat. It was proof they could actually have a conversation without trying to kill each other.

Their dinner was a combination of fire-roasted rabbit and fresh berries, and although it wasn't a huge meal, it was tasty. Tancho made sure the two sleeping guards had some put aside, and Kohaku basically picked every bone clean.

He and Soko clearly got on well, both appreciating the other's sense of adventure and humour, and Crow was happy to let them do most of the talking. He caught himself staring at Tancho across the fire a few times, and he caught Tancho staring back a few times as well.

But eventually the conversation quietened, everyone lay down, and the night was filled with crickets chirping instead. If Crow listened hard over the sound of the fire, he could make out the gentle trickle of the river and perhaps some critters that came to drink from it.

When he heard Tancho wake the guards for their change of shift, Crow closed his eyes.

THE BURNING PAIN in his wrist woke Crow just as the sun was rising. He sat up to find Tancho gone from where he'd been sleeping. Kohaku was still snoring, Soko still splayed on his back, and the two guards were saddling the horses. Karasu was sitting up, mixing something in a bowl. But Tancho . . .

Came walking back from the river. He looked tired and genuinely sorry. "Apologies. I forgot," he said. "I was still half-asleep and thought fresh water sounded like a good idea."

Crow scrubbed his hand over his face. He couldn't even be mad, because lifelong habits were ritual, and these blasted birthmarks had been joined for what? Two days? It felt so much longer.

"Fresh water sounds like a good idea," Crow said, his voice rough. He got to his feet, and together, he and Tancho walked down to the river.

The water was cold and so clear Crow could see every tiny pebble on the bottom. He knelt by the edge and splashed his face, then cupped his hands and drank. "How much time do we have?" he asked.

Tancho shrugged. "We should be leaving soon if we want to make Yura by tonight."

"What's Yura?"

"A village. There's an inn that can take us, though it's only small."

Crow didn't care how small it was. A bed and a proper meal sounded good.

"Why?" Tancho pressed. He wiped his mouth with his sleeve.

"Just wondered if I had time to take my boots off," Crow said.

"There are baths at the inn," Tancho said.

Crow got up and clapped his hands. "Then let's not waste any more time."

Tancho smiled at that and they walked in silence back to the camp. Soko and Kohaku were having a literal pissing contest at a tree, but Karasu had Maghdlm sitting up. She held a bowl to her mouth. "Just a sip," she urged.

The old woman appeared even smaller than before, and somehow even more frail. But in the new morning light, Crow could better see her injuries.

Her skin, wrinkled, swollen, and bruised, looked as if someone had pressed too hard on an overripe plum. Crow imagined it had torn much the same way. She was a healer, but how could she heal herself? How could she work her own magicks on herself when she could barely summon the energy to sip water?

Crow knelt beside her. "What do you need?" he asked. "Any herbs or seeds? Wort or hemlock, perhaps?"

Maghdlm gave a nod before she closed her eyes. "Tea," she whispered.

Crow looked at Karasu, then to Crow. "Will we find that on our path today?"

"There is a farming village not far from here," Tancho said. "We'll find fruit for breakfast as well."

When the fire was extinguished and the horses saddled, Kohaku took poor Maghdlm upon his horse with him, and they set off for the road. At first, Crow thought the sunrise was filtered through the clouds and that the sun would brighten as it climbed higher in the sky.

But it didn't.

"Does the sunlight look different to anyone else?" Crow asked. "Do my eyes deceive me? Or is the sunshine a different colour in the west?"

"Different, how?" Soko asked.

Crow shrugged. "Diffused, somehow. As if dusk approaches instead of it just being dawn."

Soko laughed. "I think your eyes are playing tricks on you, my lord. How can the sky be different? The Westlands follow the same sun and stars as we do."

Tancho shifted in his saddle. "I agree. There is a certain . . . hue."

Soko frowned up at the sky and continued to frown at the valley and at the river and at the bridges as they made their way to the farmer's village. "A hue of what?"

Karasu smiled. "Humility."

Soko gasped loudly and pulled his horse to a stop. "Is that a sense of humour? Blue skies above, she made a joke! I never thought it possible."

She turned around, not even a glance. "Want to see how funny you find it with my boot print on your britches?"

Kohaku laughed. "I would find that very funny. A nice change for her boot to be aimed at someone else."

Karasu rolled her eyes, but she did smile. Soko cantered his horse to catch up. "Should we make a wager as to who would win?"

"That's not a bet you should make," Tancho said, the corner of his lips lifting.

Soko countered with a good-natured barb and Crow smiled as they rode on, relieved and with a glimmer of hope that this motley band could get along. He doubted it would last long, but he'd take whatever small slivers of amicability he could get.

Around a sweeping river bend, a patch of buildings came into view. Homes built almost on the river, with stone foundations like bridges, white walls, and verandas under wooden shingled roofs, they were so different to Northland houses Crow was used to.

Northland homes were all stone and wood, built to hunker against the snow and cold. These homes were constructed to utilise the water, with water wheels and bridges. It seemed so . . . foreign. And peaceful and fantastic.

Soko grinned at him. "Have you ever seen anything like it?"

Crow tried not to smile too hard. "Never."

As they drew near, a villager came to the road to greet them. He had long black hair pulled back in a braid, and wore a long linen shirt over pants with a sash at his waist with sandals on his feet. "Welcome." He bowed his head, then did a double take when he saw Tancho. "My king! Welcome, an honour you bestow upon us."

Tancho slid down from his horse and took the man's hand. "Greetings to you. We require some supplies, if you would be so kind."

The man smiled as if he'd just been handed a gift. "Of course! Anything we have is yours."

There was no doubt about it. Tancho's people liked him.

"We need only fruit and bread, for which we have coin," Tancho explained. "Tell me, good man, does a healer live nearby?"

The man's eyes widened. "If you are injured, my king—"

"Not me," Tancho replied. "But a woman who travels with us. She needs care."

"Yes, yes, come this way," the man said, ushering them along. He showed them to his house and offered baskets of pears and berries and a few small loaves of bread, then sent a small child to run to the house at the end of the small village to tell the healer to prepare. By the time they made it to the healer's house, the child reappeared with an old man at his side, and everyone in the village stood to watch.

Crow noticed how the villagers stared at him and Soko. Their black cloaks stood out like their short and unruly hair. They stood taller, as well, and wore different weapons, different boots.

These people hadn't seen their kind before.

Ignoring them, Crow went to Kohaku and took Maghdlm from him, carrying her toward the healer. The old man, his long grey hair and grey eyes, gave a hard nod and held the door open for him.

Inside was warm and lamps lit the small room, and it smelled of a dozen different herbs. It reminded Crow of the healer's rooms he'd been in at home: tables with bottles and jars, glass and metal canisters, dozens of different types of dried leaves, and steaming bowls on a small fire.

"She was attacked," Crow said, laying her down on the mat by the fire and kneeling at her side. "But she survived the night."

The old man knelt at the other side and pulled back Maghdlm's shawl. He winced when he saw her injuries but inspected her eyes and gums. "I can only do so much," he said quietly.

Crow met his gaze. "You should know, she is an alchemist. A healer, from Aequi Kentron."

"From Aequi . . . ," he trailed off, looking back at the injured woman. Then he reached out and grabbed Crow's wrist, seeing the crow-shaped birthmark. "You are . . . ?"

"I am King of Northlands," Crow said.

Just then, Tancho knelt down beside Crow. "He travels with me."

The healer's eyes blazed with the light of the fire. "My king."

"Can you heal her?" Tancho asked. "We need to travel to the village of Yura by nightfall. We must return to my castle as fast as we can."

He stared at Tancho for a long second, clearly putting the pieces together, then gave a nod. "I shall do my all." He shot to his feet and went to the counter, measured and weighed a range of dried leaves, seeds, powders, mumbling as he went, and after a few moments, he took a small scoop from his trove, tipping it into a pot of boiling water.

While the tea steeped, he made a paste into a ball, wrapped it in muslin, and dotted it along the gash in Maghdlm's head. She stirred and mumbled but didn't wake. "This will numb the wound and rid infection," the man explained as he wrapped a long bandage around her head. "The tea will heal her and give her strength. Have her drink as much and as often as she can."

Then he went to the door and called for the man who had given them fruit. "Fetch a carriage from my stable for the woman," the healer ordered before turning back to his patient. "She needs to lie down, not ride on a horse. And how long could the big man carry her for?"

"As long as he needed," Tancho replied with a smile. "He would complain a lot, but he would do it." Then he gave a grateful nod. "The carriage is appreciated."

He checked the tea, stirring it. "I can only assume trouble comes," he said, "given the Golden Eclipse is upon us and you now hurry back to your home. You bring with you the alchemist from Aequi Kentron, whom someone has tried to kill, not to mention the King of the Northlands sits with you."

The statement was directed at Tancho, so Crow let him answer. Tancho paused a while. "Have you heard any news? Whispers of strange tidings?"

"No, my lord," he replied. "Though the sun cast strange light today, so I would think the Golden Eclipse nears. Can you make it to your castle in that time?"

Tancho looked at Crow. "We will have to."

"What do you know of the golden sun?" Crow asked. Maybe this old healer had learned something different . . .

The healer shot him a cautious look. "That the golden skies happen only once in many lifetimes. That all kings are to meet when the eclipse is in full effect. Except that now two kings sit in my house, so I assume trouble is on its way."

Tancho stood up and gave him that patient look that gave no emotion away. "Or perhaps it is already here. We may be walking into uncertain times but won't know until we return. So, my good man, I don't wish to appear ungrateful, but we must hurry."

The healer poured the boiling tea, leaves and all, into a pot. "This is mandragora, willow bark, wolfberry, feverfew, amongst other things. It is not for anyone else to drink, or they won't be riding anywhere."

Crow scooped up Maghdlm and carried her outside. The carriage was hooked up to a new horse, which was tethered to Unagi's horse. The carriage itself was small and was probably used to carry livestock or produce, but it had a roof and the old man was right. Kohaku would have struggled to have carried her for six more days.

As they got Maghdlm settled and comfortable and put the pot of tea in the carriage with her, Crow noticed Tancho go back into the house with the healer. Karasu stood at the door, ever the protector, but the pull on Crow's wrist dragged him close enough to the door for the pain to subside.

Soko threw him a pear and Crow ate it, pretending not to try and hear Tancho speak. Was he thanking the man?

Paying him? Or ordering him not to breathe a word of what he assumed about trouble coming lest he spread fear through the villages?

Crow then considered that it was highly possible Tancho was doing all three.

A short while later, Tancho emerged. He held his chin high, impossible to read, and gave a nod. They climbed up onto their horses and continued on their way. Crow was pleased when he saw the healer in the doorway, so Tancho hadn't killed him at least.

He had no clue what the private meeting was about, and Crow managed to put it from his mind. At least until they'd stopped at midday to give the horses a rest and to give Maghdlm some tea. The ride had been faster with the carriage, and Kohaku complained a whole lot less. With the scenery of tranquil rivers and ornate buildings, rolling green patches, and a myriad of wildlife, Crow hadn't given the healer much thought.

Until, when they were ready to ride again, he noticed Tancho's wrist. His birthmark wasn't just covered. It was bound in bandages.

CHAPTER TEN

TANCHO HADN'T INTENDED to deceive Crow. Not outright, anyway. He was going to tell him about the experiment with the healer but then wondered how long it might take Crow to realise. Would he feel it? Would he even notice it? Did Crow pay attention to him, notice things about him as Tancho noticed about him.

Little things such as the slight dimple in Crow's cheek when he smiled, the faded scar on his cheek. How his dark hair shone under the sunlight, how the muscles in his forearms bulged when he held the reins of his horse.

Did Crow notice the little things about Tancho? Sometimes he felt Crow's gaze upon him, but he'd always turn away or avert his eyes whenever Tancho tried to catch him.

The link between them, the invisible thread Samiel had talked of, was as strong as it was unexplainable. Tancho might even have liked Crow if he didn't irritate him so much. He was certainly handsome, in a roguish mountain-man way, with his size and strength and his rough-cut laugh that warmed Tancho's belly. Tancho might have even fancied a man like that in his bed, if that said man didn't question everything and gnash his teeth and threaten to kill someone several times a day.

So yes, the bond between them, as remarkable and powerful as it was, needed to be severed.

The old healer man had said a birthmark bond was an old, old magick and well outside his realm of expertise. It could take most of the day for the effects to take hold, the healer had said. If they even worked at all. Although he was dealing with the unknown, so it was mostly guessing, and it was highly unlikely it would work at all.

But Tancho wanted to try.

"Your arm," Crow said as he slid back into his saddle. He kept his eyes ahead, his jaw ticked. "Are you injured?"

Tancho pulled the sleeve of his cloak down. "No." They set a steady pace, heading west, the carriage trundling along nicely at the rear of their procession. Tancho wasn't going to elaborate on what he'd asked the healer to do, at least not until they had some privacy at the inn where they would stop for the night.

So when he said no and nothing else, he assumed it would be the end of it. But he wasn't used to being questioned and countered and argued with. Sure, Karasu and Kohaku raised questions when needed, but they knew when to drop a subject.

Crow did not.

"What did the healer do to you?" he asked. "He was still alive and standing when you left, so I can guess he didn't harm you. But you wear a bandage, so if you're not injured, then it was self-inflicted. I assume you asked him to get rid of your birthmark or to do what Maghdlm could not and break the bond." He stared at Tancho now as they rode side by side. "Did you not think it was something you should have consulted with me? Considering I am the other half to this wretched curse."

Tancho bristled immediately. "I do not answer to anyone! Let alone to you."

"What do you think should happen to me if whatever that healer has done causes pain? Did you stop to consider that your actions no longer only affect yourself? You ask some small-village healer to do the work of an ancient alchemist and expect no repercussions?"

"I had intended to talk to you about it when we had a moment alone this evening instead of every ear listening," Tancho bit back. "And I asked the healer to do no such thing. Do you take me for a fool?"

Crow turned to look at him, raising one eyebrow. He said nothing.

Tancho glared at him. *How dare he?* "I asked the healer to provide me a paste to numb the skin, if you must know."

"Like the one he made for the gash on Maghdlm's head," Crow mumbled, nodding.

"Yes! He mentioned numbing and I wondered if it would work to numb the pain and afford us more distance between us. I asked for it only to be applied to my skin. In case there were ill effects, it would only harm me. Not you." Tancho didn't even try to conceal his anger or his distaste. "But go ahead, make it about you."

"You should have told me."

"I am telling you."

Crow gnashed his teeth and growled. "You're impossible!"

Tancho growled right back. "And you are insufferable."

Crow waved his hand up ahead. "Go on, then. Put your precious distance between us. See how well it works."

Tancho snarled at him. He was tempted to pull his

katana and take out Crow's barbed tongue, but he took hold of his self-control and gave his horse a nudge with his heels instead. "Yah," he hissed, and his horse took off at a pace. He put a few quick lengths between them, and he knew the split second he'd gone too far.

The pain ripped up his arm, bone and flesh felt on fire. Searing, biting, burning. He almost came off his horse. He pulled hard on the reins, groaning through the pain, and it took him a second to realise that Crow had cried out too. He was gripping his wrist, his face etched in horror. "You fool!"

And Tancho didn't even have it in him to argue.

Karasu rode up to Tancho and took hold of his horse's bridle, keeping him on the road, at least. Somehow they all managed to keep riding. Soko quickly had his horse beside Crow's, and he was grinning. "Watching you two together is like those puppet shows we used to watch as children. Remember, Crow? Those crazy marionettes bickering and fighting, sword-fighting, making us laugh."

Karasu smiled at that, and Tancho glared at her.

Crow shot Soko a dirty look, still holding his wrist. "I'm fine, thank you for asking."

"I loved those puppet shows," Kohaku said from behind them.

Soko laughed. "Great entertainment, see?"

"I have a great idea for entertainment," Crow said. "Next one to make someone's arm feel as if it had just caught fire gets their ass kicked."

Tancho rolled his eyes and raised his chin. "I apologise."

"So we can safely assume that the numbing paste doesn't work."

Tancho shot him a glare over his shoulder. "He was unsure how long it would take for the effects to hold. It might still work."

"I dare you to try it again!" Crow said.

"You know what was best about those puppet shows?" Soko added.

"That one puppet usually got to knife the other?" Crow deadpanned.

Tancho shot him another steely glare.

"No," Soko replied with a laugh. "The best part was that the entire puppet show only lasted a short while and not a full seven-day ride."

Karasu chuckled and Tancho gave her a pointed glare. "Something funny?" he asked her.

"Not at all, my king." She smirked. "Not at all."

THEY REACHED Yura just on dark, and Tancho was glad to be off his horse. Not that he'd ever admit that in front of Crow—he was loath to show any weakness—but there was a hot bath with his name on it.

The innkeeper came to the door, his eyes widening when he saw Tancho. "My king!"

"How many rooms have you this night?" Tancho asked.

"Four, your excellency." He bowed his head. "You may take my house for the night if that pleases you. It is not much but it is yours, if you wish."

Tancho bowed his head. "Your generosity is kindly noted but not required, good man. The four rooms will suffice."

"Yes, yes," he replied. "Your horses are this way."

He led them to the stables first, then showed them to their rooms. Unagi and Iruka took charge of the horses and Kohaku carried Maghdlm from the carriage. The innkeeper was alarmed at the sight but knew well enough not to ask questions. Though his eyes almost left his head when he finally noticed Crow and Soko wearing Northland cloaks.

He gave Tancho a bewildered look. "Is that . . . ? I trust all is well, my king?"

Tancho smiled. "All is well, good man."

He kept a wary distance from Crow and Soko, taking in their hard-soled boots and broadswords, and made nervous eye contact with Tancho. "Is there anything I can do for you, my king?"

The poor man clearly thought his king was under duress by the two tall men in black cloaks. "A hot meal and baths," Tancho replied. "Our guests from the Northlands appreciate your hospitality."

He bowed his head again. "Of course. I will see the horses fed as well, my king."

He scurried off and Crow sighed. "Are we that intimidating?"

Tancho refused to admit that their height and build, their weapons and clothes meant for colder weather was intimidating. "More of a curiosity, the way a child might look at a pentatomidae for the first time."

Karasu snorted and Kohaku laughed, and Crow glared at them all. He very obviously had no clue what a pentatomidae was, but he knew it was an insult. His hand went to the hilt of his sword, but Soko rolled his eyes and sighed. "Did you mention hot food and baths?"

The inn rooms were adjoining in a line, and it was agreed that Karasu and Maghdlm would take one room, Kohaku and Tancho in one, Crow and Soko in the next room, and Hikari and Unagi in the end room, closest to the stables.

"Can you stand to be one room apart?" Soko asked Crow, teasing in his voice.

The truth was, there was only one way to tell. So with Crow in his room, Tancho walked to the door of his room. The pull on his wrist was harsh, the burn noticeable. But as he entered his room and went to the bed along the adjoining wall, the pain was gone.

Thank the sun and stars above.

Tancho didn't fancy sharing a room with Crow. But of course, Soko found something funny because he laughed. "Sleeping with a wall between you is fine. Using the baths should prove interesting though, don't you think?"

Crow glared pure rage at Soko, and Tancho inhaled deeply in an attempt to calm the sea of anger and frustration welling inside of him.

He hadn't thought of that.

"I can wait outside, if he wishes to go first," Tancho said as politely as possible, as if that offer made him a better man.

"Or I could wait while *he* goes first," Crow replied.

Soko let his head fall back and he groaned at the ceiling. "May the blue skies save me."

Karasu rubbed her temple. "I have to tend to Maghdlm. I will leave the children to bicker."

Tancho glared after her as she walked away, but Crow took that as a victory. Kohaku, like Soko, seemed to find something funny. "Soko and I will supervise." He grinned at Soko. "Should we let them have weapons?"

"No!" Karasu yelled from the door to her room.

Tancho grumbled, walked into his room, and kicked the door shut.

He knew he was acting like a child, but so help him, he couldn't seem to stop himself. Every single thing about Crow drove him to madness. He lost all reason around him. He wanted to fight and push back, and if he couldn't use his blades on him, then the very least he could do was cut him with words.

He stood in the small lodging room and took another deep breath in some futile attempt at self-control. "I am better than this," he whispered to himself. "I am stronger. I have been trained for this." Well, that wasn't exactly true. He'd been trained in many things. But being subjected to and mysteriously tethered to a man who plucked his strings like a lyre was not one of them.

Tancho was angry at himself for not having better control of his emotions. Even with his birthmark curse, and his connection to Crow, he still should have better control.

All those long hours of meditation, of blocking out all else while centring his thoughts, should have prepared him better than this.

He remembered his lessons with Asagi. He remembered all the breathing techniques and mind-calming measures. He was determined to do better, to be in control.

And that worked just fine . . . until they went into the bathhouse and he saw Crow's half-naked body before he had the presence of mind to look away. Tancho had reassured them all it was ridiculous to make everyone else wait to bathe because he and Crow were unable to be in the same room as each other. Which was ridiculous, because they couldn't *not* be in the same room as each other.

So into the bathhouse together they went. Where the only bath was a large circular tub made of stone, cut into the floor. Tancho hadn't realised they'd have to share a bath. A bathroom, yes. But a bath? He was about to raise the question with Crow and turned to face him . . .

Only to find Crow had taken off his shirt, just peeled it away without any consideration of Tancho and how it made his pulse thunder. Crow's torso was muscled and strong, pale, and sweet mercy, there was a smattering of hair on his chest.

Tancho gasped at the sight of it. Never had he seen such a man . . .

Crow turned at the sound, and Tancho quickly pretended to be untying the bandage around his wrist, which now that he thought about it, had begun to sting.

"Tancho?" Crow asked, walking over. He snatched up Tancho's wrist and made quick work of the bandage. "You sounded pained, are you hurt?"

Tancho couldn't answer. He couldn't think straight. Not with him so close, still shirtless, his beautiful chest, his strong arms, his smell . . . He was lightheaded with the thrill of it.

"No, I'm fine," Tancho mumbled, remembering Crow had asked him a question.

Crow finished unwrapping the bandage to reveal Tancho's wrist, still with the balm layered over his birth-mark but with red angry skin underneath.

"It's red raw," Crow said, a scowl across his brow. He led him over toward the bath, and taking a cloth from the water, he gently washed the balm off. "You're lucky this isn't infected."

"It doesn't hurt," Tancho said quietly. "I'd not felt it until just now."

Crow had such big hands, rough and calloused, but his touch was gentle and kind. "That balm might numb a wound, but you've only served to cause yourself more injury," he said as though he was mad—mad that Tancho should have known better—but his tone was soft as if he couldn't bear the thought of Tancho being in pain. "Does it bother you?"

Tancho shook his head. He would have answered any

damn thing to appease Crow while he touched his arm. Tancho felt his cheeks warm with a blush, so he pulled his arm free before Crow could see. "Thank you," he whispered, turning away. Keeping his back to Crow, Tancho began to unbutton his shirt. When he could trust his voice not to betray him, he said, "They'll assume we've drowned each other if we take too long."

He concentrated on undressing and was just about to take his pants down when he heard the splash of water. He turned quickly to see the back of a very naked Crow sinking into the bath. The long lines of muscle, the curve of his arse, broad shoulders . . .

Tancho was mad at himself for not turning sooner.

But while Crow had his back turned, Tancho stripped, and when Crow slid down under the surface to wash his hair, Tancho stepped in.

He was seated across from Crow when he resurfaced and blinked his surprise, but a smile pulled at his lips. "The hot water is a welcome reprieve from long hours in a saddle," Crow said.

"It is," Tancho whispered. He had to look away from Crow's impossible eyes. He felt scrutinised under that piercing stare, as though Crow saw *into* him. Being naked in a bath with him didn't help. Their difference in size had never felt more apparent than it did to Tancho in that moment.

"It's a shame they wouldn't let us bring our weapons," Crow said with a smile. "Though I'd be a fool to think you couldn't kill me with your bare hands."

Tancho met his gaze then, the steam from the water swirled between them. "You'd be a fool to think I'd even need to use my hands."

Crow's nostrils flared and one eyebrow quirked upward. He fought a smile. "Is that a challenge?"

Tancho had to wonder if they were talking about fighting. He was beginning to think they weren't. "Is everything a sport to you?"

His eyes danced with humour. "Yes."

Needing to assert some control and possibly a little cruelty, Tancho took the cloth and began to wash his arm and shoulder. He knew Crow watched every movement, so he did it slowly, deliberately, right up to his throat, craning his neck just so. Letting the water run over his collarbone, his chest, letting his hair fall into the water. He never took his eyes off Crow's, seeing them darken, seeing his jaw bulge and his lips part . . .

Sport had never been so much fun.

Just then a knock sounded at the door and Soko poked his head in, as if he was hoping to see something in particular. "Ah, excuse the interruption."

Kohaku's grinning head appeared above Soko's in the darkness outside. "Meals are ready," he said. "The innkeeper wanted you to know."

"Thank you," Crow said. Then, with all the brazen confidence, or perhaps his turn at this sporting game, Crow stood up in the bath, naked as the day he was born. He leisurely reached for a towel, then casually dried his face and hair, very deliberately leaving his cock on full display.

He was half-hard, hanging heavy and thick, and Tancho couldn't look away. His mouth went dry. He licked his lips with want, the cloth in his hand long forgotten. Crow smirked at him as he towelled his hair, his face and chest. The kind of smirk that could start a war, raise an army, and topple kingdoms . . . The kind of smirk that said yes, this sport is fun indeed.

Like the smirk Tancho had worn just moments before.

The kind of smirk that said Crow had won this round and they both knew it.

Apparently so did Soko and Kohaku, if their laughter was anything to go by. Kohaku dragged Soko away before he could comment, which Tancho was grateful for. He didn't fancy hearing anything anyone had to say.

He closed his eyes, wishing it all away, and slid down under the surface, hoping when he came up for air, everyone would be gone. Soko and Kohaku were long gone, thankfully, but Crow was still there, pulling on his shirt. He was wearing pants, something Tancho was both grateful for and bitterly disappointed about.

While Crow still had his back turned, Tancho stood and pulled a towel around his waist. He took another towel to dry himself with and padded over to his clothes and hurried to redress. Crow still wore that cursed smirk, but he thankfully didn't tease him. He sat down to pull on his boots and watched as Tancho towel-dried his hair.

"Does everyone in the Westlands have long hair?" he asked.

"Most, though not all," Tancho replied, surprised by the question.

"I thought it might have been a royal court status, with you and Kohaku and Karasu. But most villagers I've seen these last two days also have long hair."

"It's not a status symbol. It's just how we are." Tancho frowned. "It's *who* we are."

"I like it," Crow said quickly. "I wasn't implying otherwise. The colour of yours . . ."

"I have worn the brunt of many mockeries for the colour of my hair," Tancho said. "Even as king. Could you imagine what would have been said to me if I didn't hold that title?"

Crow stared at him. "They mocked you for it? And you let them live?"

Tancho sighed. "If a king cannot take insult said in jest, how does he expect to take insults thrown at him in bad taste?"

"The colour of your hair is like . . ." Crow's eyes raked over Tancho's wet tresses and he whispered, "Like a blood-ruby cut from the oldest mountain by the most skilled hand. Rich and deep and incredibly rare."

Tancho studied Crow's eyes for the humour, waiting for the punch line, the joke to follow. But he saw only seriousness and even some embarrassment. "Sorry, if that sounds . . ." Crow frowned. "But should I hear anyone mock you, I'll give them a condensed lesson in manners."

Tancho couldn't help but smile. "Condensed?"

"Very short and summarised. To the point." He looked over Tancho's hair again. "Should you dry it more? Will you catch a cold?"

Tancho almost rolled his eyes but refrained. "This isn't the Northlands."

"True. If it were, your wet hair would either be so frozen it snapped off, or it would be the death of you."

"Lucky for me this is the Westlands, then, isn't it?" He stood, smiling. "We're late for our meals. Everyone is probably waiting."

Crow rose to his feet as well. "Not Soko. He'd have finished his and started on mine by now. We should probably go."

"Sounds like Kohaku."

Crow held his gaze for a long moment. "I'll see you in the morning then. If you need to leave for whatever reason, knock on the wall between us instead of trying to sneak off and making my whole arm catch fire." He held out his wrist, birthmark facing up. "Perhaps Maghdlm will be able to separate us from this lacuna bond soon, if she's well enough."

Tancho nodded, because that should be what he wanted. He *should* want their bond severed so he could return to his castle and be the king his people deserved. He *should* want their bond severed so their lives were their own again, so he could resume his life from just a few days ago.

Except now . . .

The thought of being separated from Crow made him feel ill.

"Yes, perhaps," he mumbled. Together they walked back to their rooms in the dark, and Tancho was glad Crow couldn't see his face.

Soko and Kohaku met them outside their rooms. Having eaten already, they were going for a bath. "Meals are in our room. Thought it'd be better if you ate together," Soko said, not even trying to hide his grin. He waggled his eyebrows at Crow as they walked away, which Tancho was certain he was not meant to see.

Embarrassed, Tancho stood aside and waited for Crow to open the door. Their food had been left on the table. "I'm surprised there's anything left," Crow mumbled as he walked inside. The table was low to the ground with seat cushions on the floor, like most tables in the Westlands. And of course, Soko and Kohaku had arranged the cushions and the plates of food so Tancho and Crow would sit together.

Tancho hid his smile as he watched Crow trying to sit cross-legged on a cushion, and he poured them each a cup of tea. Crow inspected the bowl of stew in front of him. "What is that?"

"Fish stew," Tancho said. "It is a common meal here."

Crow sniffed at it and took a tentative taste. He blinked in surprise. "Oh. It's good."

They ate their stew and breads in relative silence, and after Tancho poured more tea, Crow took Tancho's hand. It startled Tancho, his heartrate took off, and his belly flooded with butterflies. His skin felt alive, buzzing with anticipation that Crow would touch him . . .

Crow lifted Tancho's hand to the lamp so he could inspect his wrist. "Is your skin still bothered by the numbing paste? It's still marked."

Disappointment sank in Tancho's belly like a stone. Of course Crow wouldn't touch him with affection. Why would Tancho think he would? Tancho pulled his hand away. "It's fine. The mahicain will wear off and the rash will be gone by morning, I'm sure."

"Are you sorry it didn't work?"

Tancho looked out the door into the darkened night and gave a nod. "I had hoped it would allow you to go home. That's all. If we could numb the pain with distance between us . . ."

Crow's brow furrowed. "Is my presence such a burden for you?"

"No." Tancho shook his head. "But I realise you mustn't want to be here with me when you could be with your own people. We face uncertainty when we return to my home, with those strange intruders. Who knows what we're returning to? Something is wrong at Aequi Kentron. I would understand you wanting to be headed home because I would feel the same way should we stand in opposite places right now."

Crow sighed deeply. "Something is wrong, I agree. But my home is well protected. My people are resilient and strong."

"We don't know this enemy or if they are an enemy at all."

"My castle is many days trek from the northern shore, across steep mountains, snow, and ice. If an invading army survived the mountains, they'd be in no shape for battle once they reached the Northlands' castle." Crow met Tancho's eyes. "Your castle is on the western shoreline?"

Tancho nodded. "We are water people. We live by the water. It's who we are."

"And of all four kingdoms, yours is the most accessible. The Eastlands is desert dunes and the Southlands is deep jungle. The Westlands is flat, accessible."

Understanding crept over Tancho like a cold mist. "So if any intruder wished to invade, the Westlands is the path of least resistance."

Crow gave a nod. "But how would a foreign army know this?"

"You think someone here told them?"

"Not here, no. But something is afoot at Aequi Kentron. Having the leaders of all four kingdoms there and intruders hit at the same time? I don't believe in that kind of coincidence. They came to the west for a reason, Tancho."

Tancho stared at him, and he knew Crow was right.

Someone at Aequi Kentron had betrayed them.

Tancho's glare hardened. "We need Maghdlm to talk."

Crow nodded. "So don't think I regret not going north. What comes at you will be coming at me next. So heading west with you, facing whatever it is we need to face, is where I need to be."

CHAPTER ELEVEN

THEY RODE out at first light and, after riding hard all day, slept under the stars by a campfire when they finally stopped to let the horses rest that night. Crow saw a new determination in Tancho to get home, to get to answers.

Maghdlm had much improved and Karasu had said she was mostly lucid when awake. The medicinal tea kept her comfortable and helped her body heal, and Crow hoped they might soon get answers from her.

They rode through some remarkable scenery. Ornate bridges, beautiful waterways, peaceful landscapes, made even more magical by the golden hue of the sun. There were trees Crow had never seen before, with pretty blossoms and fragrance he couldn't have imagined.

Trees in the Northlands were scarce higher into the mountains. Sure, there were trees and greenery in the rolling foothills, but the majority of Crow's homelands were snow-covered alps. The mountains Crow could see to the north were *his* mountains, far off and getting smaller the farther they rode.

And he loved his country. He missed it, having never been absent from it for so long, having never visited another kingdom. But he had to admit, only to himself, he'd never seen anything so magical as the Westlands.

As they rode further west, the villages were closer together and larger in size. Bustling towns built in harmony with the rivers, with kind villagers who offered their king food and fresh horses. Though the people of Westlands were wary of Crow and Soko in their black cloaks and strange clothes, Tancho reassured everyone they met that they were amongst friends.

Crow knew this was to ease his people's minds, not for Crow or Soko's benefit at all, but Crow liked it, nonetheless. They had spent the last few days and nights not more than a few strides apart, constantly in each other's company. They'd reached some kind of amicable agreement where bickering was fine, the occasional jibe was tolerated, but they hadn't drawn their weapons on each other in almost two days.

There might be hope for them yet, Crow thought.

Maybe it was the urgency with which Tancho needed to return home. Maybe it was how Crow could sympathise with him, king to king, because Tancho's homeland might be in danger. An attack on one was an attack on them all.

Maybe it was the way Crow caught Tancho looking at him from the corner of his eye, or the way he smiled or the sound of his laughter, or how his red hair caught the strange golden sunlight . . .

The next night they stayed at an old inn where the only room available was a large dorm room they would all share. It wasn't ideal, but the baths were hot and the food was good. Like before, Crow and Tancho had to bathe together, but this bath was only big enough for one. So while Tancho bathed first, Crow sat nearby with his back turned for privacy. He couldn't help but steal a few glances, catching the sight of smooth alabaster skin and errant strands of long red hair that had escaped the bun on his head.

Tancho was trim and lean, muscular like a whippet. His neck was long, his shoulders defined, and his biceps bulged as he washed. And even though he was mild-mannered and quiet, Crow didn't take that for weakness. He would never doubt Tancho's ability with his katanas.

Crow had no doubt he could best him in battle, if it ever came down to that. But he still would have liked to see him in action.

After their meals and baths, Tancho helped Karasu with Maghdlm, cleaning her wounds, feeding her broth. The frail old lady was improving. She understood questions now, giving a nod, but she mostly kept her eyes closed. She whispered her thanks after more tea and was soon sleeping.

They wouldn't get answers to their questions today, but soon. Crow hoped it would be tomorrow, the day after that at the latest. They didn't want to be riding into Tancho's castle without knowing all they could.

The thin reed mattresses on the floor of the dorm room were hardly comfortable, though Crow lay in the corner listening to Soko and Kohaku comparing swords. Soko had a broadsword, Kohaku twin daggers, and they weren't compatible for—

"Let me see what you've got," Soko said, getting to his feet. He held his broadsword with both hands, and Crow might have been concerned if it weren't for his shit-eating grin.

Kohaku leapt up, a dagger in each hand, a smile splitting his face. They sparred, struck, parried, countered, all while circling each other, laughing as their swords sung with each strike. Two different weapons and two very different fighting styles, but it was fun to watch. Then they swapped swords. Kohaku liked the weight of the heavier sword and Soko fancied the two smaller daggers but they were both hilariously unskilled at wielding them.

Everyone laughed at their antics, but Karasu found it funniest. "Kohaku, has your training taught you nothing?" she asked, laughing. "The weight of the sword doesn't make for heavy feet."

"You try it," he said, holding Soko's sword out for her. "Don't mock me until I've seen your footwork."

She jumped at the challenge, and when she took the sword from Kohaku, it almost went to the floor. She managed to hold it, needing both hands, and she shot Kohaku and Soko a glare when they laughed. "Is it made of lead?"

"Finest Northland steel. We mine the richest ore from deep in the mountains." Soko said. He raised the two daggers and bowed. "En garde, madam."

Karasu grinned and hefted the sword up, and they sparred for a few minutes. Crow had wondered if her temper might fray the mood, but she played in good sport. After a while she raised her hand. "Yield. How do you expect to fight for any length of time with this?"

"We know no other way," Soko replied. "From the age when we could hold a fork and knife, we could hold a sword."

"Here," she said, handing Soko back his broadsword and swapping Kohaku's daggers for her katana. "Now we'll see how we fare."

Soko's grin widened impossibly, and if Crow weren't

mistaken, he might have thought his friend enamoured by the challenge, by Karasu. There was a light in his eyes that wasn't there when he sparred with Kohaku.

They circled around each other, sparring, striking, and taunting, and Crow caught Tancho's smile as he watched them. His whole face lit up when he laughed, and for that briefest moment, he looked carefree . . . and devastatingly beautiful.

Crow had never seen someone so beautiful.

When Crow heard Karasu laugh, he turned his attention back to the sparring to see Soko had swapped his broadsword for a katana. "Oh, Crow, I must get myself one of these. You must come and try this."

Crow was about to decline the offer but Karasu held the hilt of her katana out to him, and he wouldn't dare offend her. He got to his feet and took the katana with a bow of his head. It was light, and after he swung it in his hand a few times, he could tell it was expertly made. The weight distribution and point of balance were sublime in the hand.

"See?" Soko said. "We need to speak to our blade master."

Crow barked out a laugh. "He would never. Even if he could."

Soko and Crow tried to spar with the foreign swords but were only good for entertainment, though thankfully they were as bad as each other.

"Here," Soko said, offering his katana to Tancho. "Show him how it's done."

Crow was about to say no, even rebuke Soko for suggesting it, but Tancho got to his feet. Lithe as a fish through water, and smiling, he took the katana and bowed his head to Soko, then took his place opposite Crow.

A thrill ran through Crow. Was it anticipation? Was it

excitement, or was it something else? His blood felt alive and his skin flushed warm at the thought of fighting Tancho. He wanted this like he'd never wanted anything.

He swung the katana, smiling at Tancho, and they began to circle.

"You know this is for fun?" Soko asked, now alarmed.

"Oh, yes," Crow replied, not taking his eyes off Tancho.

"Fun," Tancho whispered, and he lowered his stance as they moved about each other. He raised his sword, preparing to strike.

"Uh, Tancho," Karasu murmured. "Remember who you are."

From the corner of his eye, Crow saw the two guardsmen, Hikari and Unagi, get to their feet. But he didn't dare look at them. He simply couldn't draw his eyes away. He knew the others in the room were uncomfortable with this, but he was connected to Tancho by some charge between them, and he didn't want to look away. His bones buzzed with it, his blood was getting warmer, and it felt so good he hummed with pleasure.

Tancho smiled at him, much like a cat would at a mouse. "You feel it."

"I want it," Crow growled.

"As do I," Tancho replied, and he swung his blade at Crow's neck.

He was fast but Crow blocked the strike, and soon as the blades hit, the charge between them exploded. Blue sparks and a bolt ignited up the swords, as if arcane lightning struck them from the sky. The jolt blew them apart, both men landing on their arses, and Crow dropped the sword as a stray bolt of blue power zigzagged up the blade's edge.

"Crow!" Soko ran to him, just as Karasu and Kohaku ran to Tancho.

Crow sat up, his heart beating like thunder in his chest. The inside of his wrist burned, and he checked his birthmark, half expecting to see it blistered.

"Are you hurt?" Karasu asked Tancho.

Tancho sat up too, looking for Crow as Crow looked for him. "I'm okay," he whispered, holding his wrist.

"Crow?" Soko asked, worried.

"I'm fine. The birthmark burns, that's all."

Soko found a cloth and poured water over it, then wrapped it around Crow's wrist, and the burning subsided. Crow was watching Soko as he tended to him, and he hadn't paid Tancho any mind for just a moment.

"I said I'm fine," Tancho hissed at Karasu, trying to apply a wet bandage to his wrist. Then Tancho shot a rabid glare at Soko and growled, his voice low and full of warning, "Would you stop touching him!"

Everyone stared in stunned silence, and Soko slowly raised his hands and backed away from Crow. "Apologies, I forgot," Soko mumbled.

The truth was, Crow had forgotten too. That whole weird 'no one else can touch him' thing seemed so long ago. "It's okay," Crow said to Soko, then he turned to Tancho. "He means no harm."

"I know, I know," he said, his eyes squinted closed. "Apologies."

Everyone took a few moments to breathe and calm down. Hikari and Unagi were wide-eyed and horrified, and Karasu gave them an apologetic nod. "Can you please check on the horses?"

They nodded and made a hasty exit, and after a few

moments silence, Kohaku stood up, the colour bleached from his face. "What in the abyss was that?" he hissed.

"I don't know," Crow replied in a whisper. "I felt . . ."

"As if I was made of fire," Tancho replied. He met Crow's eyes. "As if we both were."

Crow nodded. "Arcane fire."

Then a quiet voice from the far corner of the room spoke, feeble and centuries old. "It is in your blood."

Everyone turned to find Maghdlm half sitting up, her head bandaged and one eye still swollen shut. "You cannot fight it."

"Fight what?" Crow asked.

"The lacuna," she replied, her voice weak. "You cannot bring harm to the other."

Everyone stared at her, and it was Tancho who spoke first. "Do you mean to tell me that no matter what he does," he said, pointing his thumb at Crow, "no matter how much he pisses me off or what he says or does, I cannot kill him?"

"Kill me?" Crow asked, staring at Tancho incredulously. "As if you could!"

Tancho bared his teeth. "I would best you—"

"You cannot," Maghdlm said, closing her eyes and laying back down. "You cannot be apart. I told you that. Not in life, not in death."

Not in life.

Not in death.

Crow was about to object and denounce this nonsense for the absurdity it was. He wanted to be angry, to rage and wreak havoc . . . but he couldn't. Because he knew. He knew in his bones, in his core, that it was true.

Whatever it was between Crow and Tancho was strange, some alchemical or astronomical oddity, but it was real. Real enough to spark bolts of blue lightning between them and real enough to burn the birthmarks on their skin.

The jovial mood from before was gone. No one spoke or laughed, and Crow was quick to go back to his reed mat on the floor even though he had no hope of sleeping this night. Not now. His mind raced and his wrist still ached, and from the way Tancho tossed and turned, Crow assumed his did too.

"Oh, for the love of the blue skies above," Soko grumbled, getting up. He trudged over to Tancho and nudged his foot with his own. "Swap beds. I can't stand the noise. If you have the bed next to him, you might actually sleep. You're keeping everyone awake."

Tancho sat up angrily, got to his feet angrily, and stomped over to the mat next to Crow's, and lay down angrily too.

But the ache in Crow's wrist went away, and he felt settled by Tancho's closeness. He was calmer, more relaxed, and at peace. His mind swam and his blood buzzed warm, drunk from just being near him. He knew Tancho had to feel it too.

"It doesn't mean anything," Tancho whisper-hissed.

Crow smiled in the dark and closed his eyes, and for the first time since this whole mess began, sleep came all too easy.

***

"WHAT DO you think Maghdlm meant when she said, 'not in death'?" Tancho asked. "What's that supposed to mean?"

They'd not wasted any time getting the horses saddled and ready for another day's ride, and even though Crow and

Tancho rode side by side for hours, they hadn't really spoken. Crow's mind ran in circles, turning over everything Maghdlm had said and what had happened with the sword fight and the crazy bolt of lightning.

Not to mention what had happened before the fight. The desire, the want. When they'd squared off against each other, there was a physical thrill that gave his blood a buzz, and Crow had been certain Tancho had felt it too.

And there was the sleeping next to each other that felt like one too many a shot of berry wine. It made him feel warm all over and his limbs heavy, and he'd slept like the dead. And that was having Tancho on the reed mat beside him. Imagine what it would feel like to have him in the same bed . . .

"Do you not wish to answer me, or are your ears for decoration?"

Crow looked at Tancho. "What?"

"I asked you a question. Maghdlm's 'not in life, not in death' comment. What do you think she meant by it?"

"I can guess, but I don't know exactly."

"And your guess?"

"Is that we cannot be apart in life or death. That we cannot cause that death. I cannot kill you because I cannot be apart from you."

Tancho sighed. "You couldn't kill me because you lack the skill."

"Perhaps," Crow replied. "But it's not for the lack of wanting to kill you."

Tancho smiled at that. "Well, that is something we have in common."

"The real question," Crow furthered, "is what happens to the one who remains should the other meet his end? For example, if you were to trip and fall on your own sword, what would happen to me?"

"Fall on my sword?"

"Yes, or lose a fight to a novice. Both of those scenarios are likely; I've seen you fight."

Tancho's mouth fell open. "Or if you should fall from your horse right now and snap your neck. Or accidentally eat some shinigami berries and, in turn, pass your innards for outtards."

"Shinigami?"

"Angel of death," Karasu answered. She and Soko were riding in front of them. She cast a smug smile in Crow's direction. "The berry is sweet and delicious, apparently. Before it turns into a fermenting acid bomb in your belly and rips your insides apart."

"Nice," Crow replied to Tancho. "But more to my point, if I were to die—in some heroic battle, of course, not because I was poisoned by a fermented berry bomb—what becomes of you?"

Tancho was quiet for a moment as he pondered this. "If I were to die before this lacuna curse is lifted, I would assume you'd follow soon after. Isn't that what she meant?"

And as if hearing Tancho say Crow would die if he died wasn't the worst part, hearing him call the lacuna bond between them a curse felt impossibly worse.

It was a curse, Crow tried to tell himself. It made a mockery of their self-control and all but set their autonomy on fire.

Crow hated that his choice was removed, but he couldn't bring himself to hate Tancho. It wasn't his fault, nor was it Crow's. And he couldn't bring himself to hate that they were in this together. So yes, a curse to some degree . . . but there was something about the way Tancho said it . . .

"This lacuna curse?" Crow said, trying not to sound like a pouting child. "Is it a curse because of the situation we find ourselves in? Or rather, who you find yourself cursed with?" he asked, putting his hand to his chest.

Soko shot Crow a pitiful look and Karasu laughed. Tancho looked at him and a slow smile spread across his face. "You sound bothered by the latter."

Crow shifted in his saddle. He knew he sounded petulant but he couldn't stop himself. "No, I just wasn't sure how insulted I should be. If you consider yourself cursed because it's me who you're linked to . . ."

Tancho chuckled at him then. "If not a curse, then what would you call it?"

Crow searched for the right word but couldn't put his tongue to it. "Okay, so maybe cursed is the right word. But for me, it is not a reflection on you but the situation we find ourselves in." He raised his chin. "At least I'm man enough to say it."

Tancho's lips quirked in a way that Crow both loved and hated in equal measure. Smug and shy at the same time, with his stupid perfect skin and stupid beautiful hair. "You know what?" Crow said, past caring for his petulance. "It *is* a curse. This whole thing is a giant curse, both the circumstance *and* the man I'm stuck here with."

Tancho's nostrils flared, his smile long gone. "Oh, is that right?"

Crow pulled his horse to a stop, making everyone come to a standstill. "Yes. Completely accurate. And you know what else? I might just decide not to go one step further. It's not me who needs to go west, it's you. But you can't go without me; so if I don't go, neither do you. I have forgone going home to my people for the sake of yours, so if you want me to take one more step, maybe you could ease up on the mockery. Some appreciation might not go astray." Tancho was rendered silent, and now it was Crow's turn to smirk. "Where's your pretty smile now, little fish?"

Tancho unsheathed his katana, and he spoke through gritted teeth. "Call me that again, blackbird. I dare you."

Crow opted to pull the dagger from his boot rather than his broadsword, ready to fight—blue arcane lightning be damned. He'd take his chances.

Soko sighed, Kohaku laughed, and Karasu got off her horse. "We're stopping here," she said, leading her horse off the road to the river for a drink. "If you two are done bickering like babes."

Soko made no attempt to defend Crow, much to Crow's chagrin. In fact, Crow thought he saw him roll his eyes. "Good. I'm famished."

Kohaku cheered. "Yes, food!"

Soko took his and Kohaku's horses to the river while Kohaku helped the guards pull the carriage off the road, and they sought about splitting the fruit and bread kindly given by the innkeeper.

Everyone milled about as though nothing was out of the ordinary, like Crow and Tancho weren't still on their horses in the middle of the road, weapons drawn. It was all rather . . . anticlimactic.

Crow re-sheathed his dagger with a huff, and Tancho put away his katana. They both swung their legs over and dismounted at the same time, both scowling at the other. They trudged in silence, leading their horses to the river; then they trudged back up to the others. They ate without a word, sitting side by side, of course. Crow would like to put a few hundred miles between them but he couldn't.

Tancho was right. This whole thing was a curse, both in circumstance and man.

And there Crow was, after a morning of amicable silence across the distance they'd covered, thinking that Tancho wasn't all bad.

"Glad you two have calmed down," Karasu said. "And I think we've learned that tempers are frayed when hungry."

Crow smiled at her. "And I learned that I like him a whole lot better when he doesn't speak."

Karasu groaned and rolled her eyes. "Oh, may the abyss take me."

Soko laughed and threw Crow another pear. "And what I learned today is that Tancho called you pretty blackbird the other day, and you called him pretty fish just before. So while there is some name-calling, there's also a lot of pretty—"

He had to duck the pear and apple Crow and Tancho threw at his head. "Shut it, Soko."

Kohaku roared laughing. "No, he said pretty smile, not pretty fish."

Tancho glared at him. "If you don't wish to find yourself cleaning the royal stables, I suggest you choose silence."

"Yes, my king," Kohaku said, though he had to shove more food in his mouth to hide his smile.

Maghdlm managed more tea and some fruit, and now that everything had calmed down and the horses had rested a short while, it was time to leave again.

As they were about to climb back onto their horses, Tancho stopped at Crow's side. "What you said before, about not having to come west with me . . ." He frowned. "That is true and I should be more grateful. You make this trip with me, not because of the birthmark on your wrist but as a king who saw my plight. I needed you to join me because my home may be in danger, and you never hesitated. I didn't mean to offend you or to seem ungrateful. It's just that this—" He motioned between them. "—has me out of sorts. I cannot control my emotions or my reactions, and that is unlike me."

"It's not easy on me, either."

Tancho's brows knitted together and he made a face as though his thoughts left an unpleasant aftertaste. "I have spent many years mastering the art of meditation and centring my mind and energy. Yet now . . ." He looked out across the river, but what he saw Crow could only guess. "Now it is all for naught. My centre seems to have shifted and I can't focus. It adds to my worry, and the way the skies now colour with gold."

Crow sighed. "To know those creatures came to your home would be worry enough. I apologise if I behaved unbecomingly of my title. I have been schooled in the art of war, how to appear unruffled in the face of horrors, and here I am acting like a spoiled child. I think I even pouted before."

That, at least, drew an almost-smile from Tancho. "Perhaps a little."

"So we can agree that whatever this is affects us both, and we should aim for patience."

Tancho nodded and he let out a relieved breath. "I feel better having spoken to you, thank you."

"I do, as well." Then Crow did the most innocent thing. He put his hand to Tancho's shoulder, just for a second, but time stood still and the sound of the world fell away. His palm was hot, their touch charged and buzzing. Tancho's eyes drifted closed and he hummed, Crow gasped at the power of it, the thrill. Tancho's blue eyes cut to Crow's and his lips parted.

When Crow's hand fell away, when contact was lost, the world closed in on them once again. Sounds flared around them: the horses being readied and Kohaku giving the guards directive and running water and Karasu talking to Soko . . .

Crow blinked, and Tancho shook his head and gave Crow an incredulous look. "What was that?"

"You felt that as well?"

Tancho nodded, breathless. He licked his lips. "Perhaps you shouldn't touch me."

Or perhaps I should touch you a whole lot more . . .

Crow's thought stunned him, and it was all he could do to nod. He hauled himself up into the saddle and Tancho did the same. They rode out in procession, Soko and Karasu took lead, Crow and Tancho next, followed by Kohaku and the two guards behind him and the spare horse pulling the small carriage. They kept a steady pace, passing through villages and towns, and rode until sundown.

The inn they stopped at was nicer than the last. The baths were bigger, the water hot, the food plentiful. Though the room was another large communal dorm with mats on the floor and low tables with cushions for chairs.

This night, Maghdlm was well enough to sit up. She drank her tea and had some bread, and after they'd eaten, Karasu undid the bandages and dabbed more numbing paste along the gash there. She didn't say much, but her wounds were still ghastly, so Crow didn't doubt the pain of her injuries.

"How are you feeling?" Tancho asked quietly.

"Alive," she replied feebly. "For which I have you all to thank."

"Kohaku carried you," Tancho said. "Up those stairs and then on horseback for a day."

She turned slowly to where the big Westlander sat near the fire with Soko. They were now comparing boots, of all things. Kohaku gave her a wave.

Maghdlm gave him a nod, then turned back to Crow and Tancho. "And Karasu here tells me we're heading west."

"Correct," Tancho answered. "We had word of strange figures approaching my home."

Maghdlm nodded but focused on Crow. "And the King of Northlands walks on foreign land."

"The King of Northlands," Crow said with a bite in his tone, "has little choice." He held up his wrist, birthmark on display. "Remember?"

"I remember," she whispered.

"Maghdlm, we have many questions," Tancho tried with more manners than Crow. "To which you hold the answers."

She nodded slowly and blinked heavily. "And I shall tell you what I know. Though I fight sleep. The tea helps my pain but makes me drift."

The old woman closed her eyes and Crow sighed, figuring that was all they'd get out of her tonight. But Tancho tried again. "Maghdlm?"

She opened her eyes but they were unfocused. "Mm."

Crow wondered in that split second what his first question was going to be. He would have bet good coin that it would be asking how to sever the bond between them, but he surprised Crow almost at every turn.

"Who attacked you in the archīvum? We found you on the floor there. Someone hit you and left you for dead. Did you see who it was?"

She shook her head and frowned. "No."

If Crow could get one question in, he was going to try.

"Maghdlm," he said. "The Aequi Kentron was deserted when we left. Everyone was gone. Do you know where they went?"

He dreaded that she would say north.

She shook her head again, her eyes barely open. "You ask the wrong question," she whisper-mumbled as sleep tried to take her. "The question is not where they went, but how."

CHAPTER TWELVE

TANCHO AND CROW both looked at each other, confused, stunned. Her words were so quiet, Tancho wondered if he'd heard her correctly.

"It's not where they went," Crow repeated. "But how . . ."

Maghdlm was fast asleep, and although Tancho hated the riddle and cryptic prophecies, he wouldn't dare wake her for explanation. The bruising that covered half her face, the swelling, was now a mottled horror show of purple, green, and yellow. It was true that the older the skin, the worse the damage, and that was true for Maghdlm. She was old and frail before being clobbered with something blunt and heavy. How it hadn't caved her skull and how she lived at all, Tancho wasn't sure. But she needed to sleep.

So they left her to sleep and went back to their mats. Soko hadn't even bothered attempting to sleep next to Crow. He left that space for Tancho, and as much as it rankled him, he was also secretly pleased.

They sat beside each other, Crow leaning against the wall with his legs outstretched, Tancho cross-legged. Crow's expression was decidedly cool, but Tancho could see the fire in his eyes. "How could they leave if not on foot or horseback?" Crow asked. "If not a procession of carriages or wagons? And we've asked every villager at every stop if they've seen anything unusual but no one has. So we can assume no one from Aequi Kentron came west before us."

Tancho nodded. "So where did they go? Are Elmwood or Samiel walking into a trap?"

Crow's nostrils flared and his jaw clenched. "I hope not."

"Do you believe they went north?"

Crow's eyes flashed to his, the fire in them dying out quickly. "It wouldn't make sense."

"None of this makes sense."

"True."

"*How* did they leave?" Crow mumbled again.

Tancho thought about Aequi Kentron, the castle itself. There was a moat but no river. So where did the water come from? What source sustained them, the lands, the people? Water was essential for all life, Tancho knew that better than anyone. The only way water could reach them . . .

They both stared at each other, seemingly coming to the same conclusion at the exact same time. They spoke in unison.

"Underground."

Crow nodded hard. "If they didn't go out and they didn't go over, they must have left by ways underneath. It is the only explanation."

"The water," Tancho added. "The moat, sustainable supplies of water for consumption, the only way they can survive without a river is for the water to come from an underground supply."

"It would make sense," Karasu said from across the room. Tancho looked around then to find all eyes on them, ears listening to their hypotheses. "The archīvum was deep in the belly of the castle, yes?" Tancho and Crow both nodded. "We found Maghdlm there. Whoever tried to kill her was on their way down to somewhere."

"Caves," Soko added. "But where do they lead?"

"They need to surface somewhere," Tancho said.

"To find where they went, we must first ask why," Crow said. "What are they after? They must require something for their purpose. Someone has something they want. Out of the four kingdoms, which is it?"

Tancho stared at Crow for a long moment. "And perhaps we should also ask who. Who leads the charge? Maybe we should look at each of the elders to see if something lies amiss. Did one betray us? Or all?"

Crow glowered at the fire, his jaw ticking, his mind clearly racing. But then something in his features changed. He turned to Tancho. "What were you taught of the Aequi Kentron? In all your studies?"

Tancho let out a low breath. "That it was always there. It was the founding council of the entire empire. Aequi Kentron means equal centre in the old tongue. For thousands of years, it has been at the very heart of our lands. Equal lands, equal rule."

Crow nodded. "That rings true for me also. The elders who govern have done so for as long as our histories were written."

"That in our ancient histories, all four lands were run as their own. There were wars and destruction in a grab for land and people," Tancho furthered. "Lawlessness and greed drove the whole kingdom into despair. The people starved, and the lack of loyalty killed more leaders in the grapple for the top than any famine ever did. A treaty was reached and the central council was formed. They provided assistance and guidance, and in allowing each land to have its own ruler for its people, yet to live under a communal law, proved beneficial for all."

"Proved beneficial the most to whom?" Karasu asked. "All four lands receive equal measure, but what do the council receive? What does Aequi Kentron get?"

"Who governs the governors?" Soko furthered.

"They have been our guiding hand for many centuries," Crow said. "It's hard to believe it's all a farce. Yet what we saw with our own eyes . . ."

Tancho studied Crow for a moment. "What were you told of the Golden Eclipse?"

Crow took in a deep breath and shook his head. "I would imagine the same stories as you. That ours was the generation of kings to live through the Golden Eclipse. That the two moons would eclipse the sun together, this once in a thousand years. That we would make a pilgrimage to Aequi Kentron to take part in the Golden Festival, some ritual ceremony to honour the kings of our pasts."

"Do you not believe that to be true?"

"The eclipse? Yes. The changing shades of the sky are proof enough of that. I believe in things that are proven. I'm beginning to think we followed blindly what they wanted us to believe. They manoeuvred us as chess pieces in a game we were never supposed to win. That is what I believe."

Tancho took a deep breath and released it slowly, feeling the truth of Crow's words fill his bones. He held up his wrist, birthmark showing. "If it is all a lie, a fiction for their gain, then what is this?"

Crow shook his head slowly and met Tancho's gaze. "I don't know."

"I'll tell you what it is," Soko said. "It was a checkmate they didn't see coming. When your birthmarks reacted that first night, when they sparked lights under Maghdlm's touch, that was unexpected. If they did manoeuvre us into their game, this birthmark bond was a blindsiding. The looks on their faces . . ." He smiled. "They didn't plan for that. It wasn't surprise on Adelais face. It was outrage."

"Did you see Aelfflaed's face?" Kohaku asked. "For a seer of truth, it was a revelation she didn't foresee, and one she didn't like."

The reality was, Tancho hadn't seen anyone else's face in that moment but Maghdlm's and Crow's. And of course, there was the burn under his skin and up his arm. Nothing and no one else in that moment existed.

But maybe Soko was right. The realisation that their birthmarks were bonded had changed the mood of Adelais. Her façade of the calm and collected Grand Speaker had slipped after that. And maybe, if it was a move the elders had not counted on, then maybe—just possibly—the bond between himself and Crow wasn't such a curse after all.

"So many questions," Tancho whispered.

"Maghdlm will talk more tomorrow," Crow said. "And hopefully provide more answers. But tonight we should sleep." He lay down on his mat, folded his arm under his head as a pillow, and closed his eyes.

He had such long lashes, and his stubble was dark against his pale skin. He was disturbingly handsome, in that rough mountain-man way that Tancho had never considered handsome before. But for all his temper when awake, his usual glower was gone when he slept. He even looked peaceful. Beautiful.

The sound of Soko's laughter made Tancho look over, and he found Karasu, Soko, and Kohaku all staring at him and grinning. "I've been trying to get your attention for two minutes," Karasu said. "You called him beautiful."

Tancho growled at them. "I did not."

They all scoffed and Karasu rolled her eyes. "Okay then." She lay down, still smiling. "Good night."

Soko lay down as well. "Good night . . . beautiful."

They all laughed, and even one of the guards in the corner snorted. Tancho threw himself down on the mat and rolled over so they couldn't see the blush on his cheeks. "How long has it been in the Westlands' history since someone received fifty lashes for mocking the king?"

They stopped laughing.

"That's what I thought."

THEY WERE BACK on the road with the rising sun the next morning. They were so close to home Tancho could almost taste it. The townsfolk cheered as they rode through, welcoming their king home. No one had seen anything or anyone untoward, no unsightly creatures, anyway, though they mostly stared at Crow and Soko, giving them a wide berth.

Soko smiled and waved at the children. His demeanour was always cheerful and it was hard not to like him. Maybe the local people could warm to him, given the chance, even though he wore royal colours of the Northlands. Karasu and Kohaku certainly appeared to like him.

Crow, on the other hand, wasn't exactly welcoming. He kept his horse close to Tancho's, putting himself between Tancho and the crowds of people. He was being overprotective, a trait of their birthmark bond, and as much as it infuriated Tancho, he reminded himself that it wasn't Crow's fault. He couldn't help it.

But that was why the people looked at him warily. He was an imposing form, dressed in his black king's cloak, with a gleaming broadsword sheathed at his side. That, and the fact he scowled at almost everyone.

But they were offered baskets of fruit and breads, and as they continued west, Tancho wanted to pick up the pace.

"We're a day's full ride from home," he said. "No one has seen anyone come from the castle. No invading armies, no creatures. Nothing. That means they haven't left the castle, surely. They're not invading, they're waiting. We must ride on through the night without rest. We must get there as fast as we can."

"Have you lost your mind?" Crow said flatly. "You would ride into an unknown scenario without sleep and on weary horses when the enemy is six days' rested? If they're prepared for battle, you wouldn't stand a chance. We must rest and plan how we approach your home tomorrow. We have to be prepared."

Tancho glowered at him as they rode. He hated that Crow was right. "Then we ride as far as we dare tonight, and rest. Then we can approach earlier than would be expected, hopefully catch them unawares."

Crow's eyes hardened, but he pushed his horse to go a little faster. "Agreed."

THE INN TANCHO chose was off the main roads, smaller and obscure, and most definitely not what a king was accustomed to. But the innkeeper was a kind woman who was grateful for the coin and offered hot baths and food, and fresh hay and carrots for the horses.

Tancho was so restless, so anxious, he didn't linger long in the baths. Not even a naked Crow could keep him there. He hurried to redress, then remembered he had to wait for Crow to finish and join him.

Seeing Tancho's impatience, Crow let out a heavy sigh, quickly finished washing himself, and towelled off. Tancho held out his clothes for him, deliberately not looking when Crow pulled on his pants. He tried not to look at his naked chest either as he pulled his shirt on over his head, seeing that broad chest and the smattering of dark hair there . . . Tancho made himself turn to stare at the door.

"Hey," Crow murmured. "I know you're worried about tomorrow. I am too. But we need to be prepared, and to come up with a plan. You know your home better than anyone, so Soko and I will follow your lead. But we must think with strategic minds and not heavy hearts. We don't know what we'll be walking into, so we must think tactically."

Tancho sighed and gave a small nod. *Must he always be right?* "I know."

"And we should see if Maghdlm is faring better for questions."

Finally something Tancho readily agreed with. "Yes, we should."

Maghdlm was sitting up and dipping some bread into broth and taking small bites. Her bruising looked no better, truth be told, but she no longer resembled a piece of rotten fruit; she had some colour and life in her now. "Karasu helped me with a sponge bath while the room was empty," Maghdlm said. "I feel better for it. And I should offer my thanks once again for your kindness, both of you."

They sat on the floor cushions beside her. "You appear in much better spirits this eve," Crow said. "If there is anything you need, any alchemical or medicinal ingredients we can source for you, please just ask."

"Thank you, my lord," she said, bowing her head. "I forgot my manners, apologies."

Tancho gave her a smile. "We do have questions," he began.

"I thought you might," she said. Her one good eye held some spark; the skin on her unmarked cheek looked like soft paper.

Crow wasted no time. "Out of all the Elder Consuls, who is the traitor?"

She smiled at him. "You don't hold back, do you?"

"We have no time for riddles," Tancho said. "We reach my home tomorrow morning and have no idea what we will find. Is it a trap?"

Maghdlm took in a deep breath and put her bowl of broth on the floor between them. "Adelais leads them in all things," she said. "The Grand Speaker. I know nothing of their plans or intentions, only that there have been whispers and secret meetings for some time. I can only assume Aelf-flaed knows because she is the Seer of Truth. If Adelais had ill intentions, she'd have known about it."

They'd assumed this much last night.

"You said last night," Crow said, "that the elders left and our concern should not be where they went, but how."

"That tea the healer made must be strong," she mused. "The elders haven't set foot outside the Aequi Kentron cobblestones in many, many years."

"So how did they leave?" Crow asked, his tone shorter than it had been.

"Enough of the riddles, Maghdlm, please," Tancho tried.

"I'll be breaking the elders' code by telling you," she said. "If any code even still remains."

"They tried to kill you," Crow reminded her. "And very nearly succeeded. There is no loyalty anymore, no matter how much you wish it otherwise."

She stared at him for a long, long moment. "Centuries ingrained is a hard habit to break, my lord. And if I break the elders' code of secrecy, they'll have me marked for death again. I'm sure they won't fail a second time."

"Murder?" Tancho asked.

"They take it very seriously," she replied. "It is a position worthy of such a standing, is it not? Ruling over all four kingdoms."

Tancho's eyes darted to Crow's, and it was clear that Crow didn't like how she said that either. But they didn't have time for that right now. The old, injured woman was fast becoming tired. "How did they leave, Maghdlm?" Tancho asked. "Where did they go?"

"There are . . . doorways," she said, making a face. "I cannot explain it. But I can show you. When we get to your castle, kind Westlands' king."

"You can show me a doorway at my castle? To explain how the elders left Aequi Kentron?"

She nodded slowly and her eyelid drooped. "Yes."

"Where did they go?" Crow repeated. "When they left. Where did they go?"

She was slow to answer, almost asleep now. "That I don't know."

Tancho tried his luck for one more question. "The lacuna bond, between Crow and myself. Our birthmarks . . . You said the distance between us is no distance at all. What does it mean? We can't be separated, we can't bring harm to each other. When Crow touched my arm, it seemed as if the world stopped turning. What does any of it mean?"

She smiled and slow blinked. "It is the lacuna. It will get stronger as the eclipse draws near."

"And after the eclipse?" Crow asked. "What of it then?"

"I tried to find the tomes," she whispered. "Where it is written, but that is when I was struck." Her hand went to her bandaged head. She was falling asleep as she spoke, so Tancho helped her lie down. "I cannot be certain, good kings. It was so long ago. But it would seem the choice has been made."

Tancho stared at her. "What choice?"

"If you shall part or be forever joined."

Just then, the door opened and Soko and Kohaku walked in, their smiles and conversation fading when they saw Tancho and Crow talking to Maghdlm. But when Tancho turned back around, the old woman was asleep. He pulled a blanket over her.

There would be no more answers tonight.

"Did you learn anything new?" Soko asked quietly.

"Only that with every answer, ten more questions arise," Crow replied. "She didn't see who hit her, though she believes Adelais to be the leader, and more—if not all—elders have conspired with her."

"And that there are secret doorways," Tancho said, giving a shrug. "Which she can't explain but will show us when we reach the castle."

Kohaku's brow furrowed. "She will show us at our castle? How can she show us a doorway at Aequi Kentron from Westlands?"

Tancho sighed. "That would be one of the ten *new* questions."

Crow got to his feet. "First, we need to lay down plans for our arrival at the Westlands' castle in the morning. All the secret doorways be damned if we are ambushed before we get there."

Tancho reluctantly agreed. He hated the thought of his home being captured or held under siege, but it would be foolish to think they would be just walking in unimpeded.

So make plans they did.

When Karasu joined them after her bath, they forged a chain of plans. And Tancho had to admit, Crow was clever with such things. Perhaps he had better perspective because it was not his home, not his people. But regardless, they went to their mats more prepared than perhaps Tancho would have been without Crow's input.

In the dark and quiet of midnight, while everyone else slept, Tancho stared at the ceiling. His mind raced too fast for sleep to take hold. He had no idea what they would face in the morning, and he feared for the worst. For all the misgivings and difficulties being bonded to Crow had brought with it, Tancho was glad he was there.

He rolled onto his side to face Crow, only to find Crow watching him. He smiled gently, patiently. "Go to sleep, little fish."

And as much as he hated that name, as much as it rankled him, for some reason he couldn't explain, he didn't seem to mind it then. When it was whispered like that, with such affection . . . He met Crow's dark eyes, his heart skipping a beat, and smiled.

CHAPTER THIRTEEN

THE BIRTHMARK at Crow's wrist grew agitated with the growing dawn. It itched and burned as though he and Tancho were in different rooms, but they were side by side. He caught Tancho inspecting his, rubbing it gently, so he knew he felt it too.

"Is it warning us of danger?" Crow wondered out loud. "Or because the eclipse draws near? The skies are more golden yet again." He finished his tea. "Or perhaps they both burn because one of us is anxious?" Tancho glared at him and stood up, about to walk away, but Crow stood as well and stopped him. "Our plan will work. It's not ideal, but lacking an army and arsenal, it's the best plan we have."

"I'd like to leave," Tancho whispered.

The sun hadn't passed the horizon yet and the guards were still saddling horses, the others' breakfast barely touched. He looked at Soko, who was still half-asleep, grumbling to Kohaku about his morning meal. Karasu was tying off her bedroll. But Tancho needed to get home, he needed to see with his own eyes and he needed to be a king for his people. And *that* was something Crow understood all too well.

Crow tipped the water out on the fire embers, extinguishing it for good. Everyone looked at him and he picked up his bag. "You heard Tancho. We leave now."

Tancho gave him a grateful nod, and after collecting his bag, they headed for the stables. And soon enough, their procession was heading out on the final leg of their journey. It would only be a few hours at most, and although Tancho had explained the layout of his castle—where they would approach from, where any vantage points might be, any weaknesses—Crow still had no idea what to expect.

He could see the change in the landscape as they rode, all the houses much closer together now, in one continuous city. They had curved roofs and white walls, and Crow just couldn't imagine a huge stone castle like his here. And when they came upon a slight crest and an arch bridge, Crow couldn't see a 'castle' at all. No, what he saw fronting the water's edge, still some distance away, was the largest building by far with high walls around it. It had to be it, but it was what Crow would call a temple.

Several stories high with many separate levels, white walls and curved ornate roofs. It had to be it. It was remarkable in its architecture and beauty, how it was huge but somehow complimented the land it stood on.

But Tancho wasn't looking at that. He was scowling at something else. The flag atop the tallest part of the castle, Crow noticed . . . the koi was upside down. And an upside-down flag meant only one thing.

A cold shiver ran down Crow's spine despite the humidity.

Tancho pulled on the reins of his horse. "Ride!" he

urged, and Karasu and Soko at the lead didn't need telling twice. They rode through narrowed cobblestone streets, along built-up water canals that were like never-ending bridges. People stopped and waved, cheered, and went back to their business.

There was no alarm, no terror or fear, no signs of distress anywhere. As if the ships out to sea weren't even there, or at the very least, were no threat at all.

Either something was very odd or they'd rushed back here for no reason . . .

But as they weaved their way through the streets, Tancho didn't slow down, and the hard set of his eyes only seemed more determined.

As they approached the high wall, the huge gates slid open and their procession filed through without incident. Only once they were all inside, they were quickly surrounded by a circle of guards in white, katanas drawn.

Everyone dismounted slowly, and an official of some sort rushed out to meet them, making a beeline for Tancho's white kings' cloak. Only, he took one look at the man wearing it, took a horrified step backward, and threw up his arm. "It is not the king!"

Every guard there closed in, brandishing their katanas and daggers and bows, and it was a tense few seconds before Tancho spoke.

"I am here," he said, from where he and Crow stood at the back of the procession in guard's uniforms. They had swapped cloaks with Hikari and Unagi and had ridden with the horse pulling Maghdlm's carriage. "Sorry for the subterfuge. We didn't know what or who would come out to meet us."

The official waved the guards away and went to

Tancho, hands out to greet him. He bowed his head. "My king. Forgive the less-than-stately welcome. Your arrival today was not expected."

Tancho turned to the nearby guards. "There is an injured woman in this carriage. See her to private quarters and have the healers come at once." Then he turned back to the flustered official. "Marin, where is Asagi? We got word of warning and returned immediately. The flag flies in distress."

Marin nodded and bowed his head again. "Yes, yes. Asagi is inside. There is much to tell you. Come, come." He began to usher Tancho toward the doors but cast an eye at Crow and stopped. "Uh, your guests?"

"My guests," Tancho said flatly, "come with me."

Crow gave Marin a curt smile. Yes, Crow wore a guard's white cloak, but it was far too small for him. And had they not noticed his clothes underneath or his boots? His broadsword? How easy it had been to fool them . . .

They hadn't needed any of their actual plan. That Tancho and Karasu would take Maghdlm's carriage to the stables and sneak in that way, or that Karasu and Kohaku would escort Soko as a pretend prisoner, or if they were ambushed, they would branch off into four separate directions and circle back.

But they'd not needed any of that.

Was it because they assumed it to be Tancho? Or was the Westlands' castle always so poorly defended?

Was Crow's Northlands any better? With a rush of embarrassment, he thought probably not. "We need to increase our security measures," he mumbled. "Everywhere. We've been unthreatened for far too long and have become complacent."

Marin gave Crow a curious look just as Hikari walked

over, removed the black cloak, and offered it to Crow with a bow of his head. "My lord. It was a privilege to wear," he said. "Yet the weight of its responsibility is too much for me."

Smiling, Crow swung the white guard's cloak off and gave it back to Hikari. "As is yours for me. Gratitude, good man." He slipped his own cloak back on, feeling more himself.

Marin realised then . . . His wide eyes shot to Tancho. "The King of Northlands . . . your guest is the king—"

"I'm very well aware of who he is," Tancho said, striding off down the open corridor to the double doors at the end, which Crow deduced led them inside the castle. "We must speak to Asagi at once."

Crow fell into step beside Tancho, as Marin scurried to keep up. Inside the castle were dark floors and white walls made from some kind of bamboo and paper, from what Crow could tell. Doors slid open instead of swinging outward, and every wall, window, shelf, vase was placed with artful precision to make each angle a masterpiece.

It was immaculate and beautiful, and there was a peace here that Crow couldn't explain.

As they turned a corner into a large room, Crow heard the whisper of many feet getting closer before a swarm of men appeared out of nowhere. Crow pulled Tancho behind him, putting himself between Tancho and the oncoming threat, and in one fluid motion, he wielded his broadsword and readied himself for a fight . . .

For a group of house staff, by the looks of them, all startled and afraid of the huge man wearing a black cloak pointing a sword at their throats. Clearly no threat, even the one closest man put his hand to his chest and squeaked.

Crow lowered his sword and Tancho stepped around him. "They mean no harm," he said to Crow.

"We come to fetch your belongings," one of them said, bowing. "Apologies. We were not aware of your arrival."

"Thank you," Tancho said. "All bags to my quarters, please. And see the horses are well tended to."

They rushed out the way Crow and Tancho had come, brushing past Karasu, Soko, and Kohaku, who were walking in.

"Care to explain why the King of the Northlands protects you like a personal guard?" a calm voice spoke from the other end of the room.

Crow spun to face him. He was a tall and thin, older man, wearing the white Westlands' robes. He had long, straight grey hair and wise eyes. He was serious for a long moment before a slow smile spread across his face.

"Asagi," Tancho breathed, clearly so very relieved to see him.

"Father," Karasu said, running to greet him.

"Uncle!" Kohaku cried. "A sight for sore eyes, you are."

Father and uncle? Karasu and Kohaku were cousins?

Asagi greeted them both fondly; then the older man bowed his head to Tancho. "My king, never have I been so happy to see you."

Tancho took his hand. "You must tell me everything."

Asagi cast a glance at Crow and Soko. "And you as well, it would seem." Then he turned to face Crow square on and bowed. "It is an honour to have you here, King of Northlands."

"Please call me Crow," he replied. "And this here is Soko."

Asagi bowed to Crow again. "Do I owe you thanks for Tancho's safe return?"

"Safe return?" Karasu said. "Father, they only stopped trying to kill each other yesterday."

Asagi's eyes went wide. "Kill him? I just saw he defended him?"

Karasu, Kohaku, and Soko all shrugged. "It makes no sense to us, either," Kohaku said. "Least of all to them."

Asagi met Crow's eyes and tried again. "Your journey has been long and arduous, no doubt. We shall have hot baths drawn for you—"

"He stays with me," Tancho interrupted coolly. "Explanations will be forthcoming, but first you must tell me, what of the creatures that came ashore? Have you seen them? Spoken to them? I'll admit, I feared my home threatened or under siege, even. Answers, please, Asagi. It's been a long seven days."

Asagi paled a little, worry etched his features. "Seen them, yes. Spoken to them? Briefly." He shook his head as though it was news too bad to repeat.

"Asagi, what is it?"

"They came ashore, my king. A hundred of them. Maybe more."

A hundred?

Crow felt cold all over.

"They came to the gates in lines of two. Not human, my king. Blue, mottled skin, their faces akin to a boar, with tusks and snouts," Asagi whispered. "They . . . took one guard, Shāyú, my king. They slayed him . . . gruesomely so. As a warning, as a threat. They promised no further harm, they simply needed safe passage."

Tancho paled. "Shāyú? What became of him?"

Asagi grimaced, his mouth a watery line. "They tore him apart. And . . . my king, some of them, those hideous creatures . . ." He paused, then whispered, "They ate him."

They ate him?

Everyone stared in disbelief.

"Like pigs at a trough," Asagi added. "I've never seen such horrors."

Clearly the Westlanders were too stunned to speak. Too horrified. "They requested safe passage?" Crow asked.

Asagi nodded, frowning. "They were big, with hands like that of a bear. With talons, sharp as any I've seen. They asked as a formality. If I'd said no . . . I have no doubt they'd have left not one person standing. What they did to Shāyú . . . Those creatures were coming in, Tancho, regardless of my answer."

"So they came in through the gates?" Tancho clarified. "Where did they go? Safe passage to where?"

"I don't know their destination, my king. Only how they got there. If I'd not seen it with a great number of our guards, I'd have thought my mind gone mad." Asagi was pale now; he looked ill with worry. "They asked their way to the grand hall. They trudged through your home like an army, my king. It haunts me still." He swallowed hard. His hands began to tremble. "The leader, the biggest of them all, he wore some kind of stripes on his shoulder. He threw some metal powders onto the compass rose. He somehow moved the tiles in the floor—he moved it like a dial—then it drew a large circle of purple sparks in the air. Like a window to somewhere else. And as true as I stand here, my king, every single one of them walked through it as if it were a doorway."

A shiver of recognition danced down Crow's spine. "A doorway . . ."

Asagi nodded. "They marched, two lines at a time, and disappeared through the circle doorway into thin air. The circle closed after the last of them, leaving a spray of sparks on the floor. I've not fallen into madness, my king, I swear. I wasn't the only one to witness it."

Tancho turned to Crow, his eyes wide. "A doorway . . ."

"Why do you both keep saying that?" Karasu asked, looking between them both.

Still looking at each other, Crow and Tancho answered in unison. "Maghdlm."

AFTER EXPLAINING the lacuna bond to Asagi and everything that transpired at Aequi Kentron, the old man needed to sit down. "Is everything we've known, all of our histories and teachings, the very fabric of who we are, is it all a fiction?" he asked. Crow wondered if it was possible for him to have aged ten years in a few minutes. "All of my teachings to you, fair king, is centuries of history and culture. Is any of it true? Or did they manoeuvre me against you?" He shook his head, paling to a shade of green. "I shall not ever forgive myself."

"No, Asagi," Tancho said calmly, patting his hand. "Everything you taught me was the truth you were given. We don't know whose untruth came first. We don't know . . . anything. All we have is questions."

Crow clenched his hands into fists and folded his arms. He considered pacing but stopped himself, though he twitched and fidgeted, his self-control near the breaking point. He knew it was unreasonable and ridiculous given Asagi's age and his relationship to Tancho . . .

It's not a relationship. Don't call it a relationship.

"Are you well, King Crow?" Asagi asked, looking at him concerned.

"I mean this with the utmost respect, good man," Crow

said, trying to smile at Asagi. But he cut a seething glare to Tancho, because he should have known better . . . "But could you please not touch him? I know it lacks reason, but I can't focus, and your hand on his causes me physical ill and I don't wish to cause anyone harm."

Tancho slowly pulled his hand back. *Was he trying not to smile?*

Asagi was confused now. "Cause anyone harm?"

Soko laughed. "In addition to not being able to stand anything more than a few feet between them," he said, stepping closer to Crow, "they also can't bear anyone else to touch the other. Here, let me show you."

Soko only got one hand on Crow's shoulder, and in the blink of an eye, Tancho was up on his feet with his two katanas crossed at Soko's throat. Soko very slowly removed his hand from Crow, looked around Tancho, and gave Asagi a smile. "See?"

Wide-eyed, Asagi put his hand to his forehead. "Oh, dear."

Crow would have laughed if it weren't for the murder in Tancho's eyes. "Soko, my brother. I would suggest you don't do that again."

Soko took a step back, away from Tancho's blades, and gave him an apologetic smile and bowed his head. "Apologies, Tancho. I meant no harm."

Tancho heaved out a breath and lowered his katanas. "Not even to joke, Soko," he whispered. "My control is not what it should be. I might not know to stop next time, and you'll find your head at your feet."

Soko nodded and swallowed hard. "Understood. My point is proven though."

Karasu chuckled at Soko. "It was a point worth making to see the Northlander fill his britches."

Soko, of course, couldn't help himself. He turned and pulled his cloak away, giving her a better view of his arse, turning this way and that. "Do you like how I fill my britches?" He grinned at Crow. "Did you hear? She likes my britches."

Crow smirked at him. "I would offer caution, Soko. If Karasu draws her katana to your neck, she won't be of a mind to stop. You *will* find your head at your feet."

Kohaku laughed. "Can confirm."

Crow noticed then that Tancho stood to the side with his back to them, his face to the ceiling, his chest rising and falling with deep breaths. Crow stepped closer, and even though he wanted to, he was careful not to touch him. "What is it, little fish?" he asked quietly.

Tancho shot him a fiery gaze that quickly melted into a half-smile. "I hate that name."

Crow's smile won out. "I don't think you do."

"If anyone else called me that, I'd slit their throat."

"If anyone else called you that, I'd slit their throat."

Tancho smiled at the absurdity and ended with a sigh. He was quiet and troubled. "I used to have better self-control than this. Before, with Soko. I almost didn't stop. And we can joke and it's all some bizarre jester's trick that I can't stand anyone else to touch you, but Crow," he whispered, meeting his gaze. "I almost killed him. I very nearly didn't stop."

Crow's smile fell away, and he gave a nod. "We shouldn't joke, and I'm sorry. He meant no disrespect. He plays a fool to lighten the mood, but he has the best heart."

Tancho sighed. "I know. I just . . . I lose all reasoning, all self-control. I need to meditate, gather my thoughts and find peace and clarity."

Meditate? Crow thought perhaps that was a load of bollocks, but Tancho clearly didn't. "Anything you want."

"My king," Karasu called out. Both Tancho and Crow turned. There were two guards next to Asagi. "The healers are done with Maghdlm. She's resting but awake if you wish to speak to her."

CHAPTER FOURTEEN

TANCHO'S MIND WAS A MESS. He was so relieved to be home and to find all was well that his heart could have burst. But now there was other madness with a magical doorway he didn't understand, and his protectiveness over Crow had gotten worse.

So had his affection for him.

And maybe that was what played with his mind the most. This was some forced bond, some alchemical trickery that they had to find a cure for. It wasn't a real connection.

But it felt real. The emotions were real. How his heart soared and squeezed when Crow smiled at him was real. How Tancho wanted to kill anyone who dared look at Crow, let alone touch him . . . That was very real.

It was messing with his head.

He needed to find some focus. But more than that, he needed answers.

Maghdlm was in a large guest room, sitting by the window, when Tancho and Crow entered. They'd brought Asagi with them, and Soko, Karasu, and Kohaku filed in and stood by the wall. She had a blanket over her lap. Her head bandage was clean and she looked much brighter.

"I trust we find you well," Crow said.

She smiled. "As well as expected. Thank you both, for bringing me here." She turned to Karasu, Kohaku, and Soko. "Thank you, all." Then her gaze fell to Asagi.

"Maghdlm," Tancho said. "This is Asagi. Trusted mentor and advisor. He witnessed something you might offer explanation to. A hundred creatures came ashore, walking out of the ocean. They trudged into this castle, killing one of my men. And then with sorcery of some kind, they drew a large circle of sparks in the air and made a doorway."

Maghdlm's eyes went wide. Even her swollen eye opened for a second. "They did?"

Tancho studied her for a long moment. "You mentioned a doorway to Crow and myself earlier."

She leaned forward, staring at Asagi. "Above the compass rose?"

He nodded. "Yes!"

She sat back and turned her sorry gaze back to Tancho and Crow. "Then it would appear we got out of Aequi Kentron just in time."

"Is that where they went?" Tancho asked. "How can you be sure?"

"I can't be certain, but I would guess."

Crow frowned. "So, for these doorways to work, they need a compass rose tiled into the floor?"

Maghdlm nodded.

Crow stood to his full height, his eyes sharp. "There is a compass rose tiled in the grand hall of the Northlands' castle."

"There will be one in every castle in all four lands,"

Maghdlm replied calmly. "It is how they travelled a thousand years ago. Our ancestors, before the wars when they were closed off and forgotten."

"We must warn them. Your people, Crow," Tancho said. "And Samiel and Elmwood."

"Yes. We must." But then his eyebrows furrowed. "Closed off?" Crow asked Maghdlm. "If they were closed a thousand years ago, how did they use this one just days gone past?"

"Sorcery," Asagi said. "I watched them do it."

Maghdlm gave a nod. "A better question, perhaps: *How did they know about it?*"

"A more urgent question," Crow said. "A door opens both ways, does it not? What's to stop them from coming back through? Right now? Or tonight when we sleep?"

That had Tancho's immediate attention. "We need to close it. Lock it. Tear it from the floor if we need to."

"We need to warn the others first," Crow said. "I must get word to my castle."

Tancho turned to Maghdlm. "Do you know how to make it work? You said you could show us. Can you open a doorway to the Northlands' castle?"

She gave a small nod. "It is a magick long lost. But I can try. Though I have no tools with me," she said. "Nothing."

"We have alchemists here," Tancho said. "They can supply you with all you need."

Maghdlm smiled wearily. "Good. Then take me to the compass. Let me see where it is they went."

ASAGI HAD a push-chair brought for Maghdlm and they made their way to the grand hall. It was a large room, with large white tiles and a huge silver compass rose in its centre. Similar to what Tancho had seen at the grand hall in Aequi Kentron.

He'd walked over this a thousand times, stood on it, even played hopping games on it as a small child. He was led to believe the compass signified all four equal lands, and Aequi Kentron at the centre. It had made sense. It still made sense.

The symbol for Aequi Kentron was the compass rose. As Tancho's was the fish, Crow's the raven, Elmwood's the tree, and Samiel's the desert wind.

But now the compass symbolised something else, and so too did Aequi Kentron.

Something Tancho wasn't sure he liked.

Tancho studied the tiles, looked at the compass itself, and it took him a moment to realise what had changed. There were two outer circles: one at the midpoints and the other at the outer points of the compass.

Had the inner circle moved? Seeing it now he wondered if it had always been this way, but surely not . . .

"The inner point circle has moved," he said, unsure. "The arrow now points . . . inward? How is that . . ."

"They went to Aequi Kentron," Maghdlm said. "The arrow points to the centre. If the inner point circle arrow pointed north, that would be their destination."

Crow let out a relieved breath. "So, how do we move the inner circle?" he asked. "I need to get a message to my people. How do we make the arrow point north?"

"Well," Maghdlm said. "That is the complicated part. Setting the compass is a forgotten magick. I read about it once, a long time ago."

"Can you do it?" Crow asked.

She gave a nod. "I will try."

Tancho was studying the compass. "The outer circle. What is its purpose?"

"It is incoming, I believe," Maghdlm answered. "From where the gate opens."

Now Tancho stared at her. "You mean anyone, at any of the remaining three points, can just decide to open the doorway and appear here? Uninvited?"

"Yes. If it begins to move, you would know someone comes. There was a way to lock it, but I would need to remember . . ." Maghdlm said, blinking slowly. She was clearly tired. "I will try to remember."

"We can take up a tile," Karasu suggested. "Surely if the compass isn't intact, it cannot be used. A key cannot open a door if the lock is broken, no?"

"Let's hope," Tancho said. "Then we can slide it back into place when we are ready."

Karasu put her sword in between some tiles outside of the compass, so as not to damage the circle or points, but couldn't get any leverage. Kohaku joined in, as did Soko, and it took a lot of work and one slightly damaged tile, but once it was removed, they could lift the tile next to it much easier. It took both Kohaku and Soko to lift the large stone tile, but they did and left the outer circle of the compass missing a piece between the north and the east.

"Should that be enough?" Tancho asked Maghdlm.

"I cannot say for certain," she replied. "Too much is unknown to me. Tancho, I trust you have a library here? Archives, perhaps?"

"Yes, of course."

"A keeper of such records? Someone who may be able to help me search the old tomes."

"You think we have something here about the compass? I've not heard of any such thing."

"You wouldn't," she replied. "For you did not know to ask."

Asagi came forward, his head bowed. "I can help. I know the archives. I've not encountered any such records myself, though there are sections with old, old books and scripts I've not yet read."

"No one would be better suited," Tancho said with a grateful bow of his head. "If you are willing. Take some guards with you for climbing ladders and heavy lifting." And to watch over you, Tancho thought but didn't say out loud.

Asagi seemed to understand and he gave a thankful bow in return. "You must be tired and hungry after your long journey. You said before it's been a long week," he said. "Eat and rest. If I find any mention in any book, I shall return at once."

"Maghdlm, do you feel well enough?" Tancho asked.

"There isn't time to waste," she answered. "The eclipse is almost upon us."

Tomorrow . . . the eclipse was tomorrow, if he'd counted the days right. It all seemed so blurred together, Tancho wasn't even sure what day it was.

Asagi and three guards led Maghdlm in her push-chair from the large room, leaving everyone else in silence. Tancho sighed. "The eclipse is tomorrow, before sunset."

"Then we should rest while we can," Crow said.

"I'm going to my quarters," Karasu said, "where I can bathe in peace and rest on my own bed without these two stinking up the place." She waved in Kohaku and Soko's general direction before she walked to the door at the far end without another word.

Soko looked to Crow, unsure of where he should be. Kohaku put his arm around him and led him out the same door. "You come with me, little Northlander. I'll show you to your room, but we'll visit the kitchen for food first, yes?"

Soko mumbled something that made Kohaku laugh, and both Tancho and Crow smiled.

But then they were, for the first proper time, alone. "I'm not sure where you wish me to go," Crow said quietly.

"With me," Tancho replied. "Our choice is removed, but I'm sure you'll find my quarters adequate."

Tancho led the way and Crow fell into step beside him, and they walked in silence through the corridors. Tancho stopped at the large, red wooden door, suddenly uneasy. He'd never had a man in his room before, and it felt oddly exhilarating to do so now. He pushed the door open and stood aside. "After you."

Crow gave a nod and stepped inside and Tancho followed him close behind. His belly was in knots and the door clicking shut behind him made him jump. His private quarters was a large set of rooms, not too unlike those at the Aequi Kentron; a meeting area for guests with long seats, chairs, and a table—which had a tray of fruit and breads on it—then a door to his bed chambers with his own private baths. Windows overlooked the ocean.

Tancho had missed his home, but above all, he missed his own private space. He watched Crow as he took in the large room, the furniture, the view. And although he craved some solitude and peace, he didn't mind that Crow was with him.

"You know," Crow mused out loud, "I'd hate for you to think more on this than what it is, but your home, your castle, is truly beautiful."

That made Tancho smile. "Thank you."

"The villages, the countryside on the journey here, I've never seen anything like it." Crow gestured to the room.

"The architecture, the furniture, the food, it's all so different."

"What did you expect?"

"I don't know." Crow frowned. "I hadn't expected anything. I'd never given much thought to what the Westlands looked like or how the people lived, to be honest."

Tancho conceded a nod, because he hadn't really studied any culture other than his own either. "And how does the Northlands differ?"

"We live in the mountains, under a blanket of white and grey, mostly. Our homes are built for our climate, to withstand the cold and the weight of snow. As your homes are built here for the breeze and the water."

"Perhaps one day I will see the Northlands," Tancho murmured.

Crow grinned at him as though the idea of that made him incredibly happy. "Then I would suggest the warmer months, or you'll require an upgrade in wardrobe."

Tancho smiled at that and looked down at Crow's heavy boots and the thickset fabrics of his pants and shirt, compared to Tancho's thinner linens and silks. "Are you overheated in your winter clothes?"

"A little," he admitted. "It's not so bad."

"Perhaps some of Kohaku's clothes would fit you. If you wish for a change."

Crow sniffed his armpit and gave him a crooked grin. "Are you trying to tell me something?"

Tancho chuckled. "Not at all." He would never admit that he liked the smell of him. "Though I do have a private bath in my room—" He gestured to the bedroom door. "—if you need. Please treat my home as your own."

Something flashed in Crow's eyes, but it was gone before Tancho could give it a name. His brows knitted together and he cleared his throat. "Did you say you wanted to . . . meditate?"

Tancho nodded. "Yes. It helps clear my mind. Would you like to do it with me?"

Crow blanched. "Uh . . . okay?" The corner of his lip pulled downward. "Though I don't know how."

"It's rather simple. Come sit with me."

The corner of Tancho's large bedroom was a cleared space where sunlight and the sound of the ocean came through the windows. There was a mat on the floor, which Tancho sat on, and he patted the floor beside him.

After unbuckling his scabbard and sword and laying it on the floor, Crow sat, but again couldn't quite master sitting cross-legged. It was awkward and adorable how he tried to hold his legs in, but after he over balanced for a third time, Tancho could only laugh instead. "Try lying down. On your back, hands by your sides."

Crow did that. "Now what?"

"Close your eyes and inhale, hold it. Exhale. Are you comfortable?"

"I think so."

Tancho was struck by how handsome Crow was, and how vulnerable he was lying on the floor, his bedroom floor, no less. With his eyes closed and a gentle smile at his lips. His dark hair falling toward the mat, his pink lips. They looked so soft and warm . . .

"What now?" Crow asked, thankfully keeping his eyes closed.

Right. Meditating . . .

"Breathe in deep," Tancho said, hoping the meditation cleared his mind of those kind of thoughts. "Breathe out slow. Now, imagine there is a silver ball in your feet."

"A silver ball?"

"Yes."

"Why is it silver?"

"This will go a lot better if you don't question me."

Crow grumbled but didn't press for any more questions. Tancho inhaled deeply and closed his eyes. "Imagine in your mind, the ball moving very slowly. Very slowly. From your foot to your ankle. Slow, slow." He kept his voice low and smooth. "Then it moves slowly, further up your leg, into your calf muscle, slow, slow, to your knee."

He was silent for a while, listening to Crow's deep, measured breaths.

"Nice and slow, up your thigh."

Those thick and masculine thighs. Thighs that filled those black pants far too well . . .

Now he was thinking about Crow's body, how close he was, how anatomically gifted he was. Tancho swallowed as silently as he could and let out a long, calming breath.

"To your hips . . ."

And your groin. I've seen how anatomically gifted that is . . .

"At the base of your spine," he said, his voice low and rough. Surely Crow had to hear the desire in his voice? Tancho was certain if Crow turned his head and looked at him through those long dark eyelashes, Tancho wouldn't be able to restrain himself.

He wanted him. Right here, in his room, in his bed. He wanted to give himself to Crow, let him have his wicked way with him . . .

But then Crow's lips parted and he began to snore, ever so quietly. He was sound asleep.

Tancho was relieved and embarrassed, and all he could do was laugh. As if that haze of lust evaporated around him, he could suddenly think clearly again. He was still aroused, and the buzz of anticipation lingered in his blood for a few beats of his heart before fading away.

He shook his head at his own ridiculousness. Then he concentrated on his own mind, his own body, clearing his mind of everything but his own breathing. He let the sound of the ocean set the pace, feeling the strength and power of the waves fortifying him.

He'd missed the water. He'd missed the rivers and the streams, and he'd missed the sound of it, the power of it, and how it calmed him by just being close to it.

But before he could fully relax, before he could lose himself in his mind, a soft knock at the door startled him. "My king," Asagi's familiar voice said.

"Come in," he said quietly.

Tancho stayed where he was, sitting cross-legged on the floor, and waited for Asagi to come into his room. Asagi stopped and stared at Crow, still splayed on the floor beside him. "Is he . . . ?" Asagi whispered.

"Asleep," Tancho replied quietly. "He tried to meditate."

Asagi pressed his lips together so as not to smile. But then he gave Tancho a nod. "I came to advise that Maghdlm found a book she thought might be of use, and she's asked that we fetch her some . . . components."

Tancho tilted his head. "Components?"

"Ingredients, elements . . . what she needs to open the doorway."

"Oh."

"They may take a while to procure," Asagi whispered. "One, in particular, is not an easy find. We have sent guards out to anyone who dabbles in alchemy. And even blacksmiths."

"Good." He nodded to the book Asagi was holding. "Is that the book?"

Asagi nodded. It was a white leather-bound book and Tancho could make out an embossed koi on the front. It looked old. "But I would call it a grimoire. It seems incomplete, and there are drawings I can't decipher, but Maghdlm was very interested in it. She asked to take it but I thought it best to ask you first."

Tancho smiled. "Good man. If she asks again, tell her to speak to me. Tell me again," he went on, "you sent guards out into the ocean where they walked out from, yes? And they found nothing?" Asagi had told them this when they exchanged information earlier, but he needed to hear it again.

"Yes, my king. There was no underwater ship, no submerged vessel. There was no sign of them at all, as though we had imagined it."

"Or, as though they had a doorway under the waves," Tancho murmured.

Just then, Kohaku and Soko appeared behind Asagi, both of them taken aback by Crow lying on the floor. Soko did a double take, then seeing he was simply asleep, burst out laughing.

Crow shot upright, and in a move that defied gravity and Tancho's eyes, Crow swung himself around and in front of Tancho while pulling a dagger from his boot. He landed, crouched in front of Tancho, dagger raised, facing whatever the threat was. Protecting him, defending him . . .

Tancho knew it was the lacuna curse, he knew it was fabricated, but he still liked it.

He put his hand to Crow's back, just a breath of a touch. "I'm fine, Crow," he whispered.

Crow seemed to come to his senses or wake up. He

shook his head, then groaned, his shoulders relaxing. "Dammit, Soko."

"What were you doing?" he asked.

"I was . . ." Crow sheathed the dagger back in his boot. "I was . . . meditating."

"Sounded like snoring to me," Kohaku said, and Soko laughed.

Now it was Tancho's turn to raise his hackles. "You'll both do well to remember to whom you speak." He leaned in closer to Crow, protective of him now, their bodies almost touching. Tancho could feel the heat of his body. Crow's smell filled his head, boosting his need to protect him. *How dare they make fun of him.* "What brings you to my quarters?" he snapped.

Kohaku bowed his head. "My king. To give the message that one of the guards has returned with two of the items Maghdlm requested."

"There are two to go," Soko added, giving Crow a curious look. Tancho had to remind himself they were close, clan-brothers even, and that Soko's main concern was for his king. "Crow," Soko said gently. "Is there anything I can get for you?"

Crow only seemed to notice then just how close he and Tancho were standing. One of Crow's feet was in between Tancho's. And yet, for how close they were, Crow never moved. "I'm fine. You startled me from sleep, that's all." He squeezed his eyes shut. "I should eat something."

"There is an array of foods on your table, Tancho," Asagi said with a bow of his head. "If anything else is preferred, I can have it arranged."

"I'm sure it'll be fine," Tancho said. "Though a hot bath would be most appreciated."

Asagi snapped his fingers and two attendants appeared

out of nowhere, then disappeared into his private bathroom to prepare the bath.

Soko pulled on Kohaku's arm. "We'll take our leave. You two can . . . eat something. Take a hot bath. Rest, on the . . ." He waved to the bed. "Very big bed. We won't interrupt again until all the items on Maghdlm's list are here."

Crow growled at him but they were already gone, then Asagi followed them out the door with another bow of his head. They were alone again, and Tancho's blood thrilled at the realisation.

Tancho made himself take a step back. "Let's get you fed." He led Crow back to the table and the trays of food and pitchers of water and nectars. It had been a long, eventful morning, and Tancho doubted Crow had slept much the night before. He needed to eat.

Tancho fixed him a plate of bread, sliced meats, cheeses, and fruit pastes, and Crow took it gratefully. They ate in silence for a while, Tancho realising he was hungrier than he'd first thought.

"I didn't mean to fall asleep," Crow said eventually.

"It's fine," Tancho replied with a smile. "You were clearly tired."

"Or your meditation skills are too strong. That silver ball thing you did to me. I could almost feel it. It turned my mind off like an extinguished oil lamp." Crow took a sip from his cup. "I'll have to remember that technique if Soko wants to tell me all about his conquests."

Tancho smiled at that. "Does he have many?"

Crow made a face. "I'd be remiss to talk about him while he's not here to defend himself, but he has a certain charm that ladies take a shine to."

Tancho took a slice of pear and bit into it. He was

aiming for nonchalant but he doubted he managed it. "And you? Do the ladies shine to your charms as well?"

Crow stared at the pear between Tancho's lips, the juice that escaped and how Tancho's tongue chased it. His eyes darkened and his voice rasped. "Not the ladies, no."

Tancho's gaze cut to his. "Have you left a trail of men behind in Northlands?" He couldn't keep the ice from his tone. "Or perhaps one, in particular, you yearn to return to?" Tancho didn't know which was worse.

"Neither," Crow replied. "I've had . . . enough to know what I like." Then his eyes flashed with daring. "And what about you? I thought you and Karasu . . ."

Tancho made a face. "She is a sister to me."

"When I alluded to that before, you never corrected me."

"Perhaps I wanted you to think that."

"To tease me?"

"To have you keep your distance."

"And how's that working out?"

Had they moved closer somehow? Crow's face was barely an inch from Tancho's now. He could feel the heat of his body, he could see the gold sparkles in his eyes.

"It's not working at all," Tancho replied in a whisper.

"Have you a trail of lovers from your bed?" Crow asked, his eyes studying the depths of Tancho's. "Or just one?"

"No," he breathed. "No one."

"Good." Crow licked his lips as though he might kiss Tancho, and oh, how Tancho wanted it. "Men or women?"

Tancho had to repeat the question in his head so he could answer it. "Both. Mostly men."

Crow hissed. "I don't like the idea of other men knowing your body."

Before Tancho could reply, before his brain could snap

out of whatever trance possessive Crow had on him, one of the attendants cleared their throats from the door. "The bath is ready, my king."

It was just enough of a distraction for Tancho to gather his wits. He stepped back, not meeting Crow's intense stare, breaking the spell between them. "The bath is for you. I will meditate; then I can bathe while you . . . rest."

"Are you telling me what to do?" There was a smile in his voice, so Tancho risked a glance.

"Yes."

Crow's smile became a smirk, as though Tancho had just put down a challenge he couldn't refuse. Maybe he had. His mind certainly wasn't his own lately.

Using every ounce of self-control, Tancho walked into the bathroom knowing Crow would follow. He went to the window, and keeping his back to the bath, he dared not turn around while he heard Crow undress.

There was a splash of water. "You can turn around now," Crow murmured. "Though I don't know why it matters. You've seen me naked before."

But Tancho didn't turn around. He was barely holding on to his thread of sanity as it was. Seeing him naked now would be his undoing. "I don't think that's a good idea," he mumbled. "Considering how things are between us."

Crows voice was low and smooth. "And how *are* things between us?"

Confusing, odd, frightening, amazing. "Tense."

Crow chuckled at that and Tancho wanted to send him a scathing glare, yet he didn't dare look. He simply sat down, cross-legged, took a deep breath, and closed his eyes. "I would prefer silence," he said instead, and thankfully Crow had the good manners to do as he was bid.

Tancho could finally shut his mind off. If it were the

sun beaming in from outside, the steam from the bath, the gentle sounds of water as Crow washed himself, or the relief of being at home, Tancho wasn't sure. But he could feel his mind centring. As he closed out the rest of the world, he could feel his inner peace and calm returning.

It had been far too long.

He didn't hear Crow get out of the bath, he didn't hear him dress or leave the room. It was the burn underneath his birthmark that drew his attention. They were too far apart, and the pain ripped him out of his meditation like a fish caught on a line. "Ah!" he cried, getting to his feet.

"Sorry," Crow said from the doorway. "I forgot. I was just trying to leave you in peace. You were so engrossed. I had a whole conversation with you and you ignored me."

"I didn't ignore you. I was meditating. I tune everything out." Tancho rubbed his birthmark. He tried to cool his temper because Crow had just tried to do the right thing. "I apologise. Was the conversation of anything important?"

Crow shook his head, and Tancho only just realised that Crow's hair was wet. He liked it wet, the way it hung down . . . "I was just telling you . . . never mind."

Tancho went to him, too scared to touch him but needing to be closer. "I do apologise. I should have warned you. When I meditate, I get lost in my head. You can speak to me while I bathe, if you wish."

"I was only teasing you," he said. "The conversation . . . I was trying to distract you because I was naked in the bath and you were trying really hard not to look. Well, I thought you were trying, but you really were meditating and didn't care that I was naked. Not even when I stood up out of the water. So I'm trying not to bruise my ego too much."

Tancho chuckled. "I fear there is enough of your ego to survive the biggest of hits."

"Perhaps," Crow said. "But I am still just a man."

Tancho studied those dark eyes, that handsome face, and he could have so easily got lost . . . "I should undress," he murmured.

"I can help you," Crow whispered, looking him up and down. "With whatever you need help with."

Tancho's pulse quickened, his skin flushed warm. He loved knowing Crow was just as affected as him, that Crow wanted him. It was a mighty powerful drug. "I fear that should we . . . do more than touch, what it would do to us. Does this connection not scare you?"

Crow's gaze went from Tancho's mouth, to his eyes, and he seemed to jolt back to his senses. "Scare me? A little," he admitted quietly. "Scares me that we will do more than touch. Scares me that we won't."

Tancho nodded quickly. *He felt it too.* Tancho didn't know if that was better or worse. He could just reach up and touch Crow, cup his face, and pull him down for a kiss. It would be so easy. He was so close, Tancho could almost taste him.

A loud knock at the door broke them apart and Tancho's heart felt it might burst out of his chest. It took him a second to catch his breath. "Come in."

Asagi opened the door and looked between the two kings, no doubt at how close they were standing. He bowed his head. "My king, apologies for the interruption. We have acquired all the elements. Maghdlm believes she can open the doorway. The tiles have been moved to the north position and we await you both."

"My bath can wait," Tancho said, then he and Crow collected their swords and followed Asagi to the grand hall.

KARASU, Kohaku, and Soko were already there, standing on the outside of the outer compass circle. The tiles had been put back into place. Maghdlm stood with her feet before the S and she held an old book in her hands. Her head was still bandaged, and she looked tired but determined.

"The compass in your castle," she said to Crow. "Is it in a hall like this?"

"There is a large compass tiled into the floor of the formal hall, yes," Crow replied. "We can expect a welcome by guards at the end of a lot of swords. I would imagine no one too pleased at the magical intrusion."

Soko stepped forward. "I will go through first. They will recognise me, and if someone's head shall meet the floor, it'll be mine and not yours, Crow."

"Wait a moment," Crow said first, his attention on Maghdlm. "How long will the doorway remain open? Can you close it? Can you open it again? Can you lock it once we're through?"

She read from the open book in her hand. "It will stay open until it is closed by incantation. I can open it as long as I have the elements." She held a small velvet pouch in her hand. "And I believe I can lock it, yes."

"You're still coming through with us," Crow said, his voice full of authority.

She looked about to object but conceded a tired nod. "Of course."

Tancho didn't have time to wonder about Crow's tone or insistence that she join them. Because Maghdlm slipped the book into the folds of her shawl, took a pinch of what was in her pouch, and spoke as she sprinkled the floor with it.

Aperi ianuam,
altera ex loco,
illam cincturam,
hoc portal,
revelare.

The tiles in the floor moved, scaring everyone into taking a step back. Scraping and grinding stone against stone, the old tiles moved around the compass. Sparks cascaded in mid-air like a waterfall of ash and fire. She chanted again and the sparks formed a large circle, spinning and growing in size until it was a doorway big enough for a grown man to walk through.

Tancho could see through the doorway and see a strange room, but Soko grinned at Crow. He liked what he saw on the other side. Crow nodded and Soko stepped into the circle, his hands raised. There was no sound, Tancho realised. They couldn't hear what he was saying or see who he was talking to. But he turned back, smiling, and waved them through.

Tancho looked to Asagi. "Keep the tiles intact in case we need to return. I will send word if I want the tiles removed to close the doorway."

Crow walked up next and waited for Tancho to stand next to him, and with a deep breath, they stepped through.

The sound hit him as though he'd been underwater and had just broken the surface. Men yelled, a formation of guards in black with swords raised, with clear confusion and fear on their faces.

"Stand down," Crow said, his voice booming. "It is I, your king." The men lowered their weapons, and after a long beat of silence, chatter began. Soko was already talking to someone, laughing, of course.

Maghdlm came through next, followed by Karasu and Kohaku, and with another chant by Maghdlm and another sprinkle of whatever she had in that pouch, the circle of sparks shrank to nothing, leaving a flourish of purple sparks on the tiled floor.

The room itself was huge, with high ceilings supported by sturdy rafters. The walls were grey stone, and there was a crackling fireplace. Ornate windows along the wall were long and narrow, and there must have been a dozen of them . . . but it wasn't the windows, per se, that caught Tancho's attention. It was the scenery outside. Something Tancho had only ever dreamed of seeing.

White, snow-covered mountain peaks cutting through pale blue skies. Ginormous and glorious, daunting and breathtakingly beautiful.

Northlands.

CHAPTER FIFTEEN

HOME.

Crow was so glad to be home. The familiar sights, familiar smells, familiar faces, familiar rooms, halls, furniture. He'd never quite realised what home meant until he'd spent too long from it. It was a true sense of belonging.

As much as the Westlands was foreign, different, and beautiful, it was Tancho's. It was the embodiment of him.

And the Northlands was Crow's. The dark grey stone walls, the men in black cloaks, the white snow outside the windows.

Their welcome through the doorway had been as warm as expected, with swords raised and much shouting, but once the guards realised who it was, shouts were replaced with cheers. Crow sent for Erelis to come at once, which he did, bringing Hitode and Iruka, the two Westland guards who had arrived just that morning with the urgent message Crow had sent them with all those days ago.

It felt like a lifetime.

The two Westlands' guards were welcomed by Tancho, Karasu, and Kohaku, and seeing the five Westlanders in a room full of Northland guards and consorts made Crow smile. He liked having them here.

Correction. He liked having Tancho here.

With his fine white boots and white cloak and his long, straight red hair and delicate face . . . He appeared slight, but Crow had seen him wield those katanas as though they were extensions of his hands. He was whisper quiet and deathly fast.

And Crow liked that.

There was something thrilling about knowing Tancho was as lethal as Crow. They were equals, and Crow *really* liked that.

Crow had explained everything to Erelis: the doorway and how they'd travelled from Westlands in the blink of an eye, what happened at Aequi Kentron, the journey to Westlands, and of course his connection with Tancho. It had taken some telling, and thankfully, Erelis took the news well. He didn't have Crow hauled off to the asylum, so he considered it a win.

By this time, Maghdlm was flagging, her headache blinding, so Crow insisted she be shown to a guest room for rest. Soko was excited to show Kohaku and Karasu the castle, and Kohaku was excited to see the kitchen. As they were walking out, Soko put his arm around Karasu and she pushed him into the doorframe. They could still hear Kohaku laughing as they disappeared down the corridor.

"I see Soko found new friends," Erelis said fondly.

"As he always does," Crow replied.

Erelis bowed his head to Tancho. "And, gracious King of Westlands, it is an honour to have you here. When your men arrived this morning, almost frozen, mind you, I wasn't sure what to make of it."

"Thank you for seeing them cared for," Tancho replied with a polite smile.

Erelis continued, "Until they gave the message that Crow said I'd meet them with scepticism and to relay how much he hated Kalevala. Then I knew the message had come from Crow."

Crow laughed. "It was one of the tamer stories from my youth."

"Indeed it was." Erelis smiled. "You also said to send a squadron of men to the northern line, my king. I've already sent them. They left mid-morning. If you want them to return, we could send a rider . . ."

"No, let them see. I want to be sure our northern shore-lines are safe."

"It would be a cruel attempt for anyone not prepared to try and cross those alps," Erelis said. "Those ranges are steep, the snow unforgiving."

"True," Crow conceded. "But we don't know what these creatures are capable of. We know they've killed one of Tancho's men. If there's more of them coming, on their way here, I'd rather be prepared."

Erelis nodded. "Of course. I will also ready our armies and await further instruction from you."

"Good. We need to get word to the east and south. Now we have an immediate mode of transport," Crow said. "Whenever Maghdlm is well enough, we'll be going."

"Understood. Though if I may be so bold," Erelis said, "it is good to have you home, my king. No matter how brief."

"As it is to be home," Crow replied.

"If there is anything you require at all before I leave you?"

"Actually, there is," Crow said. "I want Tancho to try

Northland food. Ask Scaevola to prepare him her favourites, and see them delivered to my quarters. The Westlands impressed me greatly and I'd like to return the favour."

Erelis bowed. "Of course."

"And please have my private bath filled," Crow said. Tancho had been robbed of his chance to take a long bath earlier, so Crow wanted to remedy that. "And please have the libraries searched for any tomes or ancient scripts regarding the doorway, the eclipse, or any mention of the word *lacuna*."

Erelis bowed again. "As you wish," he replied, and then he was gone.

Crow turned to Tancho and gestured toward a door at the end of the grand hall. "This way." As they walked through the halls and corridors toward Crow's private quarters, he couldn't help but smile at Tancho's wonderment.

When they entered the hall of windows, Tancho stopped. The hall itself wasn't anything but grey stone floor and walls, but the outside wall was lined with tall, narrow windows. The ornate stained glass that filled each top panel and their craftsmanship and artistry, as old as the castle itself, were lost to the view outside.

Majestic snow-covered mountaintops glistened in the winter sun, the cold wind blew flurries off the peaks, the sky behind a pale but endless blue.

"I have never seen any such thing," Tancho whispered. "It's . . . beautiful."

Crow found himself smiling, pleased and proud that Tancho liked his first impression of Northlands. "The view in this hall as the sun rises is magnificent."

Tancho's grin widened and he shook his head. "I now understand your fascination with my home," he mused.

"You found beauty in things I overlooked, having been so used to seeing them. Everything was new to you, and now here I am seeing things for the first time and I . . ." He sighed. "I can see why you found it so intriguing."

"There is a certain beauty in foreign sights, but the same could be said for coming home." Crow smiled at the mountains. "I have missed this place. And you mentioned being so used to seeing the sights of home we overlook the small details. That's true. But I don't think I'll take them for granted again."

Tancho nodded. "I'll admit I'm grateful it wasn't a two-week ride to be here. That doorway is a powerful asset. It will open new trade routes, new communications. We don't need to go through Aequi Kentron anymore."

Crow thought about that. "Do you think that's why they closed it down? Why no one has ever learned about these doorways?"

Tancho inhaled deeply. "Possibly. Perhaps there were other reasons. Our histories teach us of wars between all four lands. Perhaps they were closed down as a security measure and over time they were forgotten."

Crow's brow furrowed. "Perhaps. Or perhaps the King of the Westlands in those ancient times didn't like how dashingly handsome and funny the King of the Northlands was."

Tancho rolled his eyes and tried not to smile. "Or perhaps the King of Westlands found the Northlands' king's ego tiring."

"Or he found him attractive."

Tancho laughed, but Crow didn't miss the blush that crept up his neck.

Perhaps, indeed.

"I believe I owe you a soak in the tub," Crow said,

starting to walk again. "Though I don't think I'll try meditating again. Unless you want to hear me snore."

When they made it to Crow's quarters, one of two guards opened the heavy oak door for him. "Grateful for your return, my king," he said. "Trays of food were just delivered, sire." Crow gave him a nod but stood aside and let Tancho walk through first.

Tancho walked a few steps in and stopped, looking around, taking it all in. The room itself was huge, with stone walls, heavy oak furniture with wrought iron trims, rugs on the floor and tapestries on the walls, and the wooden bathtub by a roaring fire.

Tancho gave him a curious nod. "I am . . . impressed." *Did he blush again or was that the light of the fire?* "If a room ever personified the person, this is it."

Personifies me? "I am comfortable here," Crow admitted. "Though I would think your quarters personifies you, also."

"How so?" Tancho asked.

"Elegant, understated, without clutter."

Tancho's lips twisted in an almost-smile. "I'm not even offended."

Crow laughed. "I should think not. And how does my quarters resemble me?"

Tancho inhaled deeply and smiled. "You're a man cut from the mountain stone. Dark and formidable, yet warm and welcoming. And I had wondered what scent I caught from you, and now I know. Whatever it is you burn in your fires. It's not wood, is it?"

"No," Crow whispered. "Wood is too scarce a commodity here. We make compressed bricks from pulp scented with port berries. Are you saying I smell of it?"

Tancho's eyes met Crow's. There was that blush again.

"Yes. It's not unpleasant, I assure you," Tancho murmured. "Smokey but sweet. Subtle and . . ."

There was a long pause. "Subtle and what?"

Tancho licked his lips but turned away, walking to the fire instead. "Subtle and alluring."

Crow's blood warmed and his skin prickled all over. He followed Tancho to the fire and stood behind him, and with a slow hand and light touch, he pulled back Tancho's long hair to reveal the long line of his neck.

Tancho gasped and half-turned, his eyes dark and his skin aglow from the fire. "Your scent is alluring to me also," Crow admitted. "Like a breeze off saltwater. I could only dare imagine how you taste."

Tancho's voice was barely a breath. "So taste me then."

Crow cupped Tancho's face, tilting his chin up, relishing the feel of his beautiful skin under this touch. Entranced by Tancho's inviting lips, Crow was about to bring their mouths together when something moved out of the corner of his eye. Tancho saw it too because he turned, startled.

Tancho grabbed Crow's hand and everything slowed to a crawl. Slow motion, as if time itself were drunk. "Crow, look!"

He was still holding Crow's hand, now staring at his wrist, and Crow realised what he'd seen moving out of the corner of his eye.

His birthmark . . . the raven on his wrist . . . its wings were moving. It was slow and awkward but moving. His birthmark was moving.

"What in the . . . ?"

"Does it hurt?" Tancho asked, concerned.

Crow shook his head. The usual burn under the skin was now a pleasant buzz. "It feels . . . good."

They seemed to notice at the same time that the world around them had slowed right down; the fire was dancing too slow and it made no sound. "When we touch . . . ," Tancho said, squeezing Crow's hand. "Everything stops when we touch."

"Yet we can speak," Crow added. He curled his fingers around Tancho's, his touch quick and strong. "And we can move as if nothing has changed."

The raven's wings were still slowly moving on the upward stroke of flight. When it moved its head, both Crow and Tancho gasped, pulling their hands apart.

The world snapped back, full movement, full sound.

Crow held up his wrist and they both inspected it. The birthmark was frozen once more, though in a different position than it always had been. "That is disturbing," Crow murmured.

Tancho held up his wrist. His fish birthmark appeared normal, from what Crow remembered. "Hold my hand."

Crow slid his fingers around Tancho's and they waited, staring at the fish. Staring, waiting . . . Then ever so slowly, its tail began to move. Crow held up his wrist and the raven's wings began to move once more. He pulled his hand away and took a step back. "I don't know what any of this means," he said. "Between you and me. The distance thing was strange, and being so protective of each other was odd. And I'm sure we both agree the fact time seems to crawl when we touch is beyond strange. But this?" He held up his wrist. "This is . . ."

"Inexplicable."

"I was going to say fucking bizarre, but okay, let's go with inexplicable."

Tancho chuckled. "I'm not one for cursing, usually. But the description fits."

"How can you be so calm? Our birthmarks just moved."

Tancho put his hand to his forehead. "Because my head is still spinning."

Crow was immediately concerned. "What? Why? Are you unwell? Can I get you something? Tell me, what do you need? Do you need to lie down? Eat something, perhaps?"

Tancho put his hand to Crow's chest for a fleeting moment, yet long enough to make Crow stop. "I'm fine. Just a little dizzy because you were about to kiss me and I can't remember breathing the entire time."

"Oh." Crow laughed. "Right."

"But I could eat something. And that bath would be lovely."

"Yes, of course." Crow was flustered now. The moment to kiss him was gone. "Why don't you get in the bath while I fix you something to eat." He left Tancho by the fire and went to the table, purposely keeping his back to him. He needed to put as much distance between them as their birthmarks allowed.

His birthmark . . .

He checked his wrist again and the birthmark was still as it was before. A raven mid-flight, a mark he'd had all his life, only now it was in a different position. Its wings were higher than he was so used to seeing, frozen again on his skin.

A quiet splash of water made Crow turn around, just in time to see Tancho sink into the water. His long red hair covered his pale back, his skin flickering orange by the firelight.

Crow had never seen a more stunning sight.

"I must say," Tancho said. "A bathtub by the fire is rather genius."

"After hunting or training in the snow is when I most

appreciate it," Crow admitted, turning back to face the table should Tancho glance his way.

"I've never been in the snow," Tancho said gently.

"Never?" Crow couldn't hide the incredulity from his voice. "What about the mountains that line the northern border of Westlands? Have you never been to them?"

"From a distance. Not all Westlanders' fare too well in the cold." He was quiet a moment. "Have you ever swum in the ocean?"

Crow shook his head. "No. The northern shores are bitterly cold. We have a few fishing villages along the northern shores, but the water is cold enough to stop your heart."

"Do you visit the northern shores often?"

"Twice a year. The trek there is arduous."

"I would imagine so." Tancho hummed. "Do you think it would be possible to build another doorway there? That way you could access it whenever you needed."

"It would certainly make sense," Crow replied. "I don't recall seeing any kind of tiled compass in any of the buildings there."

"We have a lot to learn about them," Tancho said. "And about these birthmarks. I wonder if Maghdlm knows."

Crow took a deep breath. "I think we should keep it between us for now," he whispered. "About the birthmarks moving. Or at least have Asagi search your libraries, secretly. And I can ask Erelis to do the same here. But I feel the less who know about it, the better. For now at least. Until we know more."

Tancho stood up in the bath and Crow quickly turned back to the table to give him privacy. He was sure he could hear a smile in Tancho's voice. "Do you think some will think us as evil?"

"I think rumours and wild-guessing will lead to fear in our people. The unknown breeds fear, and should rumours start that we are not of sound minds or able to control ourselves, they may think we cannot govern."

"But Maghdlm?" Tancho asked. There was the rustle of fabric and Crow assumed Tancho was redressing, though he still dared not turn around. Lest he see that pale skin in the firelight . . .

"If anyone should know, it is her," Tancho furthered. "She knew what it was when she first saw it. Remember, at the initiation ceremony?"

"I remember," Crow murmured. "I would simply prefer to find our own answers. All we know so far is only what we've been told."

"So?" Tancho now stood beside Crow at the table, fully dressed. His hair was wet and he smelled clean and wonderful.

By the blue skies above, he was such a distraction.

"So," Crow said, annoyed with himself. "What if all we know is all they want us to know?"

Tancho frowned. "Who is they?"

Crow shrugged. "Maghdlm. Adelais, the entire Elders' Consul, all of Aequi Kentron? I don't know. That game of chess we were never supposed to win is made all the more difficult when we don't know who we're playing."

Tancho considered this for a moment. "Okay. So we keep the moving birthmark between us for now."

"And we learn from Maghdlm what it takes to open the doorways. Having her be the only one who knows gives her more power than I'm comfortable with."

Tancho, quiet for a moment, conceded a nod. "Agreed. It makes political sense for more than one person to know and for people from all four kingdoms. We can't be the only ones. That wouldn't be fair on Samiel or Elmwood."

Crow nodded and gave him a smile. "I'm pleased we agree."

Tancho smiled right back, then turned his attention to the table of food. "Which should I try first?"

Grateful for the change of subject, Crow picked up a small pie. "Here, try this. It is spiced meat, a favourite from my childhood. Soko and I would sneak into the kitchen and steal them. Although I'm sure Scaevola knew because she always baked a separate batch."

Tancho took a bite and hummed, his eyes lighting up. "Oh, I do like that."

Smiling, Crow picked up some bread and dunked it in his favourite sweet treat. It was syrupy though, so Crow held one hand underneath it and lifted it directly to Tancho's mouth. "This is a honey and nut mixture that Bjalla makes. It is my favourite."

Tancho swallowed down the rest of his pie and was perhaps a little embarrassed at being hand-fed. But he opened his mouth and bit into the bread and he hummed louder as the taste hit his tongue. He licked his lips, delighted, speaking with his mouth still full. "This could be the best thing I've ever tasted. What did you say it was?"

Crow was still looking at Tancho's lips, at where his tongue had just been . . . "Oh, uh."

Tancho smiled, obviously knowing damn well Crow was lost in lurid thoughts. "Did you say honey?"

Crow shook his head and had to remember the question. "Yes, honey from the northern yellow bee. They feed only on the lemon willow flower. It's a distinct flavour, yes? And the vetur nuts come from the snjor bush. It grows low to the ground in the lower regions, and only for a few months of the year." He felt foolish for going on and on about food. Crow couldn't remember ever being so nervous. But then Tancho took another piece of bread, dipped it in the syrup, and bit into it. His lips glistened and a tiny drop ran down his chin. He laughed as he wiped it away, then—because he was sent to drive Crow to the point of madness—he sucked the syrup off his finger.

Crow's mind came to a grinding halt, and it appeared he forgot how to breathe.

Tancho grinned and picked up another piece, dipping it into the syrup and putting it to Crow's lips. "Your turn."

Crow opened his mouth and took the bread, Tancho's gaze firmly on Crow's lips and he appeared dazed. Crow smiled, glad he wasn't the only one affected. "You're doing that on purpose," Tancho murmured.

"Doing what?"

"Moving your lips like that. Making them glisten with honey. And smiling. It's the smile that . . ."

"You started it. Smiling all beautiful like that. Licking your lips and sucking on your finger."

Tancho looked up at him, and for a long moment, no one breathed. "Do you think I'm beautiful?"

"Like nothing I've ever seen before," Crow whispered.

That wretched smile pulled at Tancho's lips again, and Crow was about to tell him to stop it when there was a knock on the door. "Everyone decent?"

Crow sighed. "Soko."

Without being invited, the door opened and Soko's smiling head appeared, poking around the door. He studied both Crow and Tancho and, no doubt, how close they were standing. "Everything okay? Didn't interrupt, did we?"

"We?" Crow asked.

Soko pushed open the door to reveal two human coat

racks. Well, it was Karasu and Kohaku wearing . . . Crow wasn't sure how many layers of coats. "I wanted to show them the snow and thought we'd see if you wanted to join us. Did you know they've never been in snow before? Isn't that just absurd? Anyway, they don't handle the cold too well."

"I can see," Crow said with a laugh.

Tancho chuckled. "You look like starfish."

"If I have to be subjected to such ridicule," Karasu said, "the least you can do is join us."

"Coat up," Soko said, grinning.

"I have a coat you can wear," Crow told Tancho.

Smiling, Tancho gave a small nod, then turned to his friends. "Kohaku, you must try this bread and syrup."

He and Soko hustled to the table and started shoving food in their mouths, and Karasu waddled over and tried, to no avail, to pick up a small pie. Her arms were so laden by layers of fabric she couldn't bend her arm properly. "I need my dagger," she said. "I could stab it."

Soko laughed and picked it up, delicately lifting it to her mouth. She blushed a little but ate the pie and Soko's grin was victorious. Crow didn't miss Tancho's raised eyebrow as he led him to the wardrobe. He pulled out his warmest coat and helped Tancho into it. "I think something is brewing between them," Crow whispered.

"His bravery is noted," Tancho replied with a smile. "It would take a man with a spine of steel to match her."

Crow laughed as he searched for a pair of gloves. "Then perhaps she has met her match."

Tancho's eyes found Crow's as he handed him the gloves. "If he thinks of her as his next conquest . . ."

Crow considered that. "I don't think he's *that* brave."

Tancho smiled as he fixed the gloves and coat. "This is all too big. I feel like a child wearing grown-up's clothes."

Crow fixed Tancho's collar. "You'll be warm. And I'd be lying if I said I didn't like you wearing my clothes."

Tancho's smile became a touch more sultry. "And I'd be lying if I said I didn't like wearing them."

"Are you two ready?" Soko called out. "These two are gonna melt if we don't get them outside soon."

"Can't have melted Westlanders in my castle, can I?" Crow replied, and the five of them headed down the corridors to the stairs at the southern wing.

Kohaku had taken a handful of pies. "I've never tasted anything like these," he said, his mouth half-full. "And everything smells sweet here. And the white mountains are amazing, and the snow—"

Soko had opened the outside door to a face full of icy breeze and snow flurries. Soko and Crow kept walking, but the three Westlanders had stopped, stock-still, in the open doorway. Soko laughed at their expressions. "What were you saying, Kohaku? The snow what?"

"Cold," he whispered, his breath a cloud of white steam.

Smiling, Crow took Tancho's arm and led him out into the white courtyard. Their boots crunched in the snow, and Tancho's breath plumed out from his mouth. After a moment, he turned, wide-eyed, and he smiled. "It's beautiful."

Crow took in Tancho's pale skin, his dark pink lips, how tresses of his red hair escaped his hood like ribbons of blood-red silk. "So beautiful."

He was rewarded with a rich blush, deepened by the cold, no doubt. But it made Crow's knees weak.

Tancho seemed to notice something then, and looked

down between them. "You're holding my hand," he whispered.

Yes, Crow took his hand to lead him out into the snow . . .

"Oh."

Soko, Karasu, and Kohaku were now laughing and picking up the snow. Not slowed down, not muted; time hadn't come to a crawl. Crow and Tancho were touching, but the world around them stayed the same.

"It must be the gloves," Tancho reasoned.

Crow nodded. "It must be."

Just then, a snowball came hurtling at Tancho and Crow snatched it out of the air. He turned to face whoever would dare take aim at his Tancho, to see three guilty faces, their mouths in perfect O shapes. "Who would dare to hit him?"

Before anyone could answer, Tancho had scooped up a ball of snow and shot it at Kohaku, hitting him in the chest.

"Take cover!" Soko cried as the three of them ran for the columns along the side walls. Except Karasu and Kohaku had too many layers on.

"I've never seen starfish run before," Tancho said.

Crow snorted out a laugh. "Watch for Soko's wild left. He can curve a throw."

Soko appeared from behind a column, his face one of offended horror. "I can't believe you told him! You're not supposed to tell him! I've been betrayed."

Crow grinned at him. "You chose your side, my friend."

Soko replied with a snowball that narrowly missed Crow's head.

"He plays for real," Tancho said, concerned.

Crow gestured to his face. "How do you think I got all these scars."

Tancho's eyes narrowed and he seethed, turning his glare to Soko. "He'll pay for that." He scooped up another snowball and pelted it at Soko, hitting him square in the face.

They traded insults and snowballs for a few minutes, and it was fun, Crow thought. But there were three of them against their two. "We need a plan," Crow said. "Take off your glove."

"My fingers will freeze," Tancho hissed. A snowball barely missed his head. "I wish I had my sword."

Crow snorted as he compacted two quick snowballs. "Give me your hand. Their world will slow down, ours will not. Let's see what we can do."

A wicked grin played at Tancho's lips. "Clever." He pulled off his glove and held his hand out. Crow took it, and just like that, everything around blurred to a crawl.

Crow stuck his head up to see Soko with a snowball leaving his hand in slow, slow motion. Crow handed Tancho a snowball. "Let's run past them and get them from behind."

Tancho laughed. "I love it."

"Soko is south, Karasu south-east, Kohaku south-west. We will run between Soko and Kohaku. Don't let go of my hand."

Tancho gave a nod, and they were off.

They could run, at normal speed, while everything around them was stuck in some time crawl. Soko's snowball was a few inches from his hand now, his smile wide. Kohaku was still forming a snowball in his hands, a comical look of concentration on his face. Karasu was watching Soko with a distracted smile and Crow was surprised at how peaceful she looked in a moment of complete abandon. They ran between Soko and Kohaku, and Crow saw Soko catch a glimpse of him as they shot past.

They turned, still holding hands, and threw their ammunition. Crow aimed for Soko, of course, and Tancho aimed at Kohaku, then they let go of each other's hands. Each snowball hit its target with a cold splat, and Crow and Tancho both laughed. Soko, Kohaku and Karasu all spun around, stunned and amazed.

"How . . . ?" Kohaku cried. "How did you get there, when you were just there?" He pointed to where Crow and Tancho had hidden behind a column.

"I saw you run at me," Soko whispered. "Tell me I didn't see you! How did you do that?"

Karasu noticed Tancho's hand. "He took his glove off."

"To throw better with," Tancho lied with a cool smile. "We won, by the way."

"No, for real, how did you do that?" Soko asked again, wiping snow off the back of his head and neck. "It's some birthmark magic, isn't it?"

"I don't know what you're talking about," Crow said with a grin. "But I'd say, whatever it is, it works well."

Tancho gave him a sly nod. It did work well, indeed.

The heavy door at the end of the courtyard opened and a guard appeared. "My king, Erelis requests you in the library."

Crow gave a nod of acknowledgment. "Tell him we will be with him at once."

Kohaku was still trying to get snow out of his long blond hair. "Will you really not say how you moved without us seeing?"

Tancho shook his head as he put his glove back on. "We really won't."

"Come, this way," Crow said, gesturing to the doors. "Erelis awaits."

Karasu and Kohaku peeled off a coat or two as they made their way down flights of stairs to the library, but Tancho kept his on, though he did lower the hood and the gloves went into a pocket.

Crow wasn't lying when he said he liked Tancho wearing his clothes. Perhaps Tancho wasn't lying when he said he liked wearing them. The bond between them had certainly turned a corner. He no longer wanted to kill Tancho. Oh no . . . he wanted to do many things to him. Killing him was not one of them.

The library in the castle wasn't huge like the one at Aequi Kentron. And to be fair, it was probably more of a records-keeping room, but there were books. Some newer, some old, some very old.

There was some fiction, which Crow admitted to reading only whatever was required of him in his studies. He preferred history books if he had to read anything. Actually, he preferred not to read at all.

Tancho gasped beside him, lightly touching the spine of a book on the shelf. "You have different books to us. I've never seen these before. Are they fiction?" He looked up at Crow, his eyes full of wonder.

He nodded. "This makes you happy."

"Very much."

"Then you can read any book here," Crow replied. "Any you choose. Or all, if you want."

Crow noticed Soko staring at him, a mix of disbelief and wonder on his face. "What?" Crow barked.

"Nothing," he replied with a smile, looking from Crow to Tancho and back again. "Nothing at all."

Tancho took a book off the shelf, and Crow thought he

might have been about to throw it at Soko, but no. He flipped open the cover and began reading. Soko laughed and Crow growled at him, though apparently he knew him too well to know there wasn't any bite to it because he simply kept walking.

"Tancho," Crow whispered. "This way."

"Oh," he looked up, surprised. He closed the book and held it to his chest. "May I bring this with me?"

All Crow could do was smile at him. "Of course. And when you're done with it, you can choose another."

The smile Tancho gave Crow in return was just for him, as though no one and nothing else existed. A smile that could have made Crow forget everything, as though no danger lurked through a magical doorway, as though their whole lives hadn't been turned upside down. That smile was just for Crow and nothing in the world could convince him otherwise.

"Are you two done?" Karasu stood at the end of the stacks. She must have come back for them. "It's great that you two aren't trying to kill each other anymore, and you have some weird connection now where you're all smitten and I know that must be distracting, but have you forgotten that an invading legion of creatures stormed our castle and disappeared through a compass doorway to somewhere, and we came here to heed warning, and we had intended to warn the Eastlands and Southlands—"

"We haven't forgotten," Tancho replied, cool and sharp.

And that was true. They hadn't forgotten . . . they were just distracted. "Forgotten, no. Though it is hard to think of anything else," Crow admitted. Tancho's blush was his only reply.

Karasu rolled her eyes and sighed. "Please come this way. We're running out of time."

They followed her out to where Erelis sat at a long table with books spread out and open in front of him. If anyone noticed how close Crow and Tancho were now standing to each other, they never made mention of it.

"My king," Erelis said when he saw Crow. "I have found something. I take it, given the company included here, that these matters can be discussed openly. Or should we strive for privacy?"

Given Tancho was with Crow when he'd asked, Crow assumed his mentor was referring to Soko, Kohaku, and Karasu.

"It's fine. Please continue."

"There are no records of any kind of doorway above the compass in our histories. Not as recorded data, anyway. But I found this." He slid one book on the table closer toward Crow and Tancho. "A fictional book, written a long time ago. Actually, there is no date. But it has been with the fictional tomes since well before my time."

"Fictional?" Crow asked. "A fictional book about what, exactly?" The book in front of them was *old*.

"About a circular witch-door with a secret key," Erelis explained. "Not a physical key, such as one that would fit a lock. No, this key was no more metal components and a chant."

"That's hardly fiction," Crow countered. "As I think we have all witnessed."

"Maybe the record keepers thought it to be too far-fetched to have any truth to it," Tancho offered. "The door-ways had been forgotten for many generations."

"True," Erelis agreed. "But there is a record of it. Albeit disguised as fiction."

Crow gave a thoughtful nod. "Perhaps disguising it was

the point. Does it say how they used the doorways, how many there were, and why they closed them?"

Erelis nodded. "I have only had time enough to skim the pages, but yes. There were five in total; one in each kingdom and one in the Aequi Kentron. They used the doors for matters of the high courts. Only for the kings and queens and consuls, which is why they were inside the castles. If there is a way to guard the door and decide if you'll allow entry, I'm yet to find it. I will continue to read and report what I learn."

"What else does it say?" Crow asked. "Is there anything that points to where the creatures came from?"

Erelis pushed one book aside and pulled another, larger one closer. It was somehow even older than the first. The pages were yellowed papyrus, the cover some type of ancient black leather with a raven embossed on the cover.

Tancho looked puzzled. "This is similar to the book Asagi found, only white with a koi on the cover. He called it a grimoire."

Erelis gave a nod. "A book of spells and invocations. Amongst other things." He carefully opened it. Spread over two pages was a compass rose . . . no, a map superimposed with a compass rose. As if the Great Kingdoms were a compass, the western point was Tancho's castle, the northern point, stopping before the top end of the northern border, was Crow's, and in the centre, as if the circle that held the compass arrow pin, was Aequi Kentron. The southern point was slightly inland, as was the eastern point.

"Why are the points uneven," Tancho wondered out loud.

Crow pointed to the north point. "The arrow doesn't meet the most northern point of land. It points to where we stand right now. And yours"—he pointed to the western point—"does meet the most western point because that's where your castle is. Right where the land meets the sea."

"So the points don't indicate true direction," he stated. "They indicate where the location of the castle in each kingdom."

"Or, more likely, they indicate the location of each doorway," Crow replied. He tapped the centre circle. "Aequi Kentron, the so-called equal centre. It connects to all doors."

"Hmm," Tancho frowned as he hummed. "Perhaps the elders didn't like the fact we can bypass them. By using these doors, we stepped directly from my home to yours without them running interference."

Crow gave a stern nod. "That I would believe. They've controlled every single thing between our nations for a thousand years."

"And controlled our trade and all communications," Soko said.

"And profited, no doubt," Karasu added.

"They had us believe they were doing us a favour, governing sanctions to keep us from war," Tancho furthered.

Kohaku nodded in agreement. "It is what we were taught."

"Us as well," Soko said, giving Crow a dark look. "Has everything Aequi Kentron told us been a lie? They were the ones who outlined what we were taught, weren't they?"

Crow looked to Erelis then, and with a deep frown, he nodded. "I was taught the same when I was young, and my teachers told me it was knowledge from the elders," the old man said.

Tancho gave him a smile. "Asagi, my teacher, said much the same. All blame lies with the elders for this. Not you, nor him. I would imagine that Samiel and Elmwood were taught the same. We were told only what they wanted us to know."

Crow turned the page of the book to reveal another map. It was a drawn replica of the Northlands, showing mountains, roads, villages, rivers. Then he turned the page again to reveal the Westlands. But something was off.

Tancho leaned in and inspected it. "This map is wrong." He put his finger to his castle. This point is true, more or less. But the roads and the rivers . . ."

Everyone leaned in closer to look. "It's not remotely close," Karasu said.

"Whoever drew this was drunk," Kohaku said. "Why would they put the road like this? It cuts the river."

Crow looked up at him, then to Erelis. "Because if we were to use this, we'd be lost the second we stepped foot on your land. I'd bet anything you like, if we were to find the book of maps in Tancho's library, the map of Northlands would be just as wrong. The elders are keeping us blind."

"I will have Asagi find it," Tancho said adamantly.

"Erelis?" Crow asked. "Would you be opposed to visiting with Asagi in the Westlands' castle? He and yourself are of like minds. Take the books, share knowledge, learn all we can learn. The one thing Aequi Kentron has done over the last however many centuries is keep us from sharing anything they don't want us to share."

Erelis' eyes widened. "Me? Go to Westlands?"

"For a short time," Crow amended. "I would never ask you to leave your place here. We can open the doorway and have you back in a moment. Journeys of seven days to Aequi Kentron are over."

Erelis sighed with relief. "Then yes. I would be honoured, my king. And even if you required me to leave for longer, I would. It's just that I've never set foot on any soil that wasn't Northlands."

Crow smiled at his mentor. "Westlands is a place like nothing you've ever seen. It is beautiful at every turn."

Tancho's eyes softened as he looked up at Crow, and it made Crow's heart thump against his ribs. "Asagi would be honoured. And I'm sure Hitode and Unagi would like to see home."

"Then let's see if Maghdlm is rested enough," Crow said. "We need some lessons in opening the doorway, and we need to speak to both Samiel and Elmwood before nightfall."

"Are we really going to the Eastlands and Southlands?" Soko asked excitedly.

"Don't get too excited," Crow warned. "I don't know how kindly they'll take to a magical doorway opening in the middle of their castles. There's a good chance we might find ourselves at the end of a spear or axe."

CHAPTER SIXTEEN

MAGHDLM WAS STILL tired and the bruising on her face now resembled that of a pummelled corpse. Tancho remembered seeing a dead fisherman when he was quite young; he'd been thrown by rough weather into the mast of his boat, thrown overboard, and drowned. The healers had said he was dead before he hit the water, and from the sunken mast-impression on the side of his head, Tancho would believe it.

Maghdlm looked much like that.

Tancho knew Crow didn't exactly trust her, but Tancho felt sorry for her. She was beyond old, small and frail, and someone had tried to kill her. Not just any someone, but someone from within the Elders' Consul. They might not have delivered the blow themselves, but they ordered it be done.

She was alone, betrayed, and left for dead.

And she was helping them. Somewhat begrudgingly, Tancho could admit. When Crow had asked her to teach him how to operate the doorway, she had blinked owlishly before schooling her reaction. But she had eventually obliged.

The arrows still pointed to their last location and Crow held the pouch of elements. "Potassium, lanthanum, vanadium, indium," he said, as he sprinkled a dusting of metal shavings onto the compass tiled onto the floor. And before Maghdlm could say the incantation, Crow recited it from memory. Tancho wasn't sure he could remember every word, given they'd only heard it once, but Crow certainly did.

Maghdlm couldn't hide her surprise at that either.

Armed guards stood at the ready in case it wasn't the Westlands they'd just opened a door to, and the purple sparks burst to life, forming a circle in mid-air. They could see Tancho's guards in white on the other side, katanas raised, waiting to see who should step through. Kohaku did the honours.

Crow led Erelis through with Tancho, and they introduced him to Asagi, whose eyes lit up at the pile of books Erelis carried with him. Erelis stared in wonder at the room they were in and the view outside until he remembered his mission, and within moments the two older men were already discussing the history books and maps.

Crow had two Northlands' guards attend Erelis. "It's nothing personal," Crow murmured to Tancho. "Erelis means a great deal to me, and I would feel better knowing he doesn't find himself in a strange land alone."

Tancho understood. "If I'd asked Asagi to visit your lands by himself, I'd insist upon guards with him as well."

Kohaku returned carrying three bottles of rice wine and a huge grin. "I will show Soko how we Westlanders drink." He didn't even pause as he stepped back through the doorway.

Crow laughed and Tancho sighed. "We shouldn't leave them unsupervised," Tancho said.

"True. They can't be drinking before we go to see Elmwood and Samiel." Then Crow made a face. "Unless you think they would appreciate a comedy routine."

Tancho stared at him, trying to gauge if he was serious. Thankfully Crow smiled. "Absolutely not."

"Are you ready to leave?" Crow asked.

Tancho looked around the grand hall of his castle, taking in the familiarity, and inhaled deeply before he gave Crow a nod. "We'll be back."

Crow grinned. "We will be."

Tancho gave a wave to his guards. "The tiles are to stay as they are, the doorway is to remain openable for now. I'll send word if it should be closed." Then he had a thought. "If anyone but us try to enter, pull up the tiles so the doorway is shut. If we can't enter when we try, I'll know why."

The guard gave a bow of his head. "Yes, my king."

Crow waited for Tancho and they stepped back through the doorway into the Northlands again. Maghdlm waved her hand with a dusting of elements and said, *"Claude ostium."*

The purple circle got smaller and smaller until it was nothing but a burst of sparks falling to the floor. Tancho noticed that Kohaku, Karasu, and Soko now held a bottle of wine each. "Please put the wine down," Tancho said. He gave Karasu a stern glare with a pointed nod to Soko. "Are you trying to kill him?"

Karasu smiled at that, but Soko was offended. "Oh, I can drink."

"Westlanders have been known to use that wine to light the lamps on occasion," Tancho said.

Soko shot Kohaku an affronted look. "You told me it was good."

Kohaku grinned at him. "It is."

"Yeah, for lighting lamps," Soko grumbled. "And I was going to offer you some of our winterberry mead."

Tancho left them to bicker and turned to find Crow studying the floor. "There has to be a way to move the tiles to a new destination without breaking up the floor every time," he said.

"There is," Maghdlm said, holding open the old book she kept with her. "I was going to tell you before when you asked me to teach you, but you didn't need my help, apparently."

Crow stared at her and Tancho bit back a smile. "Well, Maghdlm," Tancho said, "I would very much appreciate you telling us now."

"Move away from the compass," she said, shooing everyone back. "Where to first?"

"Southlands," Crow answered. Tancho nodded his agreement.

"*Aperire ad meridianam*," she murmured.

She didn't use anything from her pouch of elements and metals, she just repeated the chant over and over until her eyes closed, her hand moving in a circle. And with a mighty creak and the sound of stone rubbing against stone, the outside circle of the compass began to slide. Ever so slowly, it slid from the W toward the S, and Maghdlm kept chanting until the arrow was in place. She opened her eyes and smiled when she saw it had worked.

This time Tancho tried his hand at opening the doorway. He took a small pinch from the pouch and recited the incantation, and he grinned at Crow when a flurry of purple sparks ignited in front of them. As the circle grew in size, Soko, Kohaku, and Karasu took their place to walk through first.

Tancho couldn't see a great deal through the doorway as they stepped through but Soko, Kohaku and Karasu disappeared through it without any cause for alarm. Crow gave Tancho a smile that was a mix of excitement and trepidation. "Ready?"

"We are, yes," Tancho replied. "It's unlikely Elmwood will be able to say the same."

Crow smirked at that. "Let's not keep him waiting."

They stepped through, and the first thing that hit Tancho was the heat and humidity. It was like walking into a room of hot steam, heavy to breathe, and Tancho doubted Crow and Soko would like it much. The second thing to hit Tancho was the noise. There was a lot of shouting, someone screamed, and there was the sound of footsteps running, first away, then getting closer.

"We have incoming," Soko said. "I asked for Elmwood, but they ran screaming for guards."

"Keep your hands off your weapons," Crow said. "Show them we mean no harm."

The room itself was large, stone floors and walls, and suddenly filled with about twenty guards wearing dark green, armed with axes and clubs. "We come in peace," Crow said, hands out. "I am the King of Northlands, and this is the King of Westlands," he said, gesturing to Tancho. "We must speak to Elmwood. It is very important."

"What is going—" Elmwood said as he barged in. He was wearing the green pants he'd been wearing at Aequi Kentron and dark boots, but he was without a shirt. He was bigger than Tancho remembered, with arms like tree branches and a chest the trunk they stemmed from. "Crow?" he questioned, clearly confused. "Tancho? What are— How? You were heading west, and we've only been back a day . . ." And then he noticed the still-open magick doorway and he paled a little. "And what in the name of peatbog is that?"

"Yes, it is us. We have much to explain," Crow said. He glanced at the closest guard, who still wielded his axe, but turned back to Elmwood. "This is an ancient doorway which we have discovered links all four castles. We need to speak to both you and Samiel, if you would be so kind."

"We apologise for the entry without warning," Tancho added. "We are yet to figure out how to do that."

Elmwood put his hand out. "Stand down," he ordered his guards. He was still clearly shocked.

"Maghdlm, please close the door," Crow asked.

She murmured her chant and the door spun to a close, and Elmwood finally seemed to relax a little. "You can travel from your home . . . without trekking a week to Aequi Kentron first?"

Tancho gave a nod. "In a matter of minutes, we have gone from my Westlands to Northlands and now here."

A quiet gasp sounded and Tancho thought it might have been one of the guards, but it wasn't. It was Kohaku. He was staring out the window, his face etched with wonder. "This cannot be real!"

Tancho followed his line of sight to the world outside, and he understood why it took Kohaku's breath. Tancho could barely believe his eyes. They were clearly high up because for as far as the eye could see was the top of an endless green sea of jungle. Not even the golden hue of the sun could tinge the green. The castle was made from stone, but there were wooden houses built in the forest canopy with wooden suspension bridges linking trees like a spider-web, creating a network of communities in the treetops.

"Oh wow," Crow said. "Elmwood, that is a thing of beauty."

It really was. Tancho could never have imagined a place like it. Birds Tancho had never seen before, so brightly coloured and loud, and . . . "What is that? In the tree?" he asked.

"A monkey," Elmwood said. "Cheeky things they are."

"And that?" Soko squeaked. He hid behind Karasu, who promptly shoved him in front of her.

Elmwood laughed. "Giant python." Tancho noticed then what he'd originally thought was a tree branch growing along the window frame was indeed moving. "They keep the castle free of rats."

Tancho almost laughed in wonder. "Crow's right. It is beautiful."

Elmwood smiled beside them. "Thank you. But please forgive my lack of small talk. Can you please explain to me how it is you are all here? And how that sparking circle worked and how you can travel between lands? And Tancho," he said as if just remembering, "was the threat at your home attended to? We saw no one at Aequi Kentron after parting ways. We saw no one. As in, not one soul."

Tancho nodded. "Indeed, there was a threat, and the news we bring is urgent. So yes, let us not delay."

Elmwood nodded, his heavy brow etched with concern. "Come this way, to my meeting room."

Elmwood, along with Kearmore and Cardwick, the two guards that had accompanied him to Aequi Kentron, led them through some corridors to another room with two large windows facing a different view of the forest. Vines grew along the windowsill and an ocean of green trees beyond, and in the middle of the room sat a large round wooden table. It seemed to be carved from one gigantic piece of wood; each chair appeared to be cut from the same tree.

"Elmwood, my friend," Crow said. "When this is over, I would very much like to return so you can show me your amazing home and kingdom. I am enchanted with what I have seen."

Elmwood gave a proud nod and smile. "Any time."

Soko wiped his brow with his shirtsleeve. "Though there seems to be something wrong with the air here. It's hot and thick to breathe."

Crow smiled. "A far cry from the icy thin air of our home."

"You can really travel to other lands through that magick circle I saw?" Elmwood asked. "Tell me everything."

So they did.

When they'd covered everything, Elmwood was quiet for a long moment. He looked out over his jungle kingdom and sighed. "So what do we do now?"

"We seek out Samiel," Tancho said. "And we four leaders go back to Aequi Kentron, through the doorway to see with our own eyes what's going on. They won't expect us to know how to use the doorway. We will have surprise on our side."

Crow nodded. "Whatever the elders had planned with their army of creatures, they were not planning on all four kingdoms joining forces. Asagi said there were about one hundred of those creatures," Crow added. "Together, we could have ten times that."

"Do we gather our armies?" Elmwood asked.

Crow and Tancho both nodded, but it was Tancho who spoke. "Have them prepare to leave. If we need them, they can be with us in Aequi Kentron in a matter of minutes."

Elmwood gave a rather sad smile. "Men who have

trained, yes. But we've never seen a day of battle. We've never known combat or wars. We've lived in peace for hundreds of years."

"And we will live to see it again," Tancho declared. "Let's hope the elders have a fair explanation and we can see an outcome without a single weapon being raised."

"Do you have any ancient scripts in your archives or maps?" Crow asked. "Or any writings on magical doorways? My mentor found a book in our fictions that more or less explained the doorways. Tancho as well."

Elmwood frowned and had a guard relay the message to the archive keeper to search and retrieve without delay. He had tea brought to the table, which Tancho was excited to try. He'd never had tea made with tropical fruit before. He'd never had tropical fruit before! And it was with a heavy heart that he wished for more time to explore these new places, experience these new things with his new friends.

Everything had changed from all he'd ever known, and if, at the end of all this, he could still call Crow, Elmwood, and Samiel his friends, then maybe it wasn't a curse after all.

A short while later, an old man appeared at the door. He had wrinkled bronzed skin, his hair in locks like tree roots. His dark eyes were kind and wise, he wore South-lands' green, and he held a book in his hands.

Elmwood stood. "Oaken, please meet my friends. Kings of the North and West, Crow and Tancho. This is Oaken, my mentor."

"An honour," he said, his voice like the rustle of leaves. "Elmwood, boy, a shirt in the presence of company."

Elmwood grinned and rolled his eyes, and a guard appeared almost immediately, holding out the olive-green sleeveless vest Tancho had seen him wear in Aequi

Kentron. He pulled it on over his head, the fabric stretched tight over his broad torso.

Oaken held out the book. "What you seek."

Elmwood put his hand on Oaken's shoulder. "My good man, we are headed east to see Samiel, and I wish you to join me. If anyone knows what secrets our histories hold, it is you."

Poor Oaken's eyes went wide. "East?"

"Through the magick doorway," Elmwood replied. "Apparently. Days or weeks of travel now takes only seconds."

Oaken was clearly sceptical and perhaps a little afraid, but he nodded dutifully. "As you wish."

Tancho smiled at them. He really did like Elmwood, and like Crow, he would love the opportunity to come back and spend time in the jungles, getting to know Elmwood and his people, and learn his customs.

Perhaps Elmwood's thoughts had taken him down a similar path. "So, what do you think the Eastlands will be like?"

"Hopefully the air won't be so wet," Soko said, sweating and flushed. "I see now why you forgo the sleeves on your shirt."

Elmwood laughed at that, a loud barking sound. "I fear I'd freeze to death in your homelands."

Kohaku nodded. "Can confirm. So beautiful, but so, so cold."

"I will see it one day," Elmwood declared with a nod. "Though something more pressing . . . Do you think Samiel will be pleased to see us?"

Crow chuckled. "Samiel, yes. Her welcoming party, not so much."

And Crow was not wrong.

Once Elmwood and his two guards were ready, it was time for Maghdlm to open the doorway. She chanted, "*Aperire ad orientalum*," murmuring it over and over. And to the sound of many gasps in the grand hall, the arrow in the outer ring of the tiled compass moved toward the E, slowly grating into place.

With a pinch from her small pouch, she sprinkled some elemental dust onto the floor and spoke the magick words. Purple sparks lit the room and formed a circle, spinning as it grew bigger, big enough to walk through.

Tancho could see to the other side, yellow stone walls and figures in red running and standing in formation. "Do not raise your swords," Crow warned in a low voice.

Soko, Karasu, and Kohaku stepped through first, then Tancho and Crow, followed by Elmwood and his two men, Oaken, and Maghdlm at the rear. They found themselves surrounded by red uniforms, shields, spears and swords, and brave but frightened faces.

"We are allies," Crow announced. "The kings of Northlands, Westlands, and Eastlands, to speak to Samiel. If you would be so gracious as to let her know we are here. We bring word from Aequi Kentron."

From amidst the wall of shields and weapons came a single tall figure, clad in red and moving with such grace and confidence. Samiel stood there, staring, her expression neutral, her hand raised as if about to give the order for her guards to strike. And for a heart-stopping moment, Tancho thought she might do exactly that.

But then she smiled and the mood in the room relaxed immediately. "That is one impressive entrance, my friends. Now, what is this news you speak of?"

CHAPTER SEVENTEEN

THE EASTLANDS WAS JUST as beautiful as every other land Crow had seen. Whereas the Westlands was picturesque stone arch bridges over thousands of rivers, and the Southlands was jungles and forests with tree houses and sky bridges, the Eastlands was yellow and red sand dunes, mighty and striking in its own right. The golden glow of the sun made it prettier still.

Samiel's castle was made from yellow clay walls, red tiles on the floor, and spiked plants and palms. The air was dry and it was hot outside, Crow had no doubt, but inside was cool by design alone. Well, cool*er*. It was still too hot for Crow to feel comfortable, and as much as he wanted to, he didn't think it appropriate to strip out of his clothes.

But Samiel took the news of their findings, and their plans to go back to Aequi Kentron, as well as Elmwood had. As strange as it all was, and as little as they knew about each other, there was an unspoken trust between them. Being equal rulers conspired against by their trusted elders would do that. Crow asked her if she could recall any such books in her libraries of anything pertaining to doorways or maps, and Samiel sent guards off to search.

"I see the bond between you two is unbroken," Samiel said, nodding to Crow and Tancho. "You move as one."

"It is not only unbroken but stronger," Soko offered.

Karasu added, "Don't get between them, don't touch either of them, and don't threaten either of them. Unless you're done with this life and would like to move on to the next."

Samiel smiled, raising an eyebrow. "Interesting," she said, still looking at Crow and Tancho. "I thought you might kill each other."

"They tried a few times," Kohaku said. "Until it changed."

"Until what changed?" Tancho asked. "And we are sitting right here. We can answer for ourselves."

"Until something changed," Karasu said, smiling.

"And you stopped trying to kill each other," Soko added.

Kohaku grinned. "And you started trying to—"

Tancho had his dagger out from his wrist guard and pointed it at Kohaku. "Finish that sentence and it will be your last." Kohaku raised both his hands.

Samiel just laughed and waved them off. "There will be no blood spilled at my table."

Elmwood chuckled. "We see what you mean." But then he was serious and he looked at Tancho, then Crow. "It has gotten worse as the eclipse draws near?"

"Stronger," Crow clarified. Worse implied it was horrible or unwanted, and Crow was now certain it was neither of those things. "The bond grows stronger, yes."

"We cannot physically be apart without pain," Tancho explained, his cheeks tinged with pink. He lifted his chin and regained some composure. "So when we return to

Aequi Kentron, Crow and I must not be separated. Whatever plan we devise, we must factor that into account." Tancho looked at Crow, and Crow gave him a nod.

"Understood," Samiel said.

"So what is the plan?" Elmwood asked. "Apart from going back to Aequi Kentron. What do we do once we get there?"

"We find out exactly what is going on," Crow replied. "Who is behind it, who or what those creatures are, and where they come from."

"And who invited them," Tancho added. "They knew about the doorways when we did not. Someone on the Elders' Consul must have sent word to them."

"And the eclipse?" Samiel asked. "Why do they come now?"

Crow nodded. "Is it because they assumed our kingdoms would be absent their kings, at their Golden Festival? Or does the eclipse itself open other doorways?"

"Or perhaps they simply assumed we four would be all in one place?" Elmwood surmised. "Would make for an easy target."

Tancho nodded. "I fear you might be correct."

"We should pay them a visit," Samiel said, her jaw clenched and her eyes sharp. "And see which of us is the bigger easy target. Them or us."

"I say we wait for nightfall and have surprise on our side," Crow said, but then he shrugged. "Or we can go right now and start the arse-kicking in broad daylight. I don't mind."

Elmwood chuckled. "I like the way you think."

"The cover of darkness would help us if we are aiming for stealth," Tancho added. "But if we open the doorway in the middle of the grand hall, I don't think it matters which time we choose. Alarms will be sounded before the doorway is big enough for us to walk through, and we could be slaughtered on entry."

Crow growled at his own carelessness. "I didn't think of that. I should have thought of that."

"So how do we get inside undetected?" Elmwood asked.

Samiel smiled. "I may know a way. Undetected, no. Unbothered, yes."

SAMIEL'S IDEA of being unbothered was throwing a hand bomb through the barely opened doorway, knocking everyone unconscious. The hand bomb was a small clay canister filled with *yanam*, a highly potent weed found in the desert, and when dried, could be made into a paste. The paste was then set in small clay canisters with a wick, of sorts, and when lit, the yanam heated, causing the canister to explode. The gaseous emission that billowed out was strong enough to knock out anyone and everyone who had the misfortune of being in that room, be it one man or twenty. She could throw one or two through the doorway, then have it zipped closed, wait a minute or two for the gas to clear, reopen the doorway, and walk in unbothered while the guards slept on the floor.

"Will it kill them?" Elmwood asked.

Samiel shook her head. "No. They will sleep for about five hours."

Tancho held one of the yanam bombs in his hand, feeling the weight of it. "Do we want to know how you know this?"

She grinned. "There are old, old stories of goat herders who fed it to their herds and the goats fell over asleep. Then there are also stories of women who would put a tiny amount in their husband's pipe, and when he'd had too much agave wine and fancied his chances for sex, she'd fetch him his pipe and he'd sleep until sun-up." She chuckled. "Not sure which of these stories is true. Possibly both. But either way, it was soon learned that the yanam was a potent weapon. The people of Eastlands are prohibited to use it. Even before my time. But we have been practising ways to utilise it."

Crow stared at her. "And you utilised it into hand-missiles that can knock twenty men out cold?" She nodded and Crow grinned. "I like it."

"We live in peaceful times," she went on to say. "And I have known no other way. Yet in my lessons, we learned of earlier days when people were not so kind. Before Aequi Kentron governed and brought peace and fairness . . . or so they had us believe." Samiel frowned, and Crow felt the weight of her sorrow at being abandoned and lied to. Everything they'd known, everything they'd ever been told, had all been a ruse.

"We can have it again," he said. "No matter what we find out, no matter what happens at the end of this. If the elders have failed us, if they have used us, then we shall see to their end. But that doesn't mean we can't have what we had before." Crow looked at each of the three rulers. "We can forge our own consul, or something akin to it, when this is over. The truth is, what we had before worked, to some degree. I'm sure we could fine-tune it, but the model of how we lived in peace worked. We can have it again. Four lands, equal in every way. We can promise each other right now that not one of us is worth more than the other."

Tancho nodded. "Agreed. The four of us, equal, always."

"Agreed," Elmwood said.

Samiel gave a serious nod. "Agreed."

An older woman entered, with warm brown skin and grey braided hair, wearing Eastland red robes, carrying a book in her hands. It was bound in red leather, and it looked to be very old. "Samiel, I believe I have found what you're after?"

Samiel stood and introduced her as Sirocco, her mentor. She took the book and turned it over in her hands. It also looked to be very familiar. Crow wasn't the only one to think so, either. Elmwood pulled his green leather-bound book out and placed it on the table beside Samiel's. The cut, the embossed emblem, the binding, the type of papyrus . . . Apart from the colour of the covers, they appeared to be identical.

"Mine is the same," Tancho said. "But for the white cover."

"And mine is black," Crow said. "I didn't note the details, though. So I can't be certain, but it's possibly a match as well."

Elmwood turned to the first page, as did Samiel, and they both scanned each page, then looked up to Crow and Tancho. "They are the same," Samiel said. "Except mine is for Eastlands, Elmwood's is Southlands. They even look to be written by the same hand."

"What is going on?" Elmwood asked quietly.

"Everything we've been taught, everything we knew to be our truth, is what they wanted us to know," Tancho said. "We should go to my home and see what Asagi and Erelis have found. They may have discovered something we should know before we arrive at Aequi Kentron."

Crow nodded. "I agree. Darkness will be upon us soon enough."

"And tomorrow is the eclipse," Samiel added.

"Whatever they're planning must happen tomorrow before sunset," Elmwood said. "The eclipse. It cannot be a coincidence."

Crow looked at Tancho then, at his pale face and his dark, soulful eyes. "We're running out of time," he whispered.

Time for what? Time together? Or time to see the bond between them broken and their lives return to some kind of normal?

Crow wasn't sure what he wanted anymore.

"Come then," Samiel said. "Let us make our plans. Where to first?"

"Ah, my home," Tancho answered. "Westlands. It's where Asagi and Erelis are, trying to piece together what little information we have."

So they gathered their supplies, their books, and Maghdlm opened the doorway to the Westlands. Tancho's guards stood armed, forming a line either side of their entry, dressed all in white with their weapons at the ready. Crow had to admit, they looked formidable. Though they couldn't hide their relief at seeing Karasu and Kohaku enter first, and Tancho, of course. They also couldn't hide their surprise at seeing Elmwood with Oaken, Kearmore and Cardwick, dressed all in forest greens, armed with axes and swords. And Samiel and Fazluna and Addax walking tall dressed in red with spears and bows and arrows.

Elmwood and Samiel were stunned at the beauty of Tancho's castle, much like Crow had been. Or still was, he had to admit.

"I could not have dreamed of this," Samiel whispered, taking in the water, the striking architecture, and stone bridges they could see from the balcony.

"Now I see why you were so taken with the view from my windows," Elmwood murmured. His grin lit up his whole face. "I would love to see more."

"And we will," Tancho said proudly. "When trouble no longer knocks on our doors, we will have all the time in the world. And I can assure you, Northlands is just as breathtaking. Mountaintops of snow like you cannot imagine."

Crow smiled at that. "Though the cold isn't as welcoming."

"No," Tancho replied. "But the wood fires and warm castle certainly is. Hot baths and fur rugs. I cannot wait to go back there."

"And I cannot wait to take you there," Crow murmured, looking from Tancho's dark eyes to his mouth, forgetting the room around them. He wanted to take Tancho back there right now . . .

"Okay then," Soko said, clapping Crow on the shoulder. "Work to do."

Crow turned to snarl at Soko, but he was already walking out the door with Karasu, smiling as he looked over his shoulder. As much as he hated it, Soko was right. They had work to do.

They found Asagi and Erelis at a long table in the library, books open and splayed out in front of them. Their animated conversation stopped when Tancho and Crow entered; both older men standing. "My king," they said in unison, their eyes darting to the newcomers.

"I'd like to introduce you to Oaken from the Southlands and Sirocco from the Eastlands," Tancho said. "They bring with them books and knowledge of their lands and histories."

Asagi and Erelis bowed their heads. "It is an honour to meet you," Erelis said. His gaze met Crow's before he glanced at Elmwood and Samiel and back to Crow. "And these are . . ."

"Samiel and Elmwood," Crow replied.

Samiel held out her wrist to reveal her birthmark, and Elmwood did the same.

Erelis gasped before bowing his head again. "An honour."

"We have come for any information you can give us," Tancho said. "We will be leaving for Aequi Kentron as soon as we can and would consider it best to be forewarned."

Sirocco and Oaken put their books on the table, and Erelis frowned. "They appear to be exact copies," Crow explained.

Erelis pulled over the black-bound book and Asagi slid over the white. After a quick once-over, Erelis gave a nod. "Indeed."

"Have you found any other information?" Tancho asked again. "Anything at all to do with the eclipse, birthmarks, rules, maps, anything?"

Asagi gave an apologetic shrug. "Nothing, really. Though from what we learned, in our youths and as teachers, the information is . . . too similar? Too perfect, if you will."

"As though it was fabricated and sold to us?" Crow asked. Both men nodded sadly.

Tancho turned the map around and pointed to the east and south. "Samiel, Elmwood, does this map look right to you?"

It only took them a quick glance to determine it was wrong. "And this is not the map I remember," Elmwood said. "These roads do not match. These mountains, the rivers. Not just here on the south map, but I studied my map as a child, and I can tell you. Not one of the lands is the same."

Tancho picked up the white-bound book. On the front was a koi fish, embossed into the leather, the same symbol on their flag, on their capes and uniforms, as the birthmark on his wrist. He flipped through the pages and stopped, going back a few to one page in particular.

There was a drawing of the compass rose, the arrows at the W pointing toward the centre. "That's odd."

Crow opened the black book, finding the same page. Only on his compass, the arrows at the N pointed toward the centre as well. "Is it a code?"

Sirocco and Oaken flipped open the red and green books and found theirs to be the same. "There are clues here," Erelis said. "We just need to find the key."

"Maghdlm," Crow said, his voice low. "Where is she?"

"Resting," Karasu said. "She is still recovering."

"Please bring her," Crow said. "And the book she carries. She knows more than she says."

Karasu and Soko both nodded at the order and disappeared out the door, and Crow sighed. "Can we even guess the origins of those creatures Asagi described? Do we know from where they come?"

Asagi rummaged through the open books on the table until he came to one in particular. He pulled it out and handed it to Crow. "We found this."

"It's not exact," Erelis said. "And we can't know if it's what we're after, but it might be something."

The picture was of a boar-like creature on a strange planet. "This is fiction," Tancho said. "I read this book when I was a boy. It's the story of a world different to ours, they had no moons and only suns. They lived in perpetual daylight. There was a quest for them to seek a new world, but they had to wait for the suns to set. Only the suns never set."

"These creatures?" Crow asked. "And you're just remembering this now?"

Tancho shot him a glare. "I read this when I was no more than seven. I've read most of these books." He gestured to the stacks around the library. "And you expect me to remember every word?"

"Not the words, Tancho," Crow said, trying to sound calm. "But the creatures with boar-like faces seeking a new world."

Tancho shrugged, defiant. "It was the story of seeking what you cannot have. I never much cared for that book. I probably tossed it aside and read another book the very same day. And it is fiction, Crow. Perhaps if I'd learned it in histories, I might have retained it."

Crow clenched his jaw and tried to speak calmly. "Perhaps we could have saved everyone a lot of time that we do not have if you'd remembered it sooner."

"And perhaps if you'd read a book at all—"

"Ah," Erelis hedged. "My good kings, there's no need to argue."

Karasu and Soko walked back in with Maghdlm, and Soko looked from Crow to Tancho. "Oh, goodie. We're back to trying to kill each other again? I'd hoped we were past that."

Crow and Tancho both snarled at him but Soko simply grinned. "Maghdlm, as requested."

Maghdlm eyed the four older mentors.

Crow tried to simmer his temper. "Maghdlm, the book you carry with you, and the books we gave you."

"Yes?" she said, unsure. "What of them."

"We need them, if you'd be so kind," Tancho said.

Though Crow didn't know why he was being so polite about it. Two of the books she got from both Crow and Tancho. They didn't belong to her.

She walked slowly to the table and put two books on the table, giving a nod to the four mentors. Crow didn't miss how she eyed the four leather-bound books they'd brought with them.

"And the other," Crow said flatly. "The third book."

"The third book is mine," she said simply. She pulled it out from the folds in her cloak and held it. "It's mostly notes and scrawled handwriting, illegible to anyone but me, I'd say."

"If they can't read it, then you won't mind handing it over," Crow said. "They won't damage it. I'll see it returned to you. I promise."

She looked up at him as if trying to decide if she should argue. She very wisely put the book on the table. "As you wish." She bowed her head and lumbered out of the room.

The cover of the book was a mottled purple, the book somewhat bent from overuse and time. Crow skimmed the pages. He wanted to see what secrets she kept, but like Maghdlm had said, he couldn't make out the writing. It was a mix of equations and codes, and drawings, in a language he couldn't read. He didn't trust her but he did trust Erelis. Crow didn't have the time to decipher her scrawls and scratchings, and if anyone here could hope to make sense of it, it would be their four mentors. So he pushed the book toward Erelis. "We shall leave it with you."

Just then, Tancho's fingers wrapped around Crow's and the room around them froze. Tancho stepped in close, their fronts almost touching. "I need to speak to you," he murmured. "Alone."

Crow was lost to the feel of him, his touch, his smell . . . and then he was gone, his hand free.

Crow shook his head, wondering if he'd just imagined that. He shot Tancho a confused look and Tancho sighed. "I need a moment alone with Crow. Please continue to talk in our absence. We won't be long."

Tancho wasn't waiting for his input or approval; he took Crow's arm and pulled him out of the room. "Care to explain?" Crow asked.

"Not here," Tancho hissed, and they walked to his private chambers in silence.

The flames of Crow's temper fanned with every step. It was irrational and inexplicable. He had no reason to be so angry, but he felt off-kilter, misaligned, and wrong or right, that anger was directed at Tancho.

Crow stomped into Tancho's quarters and waited for him to close the doors behind them. "What is so important it required us to walk the length of your castle to speak?"

"Sit down."

"I will not!" Crow yelled.

Tancho's eyes flashed with a gleam of red that matched the fire of his hair. He pointed to the table. "Sit. Down!"

"You do not bark orders at me like a dog," Crow seethed.

Tancho surprised Crow by grabbing the front of his shirt and dragging him toward the table. He kicked a chair around with his foot and shoved Crow into it, and Crow struggled to stay upright. But before Crow could react, before he could get to his feet or shove Tancho back— before he could kill him—Tancho straddled him, and still fisting his shirt, he pulled their mouths together in a crushing kiss.

It took a moment for Crow to realise what was happening. The world around them had slowed to a crawl, but Crow's world was spinning for a whole other reason.

Tancho's mouth, his hands, his body. His touch, his taste, his tongue.

But surprise soon gave way to want and need. Crow opened his mouth and let Tancho control the kiss. Tancho cupped Crow's face and deepened the kiss, their tongues tangling, lips and hands and bodies . . .

Crow snaked his hands up Tancho's sides, around his back, and pulled him down so he straddled him properly . . . and Tancho's weight felt so good. Tancho's fingers raked through Crow's hair, rough and pulling, and he kissed harder, grinding down, and it felt so good, Crow saw stars behind his eyes . . .

Everything around them still moved in slow motion. Dust motes spun in the air like tiny planets, a galaxy moved around them as though they were the sun and the moons and nothing else mattered.

Crow had never tasted anything so sweet or felt anything so hot. He'd never wanted anything more. He'd never cared for someone the way he did for Tancho. It was more than the birthmark, the curse, the lacuna. It was more than that, deeper. Crow knew that and he was sure Tancho did too.

Tancho slowed the kiss and rested his forehead to Crow's, his long red hair spilling down like curtains. He made no move to stand or remove himself from Crow's arms, so Crow held him tighter. "You really wanted me to sit in the chair, huh?"

Tancho laughed and kissed him again, slower this time. Sweeter. When he pulled away, he kept his forehead to Crow's, his eyes closed. "We are out of time. You said it yourself. We don't know what this means, or what will happen to us after the eclipse, and I wasn't going to see this end without having kissed you. I may never have this opportunity or the excuse again."

Crow cupped his face. "Look at me, little fish."

Tancho's eyes opened slowly and he smiled. "What is it, pretty blackbird?"

Crow grinned. "I don't know what will happen once the eclipse is done. I cannot say with certainty a lot of things, but I am sure that you and I will have this opportunity again. We don't need excuses. We have reasons." He gently tucked a strand of Tancho's hair behind his ear. "And my reason is you."

Tancho's smile was breathtaking. "And mine is you."

Crow was lost in the blush on Tancho's cheeks, his kiss-swollen lips. "You are a thief of breath and reason."

Tancho kissed him again, slower this time, rising up on Crow's lap only to grind back down. Crow's hands stilled Tancho's hips and he laughed out a groan. "We don't have time for that."

"Everything slows down out there when we touch," Tancho said, doing it again. "Skin to skin."

"It's still not enough time for what I want to do to you."

Tancho's cheeks flushed and he smiled. "Then you need to promise me when this is over, you will make the time."

Crow laughed. "Days, weeks, months." He took Tancho's chin between his thumb and forefinger. "There will be nothing else but us."

Tancho took Crow's hand and kissed his palm, then looked at Crow's wrist, at his birthmark. "It's gone!"

Crow turned his wrist to see, and yes, the birthmark was gone! He pulled up his sleeve and there it was near the inside of his elbow. He couldn't help but laugh. "You made it take flight."

Tancho looked at his, and his too had moved up his arm. "Is it not the strangest thing?"

"It is."

"I have to wonder what happens," Tancho mused, rubbing his birthmark. "Where is it trying to go?"

"I don't know," Crow replied. "But if kissing you does this—" He pulled up his sleeve to show his moved-birthmark once more. "—I can only imagine where it will end up when I bed you."

Tancho made a soft noise in the back of his throat and he pressed his body up against Crow's again, kissing him and grinding on his lap.

Crow let out a pained laugh and held Tancho still. "My self-control isn't that good."

"I can feel how much you want it," Tancho whispered in Crow's ear, kissing down his neck.

Crow stood up, unseating Tancho and setting him on his feet. Then Crow had to adjust his now-aching dick. "You're killing me."

Tancho's eyes flashed with hurt and rejection. "Apologies. I thought . . ."

Crow stepped in and cupped his face. His palm on Tancho's cheek brought time to a crawl again. "You thought correct. I want you. But not now. I want to take my time with you and treat you as you deserve to be treated. If we're absent any longer, Soko will be in charge of planning strategies for our arrival at Aequi Kentron. And believe me, you don't want that."

A smile eventually won on Tancho's lips. "If Karasu would let him."

"Or Samiel," Crow added. "Or Elmwood. But my point is, we should return. As much as I wish it weren't so."

Tancho leaned into Crow's palm and closed his eyes. "Same. I've never felt for anyone what I feel for you. I don't know if it's real or if it will last longer than the eclipse . . ."

"If we both feel it, it has to be real, does it not?" Crow murmured. "I'm done fighting it or even trying to understand it. What I feel in my heart for you, little fish, is real." This time, Crow lifted Tancho's chin and kissed him, soft and sweet. "Whatever happens from here, whatever we encounter or endure, we do so together."

Tancho nodded. "Together."

Crow pulled Tancho in for an embrace. It was perhaps the first embrace they'd shared, and they fit together perfectly. Tancho's forehead pressed into Crow's neck and his arms slid around his waist. Crow held him tight and he could feel the thump of Tancho's heart.

It solidified something inside him. Whatever this was between them *was* real, and it was worth fighting for. "If we wake up when this is over," Crow murmured, "and the bond between us is broken, I promise that I'll turn up at your door and annoy you every day until you agree to see me. Does that sound fair?"

Tancho chuckled into Crow's neck. "I expect nothing less, my stubborn little blackbird."

Crow kissed Tancho's hair with smiling lips. "I am all those things. A blackbird, by name and by nature, and stubborn." He kissed the top of his head. "And yours."

THEY WALKED BACK to the library holding hands. It made everything else around them move slower and they got back to the meeting in quicker time, and they dropped hands when they got to the door.

"Oh, nice of you two to show up," Soko said with a sly grin. "We didn't keep you from doing anything . . . important, I hope."

"Shut it," Crow mumbled as they went to the table where the old mentors sat. It appeared that Soko, Karasu, and Kohaku, and the other guards from Southlands and Eastlands were stockpiling weapons, and they didn't seem to need any help. But Elmwood and Samiel, along with Asagi, Erelis, Sirocco, and Oaken were in a quiet, serious conversation, their brows furrowed with worry. Maghdlm was gone, though her book was still on the table.

"What have you found?" Tancho asked.

The four books they'd brought—the white, black, red, and green matching books—were set out on the table in what appeared to be some deliberate formation. The books were open and together, and their pages made one larger picture.

No, not a picture.

A map? But not like any map Crow had ever seen before.

All four books joined together formed a picture. It all joined together like a puzzle but Crow couldn't seem to make out what it meant. There were circles and lines and dots and . . .

"What is that?" Tancho asked.

Asagi turned Maghdlm's book around so they could see it. "The same as this."

The exact drawing, only smaller, was in Maghdlm's book. It was hand-drawn, inked in the scratchy scrawl that filled the rest of her book. Her handwriting.

Hers.

Maghdlm's very own handwriting matched the drawings in each of their own books that together made the same picture. Maghdlm's handwriting . . .

"How is that possible?" Tancho whispered. "These books are hundreds of years old, are they not? How can Maghdlm's own book be the same? By her hand?"

"We think it's a chart," Asagi said.

"A chart of what?" Crow asked. He could barely trust his voice to speak.

"A chart of the sun and moons," Erelis answered. "To an exact point in time."

"When?" Tancho asked, though he didn't need to.

"Tomorrow," Crow answered for them.

Oaken nodded. "The eclipse."

"Fuck!" Crow seethed. "I knew it! Where is she now?"

Just then, a white guard raced through the door, out of breath and alarmed. "The doorway. She opened it."

Everyone was on their feet, and Crow stepped forward. "Who? The small woman with the bruises on her face?"

Maghdlm.

He nodded. "Yes. The doorway closed behind her. She's gone."

CHAPTER EIGHTEEN

CROW WAS livid and Tancho didn't blame him. Crow had tried to warn him and Tancho hadn't listened. "I'm sorry," Tancho said. "I should have questioned her. When you had your doubts about her, I should have listened."

Crow shook his head. "It's not your fault. I didn't question her on my own doubts. I shouldn't have expected you to."

Kohaku and Soko ran back into the room. "It's gone. There's nothing in her room."

Tancho wasn't surprised, but he was disappointed. The pouch with the metal elements that they'd helped her obtain was gone.

The key to the doorway was gone.

"Not all of it," Erelis said. "When she asked the North-lands to source her the four elements, I didn't give it all to her."

"She asked for more?" Tancho asked.

Erelis nodded. "She did."

"She asked our guards as well," Kearmore said.

"And ours," Addax added.

This wasn't good . . .

"You kept some?" Crow asked.

He nodded. "I could tell you didn't trust her. I've known you every day of your life, Crow. I can read you. You helped her, you saw that she was cared for when she was injured, but you didn't trust her. I can tell when you don't like someone . . ." His gaze darted to Tancho. "And when you do."

Tancho preened a little. He couldn't help it.

"And we have more indium," Asagi said. "It was the one ingredient hardest to find."

"How can we be sure she wasn't lying?" Elmwood asked. "Why would she just give us the ingredients so easily?"

"We have her book," Asagi noted. "From what we can tell, it is the only four components required."

"She wants us to follow her," Crow said fiercely. "She wants us in Aequi Kentron. She gave us the components; we know the chant to open and close the door. She made a run for it knowing full well we'd follow."

"Then we should counteract and not do what she expects," Tancho allowed. "Let us find another way."

"We are out of time," Crow said. "I say we give her exactly what she wants."

"She knows our plans," Samiel said. "She knows we have our armies at the ready, she knows about the smoke bombs. She knows we are coming."

"Tancho," Asagi whispered. He was staring at Tancho's hand . . . no, not his hand. His wrist. "Your birthmark." His face flashed with horror and rage. "Who are you and what have you done with—"

"It is I, Asagi," Tancho said, cutting him off. He quickly took the old man's hand. "It is me, I swear it." Tancho met

Crow's gaze, knowing they couldn't keep their secret anymore. "The birthmark moves."

He held up his wrist to show the now blank skin but then pulled his sleeve right up to show the koi fish nearer to his elbow. "We discovered they are able to move. As did Crow's."

They were met by a lot of disbelieving and blank stares. Crow held his wrist up, proving it too was bare. He peeled back his sleeve to show the raven had not only moved but was also in a different frame of flight.

"And you only tell us of this now?" Karasu asked. "Tancho, my king, are you in danger? Pain?"

Tancho smiled at her, then clapped Asagi on the shoulder. "Thank you for your concern, but no. It doesn't hurt. In fact, it feels good. Like a humming under the skin. A far cry from the pain if we separate."

"How does it work?" Erelis asked. "It's not moving now."

"It moves when we touch," Crow admitted. "Skin contact."

"Oh," Asagi said, embarrassed. "Apologies for mentioning it in front of others."

Crow laughed. "Not like that. Here, we can show you." He held out his hand and Tancho slid his hand into his. Just like magick, everything around them became slow motion. Everyone stood around them, peering at their inner arms, waiting for the birthmarks to move.

They weren't disappointed.

The raven's wings fanned out slowly and the koi's fins ribboned. There were slow gaping mouths and slow-widening eyes all around them, but Tancho couldn't take his gaze from Crow's. Crow smiled at him, and while everything stood almost-still around them, in a silent and slow chaos, for a perfect moment there was only the two of them.

"Should we tell them about this?" Tancho asked. "How we can slow down time?"

Crow hummed. "Probably. I wish we could keep it as only our secret, but you're right. We should tell them. It could come in useful."

"Agreed." Tancho took his hand back and the room around them snapped back to real-time. The silence of their bubble made the room seem far too loud. Everyone spoke at once, asking questions, wondering theories out loud, but Tancho put his hand up in a plea for quiet. "There is something else."

"Something else that is without explanation," Crow said. "When we touch, the birthmarks aren't the only thing to move. In a way."

"Time moves differently for us," Tancho explained. "Everything around us is slowed to a crawl, but we remain the same."

Everyone stared, disbelieving. "Let us show you," Crow said. "We stand right here before you." He held out his hand for Tancho, and as soon as they touched and time slowed, they ran to the far end of the library, and turning back to face them, they dropped hands. "And now we are here."

Everyone stared for a long beat of silence, then erupted with questions and disbelief. "How did you do that? How is that possible? What trickery is that?"

"We cannot explain it," Crow said as they walked back. "We found it quite by accident."

"I bet you did," Soko said. Then his eyes went wide. "That's how you ran past us in the snow fight! That's how you beat us!"

Crow laughed and the sound curled in Tancho's belly. "That was the first time we tried that," Crow added.

"How can you move so fast?" Samiel asked.

"We don't," Tancho explained. "We don't move fast. We stay the same. Everyone else slows down."

"Why are you just telling us this now?" Karasu asked. "Why the secret?"

"Because we didn't know what to make of it," Tancho said. "We don't know how it works, and we thought perhaps we might need the element of surprise."

Erelis smiled at them. "Just as well you did. Because Maghdlm may know all our plans and ploys, but she doesn't know of this."

Tancho smiled at Crow. "No, she does not."

Crow's dark eyes hardened. "Perhaps she doesn't. But rest assured, she knows more about us, about our birthmarks, about the eclipse, and this lacuna—whatever that even is—than all of us combined. She's played us like a fiddle the whole time."

"Why would she teach us how to use the doorways?" Kohaku asked. "Doesn't that work against her?"

Crow shook his head. "Not necessarily. Because you know what we did? We took her to each of our kingdoms. We gave her a guarded escort to the four ends of our kingdoms."

"For what?" Elmwood asked. "What did she need?"

"I don't know," Crow answered. "She did collect her compounds. The potassium, lanthanum, vanadium, indium."

"That doesn't explain how we found her badly beaten," Samiel said. "She was near dead."

Crow nodded. "We assumed she was the victim. I'm beginning to think we rescued the wrong person."

"Who was the right person?" Tancho asked.

He shrugged. "I don't know. But we need to get to Aequi Kentron and find out. No more waiting, no more playing. There are too many unanswered questions, and let's not forget an entire battalion of strange creatures walked into this very castle and used that doorway."

Tancho nodded and turned to Asagi and Erelis. "We're going to need those element components. The potassium, lanthanum, vanadium, indium. We need to open that door."

Elmwood grinned. "Kicking arse in broad daylight. I like it."

CROW WANTED to practise opening the doorway before doing it for real. Better to fumble the opening to his Northlands than to Aequi Kentron. And just as well, because the first time the circle sparked to life but then fizzled out before it opened. Giving Maghdlm a warning shot wasn't in their plans for surprise.

They only had one chance to get this right.

But it worked the second time, and they all stepped through briefly to alert Crow's men to have the army ready at the gate. Erelis, Asagi, Sirocco, and Oaken would see the Eastlands and Southlands were told the same, then go back to studying the ancient books. They each said goodbye to their mentors, and Tancho felt strange saying goodbye to Asagi this time. It felt too final for his liking, but he pushed those feelings down as they stepped into Northlands.

Tancho needed to be focused.

But both Samiel and Elmwood stared out the windows of Crow's castle in disbelief at the golden sun setting over the majestic mountains and snow, even though their stay was all too brief. "It's beautiful, is it not?" Tancho asked. "When this is all done, we will see more, and we will *be* more, yes?"

Samiel gave a hard nod. "I would like that."

"I as well," Elmwood agreed.

Crow joined them, having refixed the arrows on the compass to point to the centre circle. "Are we ready to do this?" Everyone nodded, and then he turned to Tancho. "Are you?"

Tancho gave him a smile. "Yes. Whatever happens, we stay together. You and me."

"Together," he whispered. Then he took some of the element components and sprinkled the compass. Purple sparks lit the room as the circle spun to life. It opened just enough for them to see into. Tancho could make out a chaos of movement at the doorway opening.

"Now!" Crow yelled, and Samiel and Elmwood threw in a smoke bomb each, and Crow closed the doorway before they exploded.

And then they waited.

THE FEW MINUTES it would take the smoke to clear dragged like hours.

Tancho took in the faces around him. Elmwood, dressed in his green leathers, his axe at the ready. Kearmore and Cardwick were just as big as him, just as broad, with short brown hair and square jaws, and just as handsome. They had axes and bows and arrows, blades strapped to their legs.

Samiel stood tall and proud, her long braids tied back, her bow in her hand, quiver at her back. Her two guards,

Addax and Fazluna, mirrored their queen, the three of them dressed all in russet red.

Karasu and Kohaku, Tancho's closest friends, stood beside him. They wore their white armoured vests over their white uniforms, matching Tancho's. Kohaku's long white hair was pulled back from his face; Karasu's black hair was braided. Tancho had tied the top of his hair back to keep it from his face.

Tancho noticed that Karasu and Soko stood a little closer to each other now, and they quite often would murmur things to each other no one else could hear. He liked Soko and in a way he hoped Karasu did find happiness with him. She deserved it. Soko was roguish and charming, always with a smile, perhaps the opposite of Karasu. But just like her, he was also skilled with a sword and dagger and dedicated to his king and country. And there Soko stood, dressed in his black leather and armours with his sword in hand, ready to defend everyone who stood alongside him.

Tancho had once joked that whoever won over Karasu would need a spine of steel, and perhaps Crow was right. Perhaps they were a good match.

And Crow . . .

Dressed in black, his broadsword in hand, he had fire in his eyes, with determination to defend and protect. As if he could stalk through Aequi Kentron and conquer anyone foolish enough to stand in his way. Oh, sweet abyss, he was a formidable sight. Looking at him, standing beside him, Tancho's heart was taken.

There was no going back after this.

Whatever happened on the other side of that doorway, whatever this new day held for them, Tancho's heart would belong to Crow.

Of that he was certain.

He closed his eyes and tried to imagine, blocking everything else out, and pretended he could hear the sound of the waves of his home. The ebb and flow, the reassuring pull and push of the water's pulse gave Tancho a moment of peace and strength.

He felt Crow's warm and familiar fingers grip his own, and Tancho knew the world had slowed down around him by the lack of sound. He opened his eyes and smiled.

"Are you okay?" Crow asked.

"I am. Just taking a moment to clear my mind, that's all." Tancho looked at the people standing next to them, slowed as they were in time. "I wish we could capture this moment forever."

Crow looked around them, his eyes falling on Soko last. "I wish that as well. I am stricken to think some of us may not return."

"He'll be fine," Tancho said gently.

Crow met his gaze. "If something were to happen to you . . ."

"How can it when I'll be with you?"

Crow studied Tancho's eyes, searching for something. "You have to return with me. When we first met, I wasn't sure I'd survive one day *with* you. And now I cannot fathom a day with*out* you."

Tancho's heart soared and he chuckled. "So let us live to annoy each other another day."

Crow nodded and kissed him with so much tenderness it took Tancho's breath away. They let go of each other's hand and the room around returned to normal.

"Are we ready?" Crow asked.

Everyone nodded, so Crow opened the doorway. It was dark on the other side, but no blue guards ran at them.

"There's no movement in there now," Elmwood said, peering as closely as he dared.

When the circle of sparks was big enough, guards snuck through first, taking a defensive formation, then Soko, Karasu and Kohaku, then Elmwood and Samiel, and lastly Tancho and Crow.

Something was wrong, Tancho knew immediately. It was far too dark. He looked up to find there was no glass dome ceiling above them.

They weren't in the grand hall of the Aequi Kentron.

"Where the fuck are we?" Crow hissed.

And somewhere far off, though Tancho couldn't be sure how far exactly, a blue arcane lamp lit up. With that faint light, he could see they were in some huge cavernous space, rank with damp and aeons of time.

And someone, or something, was coming.

CHAPTER NINETEEN

THE SOUND of the approaching footsteps drew louder and the guards quickly took a spearhead formation in front.

The blue light faltered a little, from what Crow could see, as though the person coming toward them considered stopping. "I come in peace," a female voice said as she ran. "I mean no harm."

Aelfflaed came into view, the blue arcane lamp she held swaying in the darkness. Crow could see her hair in disarray, her shirtsleeve was torn, and her face marked with grime and what appeared to be a yellowing bruise on her cheek. "I am so glad to see you," she said.

"Stop right there," Soko said. He stood tall, his sword raised. "Do not come any closer."

She nodded, eyed the swords aimed at her head, and swallowed hard. "Apologies. I wasn't thinking. There are so few of us left, I . . ."

"So few of who left?" Crow asked. "Where are the others? And, where are we?"

"We stand in the old house," she explained, gesturing to where they stood. "The original Aequi Kentron, a few thousand years old, a hundred feet below the Aequi Kentron you know of today. This here is the first grand hall, and you're standing on *the* compass. The one that started it all."

"Started what?" Tancho asked.

"The doorways," she replied. "We never knew about them. I mean, we learned about them as part of our histories, the old-world myths. We never knew they even worked until . . . until it was too late and those—" Her chin wobbled and her voice cracked. "—those awful things came through."

Crow was out of patience. "I suggest you start talking without the riddles and the tears because we are out of time. And to be blunt, I'm not sure who to trust."

"You can trust us," a deep voice said in the darkness. Gabel and Adelais walked into the light, and every blade, spear, arrow, and axe was now aimed at them. They raised their hands. "Only we three survived."

"The Grand Elder, the Historian and the Truth Seer," Crow said. "Three elders from nine?"

"Four," Tancho corrected. "Maghdlm yet lives."

Aelfflaed, Adelais, and Gabel all sneered. "She's no elder. She's a traitor," Aelfflaed said as if the words tasted like poison. "I am a truth seer, as you say, but I saw nothing in her. She tricked me all these years. She somehow hid her truth."

"From all of us," Adelais said, her hand on Aelfflaed's arm. "She hid the truth and betrayed all of us."

Crow wasn't sure what to make of their display, and he sure as the blue skies above didn't know whom to trust.

Gabel gave a nervous smile. "We are very glad to see you. All of you. And from all four lands, especially. You have come to help, yes?"

"To help with what?" Crow asked. "We don't know much of anything."

Adelais straightened and raised her chin, her eyes defensive. "Please tell me it was you who sent through those smoke bombs."

"Yes," Samiel said coolly. "Though it seems they were wasted."

"Oh no, they were very much put to good use." Aelfflaed waved the lamp to one side, the arc of light showing several large bodies on the ground. Everyone flinched, and Crow put himself between the bodies and Tancho. "They're not dead."

"No, they're not," Samiel replied. "But they will sleep for hours. How are you three not affected?"

"We've been hiding in the archīvum. The entrance is that way." Gabel pointed down toward where Aelfflaed had run from. "Six of them kept guard of this compass. They would take shifts of several hours. We don't think the others above ground know some of their men are down."

"How long until the next guards come down?" Crow asked.

"Four hours, maybe," Adelais replied. "It's hard to tell. Time has been . . . strange."

"Strange?" Crow asked. "How so?"

"We don't know if it's because we have been underground all this time, but we have lost track of days." She made a face. "We think."

Maybe a few hours. At least they had some time. "We need light," Crow said. "Lamps and torches. Where are they?"

"We snuffed them to stay hidden," Adelais said, sheepishly. "These creatures, they don't see too well in the dark."

"Creatures?" Soko asked.

Aelfflaed nodded and walked over to where the six bodies were lying sprawled on the floor. The light was blue so it played tricks on the eyes, and Crow could see they wore scraps of leather as armour, barely covering their bulging muscles and huge hand-like claws. And the stench was putrid. They stank like a rancid butcher's block. But their faces . . .

They had a line of ridges down their foreheads, higher and wider cheekbones, and mottled and pallid skin. It was hard to tell because of the dark, and the blue light made them appear two weeks' dead, but the word creatures seemed an apt description.

Crow had heard Asagi's description, but he never really believed it. Not that he doubted Asagi's word, it just seemed too absurd to be real. But here they were . . .

"Where on earth have they come from?" Elmwood wondered out loud.

"Not this world," Crow said.

Gabel came back with torches and, using Aelfflaed's lamp, quickly lit them up. Light crept along the floor and walls, dissolving shadows as it went, and Crow could make out more of the huge room they were in.

It was, or had once been, a cave some two hundred feet long, perhaps eighty feet wide. The ceiling must have been a hundred feet high, the walls of dark grey stone carved by nothing but time, but there were inscriptions in an old language scratched into the rock.

The floor was stone also, but for the huge compass they stood upon. Not tiles like the other compasses Crow had seen, but these were stones, huge and worn, yet he could make out the directions. They were more runes than letters, and he had to wonder at the age of this place.

Tancho seemed to gather his wits a lot sooner than Crow and slid his katana home in its scabbard. He pointed to the compass. "We need to open this doorway again and get our armies through as fast as we can. These . . . beasts"—he pointed to the sleeping creatures—"should be restrained. We need to mark entries and exits and devise a new plan. We hadn't expected to arrive underground so we need to adapt." Then he stared at the three remaining elders that, now with more light, Crow could see were all a grimy, dishevelled mess. Tancho didn't seem to care. "And let us make one thing very clear. We are in charge now. The Elders' Consul is no more, and the four of us—Crow, Elmwood, Samiel, and me—give the orders, as do our personal guards. If anyone here with us asks you a question, answer them. If they ask you to do something, do it. We need your help to take back Aequi Kentron, so you're either with us or against us."

The three of them nodded and Aelfflaed wiped at a tear. Adelais bowed her head. "We stand with you."

"You bring armies?" Gabel asked, hopeful. "You will challenge them and take back control?"

"We're not going to challenge them," Tancho answered. "They dare walk into *my* home and demand access to Aequi Kentron? No, we're not going to challenge them. We're going to *kill* them."

The three elders blinked owlishly at Tancho, but Crow met Tancho's eyes, seeing nothing but fire and determination in them, and smiled.

SAMIEL AND ELMWOOD practised their doorway opening to all four kingdoms, and the huge cavernous and ancient grand hall began to fill with rows of soldiers. Each dressed in their uniforms of white, black, green, and red, they came with supplies and an arsenal of swords, knives, arrows, and spears.

Soko, Karasu, and Kohaku were in charge of settling the ranks and giving instructions, and for the most part, despite the number, the soldiers were quiet. The guards from east and south were in charge of restraining the sleeping creatures, and Crow wasn't bothered when they did so none too gently.

Crow, Tancho, Samiel, and Elmwood sat with Adelais, Aelfflaed, and Gabel and grilled them for information.

Though they had tried to remain hidden, they had also tried to find out what they could. The creatures had two commanders; both had a different armour to the rest of the battalion with two silver stripes across the right shoulder. They had noticed two others with one stripe, and it appeared to be some kind of rank and insignia. Apart from that, the rest of them appeared the same.

"We should aim to take out the chain of command," Tancho said.

"Their armour appears to be an old leather of some kind," Elmwood said, after another brief inspection of the sleeping creatures. "It protects the chest and neck. They wear hard boots to below the knee. So if we hit them, we aim for the knee, under the arm, and into the chest cavity, or at the base of the skull."

Crow gave him a nod, pleased. "Good assessment, friend."

"They are strong," Gabel said, fear evident on his face. "They are not like anything I've seen. They move fast and without mercy."

"We watched them kill our friends," Adelais whispered. "They simply grabbed them and ended them, without effort. Broken necks, crushed skulls. They . . . feast on the innards . . ." She paled, clearly reliving those ghastly memories. "Without mercy."

Feast on the innards? *Oh, blue skies. What kind of monsters were these?*

Tancho pursed his lips. "Speaking of crushed skulls, we found Maghdlm in the archīvum. We heard her cries for help and found her lying in a pool of her own blood. We assumed she'd survived the attack. We found no one else."

"When we heard of the invasion in the Westlands, we called an emergency meeting," Adelais said. "Maghdlm did not attend. We didn't know where she was. Then some guards alerted us to the compass in the old house sparking to life. We sent our guards but they did not return. We found them all dead at the door . . ." She motioned to the end of the hall. "Richart and Perun raced in first and were met by the two commanders, with the stripes . . . they lifted them up off the ground by their necks and ripped out their bellies . . ." Her voice trailed off.

"We tried to run," Gabel said weakly. "I grabbed Adelais and Aelfflaed and we hid in the archīvum and the creatures chased, capturing the others, killing them all. There are rows upon rows of stacks in the library. We hid amongst the books, too scared to make a sound."

"Maghdlm was there," Aelfflaed added. "She gave orders in a language I've never heard. She spoke to them in their tongue. They took to the stairs and we thought you might have been killed. We were so worried." She shook her head, teary again. "We thought we'd failed the four kingdoms. We thought for sure . . ."

"We noticed everyone was gone," Tancho said. "And after finding Maghdlm, we left without delay."

Crow frowned at the three remaining elders. "Hmm. Forgive my scepticism but I'm finding your story unlikely."

They stared back at him, fearful and almost desperate. "Which part?" Adelais asked.

"All of it." He shrugged. "And I'm trying to think of any good reason why we shouldn't kill you here and now."

Tancho reached out and grabbed Crow's hand, bringing everything and everyone around them to a near stop. "I'm not sure what to make of it either," he said quickly. "But killing them won't help us. We can use them. If they are innocent, they deserve a chance to prove it. If they are not, they may give us some information, whether intentionally or not. But we need to be patient. Hear them out."

Crow bit back his anger, because he knew Tancho was right. But something wasn't adding up. There was too much treachery, too many lies. "I don't like it."

Tancho nodded. "Nor do I. If they side with Maghdlm and their ploy is to lead us into a trap, I will help you kill them."

Crow sighed. He looked at the three elders, their faces frozen masks of horror at his threat to kill them. "Fine. But I still don't trust them."

"And I trust your judgement," Tancho said. "But let us see where they decide to lead us first."

Tancho let go of Crow's hand, and the speed of time returned to normal. "What Crow means to say is," Tancho said, "the waters of truth are muddied when we are tired and under threat. We hope that none of our questions have upset you."

Adelais raised her hand, waving him off. "We, too, understand, the ordeal you have been through. But what we say is the truth."

"If you have been down here for a week, what have you eaten?" Crow asked.

"Scraps discarded by the . . . creatures," Gabel replied.

"They don't appear to care for human food. They threw away what they didn't eat. Though they drink the wine from our kitchens and sleep when they're supposed to watch the compass."

Aelfflaed's nostrils flared. "They are loud and crude, and they laugh the most hideous sound. They are . . ."

"They are what?"

"The things of nightmares." She shuddered. "They are monsters and I don't blame you for your doubts about us, but I'm so grateful you returned. We'll do whatever we can to help you."

"I have searched the archīvum," Gabel said. "What I could search, anyway. I've spent many years studying these books and there are books here older than I can explain." He made a face.

"What did you find?" Crow demanded.

"A book written in the old tongue. A language long forgotten. I've tried to translate, but it is something that makes no sense."

"Nothing of this makes sense," Crow shot back at him. "What did you find? Where did these creatures come from?"

"A land not of this world," Gabel whispered. "A reality that is not our own."

"Not our reality?" Samiel repeated.

"How is that possible?" Elmwood demanded.

Gabel shrugged. "I do not know. How are the doorways possible? How is any of it possible?"

"Then why did they arrive at the Westlands first?" Tancho asked.

"I have no answer for that," Gabel replied.

"Maybe they couldn't access this doorway first," Adelais suggested. "Maybe they had to choose another doorway in this world first so they could access this one. We don't know."

Crow glared at her. "What do you know?"

"They are called Ascii," Gabel said, intervening. "It means to be without a shadow."

"Without a shadow?" Crow replied sharply. *What in the . . . ?*

Gabel threw his hands up. "I said it made no sense! How does one not have a shadow?"

"Because they come from a world lit by two suns," Tancho replied. "It is the same in that book of fiction I read as a boy. How can one cast a shadow when the suns shine at all angles?"

"That book," Crow said. "What else do you remember?"

Tancho shook his head. "I, uh . . . The Ascii were a race of creatures on a different planet . . ."

"You mentioned a quest," Crow pressed.

"Yes. They needed to find a new world." Tancho's pale face grew paler still. "They travelled by the stars. When the stars aligned, it created a . . . road, of sorts. I read it so long ago . . ."

"The stars are aligning now," Samiel said.

"The eclipse," Tancho whispered. "They arrive here in time for the eclipse. When the sun is blocked by two moons. It cannot be a coincidence."

Gabel nodded. "There was a chart, but it is not written in any language I know."

"Show us," Crow said. "Now we are getting somewhere. Now we are getting answers."

Gabel scurried away to return holding out a book. He began frantically flipping to a certain page and turned the book around to show them. The book was old, the pages weren't any kind of papyrus Crow had ever seen; mottled and thick, brittle and stiff. The writing, if that's what it even was, appeared to be no more than faded scratches and scrawling.

Crow carefully lifted the page and inspected it on both sides. There were fine patterns, tiny filigree lines, uneven texture. *Surely not* . . . "This . . . paper," he said slowly, "is not paper at all, is it?"

Gabel shook his head. "No. I . . . I think it is skin. The same mottled skin as the creatures. The cover is a leather, but from which creature, I don't know."

Crow shuddered. "So this is not a drawing, as such, and more of a tattoo. Inked into the skin of the creature, then cut out and used as a paper."

Gabel nodded. "It is hard to say for certain, but perhaps. I cannot guess at the age of this tome, or its origins. I don't know from where it came."

"Or how it came to be here," Adelais added with a shrug. "There are tens of thousands of books, probably others just like it yet to be found."

"Maghdlm's book had similar writing," Tancho said, drawing their attention back to the book. He pointed to the tattoo. "And this was in her book also."

The drawing was a straight line down the middle of the page, marked with a series of circles and dots. There were lines and arcs and notations in that scratchy writing that no one could read, but one thing was very clear. It wasn't a drawing, per se; it was a chart.

"What is this a map of?" Crow asked.

"The skies," Gabel answered. "At least, we think."

He pointed to the circle at the centre of the page. "This is us. The Aequi Kentron, the equal centre." Then he moved to the circle above it. "The first moon. Here is the second. This is the sun."

Crow pointed to the series of small dots at either end of the page. "What are these?"

"Constellations," Gabel said. "This one here is Corvus." And then he pointed his finger at the second one. "This is Pisces."

Crow turned to Tancho. "Corvus and Pisces," he whispered.

Tancho stared right back at him. "The crow and the fish. The constellations of us, the eclipse."

"This eclipse also aligns with the crow and fish constellations, passing directly over Aequi Kentron," Gabel explained. "This line"—he pointed to the line in the tattoo—"intersects perfectly."

"It explains the bond between you," Adelais said. "And why, when Maghdlm discovered the Corvus and Pisces connection, she left in such a hurry. When she saw your birthmarks react at the initiation ceremony, she didn't rush to the archīvum to research. She rushed through the archīvum to this old grand hall to the ancient compass."

"To send a message?" Elmwood asked.

"It is what we assume," Aelfflaed answered. "A signal, perhaps."

"If she could send a signal through the doorway," Samiel said. "Why not just open it to the creatures? Why have them go through the Westlands and alert us?"

"No," Tancho said, shaking his head slowly. "They had arrived at my castle before then. They arrived the day after we left. Asagi sent those riders with that message the day after we left. It was a six-day ride. Six days before the initiation ceremony."

"If those Ascii creatures were already down here, where

we sit right now," Crow said coldly. He stared at the three elders. "Then your story doesn't add up. Because it took us six days to ride back to Westlands with an injured Maghdlm, and that was two days ago."

The three of them stared, blinking quickly. "But it has to," Gabel said. "We're not lying."

Crow stood up and drew his sword. "And you're not telling us the truth either! So which is it?"

Adelais' eyebrows knitted. "How can it be eight days? The eclipse is four days from now. That doesn't add up."

"The eclipse is tomorrow," Tancho stated flatly. "A few hours from now."

They each shook their heads. "It can't be . . ." Aelfflaed mumbled. She became teary again and put her dirty hand to her forehead. "Nothing makes sense. Time is not as it should be."

"Time cannot change," Crow snapped. "It cannot be altered as if a toy on a string—"

He stopped cold, realisation washing over him like a flurry of ice. He sat back down, woodenly, his mind trying to make sense of what was somehow the truth.

"But it can," Tancho murmured. "Time *can* change."

He reached over and slid his hand over Crow's, as if proving a point, and everything around them all but stopped. "The more we try to understand," Tancho murmured. "The less it makes sense."

"The days are wrong," Crow whispered. "How can the days be wrong?"

"I don't know. Perhaps it's not the days so much as it is this line of the sun and the moons and the stars." Tancho studied Crow's face, finally settling on his eyes. "But I don't think they're lying. I think they believe what they've been through. They understand it no more than we do, and we're not lying."

Crow sighed again and glowered at Tancho for good measure. "You can stop coming at me with reason and common sense."

Tancho almost smiled. "That's not going to happen." He squeezed Crow's hand before letting it go.

"How can time change?" Adelais asked, not privy to Crow and Tancho's private conversation.

"Time has not been exactly true for us this last week," Crow replied. "We've not lost days though. The eclipse is tomorrow."

They sat back, slumping almost, with exhaustion and disbelief. "Then we need to act now," Gabel mumbled. "We can't delay."

"What do you know of the eclipse?" Tancho asked. "And the lacuna? Maghdlm called it by that name but gave nothing but riddles after that."

"I heard her say that," Adelais said. "A lacuna is the space between, or a gap between. How that relates to you and your birthmarks, I do not know. When the marks at your wrist reacted at the initiation ceremony, it was the first we knew of it. It was unexpected to say the very least."

"Unexpected to everyone but Maghdlm," Tancho replied.

Crow turned to Tancho. "She said the space between us is no space at all. That's what she said. Before she ran off."

"What do you think she meant?" Tancho asked.

"I have no idea. But I'd really like to go up to the ground level, find her, and . . . ask."

Tancho smiled, a little sinister, a lot handsome. "Same."

Samiel cocked her head with a frown. "If this is the *old* grand hall and compass down here, what is the new one in the new grand hall for? Does that compass work as the others do?"

That was a really good question. Everyone looked to Adelais, given she was the leader of all the elders.

"We don't know," she answered apologetically. "We weren't aware the compass could even be a doorway. And we haven't been to ground level since . . . since . . ."

"I think it's safe to assume whatever its purpose isn't for our benefit," Crow said.

"Then let us go," Samiel said, getting to her feet. "The answers we seek are above us."

"Agreed," Elmwood added as he stood. "Let's see this done."

They turned to face their rows of soldiers waiting patiently for their orders. The long hall was pitch black where light couldn't reach, and Crow didn't like that. The sooner they were above ground, the better.

"What is that way?" Tancho asked, pointing to the back of the hall.

"There was an exit but it was sealed a long time ago. Hundreds of years ago, to be sure," Adelais said.

"Where does Aequi Kentron source its water?" Tancho pressed.

The three elders were clearly taken aback by the question. Random, perhaps, but Tancho was from the Westlands, a kingdom built around water.

"I, uh . . ." Adelais said, "I believe there is a well."

"You believe?" Tancho asked, his head tilted just so.

"There have been maintenance teams who take care of such things," she replied.

Tancho went to his knee and put his palm to the stone ground. He closed his eyes and inhaled, and Crow found himself standing closer, protecting him while he made himself vulnerable.

"There is water below us," Tancho said, standing up.

"You can feel that?" Crow asked.

He nodded. "I can."

"What does that mean?" Samiel asked. "The water, it is significant?"

Tancho looked at the three elders when he answered. "It means there may possibly be another entry point." He turned to the darkened end of the hall. "I think we should go that way."

Crow considered this. "Splitting up has its advantages, but we don't know what lies that way. At least we know what we'll face this way."

"We sit here with one exit," Tancho replied. "Cornered and without any other means of escape."

"Shh," Karasu hissed. "Listen!"

Crow couldn't hear anything, but Tancho, Karasu, and Kohaku could. They drew their weapons. "It's too late now," Tancho said, pulling Crow behind him. "We have company. Heavy feet, maybe six of them."

Kohaku, Karasu, and Soko took two men from each army, signalled for them to be quiet, and they raced down toward the entry. Six Ascii burst through without a care, complacent in their approach. Large creatures, as tall as Kohaku but bigger, stronger.

Caught by surprise and with no chance of sounding a warning, they were slain before they realised what was happening. Kohaku and Karasu were fluid and graceful, the two Eastlanders were swift, and the Southlanders were strong. The Northlanders, including Soko, were beautifully brutal.

The only sounds the Ascii made were the bodies hitting

the floor. Not even a quiet gasp of surprise, not even a gargle of blood from an open larynx.

They pulled the bodies out of view and ran back to formation. Soko held up his sword to show it was covered in blue-green blood. "Safe to say they are not from here."

"They smell," Karasu said, her expression one of disgust. "Worse than acrid."

"Their flesh does not pierce easily," Kohaku added.

"We attack now," Tancho said. "There is no more time for back up plans. The creatures who are asleep were to finish their shift and will be missed any minute. Others will come looking and we can't be caught here. We're cornered here with only one way out."

Crow nodded. "Agreed." Then he looked at Samiel, Elmwood, and the guards. "Remember our plan. Stick together, and be safe. Watch your backs."

They all nodded. "You two, as well," Samiel said. Then she nudged Elmwood. "Come. We'll take the east and south."

"And that leaves the west and north for us," Tancho said to Crow. Then his smile faltered. "Stay close and don't you dare get hurt."

Crow couldn't help but smile. He lifted Tancho's chin, slowing time for just a moment, and stole a quick kiss. "Same goes for you, my little fish."

CHAPTER TWENTY

THE PLAN WAS SIMPLE. Well, as simple as a plan could be when they'd had only a few minutes to draw one. Upon reaching ground level, Samiel and Elmwood would go southeast, Crow and Tancho would go northwest. Their scores of armed soldiers would split equally with them, and they would flank back to the new grand hall where they expected Maghdlm and her men to be.

The new grand hall was where it made sense for them to be, for there was the biggest compass in all the kingdoms.

Whatever she had planned to come through it was either large or large in number.

They were to take out as many of the Ascii creatures as they could, all if they were able.

Tancho could suspend disbelief enough to reckon these creatures, these Ascii monsters, were not of this world. As if their appearance was not enough to convince him, but they bled green blood.

Whatever they'd come here for, they would not get it. Tancho and Crow and Samiel and Elmwood would make sure of that.

As they ran into the archīvum, they went their separate ways. Crow and Tancho ran for the stairs they'd taken when they found Maghdlm and they would hold point while every last soldier made it to the top.

The armies were a deliberate mix of white, black, green, and red. Each had differing skillsets, different weapons, and Tancho liked how they came together for one cause.

There was no single flag they fought under. They were a united kingdom, if but for one day. It filled Tancho with a pride he'd not believed possible.

"These walls," Crow said. "The dark grey stone, it matches the cave walls below. The new grand hall is sandstone. One has to wonder when it was built."

Tancho nodded. "And why."

"Do you get the feeling this day has been coming for some time?"

"I do." Tancho grit his teeth. "I get the feeling we were primed for this. Subject to this fate by our birthright."

Crow frowned but conceded a nod. "Whatever Maghdlm has set into motion, we will stop."

The last of the soldiers came up the stairs and Tancho and Crow ran through their lines to the front. They ran back out the way they had gone when they'd left Aequi Kentron the week before, through a small courtyard toward the stables.

The light of the sun was strange. Golden and muted, as though someone had put a gold silk curtain across the sky. There were no sounds but the fall of their feet on the stones. Not a bird, not another soul, creature or human, and as they neared the stables. Tancho realised not even a horse made a whisper.

And the smell soon told Tancho why.

In the stables, any horse that had remained was now

dead in its stall. Slaughtered . . . No, not even slaughtered. Butchered without respect for the life that was lost. Hacked open, innards spread and ransacked, limbs and skin hewed off, leaving only the peeled and rotting remains.

"I think we just found out what those creatures have been eating," Crow said, his mouth a grim line.

Tancho hadn't expected alien creatures to be well-practised cooks in a human kitchen, but this . . . this was a cruel carnage.

Crow raised his hand and gave the signal for the soldiers to keep moving. They made their way through the stables in lines of two, along the cobblestone paths toward the entrances they'd been shown to when they'd first arrived.

That's when they heard it.

Cries of battle and the bellows of monsters from the other side of the castle.

"Samiel and Elmwood," Tancho whispered. "They've encountered the Ascii."

"Then now is our chance," Crow whispered. "The grand hall will be left empty if the creatures run toward the fight."

Tancho nodded, his heart in his throat, and together he and Crow ran side by side into the main building of the Aequi Kentron . . . and right into a legion of Ascii monsters.

Tancho and Crow both skidded to a stop before them. Their huge shoulders and arms were like boulders, their hands the size of baskets, with talons for nails. Those ugly ridges down their foreheads, their eyes too far apart, they had teeth like wild hogs. They wore their blue armour over blue mottled, skin and one of them opened its jaw and screamed. The sound was so loud and awful, so piercing it raised bile in Tancho's throat and turned his belly to ice.

He almost dropped his katanas to cover his ears, but

Crow swung his sword, almost pirouetting like a dancer, slicing the creature's throat. The scream cut off with a gurgle and then all bedlam broke loose.

The soldiers advanced and swung and sliced, pierced and punctured. Necks, knees, and under the arm, as they'd been told.

Soon enough, twelve Ascii creatures lay in pools of green and blue blood and guts, to the stench of sulphur and rot. Only two of their soldiers had been injured, with gashes across their arms and a graze to the neck.

Uninjured, Tancho could hardly catch his breath. "What was that noise?"

"I don't know," Crow murmured. "But a warning sound if I had to guess. We can expect more." He touched his shoulder, and while time didn't slow down because it wasn't skin to skin, the touch itself gave Tancho strength. "Are you well enough to continue? You were worse affected than I."

Tancho nodded. "I am. Apologies for my inaction. I'll be better prepared next time." He took a smoke bomb from his stash Samiel had given them. "And I'd rather hear them sleep than scream."

Crow nodded and they moved on, into the corridors of the Aequi Kentron that now seemed neither familiar nor welcoming.

Gone was the pristine appearance and immaculate cleanliness, and in its place was dirt, discarded and half-eaten rotting food thrown to the floor and kicked out of the way or trampled into the stone tiles. The stench was cloying and thick, and it stuck to the back of Tancho's throat.

They rounded a corner, nearing the western quarters Tancho had stayed in, where the corridors diverged into two. Crow signalled for half the soldiers to head along the northern hall, while he and Tancho made their way to the grand hall. About halfway along, another team of Ascii creatures came running toward them.

They were still some forty metres away and Tancho signalled for the Southlander with a bow and arrow to take aim. Tancho threw a smoke bomb high and fast above the creatures, the arrow pierced it perfectly, spilling sleep-inducing smoke over them like a morning mist.

They stopped, swayed, spluttered, and one of the creatures opened his pig-like mouth, and just when Tancho expected an ear-piercing scream, it staggered back and fell, taking its hoard of friends down like sleeping dominos.

They had to wait a minute or two until the smoke had dissipated, and every second felt like a day. "How many more of those smoke bombs do you have left?" Crow asked.

"Three."

"Shame it's not three hundred."

"If Samiel had more time . . ."

Crow made a face. "How do you think they're doing?"

"I have faith in them," Tancho replied. "They have skill and numbers."

Crow didn't look convinced. "I'm second-guessing our decision to split our teams."

"It was the right decision," Tancho murmured. "Tactically, and practically."

He winced. "I worry for them."

"As do I. But we need to worry about us right now. And I don't like standing still here. I feel caught."

Crow gave a nod. "Cover your nose and mouth." He ran toward the pile of sleeping Ascii with his hand over his nose to shield what remained of the smoke, and as he reached the last creature, it stirred, reaching for Crow's foot and raising its head. Crow stuck his sword through its throat, and as the soldiers ran through, they took care of all the others.

None of them would wake from that slumber.

Tancho heard the clang of metal ahead, the sounds of fighting, yelling, screaming. Not the Ascii scream, either.

Human screams.

"This way!" Crow yelled, bypassing the grand hall, and together he and Tancho ran at full speed toward the sounds of war.

The stone corridors were lit with familiar windows, the golden light casting an eerie glow. They had come this way with Adelais once last week, to have some fun with mock fights and displays of skill and ego. But this time, when they got to the stairs to the courtyard, they came to a halt.

There were no mock fights there now. No fake shows of skill or ego.

It was a fully-fledged battle. So many creatures, more than the one hundred Asagi had said walked through the doorway.

Soldiers fought with swords and blades, bows and arrows, axes and spears.

The Ascii creatures didn't need weapons. They had knives for nails, huge arms that could outreach a sword. There were bodies . . . creatures, dead, yes. But also bodies in white, black, red, and green.

Some only injured, trying to crawl away. Some with their throats ripped open, some missing limbs.

A massacre.

Tancho could see Samiel, a fierce sight with her blade and spear, as she slay the creature before her. It took him a moment to find Elmwood, but there he was, hacking his axe through an Ascii as if he were felling a tree.

Tancho flooded with relief that his friends were unharmed.

Crow raised his hand, signalled for the soldiers behind

them to join the fray. Then he turned to Tancho, and Tancho was certain the horror he saw on Crow's face matched his own.

"You stay by me," he hissed, fierce and determined.

Tancho nodded, numb to the realisation of what they were about to do. "Always."

Then Crow turned to Soko. "Fight well, my brother."

Soko gave a grim nod. "I will fight beside you."

Karasu spun her katanas in her hands and narrowed her eyes at Tancho. "And I will fight beside you."

"As will I," Kohaku said, his knuckles white on the hilt of his sword.

Tancho gave a nod. "For Westlands."

Tancho and Crow watched as Soko, Karasu, and Kohaku flew down the stairs, their weapons raised. And as Crow and Tancho neared the bottom step, Tancho took his katana in his left hand and held his right out for Crow.

As soon as they touched, skin to skin, everything around them slowed to a crawl.

Everything except for the Ascii creatures.

They kept moving and several of them let out that awful, ear-piercing screech and Tancho saw one of them grab a frozen-in-time red soldier and slash his throat.

Tancho dropped Crow's hand, the world around them coming to life at a dizzying pace and they found themselves in the middle of battle.

"What in the abyss was that?" Tancho yelled, slicing his katana through an Ascii creature's neck. Green blood sprayed from the wound as it fell to the ground.

"I don't know," Crow answered, as he swung his sword into the head of a creature. The heavy broad sword cut through it like butter. "They're not affected by time."

Their time-slowing trick, their one and only plan, was useless against them.

Tancho didn't have time to think. Another creature came at him, huge hands like battering rams, and Tancho ducked low under its swinging arm, and spinning on his foot, plunged his katana up under the creature's armpit, piercing its chest.

He stood tall as the creature fell and Crow smiled at him as he swung his sword at another creature's arm, slicing it off at the wrist. The creature screamed and Crow silenced it by taking off its head.

He was strength and sheer brute force, and Tancho couldn't help but admire him as he fought. Even sprayed with green blood, Crow was a glorious sight.

But he didn't have time to admire for long. Another creature came at him and Tancho took out his second katana, a sword in each hand, and as the creature came at him, hulking and clumsy, Tancho crossed both blades at its throat at sliced its head off.

And another, and another. He swung, he sliced, he plunged. The creatures seemed unending. There were so many . . . too many.

He saw Karasu and Kohaku holding their own, graceful and lethal, fighting as he knew they would. Soko fought like Crow, the same style, the same type of weapon. How they could be so agile with such a heavy weapon, Tancho would never know.

But as Tancho took on another creature, this one bigger and angrier, he stepped away, vying for a better angle, and he stepped too far away from Crow.

His wrist burned, more painful than he could remember it ever being. And they weren't that far apart.

Had the distance closed even further with the approaching eclipse?

"Crow!" Tancho yelled, his voice taut with pain.

"Tancho!"

But now there were two beasts separating them . . . and another, and the pain was almost unbearable. Tancho could barely hold his sword, let alone use it. The creature took a closer step, its hog-mouth open in a wicked smile, knowing it had the advantage . . .

Tancho dropped his katana, unable to stand the burning pain up his arm one second longer. It was burning him from the inside, turning his bone and blood to ash, he was sure of it. The pain was blinding, all-consuming, and for one split second, he wished for Crow with all his heart. He wished he'd told him how much he loved him, and he wished they'd had more time. But above all, he wished the creature would kill him now just to end the pain.

Tancho held his wrist, fell to his knees, and screamed.

CHAPTER TWENTY-ONE

CROW COULDN'T SEE outside the searing pain. His hand, his arm, felt as though it had been immersed in lava. He wondered how much more he could endure before it killed him . . . He almost wished it would.

Even with two creatures surrounding him, he couldn't think . . .

He needed Tancho. He needed to be near him, to be with him, to hold him.

He needed the pain to end.

But none of that compared to hearing Tancho scream. He'd take the pain every second of every day, he'd take both his own and Tancho's if it meant Tancho was without it.

But it was too much. Excruciating, bewildering, his sword fell to his feet, and he went to his knees. Holding his wrist, he looked up at the golden sun, as the moons closed in on it, the fighting around them, at the two Ascii beasts in front of him.

"Tancho," Crow whispered as the creature raised its talons aimed at Crow's head, ensuring Tancho's name would be his last breath.

Crow waited for the blows to come. The pain of dying this gruesome death would be a relief to the burn that consumed him. It travelled up his arm now, the pain seeping into his chest.

Oh, by the blue skies, if I die here, let Tancho live . . .

But the blow never came. The first creature's eyes went wide as a blade stuck out from its throat. The second creature's head tilted at an odd angle, green blood gushing as a blade sliced through its neck.

Through the haze of pain, Crow could see the figures in white standing where the creatures had been. Karasu and Kohaku . . .

Karasu hooked her arm under Crow's and heaved him to his feet. "Get him closer," she said, as Kohaku's stronger grip picked Crow up and all but threw him on the ground near Tancho.

The pain was gone, but the breathlessness, the haze remained. But Tancho was alive. A gasping mess on the ground, much like Crow, but alive.

Crow groped for him, feeling his chest, his arms, his face, and pulled Tancho in for a kiss. "Thank the blue skies," he murmured.

"Soko saved me," Tancho whispered. He had lines of tears down his face. "I thought I'd lost you."

"The pain is worse," Crow mumbled.

Tancho nodded. "I wanted death."

"We cannot be separated again."

Tancho shook his head and wiped his sleeve across his face, smearing dirt and green blood across his cheek.

Karasu threw Crow's sword to the ground beside them. "Stay together, for the love of the abyss."

Crow looked up at her and Kohaku. "Thank you. I owe you my life."

"Thank me by getting on your feet," Karasu said, turning to fight another creature. Kohaku was already pulling his sword out of the gullet of another.

Crow got to his feet, not even sure they'd hold him, and helped Tancho get to his. They picked up their weapons and Crow searched for Soko . . . he looked for his black uniform but couldn't see him. "Where is Soko?"

Tancho spun to search for him, just as a huge creature fell slowly to its knees, revealing a green-splattered Soko behind it. His chest was heaving, but he grinned at them, just as another beast came up behind him.

"Soko, look out!" Crow cried.

Before Soko could raise his sword, before he could ready his stance, the creature swung for him. Its huge talons aimed for Soko's head, and Crow's breath caught in his lungs . . .

Not like this.

Tancho's arm flung outward and a small blade hit the creature right in the eye, the handle protruding from its socket. It fell to the ground and Soko turned to face him, a shade paler than before and his eyes wide, and gave Tancho a nod.

Karasu flew in and ripped the blade from the creature's skull and pointed it at Soko. "Never turn your back, you damned fool. I'll be so pissed if you die out here, you'll be glad to be dead, you hear me?"

He nodded woodenly, still shaken. He took his sword in hand and when she'd turned back to fight another creature, Soko gave half a smile at Crow and Tancho. "She likes me."

Karasu swung around, aiming her sword at Soko. "I'll show you how much with my blade up your—"

Kohaku had to leap in and finish off her kill. "Are you

all done trying to die?" he roared. He waved his sword around them. "Look where you are."

Kohaku was right. It had been too close a call for all of them.

"Stay close," Crow murmured to Tancho. And they took down more monsters, not risking more than an arm's reach between them. It wasn't ideal, but Crow liked having Tancho at his back. They were stronger together, that much was very clear.

Though he could hardly spare the attention, he loved watching Tancho fight. He moved like water, smooth and with deceiving force. He might have been smaller and lean, but he bore the strength of a tidal wave.

But Crow noticed that Soko, Karasu, and Kohaku were fighting more cautiously now. Thinking smarter and not taking risks like before. But these Ascii creatures didn't seem to stop coming.

"Can we use the smoke bombs out here?" Crow asked.

"No," Tancho said. "If the open air didn't make it useless, it would take down as many of us as it would of them, and they'd slaughter those of us who went to ground asleep."

Crow growled. "How many of these do we have to kill?"

"I think we are besting them," Kohaku said. "I see more of us than them."

"Look!" Soko said, pointing back to the stairs. Some of the creatures were escaping, retreating. "They know they're beaten."

"They're not beaten yet," Tancho said, working his two swords through a beast as it charged.

But they were thinning, Crow realised. There were more human soldiers than rancid beasts now, and they killed them quicker working in teams. Other beasts ran for the stairs and soon enough it was only a mass of bloodied white, black, red and green.

There were bodies everywhere though, human and Ascii, some injured, mostly dead. Soko, sweaty and bloodied, knelt by a slain Northlander, his hand on the dead man's chest. He hung his head for a moment before he stood, meeting Crow's gaze. "Keissi," he claimed, and Crow's heart sank.

He knew that man.

They'd laughed with him a time or two in training rounds, and looking around at the carnage, Crow was certain they'd know a lot more names yet.

"Ah, it is good to see you!" Samiel said as she stepped over the corpse of an Ascii beast. She offered Crow her hand to shake. "Never have I been so grateful than when I saw you all racing down the stairs to join us."

Elmwood soon joined them, mostly covered in green blood, though he had a decent gash on his shoulder. He was breathing hard but smiling. "When I was a boy," he said, "I yearned for excitement and war." He shook his head. "I was a fool."

Crow laughed with some humour but mostly with relief. "You are wounded."

Elmwood looked down at the gash. "I'll live." He turned back to where he'd walked from. "Though I have some injured men. Kearmore needs a healer."

Kearmore was his closest guard, he was what Soko was to Crow. "Is he okay?" Crow asked.

Elmwood nodded. "He took a hard hit. He's tough, but I want him seen to."

"Yes, of course."

Tancho nodded. "We need to get the wounded back to

the doorway. Send them to Westlands where our mentors are. They'll know what to do."

Crow turned back to the building, to the stairs. "We need to finish what we started. There were more than the number that arrived at Westlands. We need to find where they came through and close it off before more arrive."

Samiel pointed her spear to the stairs. "We need to find Maghdlm and put a stop to it all." She looked up to the sky, where the two moons were closing in on a total eclipse of the sun. "We are fast running out of time. The light is doing strange things and the eclipse draws near."

It was true. The sunlight was strange. Golden, yes, but more than that . . . something was off.

"Look," Tancho whispered. "Look at the ground."

Everyone turned their gaze to their feet. The stone tiles, the green blood, the red, and it took Crow a second to realise what was wrong.

"We are without shadows," Tancho murmured, stepping in closer to Crow, their bodies almost touching. "I don't like it."

Crow put his arm around him and pulled him into his side. There were no shadows, no play of light and dark on any surface. Everyone appeared to be two dimensional. "I don't like it either. We need to end this, and end it now. Before the eclipse opens doorways we cannot close."

Tancho, Samiel, and Elmwood all agreed.

"Gather the men that can hold weapons," Samiel said to one of her red guards. "And see the wounded cared for."

The soldiers able to fight were two-third the number than when they started, but those who remained were driven by anger and revenge. Typically not emotions Crow would encourage going into a fight but he hoped it was enough fuel to sustain them.

As they made their way back to the stairs with their legions of blood-splattered troops behind them, Crow gave Karasu a nod. "I still owe you a debt of gratitude for saving my life back there," he said.

The corner of her lip lifted in an almost-smile. "It wasn't for you. If you die, Tancho dies," she replied. "See him live and I'll consider all debts paid."

Crow chuckled. "Done."

"I saved Tancho," Soko said, a clear attempt at trying to get in Karasu's good graces.

She glared at him for his efforts. "And you almost got yourself killed in the process."

"If you have any feelings for me, you only have to—"

Karasu stopped walking and aimed her sword at Soko, making the whole procession of soldiers come to a stop behind them. "I've not seen a man be parted from his ego, but I will—"

"Karasu," Tancho hissed. "Not the time."

"Not the place," Kohaku added as if it was something they'd both said to her a thousand times.

They began walking again and Soko smirked at Crow. "Told you she likes me," he murmured.

"She'll see you parted from more than your ego if you don't hold your tongue," Crow warned.

Soko laughed and Karasu growled at him, but as they began down the corridor toward the grand hall, they fell silent.

And the more Crow listened, the less he heard. The whole of Aequi Kentron was far too silent. "I can't hear them," he said.

"Neither can I," Tancho whispered as they crept forward.

"Where did they go?" Samiel wondered out loud, her hold on her spear and blade tightening.

Elmwood grunted. "Hopefully back to the pits of darkness from which they came."

Crow didn't think that was likely, as much as it was wishful thinking. But they never saw another living creature along the way. Were they all in the grand hall, waiting? Was this an ambush?

"I feel as though we're walking into a trap," Crow mumbled as they approached the huge wooden doors to the grand hall. "When these doors open, be prepared for anything."

As the huge doors opened at their arrival, the four kings stood back and allowed guards of all four colours to take the lead. They advanced into the large room and Crow waited for the sound of a strike . . .

But it never came.

A white guard reappeared at the door and shrugged. "It's empty, sires."

Empty?

Crow and Tancho looked at each other, confused, before they walked into the middle of the very empty and quiet grand hall. It looked just as it did their first night here: pristine, huge, the tiled floor gleaming, and the dome light above shining a golden spotlight onto the compass tiled into the floor.

"She was supposed to be here," Crow said. "The compass, the glass dome above it to show the eclipse . . ."

"If they're not here . . . ," Tancho said.

"Down in the old hall," Samiel said quickly. "The ancient compass."

"Where Adelais and the others are," Crow said, his nostrils flaring with his temper. "If they've lied to us . . ."

Tancho ordered the soldiers to about-face and run back to the underground. Now they were at the rear of the legions and Crow was pissed. Kings should be at the front, the spear's tip. Leaders should lead. "Dammit."

"Should we smash the compass anyway?" Elmwood asked, swinging his axe in a circle as if it weighed nothing. "They can't let in more of those hideous pig-Ascii if we break the door."

Crow shrugged. "It certainly can't hurt."

Elmwood grinned and swung his axe high above his head, bringing it down to the tiles with a jarring crash. The blade cleaved into the stone, directly at the heart of the compass, the sound echoed, resonated in the huge room, but then the sound became something else.

The ringing became laughter and Maghdlm appeared in a circle of sparks as though she'd made a doorway just for her . . .

The small old woman stepped out of it, her cloak pulled up, her smile sinister. She wasn't injured or frail. She was pure evil. "I don't need the compass now," she said, lifting her arms up toward the glass dome. "Now I can command the doors as I wish, with thanks to you, Corvus and Pisces."

Tancho flung his arm out, sending a small blade whistling through the air so fast. But Maghdlm simply disappeared out another door and appeared in another just a few metres away.

The blade clanged and skittered across the floor, and Maghdlm smiled. "The lacuna is mine to command."

"The lacuna?" Crow asked.

"The space between is no space at all," she replied. "Once you know how to use it. Space and time mean nothing when you can step between them. And this? Was never what it seemed." She waved her hand and the room around them shimmered, blinking in and out before it changed. Gone was the pristine grand hall, its gleaming white tiles and perfect columns, and they now found themselves surrounded by old grey stone, dark and drab. And not only that . . . Maghdlm's human form was gone now too.

Her size didn't change at all, but her skin was now a mottled blue, her nose a muzzle of hog-like teeth. She wasn't Maghdlm, she wasn't a frail healer or a grand elder.

She was Ascii.

"What do you want?" Tancho asked her.

"What is rightfully mine," she sneered. "What should have been mine a thousand years ago."

"Death?" Karasu asked. "Because we can give you that."

Maghdlm hissed, an ugly snout of tusks and tongue. "The last Golden Eclipse, a thousand human years ago, was fought in the Great War. The doorways were closed, but I still remained. Left behind, I summoned the power of alchemy and the stars, putting a glamour over Aequi Kentron, the largest doorway. I made the Consul, I made your kingdoms what they are today. I spent my time in the catacombs below, building our new cities. Allowing you on the surface to grow and breed, a rich feast for my kind. For this day. The day of the Ascii has come."

"The only thing that comes for your kind is death," Tancho spat.

"How many men do you have left?" Maghdlm asked, her voice as cold as her eyes. "Because I have a whole world of Ascii. Tens of thousands of them, just waiting—"

Crow raised his sword at her. "What do you want?"

"I want it all," she replied, her voice raised. "Every land, every man, woman, and child. Every flag, every coin, every mountain, every river, every tree, and every grain of sand. I want it all."

Tancho raised his two katanas. "You will get what you deserve."

Maghdlm smiled, much like a spider greets a fly. "As will you! You've all served your purpose. I needed a part of the key from each kingdom and you gave me a royal tour."

"The four metal elements," Tancho said.

Maghdlm tilted her head before a smile crossed her awful features. "They were helpful, but that was not what I mean. A part of the key from each kingdom isn't the metal elements, you foolish man."

"The books," Crow answered. "You were after the four books."

Her smile became something else. "And now I don't need you anymore. The crow and the fish will know the pain of the lacuna for an eternity."

Then, as quick as a blink, she threw out her hand, and with a force that Crow couldn't see, she sent Tancho sliding across the floor. He scrambled to stay on his feet, but as they had too much distance between them, Tancho fell to his knees, grabbed his wrist, and screamed.

The pain gripped Crow instantly, excruciating fire seared up his arm. It was blinding, sharp and insufferable, and if the pain didn't kill him, the madness would. But through the haze of agony, he heard Maghdlm's maniacal laughter and watched as she worked a large purple circle of sparks and sent it spinning toward Tancho.

She was going to send him through some doorway, to some far-off place, putting a distance between them that would surely kill them both. It closed in on him, the circle, the doorway, slid over him, taking Tancho from view.

And even as the pain burned him as it stole his breath and mind, Crow did the only thing he could.

He scrambled to his feet and ran as fast as he could, and

as the circle of purple sparks began to close—just a small burrow of a hole remained—Crow dived through the doorway.

He heard yelling behind him as Maghdlm screeched, "Nooooo," and Soko and Karasu both cried their names, but then the circle closed and the doorway shut behind them.

He had no idea where he was going, whether he would find himself on some different world or at the bottom of the ocean to drown, or if he was diving directly into the sun . . .

Because it didn't matter. No matter what they'd face, they'd face it together. If they died, they'd die together.

Crow would go with Tancho, this day and for always.

CHAPTER TWENTY-TWO

TANCHO NOTICED the absence of pain first. Then the resounding darkness, then the cold, hard ground he'd landed on. The silence, but the darkness . . . oh so dark. Then a harsh grunt beside him. "Fuck."

Tancho sat up. "Crow?"

"Tancho," Crow breathed. "Thank the blue skies. Are you okay?"

"I think so." Tancho shook his head, unsure of what had just happened. Everything was so dark, he couldn't see his own hands in front of him, but he reached blindly for Crow, feeling his back and shoulder. Crow sat himself up with a groan and Tancho felt along his arm and pulled him closer. "What happened? I was flung across the room, away from you. Oh, the pain of it. And then . . ."

"And then that bloodsucking mudworm Maghdlm opened a doorway and threw it at you," Crow said. "So I ran. I almost didn't make it."

Tancho almost cried, grateful, sorry, overwhelmed. He put his head on Crow's shoulder and clung to his arm. "Thank you."

Crow wrapped his arm around Tancho, pulled him in, and kissed the side of his head. "I wouldn't be anywhere else."

"Where are we? It's so black I can't see anything."

"I have no idea. I think my eyes are adjusting to the dark, but I still can't see much of anything. Somewhere damp and underground, I'd say."

"Somewhere cold," Tancho said. "And somewhere our friends are not. Karasu and Kohaku . . ."

Crow's hold on him tightened and he rubbed his back for warmth. "I know. Soko, too. But they'll be okay. They're smart and they'll know what to do in our absence."

"What if Maghdlm—" He sucked back a breath. "I can't bear to think about what she might do to them."

"Oh, Tancho," Crow murmured with another kiss to Tancho's temple. "Don't torture yourself with the unknown. Let us get out of this mess first, and when we see Maghdlm again, we'll make sure she regrets the day she was born."

Tancho inhaled deeply, feeling marginally better, more reassured and not so frightened. In its place was an anger he'd never felt. Anger at Maghdlm, at the lies and deception. "I'm going to rip out her spine and wear it as a necklace."

Crow chuckled. "There you are. My fierce little fish." He sighed and gave Tancho a squeeze. "Come on. We need to get out of here. First, we need to find where *here* is."

Crow slowly got to his feet and helped Tancho to his. "I can't see anything," Tancho whispered.

"My eyes are adjusting," Crow said. "We're in some kind of cave, but we need a torch."

Holding Tancho's arm, he led him along for a short while. "How can you see?"

Crow snorted. "Same way you can hear things I cannot."

"I hear water," Tancho said. "I think it is below us, though I'm disoriented . . ."

Crow stopped walking. "I can't hear anything. But water is good, yes? Isn't that what you said once? It means it has to come in from somewhere."

"Usually, yes. Unless it seeps up from the earth."

Crow took Tancho's hand and lifted it out to their left, putting his palm on something solid and cold. "The cave wall. It will help you get some bearing."

After they'd walked a while, Crow stopped. "There's something on the ground, to our right."

Tancho froze and leaned into Crow. He hated being blind, hated being so defenceless. "What is it?"

"Stay here." Crow took his sword and left Tancho with his back pressed against the wall.

"Crow, I can't see you," Tancho whispered, his voice tight. He couldn't see a thing, and he'd never been so frightened . . .

"I'm right here," Crow replied, and the burn of Tancho's birthmark told him Crow couldn't go much further. "Look," Crow said, coming back to him. "I think it's old driftwood. Like, very old. Petrified, almost."

Tancho's heart still hadn't stopped thundering. "Please don't leave me like that again."

"I apologise," Crow said warmly and leaned in so Tancho could feel his body. "But this is a good find. Can you hold it?"

He put the long piece of driftwood in Tancho's hands. It was light and smooth, but then the sound of ripping fabric scared Tancho. "What are you doing?"

"Using my sleeve," Crow replied, and then Tancho

could feel him jostling the driftwood as he held it. "Now, let me use a little of this . . ." There was more movement and noise, though Tancho could still not see, but then there was a familiar scent. The metal elements from Crow's pouch. "The potassium and indium should burn," Crow mumbled, making a rubbing sound.

Oh, how Tancho wished he could see . . .

Then, so very bright in the darkness, purple sparks ignited. But they faded slowly and far too quickly, then Tancho could see some embers . . . and then more, and more, until suddenly there was light. Bright and burning, it took a moment for his eyes to adjust. He could have cried with relief.

He could see now that Crow had made a torch from wrapping his shirtsleeve around the end of the driftwood. Crow's smiling face illuminated beside him and Tancho hugged him tight. "Oh, thank you."

Crow rubbed his back. "Can you see now?"

Tancho looked around the space they were in and nodded. "There's nothing to see," he whispered. "Where in the abyss are we?"

Where they were was in a large circular cave, with no in or out. The floor was a mix of dirt and stone, uneven, with ledges and jagged rock formations. "We walked in a circle."

"But look," Crow said, pointing to more driftwood that must have been caught on the jagged rocks at some point. "There once was a way in or out. Water carried this in from somewhere."

"How many thousands of years ago," Tancho murmured. "It is sealed in every direction."

Crow sighed and pulled Tancho into his arms. "We'll find a way."

Tancho nodded against Crow's chest, though he didn't

think it likely. They were in some underground vault, and they would, Tancho realised, probably die here. And it wasn't even that realisation that haunted him. It was knowing they'd failed. Knowing he'd left their friends to fight and defend their kingdoms alone that sent a shiver through Tancho's bones.

"You're cold," Crow whispered into Tancho's hair. "Let's gather this wood in a pile and make a fire before the torch dies."

With a solemn nod, Tancho helped collect the few pieces of driftwood, and while Crow made a campfire, Tancho plonked his ass in the dirt and watched.

He was exhausted, and he was devastated. He'd let everyone down. He hadn't just failed his friends. He'd failed his people. As the fire took and the shadows played on the walls around them, Tancho could think of nothing else.

"Tancho," Crow whispered, scooting over to sit on his haunches in front of him. He lifted Tancho's chin and wiped away a tear. "We'll be okay."

He pulled his face back and used his sleeve to dry his face. "A moment of weakness, sorry."

"No apologies necessary," Crow murmured.

"Maghdlm knew exactly where she was sending me," he said quietly. "And you chose to join me."

"It was never a choice, little fish. I had to be with you."

"Because of the bond."

"No. Because of you. I would choose you, bond or no."

Tancho's eyes burned and another tear escaped. "I can't imagine being here without you," he admitted, wiping his face. "I'm so thankful for you, even if it means our end."

"Our end?" Crow smiled sadly. "This isn't our end."

Tancho rolled his eyes at Crow's optimism but was

grateful for it all the same. But then he let out a shaky breath. "I'm sorry for the tears," he said, wiping his face once more. "I failed my people. I failed my friends, my family. It wasn't supposed to end like this, Crow. This was not . . ."

Crow took Tancho's face in both his hands. "This is not our end," he murmured, before kissing him. Tancho welcomed the warmth, the touch, and the emotion he could feel in Crow's kiss.

In that moment, in his entire life, he'd never needed anything more.

He pulled Crow closer, deepening the kiss. Opening his mouth and tasting his tongue, but it still wasn't enough. Not breaking the kiss, Tancho lay back and pulled Crow with him until Crow's weight settled on him.

Yes, this was what he wanted.

What he needed.

He needed to feel, to feel something good, something borne of passion and desire.

Crow's weight, his strength, his entire body pressing Tancho into the cold ground. Their mouths fused and tongues entwined. Tancho held him tight, clinging to his broad shoulders, his waist, his arse, grinding their erections together as they kissed, drinking each other in. But it wasn't enough. Tancho needed more. He pulled at Crow's armour, his shirt, his belt, and Crow helped him make short work of it all, their naked bodies soon gleaming in the firelight.

This was what he needed. Something to help him forget.

Something worth dying for.

Something worth living for.

And Crow held him, kissed him, ground against him

with all the passion Tancho needed in that moment. He felt wanted and worthy, and his whole body was on fire.

Heat licked at his veins and burned in his belly. Fire like he'd never known, his bones were embers of pleasure so intense, he thought he might combust. Tancho was so close, so close to tipping over the edge, he was so close he ached for it. The feel of Crow's hot and hard cock, slicked with precome, sliding between them, made Tancho beg for it. He wanted it inside him.

He needed it.

Crow slipped his hand between them and gripped his erection. He pumped him, his grip twisting and tight, and just when Tancho was about to tumble over the edge, Crow took his now-slicked fingers and went lower and lower, rubbing, and finally—finally—pushed his fingertips inside him.

Sparks exploded behind Tancho's eyelids and he gasped as pleasure rocketed through him. Searing and scorching every inch of his body, an ecstasy unlike no other he'd ever felt, Tancho's whole body went rigid, he tried to scream, to beg, to plead, but could make no sound.

If this pleasure was a fire, he wanted to burn forever.

Somewhere far off but warm in his ear, he swore he could hear Crow murmuring his name, chuckling and smug. And in his bliss-addled brain, Tancho knew Crow was between his thighs, slicking his hole. He knew Crow was using Tancho's spend to slick his cock, then press it against him. But he still couldn't form words, his bones were made of sea sponge, and he couldn't even lift his hand.

Crow leaned over him, pressing against him but waiting . . . waiting. "Is this what you want?"

Tancho groaned and rolled his hips. "Not want," he managed to whisper. "Need."

Crow's eyes flashed by the light of the fire. He lifted Tancho's leg and pushed into him, so slow. Too slow, torturously slow, painfully slow.

Tancho's senses came back to him in a rush and he gasped, his eyes wide. Crow kissed him, plunging his tongue into his mouth, while he filled Tancho's arse with his cock, and yes . . .

No. *This* is what Tancho wanted. What he needed.

His eyes rolled back in his head and he gave himself to the pain, to the pleasure, to the sensation of being claimed and owned.

He gave himself to this man.

Crow held him, kissed him deeply as he filled him, over and over and deeper with every thrust. It was slow and tender, desperation in his digging fingertips to go deeper and harder, etched with restraint and letting go.

This was giving and taking in equal measure, an ebb and flow of body and heart. And Tancho gave all he had and took all Crow gave him. They moved as one, breathed as one, became one.

Crow's thrusts grew harder and deeper, faster, and he trembled as he tried to hold back.

"Give yourself to me," Tancho breathed.

Crow thrust one last time, buried to the hilt, swollen and rock hard, and he groaned as he gave Tancho what he asked for. Tancho could feel the pulse, could feel Crow's heartbeat, his seed, and in that moment—that perfect moment—they were one.

Tancho held Crow in place, never wanting him to leave his body, never wanting to be apart again. He would have this man inside him forever, for nothing in the world had felt like this.

He felt complete and whole. He felt unified and fulfilled, and as Crow kissed up his neck, over his jaw, and found his lips, he was certain Crow felt the same. It was slow kisses and tender touches, reverent, and Tancho tasted love in every touch of his tongue, felt his destiny in every touch of his hands.

When Crow pulled out of him, he quickly wrapped Tancho up in his arms and nuzzled into his neck. Whispering sweet nothings, murmuring contentedness, and humming sleepily. The fire cast the cave in an orange glow, with flickering shadows and warmth, and Tancho snuggled into Crow's body.

Crow smoothed out an errant strand of Tancho's hair, tucking it behind his ear. He planted soft kisses along his forehead, his closed eyelids, before tilting his face up for a soft kiss. "We have an old saying in the Northlands," he said, his voice warm and gruff. "We wander lost until our heart finds a home."

Tancho smiled into Crow's neck. "My heart feels at home with you."

Crow sighed and pulled Tancho closer, rubbing his back until he was drawing loose circles and patterns on his skin. And then the pattern changed. He drew a large cross, then put a line through it. Then he drew a line from the tip of the centre line to the tip of the first spire, and Tancho's breath caught.

That couldn't have been random. No, it was deliberate. It had to be.

Tancho pulled back to look into Crow's eyes, and he saw truth and vulnerability, but there was no fear.

"You know what that means?" Tancho asked, though it wasn't really a question.

Crow nodded. "And I meant it."

Tancho kissed him then. Hard and with every ounce of emotion his heart could hold.

Crow had just drawn an old rune symbol on his back. A language old as time itself, but timeless in its meaning.

Love.

Crow had drawn the symbol for love.

"I love you," Tancho murmured. "Our birthmarks might have drawn us together, but my heart is yours."

Crow put his palm to Tancho's cheek. "And mine is yours. The distance between us is no distance at all. Maghdlm can call the lacuna whatever she pleases. I know what it means," he kissed Tancho softly. "There is no distance between us, not now, not ever."

Tancho took his hand, kissed his palm and down to his wrist and forearm where his birthmark . . . wasn't.

Tancho laughed. "Uh, your raven has flown away." He lifted Crow's arm, and not seeing the birthmark anywhere, he sat up and searched his chest, his neck. "I can't find it." He pulled Crow over onto his stomach so he could search his back, but Crow stopped him.

"Tancho," he said slowly. "Stop looking."

"Why? If it's on your body, I will find it."

"It isn't," he replied. "It's on yours." His gaze fixed on Tancho's chest and Tancho looked down . . .

He gasped, almost falling back on his arse. "What in the abyss?"

There on his chest, right over his heart, was his koi birthmark. And above it, with its wings outstretched, was Crow's raven.

"How is that possible? How is this . . . ?" He stared, wide-eyed at Crow. "What does this mean?"

Crow sat up and touched the bird now marked into Tancho's skin. "I don't know."

Tancho took stock of himself and how he felt. "I don't feel any different. I mean, I feel amazing after what we did. But that was all your doing." He shook his head, then slowly touched the bird and the fish on his chest. "I don't feel any different in regards to this."

Crow surprised him by laughing. "Maybe he liked your body better than mine. I can't say I blame him." He lifted Tancho's hand and kissed the inside of his arm. "Your skin is perfection."

He looked up at Tancho, his eyes filled with something Tancho couldn't quite name. Possession? Love?

"I will admit to you," Crow said, his voice like velvet. "Seeing my mark on your skin speaks to some primal part of me." He crawled toward him, pushing Tancho back to the floor, lying atop him again, and kissing him once more. "I could take you again, right here, like this."

Tancho grinned at him, a new fire igniting low in his belly. "Draw that rune on my chest beside your raven, and you can take me anytime, anywhere, my love."

Crow laughed and kissed him, then trailed his lips down to Tancho's chest. He drew his tongue in a cross, the start of the rune for love, but then he stopped, his eyes meeting Tancho's, now with a different kind of fire.

"What is it?"

"The rune."

"What about it? And if you say you're going to take me and then stop? I'll be disappointed and displeased. You shouldn't promise—"

Crow laughed and shot to his feet. "Get dressed."

Now thoroughly confused, Tancho sat up. "What are you—"

Crow pulled on his pants, then picked up his boot. "I have an idea. Something you said."

"An idea for what?"

"For how to get us out of here."

Tancho dressed, ignoring how dirty his white clothes now were. They were far from his usual stately self. Not only was he sprayed with green Ascii blood, he was also smeared with dirt and dried sweat and the product of their lovemaking... "Crow, I—"

Crow's second boot seemed forgotten as he turned his gaze to Tancho. "Do you regret what we did?"

"No, I . . . I was just going to say the opposite, actually. I have no regrets. Apart from being exiled to a hole underground, separated from our friends and family when they needed us the most . . . But what *we* did? No, I most certainly don't regret that. I will cherish it forever."

Crow took hold of Tancho's face and kissed him with so much fervour that Tancho almost dropped his shirt. "I will cherish it also. And every time we share that again, from now until forever."

Tancho smiled and leaned into Crow's palm, and Crow thumbed Tancho's cheek. "This blush on your pale skin . . . it is the most beautiful thing," Crow whispered. Then his fingers brushed over the two birthmarks now taking up residence on Tancho's chest. "Only bested by this. You wondered where the birthmarks were moving to when they started to move up our arms. Well, now we know." He kissed Tancho softly. "Mine wanted to be where it belonged. With you." Then he made a face. "Though I'm a little disappointed your fish didn't want to swim onto me."

Tancho chuckled, taking Crow's hand and kissing his knuckles, and he was going to jibe him about his possessive streak when something occurred to him. "Wait a second," Tancho said, pulling his shirt on. "Stay here."

He slipped his boots on quickly, and facing Crow, he

took a step backward, then another, and another until they were several metres apart. When Crow cocked his head, baffled at what Tancho was doing, Tancho's smile became a grin. "Don't you see?" he asked.

"See what?"

"How far apart we are," Tancho said, taking another few steps backward. "And you feel no pain?"

Alarmed, Crow looked to his wrist and arm, then to Tancho. "No, I don't . . ."

"Because I carry both marks. They are no longer separated. There is no distance between them, no gap, no space between."

Crow took a few long strides back, putting more distance between them now than they'd had since the moment they met. Tancho could barely see him in the dark, away from the fire. But then Crow ran back to him, grinning. He put his hands to Tancho's shoulders. "Do you know what that means?"

"Yes. That we could go our separate ways. If we weren't confined to this cave for all of time."

Crow's face fell, first into sadness, then slid sideways into anger. "Is that what you want? Is that the first thing you would do? You would leave me? After what we just did? What I said to you?"

"No, I—"

Crow pulled his hands back and took a step back. "Because I would choose you, still. I would go with you, still. What we shared before changed something inside me, yet the first thing you think of is leaving me?"

Tancho reached for Crow, sliding his hands to his face. "I would not leave you. I would choose you, also. Crow, I would go with you. Bond or no, that is what I told you before. And that is what I now know to be true."

"Then why would you say we could go our separate ways?"

"Because Maghdlm would not expect it."

Crow blinked. Then the corner of his mouth lifted. "We would have that element of surprise."

"But it does us no good in here," Tancho allowed. "The fire is losing light, and after it dies, we are thrown back into darkness."

"Well, that's what I thought of earlier. What you said, that gave me an idea. And we'll need to be quick to see if it works."

"To see if what works."

"The rune." Crow took out his sword and began to draw a large circle in the dirt. "Drawing the rune on your skin, and you saying it could take you . . ."

Tancho watched as Crow drew a large cross in the circle.

"If Maghdlm can control the compass, then why can't we?" Crow said. "We have these components from all four kingdoms, just like her."

"How do you know which way is north?"

"I don't, not from in here. I don't think it matters. Not on this. We've always thought it to be a direction, and to us, it was used as one. But on the doorway, it's a location."

Tancho felt the hairs on the back of his neck rise. The possibility . . . the truth. "Do you think we can make our own compass? Our own doorway?"

"I can't see why not. And on this day, the day of the eclipse, if there is one day in a thousand years it might work, today is it."

Tancho took out his scabbard and helped Crow finish the compass. They drew the N, the W, the S, and the E.

They drew the centre circle, the Aequi Kentron, and the inner circle with the arrows . . .

"But we don't know where we are," Tancho said, knowing they had to point the arrow on the inner circle from their starting point.

"Open them all," Crow suggested. "And see where we land. We just need one door to open. If we come out at any castle, we can get back to Aequi Kentron. We just need to get out of here."

Tancho nodded, quickly adding an arrow from every starting point. It couldn't hurt, and they certainly had nothing to lose.

When they were sure they had the compass as best as they could make it, Crow reached into the small pouch on his belt. "I don't know how many attempts we have," he said. "My supply is low."

"Let's hope this works," Tancho said.

They stood at the S, where they'd always stood, and Crow sprinkled a small amount of the element mix onto the compass. He cited the chant and . . .

Nothing.

Tancho's heart was pounding, and he clung to hope as though it was a lifeline. "Try it again."

Crow shook his head. "You try it. Perhaps now that I don't bear the birthmark . . ."

"But Maghdlm can do it and she bears no mark."

Crow sneered. "If I get out of here, she will bear a mark. Right in the middle of her forehead. My sword, or my boot. I can't decide."

"And I will help, but first we need this compass to work," Tancho said. He took a small pinch of the mix and recited the chant, imagining the purple sparkling circle bursting to life, willing it to become a reality . . .

Nothing.

"Curse that hag," Crow hissed.

Tancho shook his head. This was the right idea. They were just missing something . . .

"Did Maghdlm say something when she pushed me away from you?" Tancho asked. "Did she chant something different before she opened the doorway.?"

Crow made a face. "I can't remember. The burning pain made it impossible to focus. It took every ounce of strength I had just to focus on getting to you. But no, she didn't. She was laughing."

Tancho snarled. "What about when she opened the doorways to the other kingdoms. It was in the old tongue," Tancho said, searching the far reaches of his memory . . .

"*Aperire ad meridianam*," Crow said. "Open to the south. Or *occidens* is to the west."

Tancho tried both but to no avail. He growled in frustration. "Dammit. Perhaps we can't use a direction because we don't know where we are."

"It shouldn't matter where we are," Crow said. "But where we need to go. Back to Aequi Kentron, the equal centre." He frowned as he shook his head. "Uh . . . I can't be sure. I think it's *aperire ad centrum*."

But his words died when the metal powder sparked purple flashes on the ground, bright compared to the dying firelight. Crow gripped Tancho's arm. "Say it again."

Crow sprinkled a touch more of the powder and recited the chant, louder this time, if that made any difference.

But this time the purple sparks ignited. Fizzing and flickering, until they finally took hold.

Crow laughed. "If we ever see our mentors again, remind me to thank Erelis for all those lessons I hated on the old languages."

The swirling and spinning circle grew larger, illuminating every corner of the dark cavernous hole they'd been stuck in.

They could see now, the old and faint writings on the walls, the same letters and shapes which adorned the walls in the old grand hall. "Look," Tancho whispered. "It's the same as underneath the Aequi Kentron. We have to be close. Down where Adelais had said it had been blocked off hundreds of years before."

"It certainly looks like it." Crow turned back to the circle of purple sparks. "Let's get out of here."

The doorway was big enough for them to walk through now, though Tancho couldn't see exactly where it was they were going. "It looks dark in there."

Crow gave a nod and squinted as if to see clearer. "It does." He drew his sword, so Tancho did the same. And together, they stepped into the unknown.

CHAPTER TWENTY-THREE

CROW DIDN'T KNOW where they were going, but it had to be better than the hole they had left. Maghdlm had fully intended to send Tancho into that cold dark cell all by himself, with no hope of getting out alone.

Without Crow, without the elemental powder to open the doorway, Tancho would have died in there.

And for that, Maghdlm was going to pay.

They stepped through the doorway and found themselves standing in the middle of the old grand hall, down in the bowels of Aequi Kentron. They stood on the old stone compass, though Adelais, Gabel, and Aelfflaed were nowhere to be found, and neither were the once sleeping Ascii creatures they'd restrained in the corner.

The huge hall was dimly lit, two of the torches they'd found still gave light, but it was empty. There was not a sound, not a heartbeat. "No one's here," Tancho whispered.

Crow didn't like this at all. He tightened his hold on his sword. "We need to get up to ground level, the grand hall."

"Wait!" Tancho pointed to the darkened end of the

cave. "I want to see what Adelais was hiding. She didn't want us to go there."

Tancho grabbed a torch, and staying close to one wall, they followed the tunnel along. The path turned downward, old stone steps were cut into it in some sections, and smaller tunnels branched off in opposite directions like blackened honeycomb. He paused, cocking his head to listen, then holding the torch out in front of him, Tancho turned into one of the catacombs.

The dark stone walls were damp, glistening in the torchlight, revealing writings in the stone. Just a few more steps in and there were pockets in the walls, and Tancho froze, putting his hand up to stop Crow.

"What is it?" Crow whispered.

Tancho held the torch out and Crow could make out the horrors on display. Bones lined the walls like decorative stacks. Human bones, skulls. Some were darkened by aeons of time, others gleaming fresh.

There were yellow cloaks and blood-stained clothes on the floor and old, old blades. Tancho picked one up. "These are made from bone," he whispered. "Look."

He held up the handle and Crow could see an insignia carved into it. Not just any insignia, but his.

A crow.

Crow couldn't believe his eyes. "What in the blue skies . . . ?"

"Here's another," Tancho said, picking one more up from the dirt. "This one has a tree."

They were old, so old, in fact . . . "Do you think these are from the Great Wars?"

"I think, yes." Tancho inspected the Southlands' bone blade. "Remember how Maghdlm turned Kohaku's blade to rusted iron?"

Crow nodded, understanding dawning. "These can't be turned."

Tancho slid the blade into his belt. "Let's go back."

They went back down the short tunnel to the main path. A path that appeared too well-trod for something that hadn't been used in centuries. "This path has been well used," Tancho whispered.

Crow growled. "Which means Adelais lied."

The sound of water got louder, their footsteps echoing, and Crow was certain this would not end well. Tancho slowed as the tunnel opened up into another huge underground hall, only this time the ground met a vast pool of murky blue water. It was a subterranean lake.

Crow could see three figures were lying dead near the pool's edge, as though they'd tried to escape but didn't get far enough. Adelais, Gabel, and Aelfflaed had been slaughtered. Huge, razor-like talon marks slashed their throats and chests. Pools of dark red made macabre haloes around them.

The scribing carved into these walls was the same as the old grand hall, and in that tomb they'd been banished to. A rune-like language Crow had never seen before he came here.

"What is this place?" Crow whispered.

"I don't know." Tancho nodded to the three slain elders. "But did they die protecting us? Or hiding something from us?"

"I would guess the latter. The lamps don't add up, their count of days don't add up."

"Their lamps?"

"The lamps and torches are blue. Arcane light which is Maghdlm's work."

Before Tancho could reply, the water began to swirl and bubble. Crow took Tancho's torch and threw it on the ground near the mauled bodies and pushed Tancho back into the darkness of the shadows along the wall.

And out of the water came five Ascii creatures. Huge, hulking, with their boar snouts and tusks, their club fists with talon nails, blue mottled skin. They snuffled and growled, sniffing the air, and Tancho's hold on Crow's arm tightened.

One of the creatures stopped at the corpses, sniffing, then to Crow's abject horror, it rummaged around through the innards of poor Gabel. It riffled through and picked up a clawful of entrails, shoving them in its mouth. The other four joined in, trawling through the other two bodies, just as Asagi had said. Like pigs at a trough.

Tancho buried his face into Crow's back, gripping his shirt, and Crow stuffed his hand in his mouth to stop from gagging. He daren't make a sound.

When the Ascii had had their fill, one of them bellowed that horrendous noise and they scampered up the corridor leading to the old hall. Crow took some quick breaths, loud in the silence. "They came out of the water," Tancho whispered. "As Asagi said they did."

"But how?" Crow couldn't get his head around it.

Tancho's eyes went wide in the dark. "If there are doorways on the seabed or underwater. There's no reason to think all of those ancient compasses are on land. This is how there was more than one hundred. Once they got here, they found a way in."

Crow shuddered. Underwater doorways? His quota for the absurd was well past reached. "We'll deal with those later. We need to stop Maghdlm first."

"The new grand hall," Tancho said. "We need to get upstairs."

Crow agreed, but it meant running through the old hall,

taking that spiral staircase, running off through the stables and back through the entrance. It meant being exposed. "Oh, how I wish there was a magick doorway that took us up there. I don't want to think about how many of those monsters we need to go through."

"Stay beside me," Tancho said. "We're stronger if we fight together."

Crow lifted Tancho's chin and kissed him. "Don't you dare die."

Tancho met his gaze, serious despite the curve of his lips. "Not now, not when I have so much to live for."

Crow kissed him one more time for good luck, and they ran back up the corridor to the old hall. They clung to the shadows, though they couldn't see anyone or anything, it was still best to stay hidden. "None of them are down here guarding the old compass," Tancho whispered.

"Perhaps their attentions have been drawn elsewhere," Crow replied. His thoughts turned to Soko, and Karasu and Kohaku. "We need to hurry."

They made it to the archīvum undetected, but a few steps in, Tancho pulled Crow in behind some stacks, crouching low in the dark. Sure enough, a team of snuffling Ascii trampled through, heading back down to the old hall.

"We must be quick," Tancho whispered. "Before more of them come. We don't want to get caught on the stairs."

They could go around, the way Elmwood and Samiel went, but it would take time they didn't have. "We need to find our friends," Crow replied, unable to keep the worry from his voice. "We've been gone long enough."

Tancho took the lead and made it to the stairs first, not even pausing as he began the climb. The spiral staircase was tight and dizzying, and if Crow never climbed them again, it would be too soon. His legs burned; his lungs squeezed. He couldn't remember when he'd eaten last or slept. This day had lasted forever and he could feel exhaustion wresting his bones.

But he didn't dare stop.

Tancho got to the top landing and paused, then, to peer around the corner. His chest was heaving, but he gave Crow a nod that it was clear to keep going. They ran along the dark grey stone corridor, and as they neared the light outside, Crow could already see everything was a burnished bronze hue. As they made it to the small courtyard before the stables, Crow looked up at the sky.

It was . . . mesmerising, beautiful, and frightening.

Both moons were moments away from a total eclipse of the setting sun, and the huge yellow orb was almost blacked out but for a golden outer ring. But the light was refracting at every angle, sharp shards of golden light as though the sun had been skewered by a hundred cosmic swords.

In a few minutes, it would be complete, and it would be spectacular.

Tancho pulled on Crow's arm. "We don't have time."

He ran, fast and light on his feet, and Crow had to push himself to keep up. They ran around the stables this time, not wanting to be surprised by any Ascii who might have gone back to finish off the horse carcasses.

As they made it to the huge entry door, Tancho finally stopped for a breath. Crow gasped back deep breaths of air, ignoring how heavy his legs felt. "Your heavy swords and armour wear you down," Tancho whispered.

All Crow could do was roll his eyes.

Tancho opened the door a crack, peeked inside the foyer, and quickly pressed himself back against the wall. "Twenty, perhaps."

"Fuck."

Tancho smiled. "Later." He pulled a smoke bomb from his belt, opened the door, and threw it inside with enough force to smash it.

A deafening raucous broke out, screeching, stomping, fighting, and then it faded out to eventual silence.

Tancho opened the door, wide and fast, and Crow had his sword at the ready. A group of Ascii creatures were piled up at the door, fast asleep.

Crow pulled the top creature by its foot and out the doorway, piercing his sword though its throat before he realised that Tancho had jumped up onto the pile and was already inside. But another screech from inside told Crow not all the creatures had succumbed to sleep, and for the love of all that was right in the world, Tancho was in there alone with them.

Desperate and close to panicking, Crow clambered over the bodies to get to Tancho. He landed on his feet to see Tancho being cornered by two Ascii beasts.

And without thinking, without any thought for his own safety, Crow swung at the first creature, his broadsword hacking into the creature's knee, sending it screaming to the floor before he silenced it with another blow.

Tancho swung his katana at the other creature's huge arm, sending a spray of green blood across the floor. But the blow didn't maim it, only seemed to anger it, and it roared as it swung its blade-like claws at them, catching Crow's chest plate and slicing four lines downward.

It was so close.

Too close.

Tancho roared in response, swiping his katana through the creature's armpit, and Crow swung his sword at its neck, taking the creature's head off. Green goop oozed from its open neck and it fell to the ground like a boulder.

Crow touched the claw marks down his chest armour. If he'd been an inch closer or if his armour had been any lighter, the creature would've cut through him like a butcher. "How do you like my heavy armour now?"

Tancho conceded a breathless nod. "Thank you."

Just then, more creatures came running down the corridor toward them, and Crow gripped his sword in both hands, readied his stance, Tancho by his side.

He would take them on the best he could. They were outnumbered, out-sized, but Crow held his head high. "For the Northlands."

Tancho nodded. "For us."

But just then, a batallion of soldiers arrived in a swarm of red, green, white, and black. They cleared the sleeping creatures from the doorway and mowed into the Ascii like a multicoloured cloud of death.

One green-clad soldier pointed his axe down the corridor. "The grand hall," he said, before chopping into a creature who came for him.

Crow and Tancho didn't need telling twice. They raced past the swarm of battle, but as they neared the huge double doors, another herd of creatures were ravaging the remains of fallen soldiers. If they wore red, green, white, or black, it was hard to tell now. There was so much blood and gore, Crow's stomach soured, and the only thing that kept his bile down was the anger and fury that replaced it.

Tancho aimed another smoke bomb at them, and the creatures' panic and attack were quelled by the smoke. They scrambled to charge but fell over themselves, asleep in a few moments.

"I will make every last one of them pay for what they have done," Crow said, his jaw clenched. And he felt no remorse at all for hacking into their sleeping bodies. He could see now the uniformed soldiers had been black and green. His men, Elmwood's men . . . "I will kill them all."

"And I will be by your side as we see it so," Tancho said. He pulled Crow's arm toward the door. "Don't look at them. There's nothing to be done for them now."

"I want Maghdlm," Crow whispered, seething with a rage he could barely contain.

But the doors wouldn't open. They'd always opened as someone approached, but as they stood in front of them now, nothing moved.

Crow aimed his sword at the ancient wood. "*Aperi ianium!*" he roared. "Open the fucking door."

And, as though the doors had been under the same spell as the magical doorways with Maghdlm's chant, they opened at his command.

Opening wide, they revealed the new grand hall like Crow couldn't have imagined.

The room was cast in an eerie golden glow now, the eclipsed sun and moons were directly overhead the glass-roof dome. The total eclipse was straight above them, and a shaft of golden light beamed directly through the dome onto the centre of the compass on the floor.

It was time.

Whatever Maghdlm had planned was happening.

She stood at the top of the compass, her arms outstretched, chanting something in a foreign tongue. Three circles of purple sparks spun in mid-air. Not one, but three! Ascii creatures stood around, watching, waiting . . .

A burst of husky laughter rasped from the corner, and Crow risked a glance at the sound, to see Soko on his knees, smiling at Crow. His hands were bound, his face was bloodied, his eye swollen. He laughed again, this time at the Ascii creatures. "Now you arseholes are in trouble."

Maghdlm glanced up, surprised to see Crow and Tancho. Pointing at them, she yelled. "Get them, bring them to me!"

One of the creatures backhanded Soko and knocked him to the ground, and Crow swung his sword, leaping at the Ascii. Tancho did the same, unleashing his two katanas and slaying any beasts that charged at them, but there were too many.

Soldiers filed in behind Crow, men and women in black, white, red, and green, and they swung, sliced, skewered, and stabbed. But Maghdlm had a doorway open, a sparkling purple circle that Ascii creatures were crawling through.

"The doorway," Crow called.

Tancho took his last smoke bomb from his belt and launched it at the doorway. A second later, smoke seeped out and a beast fell out of the doorway and onto the floor.

Maghdlm roared and the door closed, and she focused her narrow gaze on Tancho. "Separate them! They cannot survive a distance between them."

The creatures tried to fend off the soldiers, aiming for Crow and Tancho, and there was so much commotion, so much distraction, Crow hadn't realised Tancho was edging around to the corner of the room.

Crow then saw why.

Karasu lay on the ground, Kohaku by her side. Neither of them was moving and Kohaku had a large red wound on his side.

Oh, please, please no.

Tancho put his katana through one Ascii throat before he reached his friends, sliding on his knees at their sides. Neither of them moved at his touch.

Then Crow noticed Elmwood and Samiel at the far end

of the room behind Maghdlm, near the stage area. They were restrained, on their knees, badly beaten, bruised, bloodied, but both alive. Their swords were now crumbled rusted iron on the floor beside them.

Crow ran to Tancho. "Are they . . . ?"

"Alive," he whispered. "Though barely. Crow . . ."

Crow looked to where Soko was lying, slumped on the floor—where they could see his chest rising and falling—and Crow nodded. "We kill them all."

Tancho stood, fire and rage in his eyes. The golden glow made him look ethereal and really, really pissed off.

He leapt again into the fray, helping a red soldier slay one creature, and Crow was quick to follow. They were separated now, the distance between them clearly a surprise to Maghdlm, but she had another door open and more creatures came through.

It was a fight they couldn't seem to win.

Crow had to put a stop to her, to the doorways, to the carnage.

He began to chant the incantation to close the door and one of the doorways sputtered and slowly began to shrink.

Maghdlm only spoke louder, urging the door to open again.

"Crow, look out!" Tancho yelled, and Crow turned just in time to see an Ascii swing its huge fist. He ducked back, the dagger-like claws missing his face by a hair's breadth.

Crow heaved his sword upward, gutting the creature like a wild boar. It stood, stunned, for a long moment, and Crow kicked it over. But then another came at him and, after that, another. More of their soldiers were gored, killed, more Ascii were coming and Crow was so exhausted he could barely lift his sword.

And for the first time since this whole ordeal began, all those days ago, Crow had the sinking realisation that they would not survive this.

He would die here, with Tancho at his side.

When Crow had said he'd be beside Tancho until the end, he didn't expect the end to find them so soon.

He wanted more time with him.

He wanted a life with him.

And these hideous creatures and that evil Maghdlm were going to take it all from him.

Crow raised his sword and roared as he killed one more creature, cutting its head off through the ear. The top of its head hit the tiles like a gruesome helmet. Crow picked it up, and with every ounce of strength he had left, he threw it at the glass dome above them.

The dome broke, sending shards of broken glass down onto the compass. The light in the room changed and Maghdlm turned to him, her face a mask of fury. And just when Crow thought he might have had a small victory against her, a creature grabbed Tancho and flung him toward Maghdlm like a rag doll. He hit the ground near her feet with a sickening thud. There was a good twenty metres between them now . . . more distance than there had been in over a week. Maghdlm grinned at Crow, and Crow screamed just as more sparks burst into life and another doorway opened.

She waved her hand with a sinister grin and Crow's sword crumbled to rusted dust.

Crow knew it was over then.

If more creatures came scrambling through, with a fresh thirst for blood, it was over. He could see four blurry figures coming through.

Exhausted, defeated, bereft, Crow fell to his knees, and keeping his eyes on Tancho, he made a vow for all to hear.

"In our next life, my love."

He took a deep breath, closed his eyes, and waited for the Ascii—and death—to come.

CHAPTER TWENTY-FOUR

EVERYTHING HAD GONE WRONG. There were too many of them, they were too strong and too brutal.

The doorways kept opening, creatures kept coming through, and while Tancho and Crow, and all the soldiers were tired and losing strength, the Ascii were fresh and desperate for blood.

Tancho had risked a glance at Crow, and in that split second, just half a second distraction, Tancho was hit.

The air left his lungs with a whoosh, his head snapped back, and then he was careening through the air. He hit the ground far too hard; his ears rung and his vision swam, darkness ebbed in his mind like high tide.

But then he heard Crow's scream.

The sound struck Tancho harder than the Ascii had. He fought to stay conscious. He tried to fight unconsciousness. He refused to die without the chance to raise his sword in defence. He refused to die without seeing Crow one more time.

He refused to die lying down.

Tancho put his hands to the floor and pushed himself

up to his knees. His head was aching, his vision was blurry, and he swayed, but he knelt back on his haunches. He focused on Crow, who was also on his knees. A creature had its huge claw on his shoulder. Crow's gaze met his, and he gave a defeated nod.

Whoever or whatever was coming through the doorway would be their end.

The doorway seemed to burn brighter, the light behind was bright and blinding. Tancho had to squint, the pain in his head piercing now, matching the ringing in his ears.

But then the figures stepped into the room, as if moving in slow motion, and the doorway snapped closed behind them. They were no creatures, no monsters from another realm.

It was their mentors. The old teachers who had raised them. And they walked into the room like royalty.

Asagi's long white cape flowed like water as he lifted his two katanas. Erelis, all in black, swung his broadsword. Sirocco in red, lifted her crossbow to aim, and Oaken wielded an axe in each hand.

And like something from a dream, the four mentors unleashed an unholy display of skill and violence. They hacked, carved, pierced, and chopped. Effortless and without mercy, as fast and as silent as a ray of sunlight, the mentors truly schooled their students. The carnage was swift and complete, slaying every creature in the grand hall where it stood.

Except for Maghdlm.

She stood, horrified and stunned, motionless. With an almighty screech, she waved her hands and mumbled a curse and all the blades, all the swords and steel, turned to rusted iron. Crumbling and breaking apart in their hands.

If more creatures came through now, they had nothing to fight them with.

Crow scampered to his feet, sprinting across the hall, and tackled Maghdlm. They slammed into the tiled floor and slid, and the old Ascii woman kicked and screamed, but Crow pinned her face-down, her arm lifted behind her back. She was strong, but Crow was gloriously angry.

Erelis and Asagi both threw their broken swords to the ground and turned to the doorway openings. They threw a handful each of a powdered mixture and recited a chant Tancho hadn't heard before, and as the powder came into contact with the sparks of the spinning doorways, there was a loud bang! A bright orange cloud of flame billowed out and shrunk back in on itself until nothing remained, and the doors were simply gone.

Above them, the eclipsed sun and moons' light moved, no longer a direct beam through the dome above. The eclipse was no more.

And just like that, it was over.

Tancho heard ·cheering, the soldiers' cries of elation rang distant in his ears. He turned to find Crow pulling Maghdlm to her feet, guards quickly securing her hands behind her back.

Asagi went to Tancho, helping him stand. "Are you well, my king?"

Tancho managed a nod. "Please see to Karasu and Kohaku," he said, looking over to where they lay.

Samiel and Elmwood were freed from their restraints. Samiel limped badly, her temple bleeding. Elmwood had taken a large gash to his arm, and his swollen face was already bruising.

But Crow, sweaty, dirty, one sleeve torn off at the shoulder, bleeding from a scratch down the side of his neck, walked through the swarming crowd, his eyes fixed only on Tancho. He collected him in a crushing hug, holding him far too tight and nowhere near tight enough.

And there, in front of everyone, Crow took Tancho's face in his hands and kissed him. He tasted of every emotion, every word he could not say, and Tancho nodded because he understood.

When Crow pulled back, he tucked Tancho into his side and faced Erelis. "A teacher's job is never done," Crow said, his voice raspy. "Never have I been more grateful for a lesson."

Erelis grinned and hugged Crow. "A lesson for us all, I believe."

Asagi came over, helping Karasu and Kohaku as they limped over. Tancho rounded his friends up in an embrace. "I thought you dead."

"Us?" Karasu asked. "We watched you be thrown into some unknown portal. And Crow dived in . . ." She scrubbed a tear from her blood-stained, dirty cheek. "We thought you both gone from this world."

"We almost were," Tancho said. "If Crow hadn't have joined me, I would be." Then Tancho went to Asagi, surprising him with a hug. "My good man. I was saved by you, also."

The old man smiled. "We will tell you everything."

Crow went to Soko and helped him stand. He was badly beaten, limping, bloodied and bruised, and they whispered quietly to each other as they walked. Soko went straight to Kohaku and clapped him on the shoulder, but then threw his arms around Karasu, and much to Tancho's surprise, she held Soko just as tight.

Tancho was so grateful they had all survived this. Though many had not, and he would recount those losses a thousand times, but right now, he would celebrate with those who lived.

Kohaku looked at Tancho but nodded to Crow. "How can you be apart? And you can embrace other people without wanting to kill everyone. Is the bond broken?"

"We have much to tell," Crow said, pulling Tancho back in close. He held up his now blank wrist. "No birthmark."

"How is that possible?" Erelis asked.

Tancho thought it would just be easier to show them, so he unbuttoned his shirt and pulled at the fabric to reveal the koi and crow on his skin over his heart. "And I have two."

Everyone gasped, wide-eyed, with disbelief. But Asagi's surprise was more alarmed. He shot Erelis a wild look, then turned back to Tancho. "Do you know what this means?"

Tancho felt his cheeks heat. "I know how we made it happen, but I don't think we need to discuss that for all ears to hear."

Soko snorted out a laugh behind them. But Asagi didn't smile. Again, he looked to Erelis as if for explanation. Crow's teacher stepped forward, his expression as grave as Asagi's. "The one who bears the mark wears the crown."

Tancho shook his head. That mantra had followed him since the day he was born. "What about it?"

Tancho felt Crow stiffen beside him and he turned to Tancho, realisation drained the colour from his face. "Oh."

"What am I missing?" Tancho asked, putting his palm to Crow's cheek. "What's wrong?"

"The one who bears the mark wears the crown," Crow whispered. "I am no longer the King of Northlands." He swallowed hard. "You are."

Tancho stared at him, his heart banging in his chest.

"No, I am not. I am Westlands, through and through. They are my people, my home."

"You bear the mark of both," Asagi murmured.

Then, disrupting their conversation, Maghdlm let out a loud shrieking sound, maniacal and menacing. She fought against her hand restraints and struggled with the guards but they held her still.

"What do we do with her," Samiel asked.

"Kill her," Elmwood said with a sneer. "A cut for every one of our men who died."

Tancho nodded. He liked that idea.

Crow scowled at her. "Gut her like a pig and hang her carcass from the bell tower."

Tancho liked that idea too.

"She could prove useful," Sirocco said. "She knows more about the doorways than us. If she could be trusted to teach—"

Maghdlm tossed her head to the side, chanting in her foreign tongue, and then beside her a flurry of sparks ignited in mid-air. Screeching sounded from the other side and almost everyone in the room shied away from the sound. But as the new doorway began to open, Tancho took the bone blade from his sleeve and Crow took his bone blade from his belt, flinging their arms out, throwing the blades straight at Maghdlm.

She fell to the ground with one blade in her chest and one in her eye.

Tancho and Crow stood tall together, facing their target, breathing hard and knowing that it was now, finally, over.

Erelis closed the doorway with that new chant, rendering it to nothing but fading sparks scattered on the floor, and all that remained was utter silence.

"*Now* it's over," Samiel said.

Tancho nodded. "There was nothing we could have learned from her." He turned to Asagi. "There has been so much death today, but for hers, I'm not sorry."

"She took much," Elmwood said.

Crow turned to Erelis. "There is a doorway in the water beneath us," he said. "It needs to be dismantled somehow. Those Ascii came out of it. We need to close it."

"We discovered many things," Oaken said. "How to close a doorway permanently being one of them."

"How?" Tancho asked. "How did you know to come? How did you get to this doorway?"

"The books," Sirocco replied. "But not from one book. We needed all four. One book by itself was just a quarter of what we needed. Together, all the information, all the history, the maps, the incantations, made sense. They each had a quarter of all we needed to know."

"Maghdlm said she needed the books," Crow said flatly.

"We'll explain everything," Erelis said.

"We need to clean this place," Tancho replied. "Burn all those Ascii bodies, and bury our dead. There are so many . . ."

Crow slid his arm around Tancho's shoulder. "And we will."

"But first, maybe we could sit and rest a while," Elmwood added wearily.

"And eat," Kohaku added.

"And raise a glass," Samiel added. "To victory."

Tancho nodded. "And to those who will drink no more."

Crow pulled him in for a hug and Tancho clung to him. He was hungry, exhausted, and emotionally wrecked. "I thought you were dead," Tancho whispered. "I thought we all were."

Crow squeezed him and rubbed his back. "I thought the

same. I cannot believe we stand here. And even if it cost me my kingdom, it is a tithe I'd gladly pay."

Tancho pulled back and shook his head frantically, tightening his hold on Crow's arm. "No. Don't say that. Northlands is yours."

Crow traced his finger down Tancho's neck and chest, pulling the fabric out of the way to reveal his raven birthmark. "Who bears the mark wears the crown," he whispered. Sadness and loss swam in his dark eyes. "For what it's worth, I'm glad it's you."

Tancho shook his head again. "You are the rightful king. Now and for always. I could not. I would not . . ."

Erelis put his hand up. "A formality to discuss later, perhaps. When we are fed and rested and what remains of this nightmare is gone." He glanced to the dead Ascii on the tiled floor, to the pools and splatters of green blood. "We have much to tell."

The remaining guards went to search for their injured comrades and finish any Ascii that might have survived. There was so much to do. It was overwhelming, if Tancho was being honest. Aequi Kentron had been left to ruin, given some magical glamour façade to fool them all.

But surely it could wait a day.

Everyone was exhausted and beaten, having barely survived. "Let's find a place to sit," Soko said. He was holding his side, and even as banged up as he was, he managed a smile. "Not that I propose to give kings or mentors orders, but not standing up right now would be great."

Crow put his hand to Soko's chin and inspected his swollen eye. "You'll have battle scars to gloat over," he said warmly.

"And you," Soko replied, poking his finger into a talon gouge in Crow's armour. "That was close."

"Too close. But this chest plate will look good on the wall in my castle."

Soko snorted out a pained laugh. "I wasn't kidding about needing to sit, Crow." Crow caught him and Karasu was quick to shoulder Soko's weight.

And together they shuffled their way out of the grand hall. Karasu had her arm around Soko, helping him walk. Elmwood and Samiel limped together, Kohaku and two of Samiel's guards shuffled behind them, and the four mentors strode with grace and poise, as always.

Tancho put his arm around Crow's waist, Crow's arm slung over his shoulder, and they followed. Tancho smiled up at Crow, and Crow's lopsided smirk yanked at Tancho's heart.

"Where is the kitchen?" Kohaku asked. "There has to be a kitchen."

Karasu quipped back some remark, and Soko mumbled something in response that earned him a shove. He groaned and almost fell, clutching at his side. Karasu was quick to grab him, pulling him close and fussing over him, and Soko clearly loved every bit of it.

Tancho laughed, and Crow chuckled as he kissed the side of Tancho's head, and they followed their friends—their family—down the corridor.

THEY FOUND the kitchen and finished off the food the Ascii hadn't eaten. Those hideous creatures apparently opted for the organs and intestines of anything with a pulse and had no appetite for bread or fruit. Something Tancho was profoundly grateful for.

He hadn't realised just how hungry he was.

They sat on the floor of the kitchen, leaning their backs against the cabinets, passing around chunks of bread and cheese, some grapes and apricots, and they washed it down with a few bottles of berry wine. Tancho and Crow sat side by side, of course, and Tancho found himself leaning against Crow as exhaustion settled into his bones.

They explained what had happened when Maghdlm threw that doorway at Tancho, and Crow had blindly followed him into it. They explained the cave-tomb, the writing on the walls. They had left out the details about just how exactly there had been an exchange of birthmarks, suffice to say they said enough without making Asagi blush more than Tancho.

Kohaku and Soko both laughed, holding their injured sides from the pain. Crow threw a chunk of bread at them.

They had described the lake of water underneath them and explained how Adelais, Gabel, and Aelfflaed had been butchered at the water's edge, though they were none the wiser whose side those three were on. Crow didn't trust them, and while his argument about the use of arcane lamps was valid, Tancho was undecided. He thought their fear was real. Though perhaps now, they'd never know.

Erelis and Asagi explained how the four grimoires had formed one tome, one giant book filled with runes, rules, rights, and regulations for all kingdoms. As though the book had been divided into four, and each kingdom was given equal knowledge that would only be complete when rejoined. "We have much to learn yet," Erelis said.

"We knew we had to shut those doorways, for good," Asagi said. "There was a poem in old runic, and it took some time to decipher. The language is old and stilted. Almost in point form, and first we have to translate the runic to our old tongue, then to something readable today."

Oaken sipped his wine. "*Portalis, in lucem.*"

"Doorway, into the light," Crow translated.

Erelis repeated the chant he and Asagi had used to close the door.

De lumine,
   Ad tenebrus,
   et semel, et pro omnibus
   apage!
   Claude ostium, aeternum.

Sirocco explained, "We had to translate it from runic to our old tongue. It doesn't translate too well today, but it basically reads as 'From light to darkness, once and for all, be gone. Close the door, forever'."

"And the powder mixture you threw at the doorways?" Crow asked. "It exploded and took the doorways with it."

"A mixture," Erelis replied. "Selenium and radium. Not a safe mixture by any accounts, but effective."

"I regret sleeping through those science lessons," Crow said, before he took a long swig of wine and handed the bottle to Tancho.

Tancho sighed, taking the bottle. "I fear we'll all find ourselves back in the classroom."

Asagi smiled at that, but then he said, "Maghdlm had written all the alchemical formulas and equations in her book. Deciphering her scrawls then translating them was not easy."

Tancho growled as he finished a mouthful of wine. "I cannot believe Maghdlm was one of them all along. Waiting for the right time."

"There are mentions of the Ascii," Sirocco said, "in the grimoires. Those without shadows."

"And in that book of fiction," Asagi added. "Which is not fiction, after all."

Sirocco nodded. "We can assume our ancestors hid the facts in fiction after the Great Wars so it would not be destroyed."

"There is so much we don't know, be it fact or fiction," Oaken said wearily. "But now we have time to learn."

"Before, we wondered how can they have no shadows," Tancho said flatly. "I suggested it was because they have two suns. In that fiction book, it was explained that way." He shook his head. "But after seeing what they did to those people . . . I now think they had no shadows because they are the darkness."

No one spoke for a long moment, and Tancho put the bottle to his lips and drank.

"They were more than the darkness," Crow whispered. "They were devoid of all light. Absolute and infinite darkness."

"And they cannot return?" Samiel asked.

The four mentors shook their heads. Sirocco smiled. "No. Those doorways to their world are closed for good. We couldn't reopen them even if we wanted to."

"There are still the underwater doorways," Crow said. "We need to find them all and destroy them."

Erelis nodded. "We will go do that now."

"There are catacombs down there, filled with bones and history." Crow let his head fall back as the exhaustion was too much to ignore. "Lies or truth, I don't know."

"There are bone blades down there, too," Tancho added. "From all kingdoms, it would seem. I think our four kingdoms tried to defeat the Ascii before, and the Great War was not us against each other, but against them. Our ancestors were bested by lies and deception."

"We know better now," Samiel said, a quiet determination in her voice.

Elmwood bit off a chunk of bread and nodded. "If they thought dividing us all those centuries ago was an effective ploy to conquer us, to make us fear each other, they were wrong. Our differences made us stronger today."

Crow smiled at that. "Well said."

Tancho's expression became thoughtful. "The doorways to the outside are closed, but the doorways between our kingdoms remain, yes?"

Asagi nodded this time. "In this world, yes."

Tancho sighed. "Good." He slowly got to his feet and held his hand out for Crow to take. "Because we need to open a doorway to Northlands."

"You can't leave," Asagi said. "We have much to discuss! Who will replace the Grand Consul? The elders are gone. We need to establish—"

"I think we have our new Grand Consul," Tancho said, looking at the four mentors seated around the floor with them. "The four of you have proven yourselves above and beyond, and I can think of no one more worthy of such a title."

Elmwood and Samiel both grinned. "I second this," Samiel said.

"Thirded," Elmwood said, banging his hand on the floor. Everyone laughed . . . except the four mentors, who were stunned.

"Crow and I won't be gone long," Tancho said. "Think

over your new titles and we can hear any concerns when we return. We need to rest before we decide how best to proceed in the best interest of all four kingdoms. We have a lot of work to do, but there is something we must tend to first."

"Where are you going?" Asagi pressed.

"We'll be at Crow's, where we have urgent regal matters to address." Tancho pulled on Crow's arm, leading him to the door.

"Urgent matters?" Asagi asked.

"Very urgent," Tancho replied with a smile. "I'm going to give him back his kingdom."

CHAPTER TWENTY-FIVE

THE FIRE WAS the only light in Crow's quarters, making the shadows dance on the walls and filling the room with a sweet perfume. His huge bed was soft and warm, his heavy blankets and furs a tangled mess around their bodies, and Crow had never been happier.

He'd never felt so complete, so in love.

He remembered how Samiel had talked of a red string, invisibly binding them to each other, and it made Crow smile. He could feel it, the binding, the bond between them that had nothing to do with birthmarks.

Tancho slept soundly on his stomach with his hands up under the pillow. His pale skin and long red hair were worthy of a poet's pen.

The raven birthmark was now perched upon Tancho's shoulder blade, and the koi birthmark swam on Crow's neck.

They'd swapped kingdoms a few times over the hours, laughing every time the birthmarks turned up somewhere new. But as soon as they touched, time slowed once more, and they could make love, and what would be hours for

Crow and Tancho would be mere minutes for everyone else.

Yet Crow still wanted more.

He wanted to be inside him forever. He wanted to spend his life with Tancho, every second of every minute of every day.

And when Tancho was laying in his bed, naked and beautiful, Crow was too weak to resist.

He snuggled in closer and kissed Tancho's shoulder, and then he kissed over his back and to the raven with its wings outstretched. Crawling on top of him once more and pressing his weight on Tancho, he kissed the back of his neck.

Tancho stretched underneath him, smiling as he woke and opening his legs wide. "What time is it?" Tancho asked, his voice croaking.

"I have no idea," Crow murmured, as he positioned himself, pressing his erection to Tancho's entrance. "I cannot get enough of you."

Tancho rolled his hips, lifting his arse, urging him to push inside. "Don't tease me."

Crow chuckled warm in Tancho's ear, not quite ready to give in just yet. He wanted this to last. "Teasing you could be fun."

Then before he knew it, Tancho had rolled him off and pounced on him. Crow was now on his back, Tancho straddling him, pinning his wrists to the mattress beside his head. "If you tease me, I will take it."

Crow laughed with disbelief, and shock, if he was being honest, that Tancho could have thrown him off so easily. But the laughter died in his throat when Tancho sank down on his cock.

He leaned forward, his red hair a curtain falling over his

face, lips parted, eyes closed . . . His body took Crow as he had every other time. A tight heat and pleasure so consuming, nothing else in the world existed.

Crow ran his hand up Tancho's pale chest, and Tancho let his head fall back, his neck corded, his cock hard, and a low groan spilled from his throat.

And then the raven birthmark flew to the top of Tancho's shoulder, its wings moving slowly, in full, glorious flight. It swooped down toward Crow's hand, and crossed onto his fingers, flying over his hand and around to his wrist.

The koi birthmark on Crow's neck flicked its tail and dived under the surface, re-emerging down his chest, then swimming downward. His skin appeared to ripple when the fish broke for air before it disappeared again, swimming down past his navel. After a moment it reappeared on Tancho's hip, and he laughed.

Tancho took Crow's hand and kissed the inside of Crow's wrist and this dance, this marking and remarking each other, making love and owning each other's bodies . . . was all Crow would ever need.

When they were both sated and spent, they bathed by the fire, facing each other in the tub. Tancho sank down to his chin in the water, smiling. His red hair was tied off in some gravity-defying knot on the top of his head, and his foot was on Crow's thigh under the water, Crow massaging it gently. "Why do you look at me like that?" Tancho asked.

Crow kept his gaze fixed on Tancho's. "Because my heart belongs to you."

Tancho's smile became something else, something akin to magick. "As mine belongs to you, Crow, King of Northlands."

"How do we move forward from here?" Crow asked.

"You have your kingdom, I have mine. We have obligations, responsibilities . . ."

"And we have a doorway from your house to mine," Tancho said simply. "And when we're together, time is kind to us."

"When we touch," Crow amended warmly. "Skin contact."

"Then you best make sure you're always touching me," Tancho added with a sly smile. But then he sighed. "Truthfully, Crow, you and I can appreciate our birthrights more than anyone else could ever dare to. I understand your obligations and the weight of responsibilities you bear. And you understand mine. Our people come first."

"Agreed."

"There will be times when it won't be easy."

"Agreed." Crow sighed, digging his thumbs into Tancho's perfect foot. "But it will be worth it."

Tancho sat up in the bath, and with his arms around Crow's neck, he straddled his hips. He gave him a smiling kiss. "It will be worth it."

Crow put his hands on Tancho's hips and stilled him. "We should check in," he said. "You said we wouldn't be gone long."

"But we've spent all this time making skin-to-skin contact," Tancho murmured. "Time has been but a crawl for everyone but us."

Crow chuckled. "Have you not had enough?"

Tancho pressed himself against him, letting him feel his arousal. "We don't know how long we'll have the ability to slow the world. I'd hate to waste it."

Surely their ability to affect time was a direct correlation to the eclipse, and their slowing of time when they touched would lessen the further the axis of syzygy fell from the Corvus and Pisces constellations. Only time would tell. Though Crow hoped they'd have it forever.

He grinned at Tancho, then stood up in the bath. Tancho held on, wrapping his legs around him, and Crow carried him out of the tub and laid him down in front of the fire so they could get dry and keep warm. He covered Tancho's body with his own, and Tancho gasped as Crow kissed his way down Tancho's pale skin. Delicious skin illuminated by the fire, and while the fire roared in slow motion and the snow flurries outside the window hung in mid-air like ornaments, a small blackbird and brazen koi fish took flight in real-time on their skin.

"THIS IS TOO big and exactly the wrong colour," Tancho griped, buttoning one of Crow's shirts. "A part of Asagi will die when he sees me in black."

"If it pleases you any," Crow countered. "A part of me likes it very much to see you in my clothes."

Tancho clearly tried to be annoyed, but a smile won out. "And if it pleases you any, I like it very much to wear them. Though if you tell anyone I said that, I will deny it."

"You could always wear the clothes you wore yesterday." Crow gestured to the pile of dirty, blood-spattered and torn clothes strewn across the floor near the bed.

Tancho smiled, smug and lovely. "I have fond memories of how those clothes came off but I don't think they're salvageable."

"No," Crow said, picking up his chest armour from near the door. He inspected the four huge talon marks gouged across it, shaking his head. "Close call, huh?"

Tancho frowned at that. "You were protecting me."

Crow shrugged. "Of course I was. And you protected me."

"I hate that she destroyed our swords," Tancho murmured. "I feel naked without a blade."

Crow went to his display of weapons on his wall and took a dagger and stood in front of Tancho. "This blade means the most to me. Given as a gift from Erelis when I was a boy, handcrafted just for me." He marvelled at the raven insignia carved into the hilt, turning it just so to catch the intricacy in the firelight. "I want you to have it."

"Crow, I . . ."

"You have my heart," Crow murmured, placing the dagger in Tancho's palm and closing his hand around the hilt. "Never has someone captured me so completely. Never has someone been worthy. But you . . . my little fish. You are all there is. Keep this close to keep you safe. That way I'll protect you even if I cannot be near."

Tancho's eyes glistened and he nodded, taking the dagger. He slipped it into his wrist guard. "I accept this gift, though it's not taken lightly. I am honoured, Crow."

Crow ran his thumb along Tancho's cheek. "You are loved."

Tancho's cheeks flushed and he smiled, shy and lovely. "As are you."

Crow kissed him softly. "Come on, we've been gone long enough."

They reopened the gate to Aequi Kentron and found Asagi, Erelis, Sirocco, and Oaken at a large round table with scrolls and books spread between them and a few pots of coffee in the middle. "We told the guards to alert the others upon your arrival," Asagi said. He looked Tancho up and down a few times, visibly distraught to see him wearing black, but let it go with a long sigh.

"I'm still King of Westlands, no matter which colour I wear," Tancho said. "And you'll all be pleased to know the Northlands' birthmark has been returned to its rightful owner."

Crow laughed at Erelis' expression, and Asagi's wasn't much better, but despite the parental admonishments, they were clearly tired but in good spirits, happy to see Crow and Tancho.

Or maybe it was the basket of Scaevola's baked goods they brought with them. "I have asked her to prepare enough food to feed an army," Crow explained. "We should feed the soldiers the biggest breakfast they've ever had."

It would be dawn soon and the new sun would shine a light on the true damage they'd incurred yesterday.

Kohaku and Samiel came in next, looking battle-worn but wearing clean clothes and fond smiles. Elmwood was next to arrive, helping a bandaged and bruised Kearmore into a seat. "Heard you were back," Samiel said.

"It is so good to see you all," Crow said. "Kearmore, I trust you are well?"

Kearmore nodded slowly. "I am, thank you. Just well reminded that we battled monsters."

"And Elmwood? Your arm?"

He flexed his huge biceps and the bandage around it stretched tight. "Just a little bark off." Crow smiled at that.

"Where is Karasu?" Tancho asked.

Crow looked around the room. "And Soko?"

Kohaku laughed. "I believe he spent the night in her quarters."

And right on cue, Karasu walked into the room and threw a savage glare at Kohaku. "Because he needed somewhere to stay and someone here had to be hospitable."

Soko limped in, trying not to grin, and Crow was quick

to wrap him up in a fierce embrace. "Soko, my brother. How injured are you?"

Someone behind them cleared their throat and they turned to find Tancho staring at them. "Well, I see we're back to being jealous boyfriends, but at least you didn't attempt to take off my head," Soko said. Then he noticed what Tancho was wearing. He grinned. "Black looks good on you."

Tancho growled but it ended with a smile. He put his hand on Soko's shoulder. "I am glad to see you well, friend."

Soko noticed the blade Tancho had in his wrist guard, his eyes flashed with recognition. "Wow."

"A gift," Tancho replied quietly.

"I bet it was," Soko said with a laugh. But then he noticed the basket of food and made a beeline toward it, though he had to bump Kohaku out of the way to get at it.

Crow smiled as he put his arm around Tancho, pulling him in for a hug, making sure to have skin contact so the room slowed down around them. "Are we ready to do this?"

"More than ready," Tancho replied. "We have a lot of work to do."

Crow cupped his face and kissed him. "I'm excited to begin this with you."

Tancho smiled serenely. "As am I."

They separated and time snapped back to normal. They pulled out seats at the table but stayed on their feet, and everyone fell quiet waiting. Someone had to take charge of beginning this new era of leadership, and Crow assumed he would.

Apparently Tancho assumed the same, because they spoke at the same time.

"I think we—"

"Perhaps we could—"

Crow and Tancho stopped and looked at each other, and Crow gestured for Tancho to continue. "Please, go on," Crow said, taking his seat.

Soko laughed because Crow never conceded to anyone, and Crow shot him a warning glare because allowing Tancho to speak first was not conceding. Soko snorted and Crow kicked him under the table.

"Yes, as I was saying," Tancho said. "Perhaps we could begin by acknowledging what we achieved when our four kingdoms came together for one cause. Moving forward, I want us to never lose sight of that. For all the faults of the elders and Aequi Kentron, they did one thing right. They made our four kingdoms equal in every way. We couldn't be more different, but what Elmwood said yesterday was true. There is strength in our differences, and we are stronger when we stand together. I believe we can learn a great deal from each other, and I very much look forward to learning more about your cultures and what gives your people heart. And please know you are all welcome in my home any day."

He sat down to a round of applause and a few shouts of agreement, and Crow slid his hand onto Tancho's thigh and leaned in. "You're very good at that," he whispered.

Then Crow noticed everyone was now looking at him, given he was going to speak earlier but had graciously allowed Tancho to go first. He shot to his feet. "Right, yes. As I was saying . . . I think we need to ask our mentors if they accept their roles as the new Grand Consul."

Crow took his seat, and it was Sirocco who stood. "We have decided. It was unanimous. We will each accept this new role." She put her hand up before anyone could get too excited. "We agreed to accept for an initial two years. That should see any new legislation, new rules, into effect. After the two years have passed, we'll vote again to see if we'll do another two years."

Everyone clapped and Crow gave Erelis a proud nod. The man had been a father to him, a mentor and advisor, the voice of reason and a Northlander to the bone. There was no one more suited to speak for their people.

They spoke until sunrise, going around the table and voicing concerns and expressing opinions. Samiel suggested using the Aequi Kentron business model as a base to build from. The exports and imports between kingdoms had worked for many years, and while it could probably be improved upon, it was a good place to start.

Elmwood voiced his concerns over taxes and just what the old Consul had done with the money. Was it accounted for properly? Or were there no records of it at all?

Tancho's most immediate concern was the doorways. They should implement some kind of schedule for regular passageway rather than just turn up unannounced. Barring an emergency of course, only permitting the doorways to be open at certain times or days made sense. And could anyone access the doorways? What if a villager in Westlands decided he wanted to trade wares with a villager in South-lands, should they have unrestricted access? If so, should they implement some kind of record that documents people coming and going?

So many things that Crow hadn't yet considered.

"What about you, Crow?" Asagi asked. "Your imme-diate concerns for us to address?"

Crow took in a deep breath and let it out with a sigh. "My immediate concern is that the sun is about to rise. We need to feed our soldiers, make sure our injured are tended, and our dead have been taken care of. We need to clean this castle, we need to address our people and let them know what happened and that they are safe and there are bright days ahead. We need to find any other possible doorway, on land and underwater, and we need to dismantle them. We need to plan a memorial ceremony for all the fallen, so we can honour those who came to fight yesterday and never made it home. We need to explore those catacombs below us, and read every history book we can find. We need to drag all those Ascii dead into the courtyard and set them on fire. And about another few dozen things, but we need to do what Tancho said." Crow smiled at him. "We need to stick together, no matter what. All of us equal, always. We need to listen to each other and be willing to learn. So when we face a new enemy, be it in perhaps another ten years or a thousand, we will face them together again. And we will kick their arses again."

Elmwood, Samiel, and Tancho all grinned at him. "You're good at this, also," Tancho said.

But they'd talked enough for now. Leaving the new Elders' Consul to their work, Crow, Tancho, Samiel, and Elmwood began theirs. They led the way, limping, walking stiffly and sore, to the courtyard. Soko, Karasu, Kohaku, Kearmore and Cardwick, and Fazluna and Addax followed.

The remaining soldiers had made a start: dead Ascii lay in disregarded piles, while the fallen soldiers were laid in respectful lines. The injured soldiers ambled slowly, giving a round of applause to the kings and queen as they came down the stairs. They cheered even louder when the food arrived, and as the sun crept over the horizon, the soldiers rested and the kings' and queen's work began.

The two sSister Moons were parting ways from their Brother Sun, another thousand years until they would meet again. Another thousand years too soon, Crow thought. He smiled at Tancho as the sunlight caught his flame-red hair, shining a light on this new dawn, this new life, and on the man he hoped to spend it with.

The space between them was a mere few feet, but the emptiness—the lacuna—that once lived in his heart, was full.

<hr>

Two months later

Crow and Tancho had spent a week with Samiel visiting with Elmwood in the Southlands, deep in the jungles and stifling humidity. Crow tried not to complain too much and had resorted to wearing only a sleeveless shirt with his pants and boots, matching the standard attire of all the South-lands' men.

Tancho had pretended not to approve, but Crow caught his gaze wandering down his biceps a few times too many to believe him. They learned how to throw axes and use flying foxes, they climbed the sky bridges and marvelled at the brightly coloured birds and tasted the amazing tropical fruits. They swam in pools under waterfalls and cooled down in tepid baths.

Elmwood then joined them for a week in Eastlands with Samiel. It was a dry, baking heat that Crow could only describe as oven-like. The sun shone with an unforgiving touch, the wind barely a relief. But Crow had never seen such beauty in a landscape that moved; giant sand dunes of red and gold that rose and swelled with the wind like slow-moving water. The winds whistled at night, strange howls and moaned sounds, and Samiel told them stories of how long ago, men would go looking for lost souls in the dark, only to become lost themselves.

They rode absurd desert beasts with huge humps that bellowed and spat; they found magical water oases with sparkling water and the tallest palms. They practised spear-throwing—in which Crow bested Tancho—and Crow enjoyed the crossbow even though Tancho schooled him in every attempt. They ate foods with spices Crow could not have dreamed of, and he soon learned the sun was not the hottest thing in Eastlands. Crow would rather take on an Ascii creature with his bare hands than eat the *qutil* chili ever again.

But at least he provided good entertainment for his friends when his head felt as if it were melting and on fire at the same time.

They next spent a week in Westlands, and both Samiel and Elmwood were enamoured with Tancho's palace, his land, and his people. The pace of it, the food, the wine—and yes, Kohaku and Soko both lost that drinking contest to Karasu, who left them both slumped under the table while she finished off the last bottle.

They walked amongst sugar blossoms and ponds with lily pads, they swam in the ocean, and they set lanterns aloft on the River of Wishes; a Westlands' tradition where small rice-paper lanterns with a gentle flame inside were let go on the shore with a wish. They practised their swordsmanship with katanas, and Tancho, Karasu, and Kohaku showed off their skills at stealth and silence.

And lastly, they all spent a week at Northlands with Crow in his home. They were mesmerised by the mountains, and by the snow, how the flurries would dance with the wind, and how those winds sang a different song. They'd never seen anything like it, and Samiel and Elmwood both apologised profusely for laughing at Crow's low tolerance of their heat and humidity as they sat by the open fires, defrosting fingers and toes.

He took them hunting in the snow, and they had huge feasts by roaring fires in the castle. He took them to his sword master's forge and gifted a small blade of the finest Northlands' steel to all of them. It filled Crow with such pride to be able to show them his home and to have Tancho at his side while he did it.

But it wasn't all vacations and sport.

They also assisted in establishing the new groundwork for the Aequi Kentron. They'd sent diving scouts to search the seabed near Tancho's castle for the underwater door-way; though they hadn't found it yet, they kept searching. The doorway at the bottom of the water pool underneath the catacombs had been found and dismantled, and so the search began for any more in all the four kingdoms. The catacombs, they had discovered, were vaster than first thought. They'd found more blades and more books and more bones, all, of course, taken for further study.

Though Crow had to wonder if they'd ever know the true histories. What they'd learned and all they'd been taught seemed more fiction now, and the truth lay out like a puzzle with more pieces than they could count.

They had all arrived back at Aequi Kentron and were discussing the options for structural maintenance. Since Maghdlm's glamour spell was dissolved, gone was the façade of pristine tiles and clean walls, and in its place was the old grey stone building, worn by time and neglect. It was true, it did need some work. Well, a *lot* of work, Crow allowed, but there was a beauty in its age and history. And perhaps keeping the not-pristine façade would serve as a reminder of the lies they'd been fed for hundreds of years.

"Well, I'd like to request tubs next to the open fires in

our quarters," Tancho said, not even remotely embarrassed. "The one in Crow's bedroom is my favourite thing."

Everyone laughed, though their humour could have been aimed at Crow's expression. "Perhaps not everyone wanted to know that," Crow had added, horrified.

"Nor did we want the mental imagery," Samiel said with a grin.

"It's not your favourite thing in his bedroom, surely," Elmwood said, nudging Tancho with his elbow.

Crow bit back his flare of anger at Elmwood's innocent touch, though his glare must have said enough. Elmwood only laughed, much the same way Soko and Kohaku did. Crow and Tancho's bond hadn't lessened a great deal, though whether if it was declining or if they were becoming attuned to dealing with it, it was difficult to tell.

But they still had the ability to slow time down with just a touch, and that made up for any misgivings in Crow's ledger of give and take. It gave them hours upon hours of a night to spend as they wished, and oh how they used them well.

Erelis, Asagi, Oaken, and Sirocco joined them, carrying the four books they'd brought with them from their homelands. Crow recognised them easily by the coloured leather bindings, and the Northlands' black book with a raven made him smile.

"We bring news," Erelis said. "The maps we discovered in these books, the ones we had of each kingdom in which we said the roads and rivers were incorrect? Well, they may not have been as wrong as we first suspected."

Crow frowned at him, because those maps of Northlands in the three other books didn't match any map he'd ever seen. "How so?"

"They are maps," Asagi said. "Just not the maps that we are accustomed to. Not of roads and rivers, at any rate."

"Then what do they chart?" Samiel asked.

Sirocco laid the red leather book down on the table, then Oaken added the green leather book, Asagi the white, and lastly, Erelis put the black book down. All open to the same page and configured in a way that all four maps made one larger map. "We believe these points," Sirocco said, pointing to certain points over the combined maps, "could be a map of more doorways."

Crow stared, everyone stared. "More doorways?"

Erelis nodded. "Each site is an old town, abandoned a thousand years ago. I don't think much remains of any of them, lost to the wilds. But it's too coincidental to dismiss. If there are ancient compass stones, we need to find them."

"And destroy them," Elmwood added.

Oaken nodded. "And something more troubling, perhaps," he said, pulling out Maghdlm's compendium and flipping to a page at the back. "Another chart."

"Another chart of stars?" Tancho whispered. "Like the Golden Eclipse?"

Asagi nodded. "Another syzygy; an alignment of celestial bodies, coinciding with our sun and moons."

Crow felt the colour drain from his face. "Another portal opening? When?"

Erelis nodded gravely. "We don't know. We're studying our astronomy charts to see if we can determine it, but we still have more to learn. Maghdlm's compendium is hard to decipher. And we found this in Maghdlm's archīvum," Erelis said, collecting a statue of sorts from the stand in the corner and placing it on the table. It was a golden globe with several movable gold rings, all suspended around it.

Crow had never seen anything like it. "What is it?"

"According to Maghdlm's compendium," Sirocco answered, "it is called an armillary sphere. It charts the constellations and planets, though we are still learning how to use it."

Tancho's eyes narrowed, and he asked something more specific. "Which stars? Which constellations are to align in the next syzygy you mentioned?"

It was Asagi who answered, a little proudly, if Crow could read him right. Proud that it was Tancho who thought to ask. "Pyxis Nautica and Circinus."

"Oh, blue skies," Crow whispered. "That's . . ."

"Concerning," Erelis replied. "To say the least."

"What is Pyxis Nautica and Circinus?" Elmwood asked. "I understood why the crow and the fish were a concern, but what are these other two?"

Erelis took a deep breath and looked at each of them. "They're both a type of compass. One for water, one for land."

"Compasses?" Tancho whispered. "And a nautical one? As in, underwater like the one at Westlands?"

Asagi nodded. "And the one here, in the pool below."

Crow shook his head slowly. "*That* is the real reason Maghdlm wanted those books."

"There is a lot we don't know yet," Sirocco said. "We are reading everything we can find, translating is slow."

"Tell us what you need us to do," Samiel said. "And we will see it done."

"We need you to be the kings and queen you were born to be," Erelis said. "Tell your people nothing until we know more. Fear will serve no purpose but create widespread panic. Until we can give them answers, we go on about rebuilding our foundations. With luck the event will pass us by without incident, or it may not be yet for another thousand years."

Crow gave a nod, determined. "We'll be ready. Whenever it is."

"A tetrarchy," Tancho replied with a smile. "Four equal kingdoms, four equal rulers." They each stood and put their hands atop of one another in between them.

The four of them spoke in unison. "For always."

~ Fin

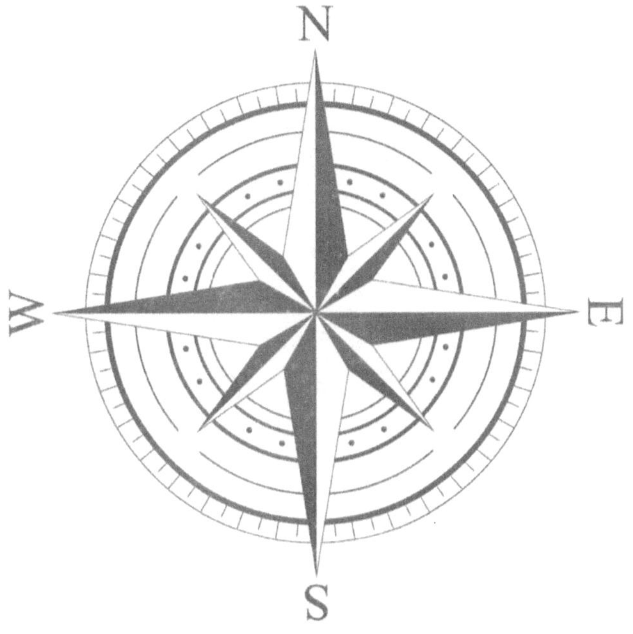

ABOUT THE AUTHOR

N.R. Walker is an Australian author, who loves her genre of gay romance. She loves writing and spends far too much time doing it, but wouldn't have it any other way.

She is many things: a mother, a wife, a sister, a writer. She has pretty, pretty boys who live in her head, who don't let her sleep at night unless she gives them life with words.

She likes it when they do dirty, dirty things... but likes it even more when they fall in love.

She used to think having people in her head talking to her was weird, until one day she happened across other writers who told her it was normal.

She's been writing ever since...

ALSO BY N.R. WALKER

Blind Faith

Through These Eyes (Blind Faith #2)

Blindside: Mark's Story (Blind Faith #3)

Ten in the Bin

Gay Sex Club Stories 1

Gay Sex Club Stories 2

Point of No Return – Turning Point #1

Breaking Point – Turning Point #2

Starting Point – Turning Point #3

Element of Retrofit – Thomas Elkin Series #1

Clarity of Lines – Thomas Elkin Series #2

Sense of Place – Thomas Elkin Series #3

Taxes and TARDIS

Three's Company

Red Dirt Heart

Red Dirt Heart 2

Red Dirt Heart 3

Red Dirt Heart 4

Red Dirt Christmas

Cronin's Key

Cronin's Key II

Cronin's Key III

Cronin's Key IV - Kennard's Story

Exchange of Hearts

The Spencer Cohen Series, Book One

The Spencer Cohen Series, Book Two

The Spencer Cohen Series, Book Three

The Spencer Cohen Series, Yanni's Story

Blood & Milk

The Weight Of It All

A Very Henry Christmas (The Weight of It All 1.5)

Perfect Catch

Switched

Imago

Imagines

Red Dirt Heart Imago

On Davis Row

Finders Keepers

Evolved

Galaxies and Oceans

Private Charter

Nova Praetorian

A Soldier's Wish

Upside Down

The Hate You Drink

Sir

Tallowwood

Reindeer Games

The Dichotomy of Angels

Throwing Hearts

Pieces of You - Missing Pieces #1

Pieces of Me - Missing Pieces #2

Pieces of Us - Missing Pieces #3

Titles in Audio:

Cronin's Key

Cronin's Key II

Cronin's Key III

Red Dirt Heart

Red Dirt Heart 2

Red Dirt Heart 3

Red Dirt Heart 4

The Weight Of It All

Switched

Point of No Return

Breaking Point

Starting Point

Spencer Cohen Book One

Spencer Cohen Book Two

Spencer Cohen Book Three

Yanni's Story

On Davis Row

Evolved

Elements of Retrofit

Clarity of Lines

Sense of Place

Blind Faith

Through These Eyes

Blindside

Finders Keepers

Galaxies and Oceans

Nova Praetorian

Upside Down

Sir

Tallowwood

Imago

Throwing Hearts

Sixty Five Hours

Taxes and TARDIS

The Dichotomy of Angels

The Hate You Drink

Pieces of You

Pieces of Me

Pieces of Us

Free Reads:

Sixty Five Hours

Learning to Feel

His Grandfather's Watch (And The Story of Billy and Hale)

The Twelfth of Never (Blind Faith 3.5)

Twelve Days of Christmas (Sixty Five Hours Christmas)

Best of Both Worlds

Translated Titles:

Fiducia Cieca (Italian translation of Blind Faith)

Attraverso Questi Occhi (Italian translation of Through These Eyes)

Preso alla Sprovvista (Italian translation of Blindside)

Il giorno del Mai (Italian translation of Blind Faith 3.5)

Cuore di Terra Rossa (Italian translation of Red Dirt Heart)

Cuore di Terra Rossa 2 (Italian translation of Red Dirt Heart 2)

Cuore di Terra Rossa 3 (Italian translation of Red Dirt Heart 3)

Cuore di Terra Rossa 4 (Italian translation of Red Dirt Heart 4)

Natale di terra rossa (Red dirt Christmas)

Intervento di Retrofit (Italian translation of Elements of Retrofit)

A Chiare Linee (Italian translation of Clarity of Lines)

Senso D'appartenenza (Italian translation of Sense of Place)

Spencer Cohen 1 Serie: Spencer Cohen

Spencer Cohen 2 Serie: Spencer Cohen

Spencer Cohen 3 Serie: Spencer Cohen

Spencer Cohen 4 Serie: Yanni's Story

Punto di non Ritorno (Italian translation of Point of No Return)

Punto di Rottura (Italian translation of Breaking Point)

Punto di Partenza (Italian translation of *Starting Point*)

Imago (Italian translation of *Imago*)

Il desiderio di un soldato (Italian translation of *A Soldier's Wish*)

Confiance Aveugle (French translation of *Blind Faith*)

A travers ces yeux: Confiance Aveugle 2 (French translation of *Through These Eyes*)

Aveugle: Confiance Aveugle 3 (French translation of *Blindside*)

À Jamais (French translation of *Blind Faith 3.5*)

Cronin's Key (French translation)

Cronin's Key II (French translation)

Au Coeur de Sutton Station (French translation of *Red Dirt Heart*)

Partir ou rester (French translation of *Red Dirt Heart 2*)

Faire Face (French translation of *Red Dirt Heart 3*)

Trouver sa Place (French translation of *Red Dirt Heart 4*)

Le Poids de Sentiments (French translation of *The Weight of It All*)

Lodernde Erde (German translation of *Red Dirt Heart*)

Flammende Erde 2 (German translation of *Red Dirt Heart 2*)

Vier Pfoten und ein bisschen Zufall (German translation of *Finders Keepers*)

Ein Kleines bisschen Versuchung (German translation of *The Weight of It All*)

Ein Kleines Bisschen Fur Immer (German translation of *A Very Henry Christmas*)

Weil Leibe uns immer Bliebt (German translation of *Switched*)

Drei Herzen eine Leibe (German translation of *Three's Company*)

Sixty Five Hours (Thai translation)

Finders Keepers (Thai translation)